SNOTGIRL: GREEN HAIR DON'T CARE

Script: BRYAN LEE O'MALLEY
Art: LESLIE HUNG
Colors: MICKEY QUINN
Lettering: MARÉ ODOMO

Created by
BRYAN LEE O'MALLEY & LESLIE HUNG

IMAGE COMICS, INC.
Robert Kirkman—*Chief Operating Officer*
Erik Larsen—*Chief Financial Officer*
Todd McFarlane—*President*
Marc Silvestri—*Chief Executive Officer*
Jim Valentino—*Vice-President*

Eric Stephenson—*Publisher*
Corey Murphy—*Director of Sales*
Jeff Boison—*Director of Publishing Planning & Book Trade Sales*
Chris Ross—*Director of Digital Sales*
Kat Salazar—*Director of PR & Marketing*
Branwyn Bigglestone—*Controller*
Susan Korpela—*Accounts Manager*
Drew Gill—*Art Director*
Brett Warnock—*Production Manager*
Meredith Wallace—*Print Manager*
Briah Skelly—*Publicist*
Aly Hoffman—*Conventions & Events Coordinator*
Sasha Head—*Sales & Marketing Production Designer*
David Brothers—*Branding Manager*
Melissa Gifford—*Content Manager*
Erika Schnatz—*Production Artist*
Ryan Brewer—*Production Artist*
Shanna Matuszak—*Production Artist*
Tricia Ramos—*Production Artist*
Vincent Kukua—*Production Artist*
Jeff Stang—*Direct Market Sales Representative*
Emilio Bautista—*Digital Sales Associate*
Leanna Caunter—*Accounting Assistant*
Chloe Ramos-Peterson—*Library Market Sales Representative*
IMAGECOMICS.COM

SNOTGIRL, VOL. 1: GREEN HAIR DON'T CARE. First printing. February 2017.
Contains material originally published in single magazine form as SNOTGIRL #1-5.
Published by Image Comics, Inc. Office of publication: 2701 NW Vaughn St., Suite 780, Portland, OR 97210.
Copyright © 2017 Bryan Lee O'Malley & Leslie Hung. All rights reserved. "Snotgirl," its logos, and the
likenesses of all characters herein are trademarks of Bryan Lee O'Malley & Leslie Hung, unless otherwise
noted. "Image" and the Image Comics logos are registered trademarks of Image Comics, Inc. No part of
this publication may be reproduced or transmitted, in any form or by any means (except for short excerpts
for journalistic or review purposes), without the express written permission of Bryan Lee O'Malley & Leslie
Hung or Image Comics, Inc. All names, characters, events, and locales in this publication are entirely fictional.
Any resemblance to actual persons (living or dead), events, or places, without satiric intent, is coincidental.
Printed in the USA. For information regarding the CPSIA on this printed material call: 203-595-3636 and
provide reference #RICH—718713. For international rights, contact: foreignlicensing@imagecomics.com.
ISBN: 978-1-5343-0036-1.

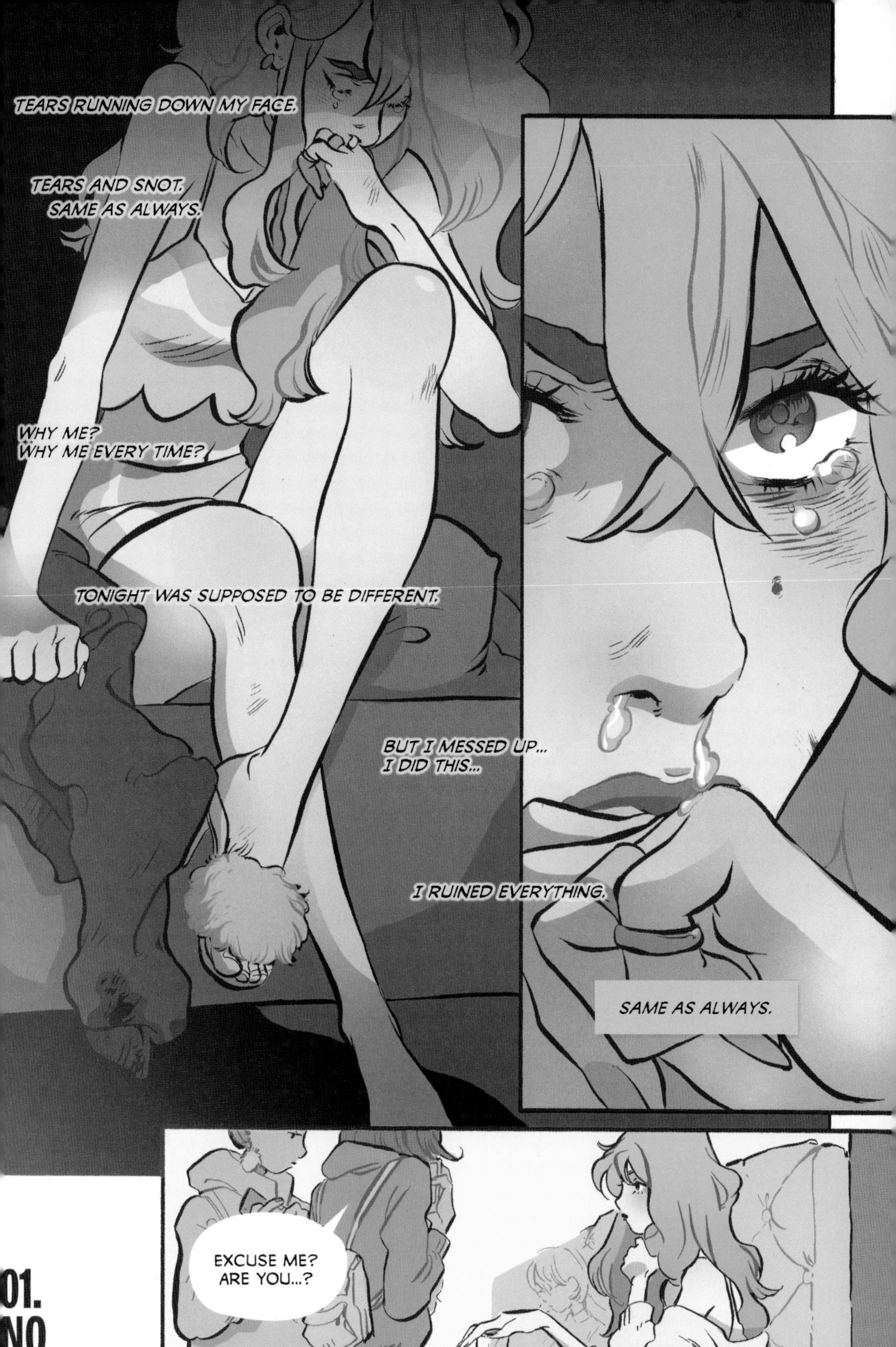
TEARS RUNNING DOWN MY FACE.
TEARS AND SNOT. SAME AS ALWAYS.
WHY ME? WHY ME EVERY TIME?
TONIGHT WAS SUPPOSED TO BE DIFFERENT.
BUT I MESSED UP... I DID THIS...
I RUINED EVERYTHING.
SAME AS ALWAYS.

01. NO NEW FRIENDS

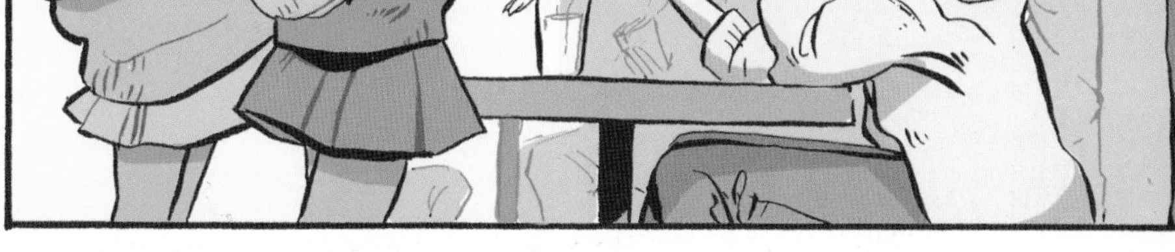
EXCUSE ME? ARE YOU...?

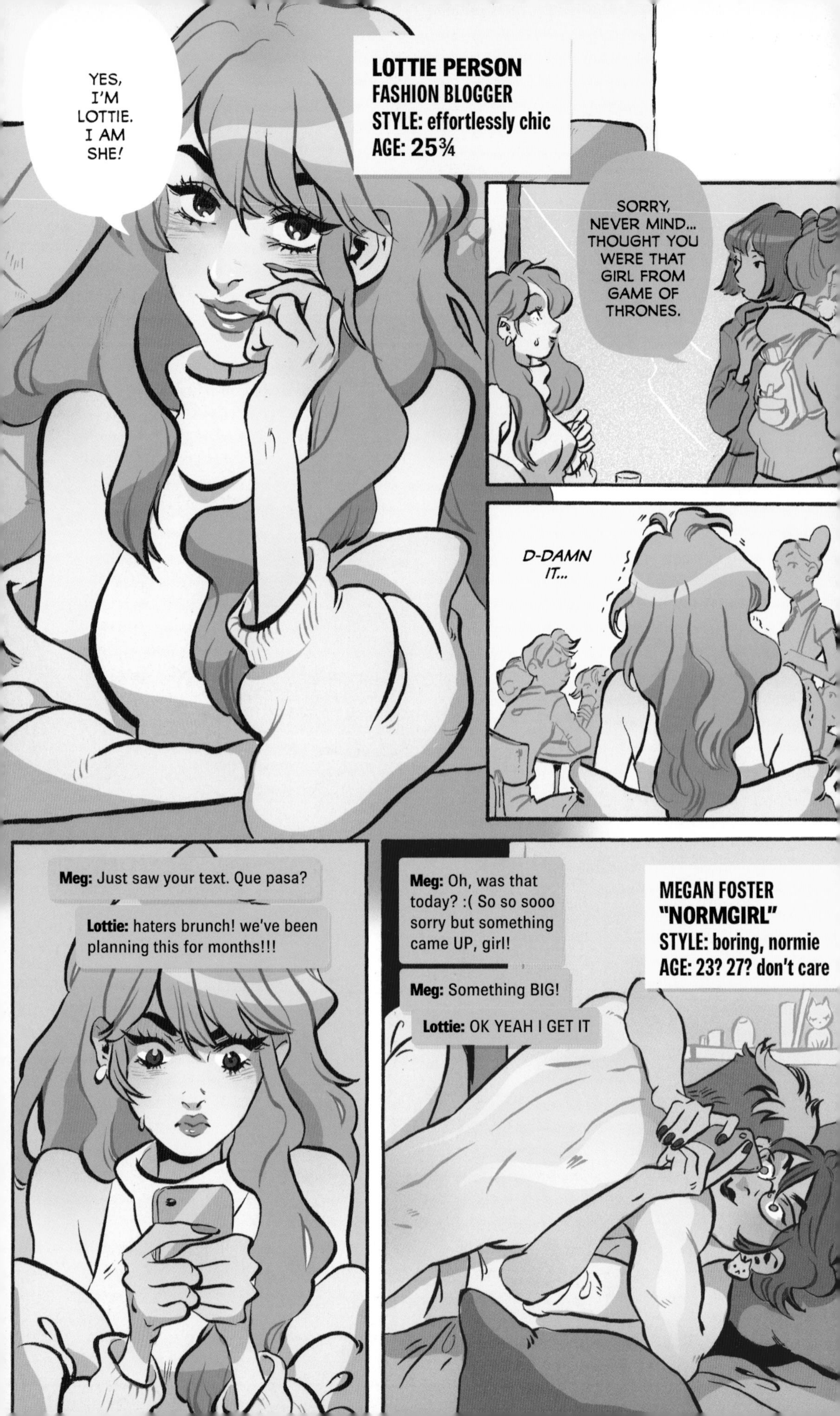
YES, I'M LOTTIE. I AM SHE!
LOTTIE PERSON
FASHION BLOGGER
STYLE: effortlessly chic
AGE: 25¾
SORRY, NEVER MIND... THOUGHT YOU WERE THAT GIRL FROM GAME OF THRONES.
D-DAMN IT...
Meg: Just saw your text. Que pasa?
Lottie: haters brunch! we've been planning this for months!!!
Meg: Oh, was that today? :(So so sooo sorry but something came UP, girl!
Meg: Something BIG!
Lottie: OK YEAH I GET IT
MEGAN FOSTER
"NORMGIRL"
STYLE: boring, normie
AGE: 23? 27? don't care

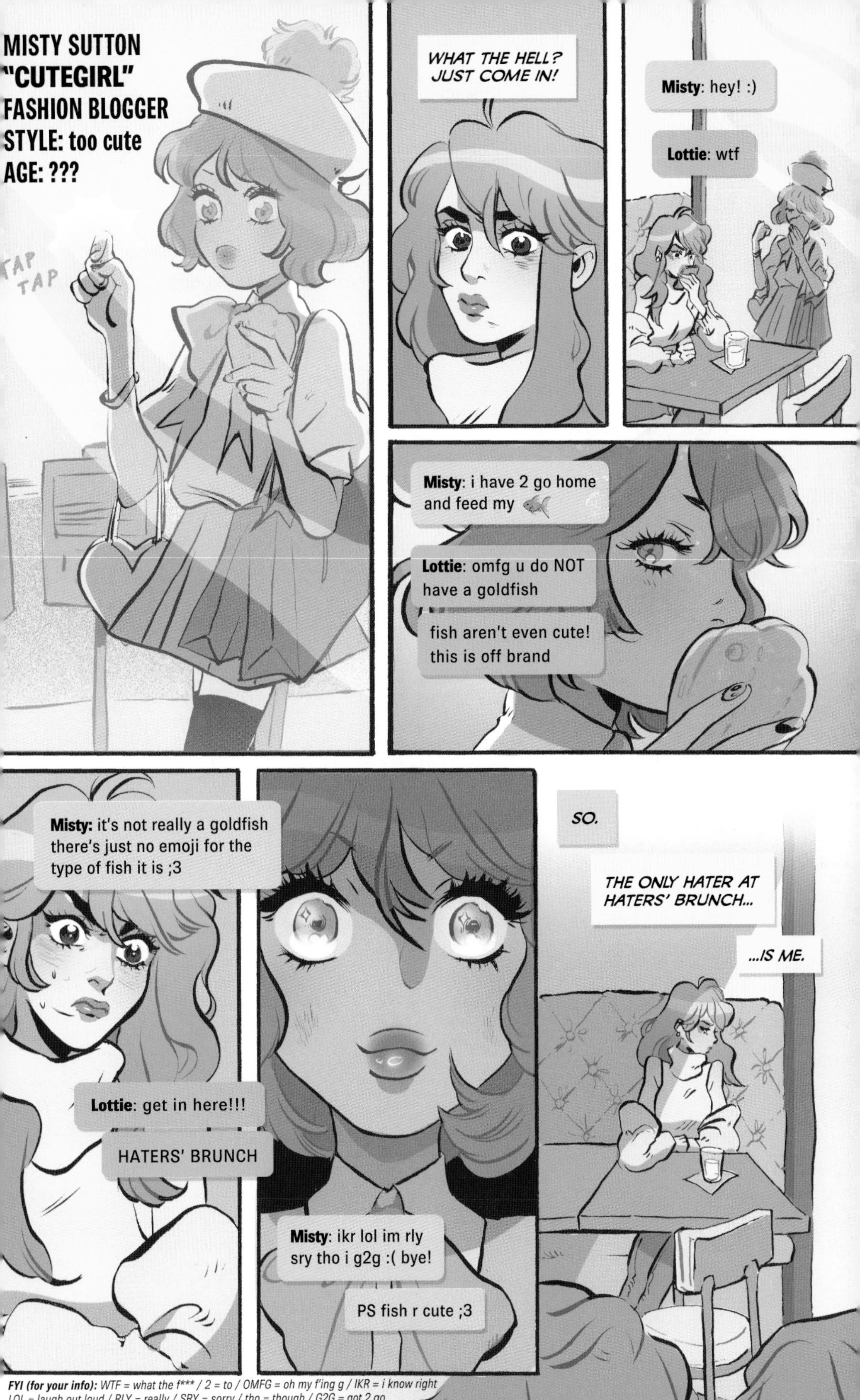
MISTY SUTTON
"CUTEGIRL"
FASHION BLOGGER
STYLE: too cute
AGE: ???
TAP TAP
WHAT THE HELL? JUST COME IN!
Misty: hey! :)
Lottie: wtf
Misty: i have 2 go home and feed my 🐟
Lottie: omfg u do NOT have a goldfish
fish aren't even cute! this is off brand
Misty: it's not really a goldfish there's just no emoji for the type of fish it is ;3
Lottie: get in here!!!
HATERS' BRUNCH
Misty: ikr lol im rly sry tho i g2g :(bye!
PS fish r cute ;3
SO.
THE ONLY HATER AT HATERS' BRUNCH...
...IS ME.

FYI (for your info): *WTF = what the f*** / 2 = to / OMFG = oh my f'ing g / IKR = i know right*
LOL = laugh out loud / RLY = really / SRY = sorry / tho = though / G2G = got 2 go

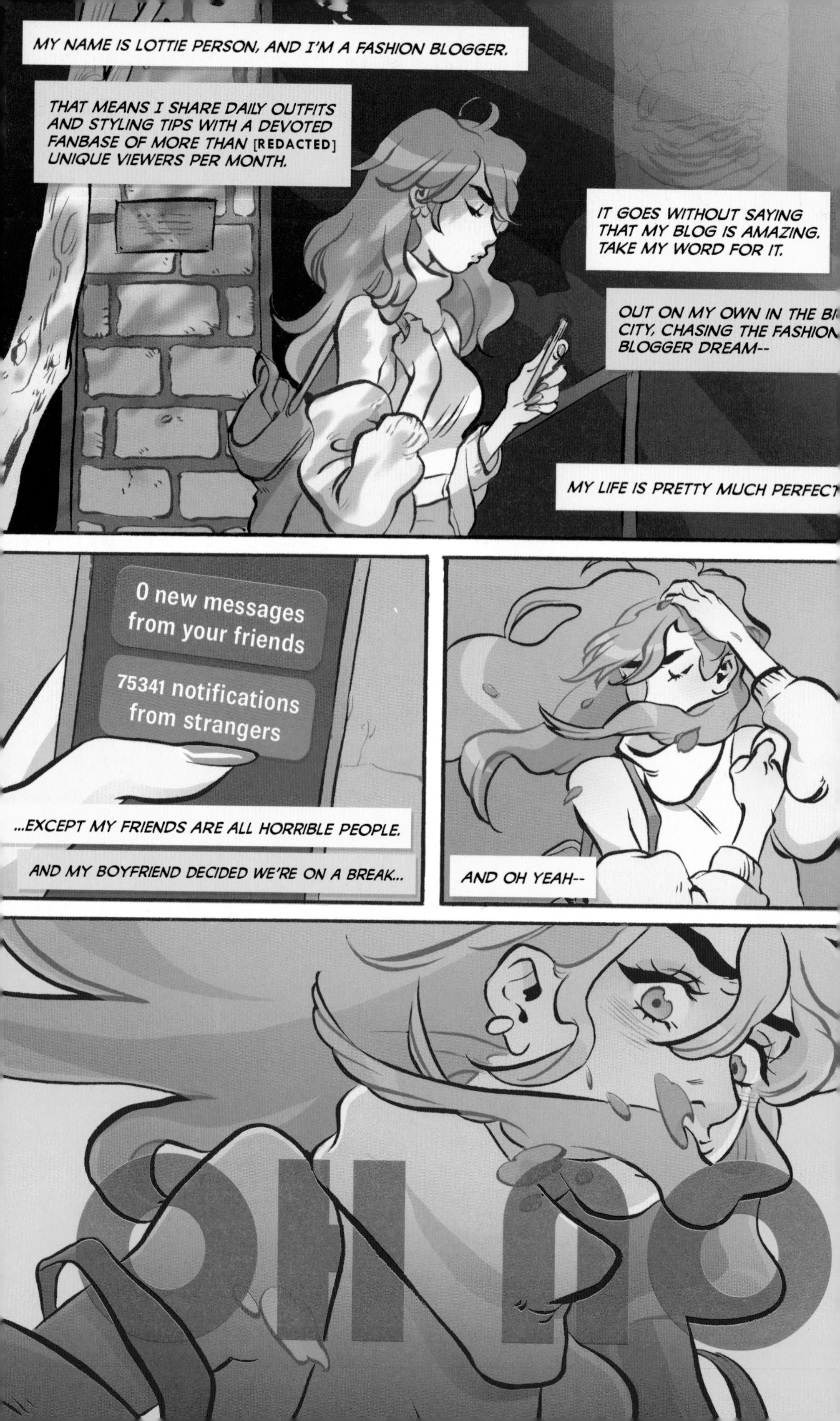
MY NAME IS LOTTIE PERSON, AND I'M A FASHION BLOGGER.
THAT MEANS I SHARE DAILY OUTFITS AND STYLING TIPS WITH A DEVOTED FANBASE OF MORE THAN [REDACTED] UNIQUE VIEWERS PER MONTH.
IT GOES WITHOUT SAYING THAT MY BLOG IS AMAZING. TAKE MY WORD FOR IT.
OUT ON MY OWN IN THE BI CITY, CHASING THE FASHION BLOGGER DREAM--
MY LIFE IS PRETTY MUCH PERFEC
0 new messages from your friends
75341 notifications from strangers
...EXCEPT MY FRIENDS ARE ALL HORRIBLE PEOPLE.
AND MY BOYFRIEND DECIDED WE'RE ON A BREAK...
AND OH YEAH--
OH NO

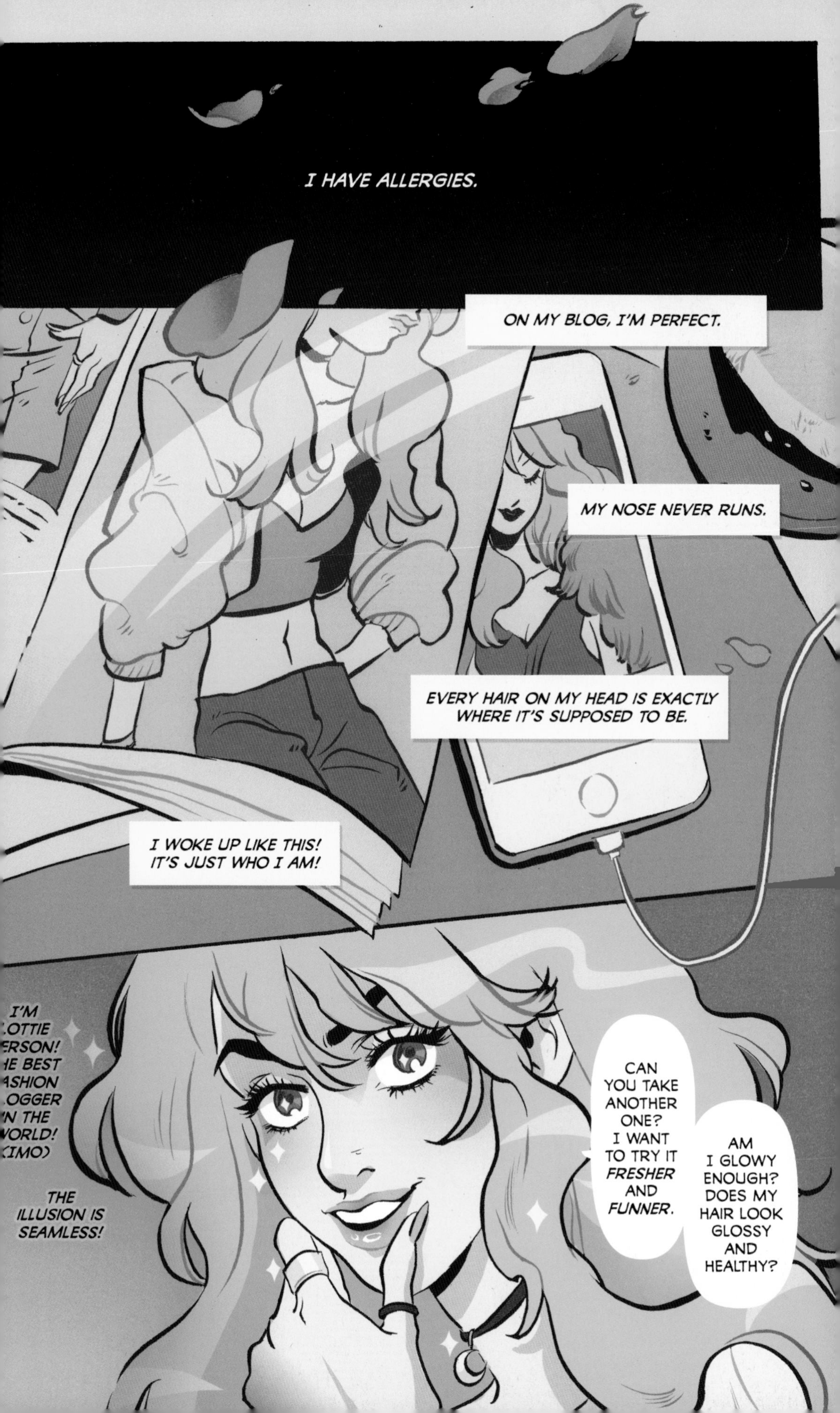
I HAVE ALLERGIES.
ON MY BLOG, I'M PERFECT.
MY NOSE NEVER RUNS.
EVERY HAIR ON MY HEAD IS EXACTLY WHERE IT'S SUPPOSED TO BE.
I WOKE UP LIKE THIS! IT'S JUST WHO I AM!
I'M
THE ILLUSION IS SEAMLESS!
CAN YOU TAKE ANOTHER ONE? I WANT TO TRY IT *FRESHER* AND *FUNNER*.
AM I GLOWY ENOUGH? DOES MY HAIR LOOK GLOSSY AND HEALTHY?

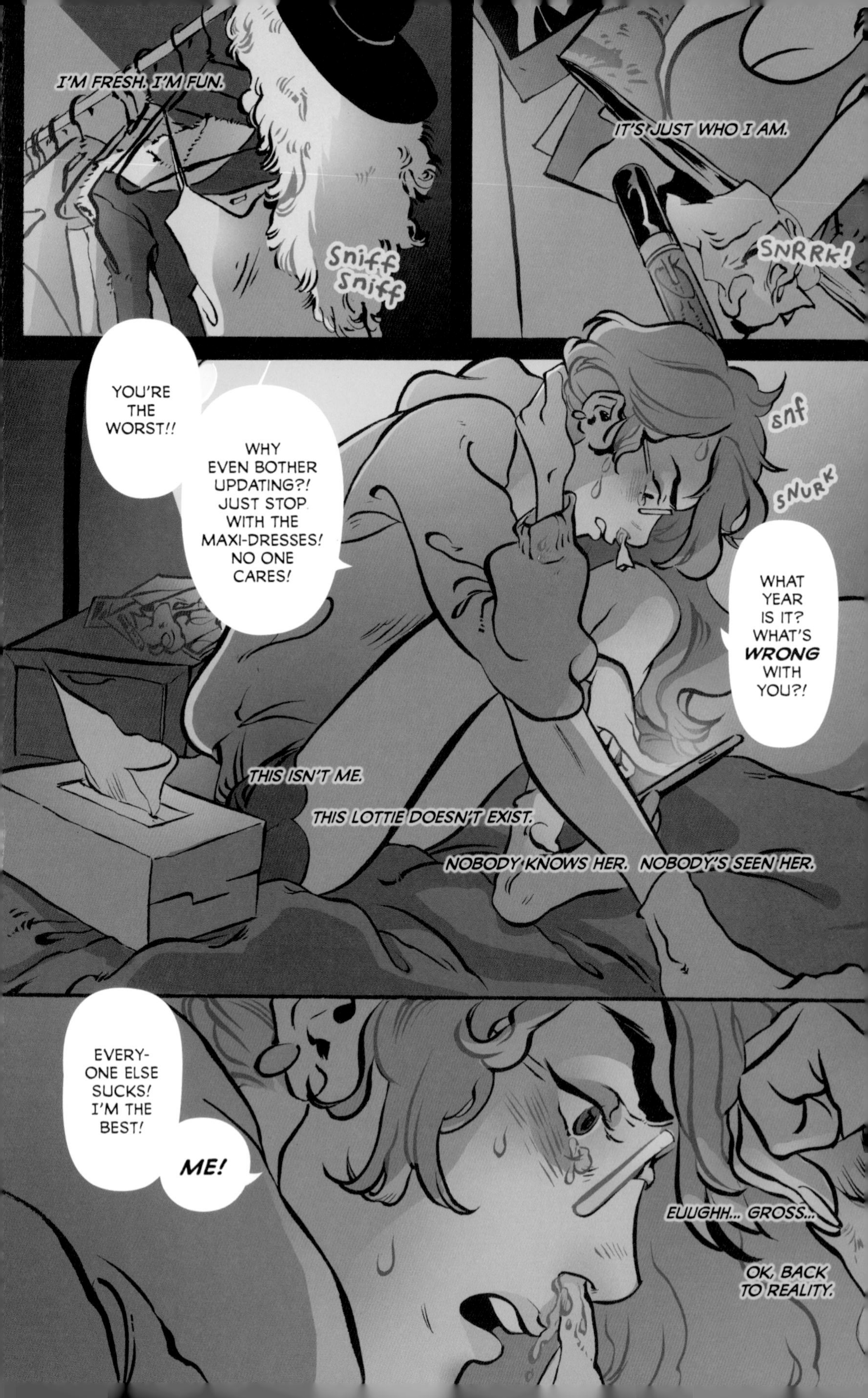

I'M FRESH. I'M FUN.
Sniff Sniff
IT'S JUST WHO I AM.
SNRRK!
YOU'RE THE WORST!!
WHY EVEN BOTHER UPDATING?! JUST STOP WITH THE MAXI-DRESSES! NO ONE CARES!
snf
SNURK
WHAT YEAR IS IT? WHAT'S WRONG WITH YOU?!
THIS ISN'T ME.
THIS LOTTIE DOESN'T EXIST.
NOBODY KNOWS HER. NOBODY'S SEEN HER.
EVERY-ONE ELSE SUCKS! I'M THE BEST!
ME!
EUUGHH... GROSS...
OK, BACK TO REALITY.

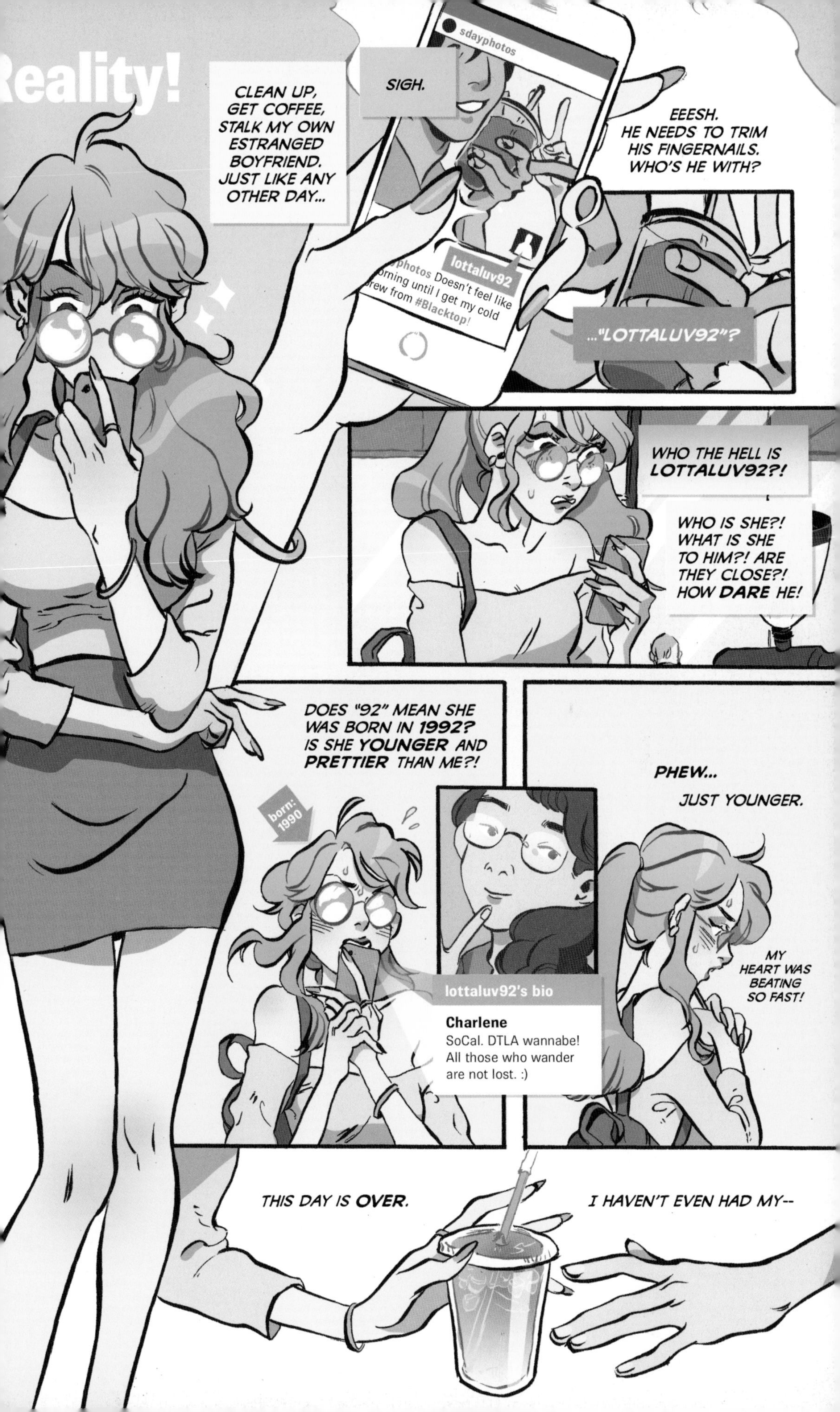
Reality!
CLEAN UP, GET COFFEE, STALK MY OWN ESTRANGED BOYFRIEND. JUST LIKE ANY OTHER DAY...
SIGH.
sdayphotos
lottaluv92
sdayphotos Doesn't feel like morning until I get my cold brew from #Blacktop!
EEESH. HE NEEDS TO TRIM HIS FINGERNAILS. WHO'S HE WITH?
..."LOTTALUV92"?
WHO THE HELL IS LOTTALUV92?!
WHO IS SHE?! WHAT IS SHE TO HIM?! ARE THEY CLOSE?! HOW DARE HE!
DOES "92" MEAN SHE WAS BORN IN 1992? IS SHE YOUNGER AND PRETTIER THAN ME?!
born: 1990
lottaluv92's bio
Charlene
SoCal. DTLA wannabe! All those who wander are not lost. :)
PHEW...
JUST YOUNGER.
MY HEART WAS BEATING SO FAST!
THIS DAY IS OVER.
I HAVEN'T EVEN HAD MY--

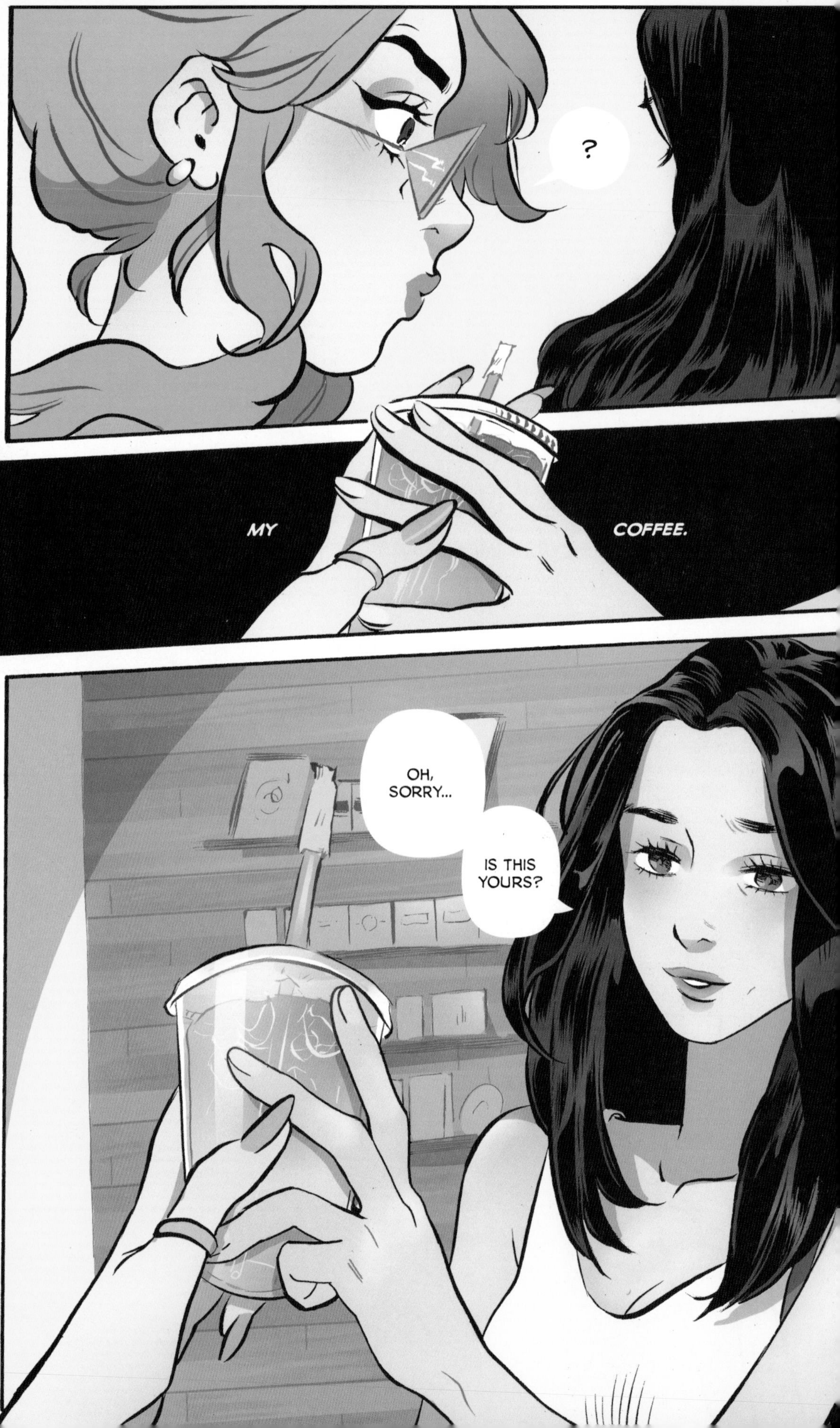
?
MY
COFFEE.
OH, SORRY...
IS THIS YOURS?

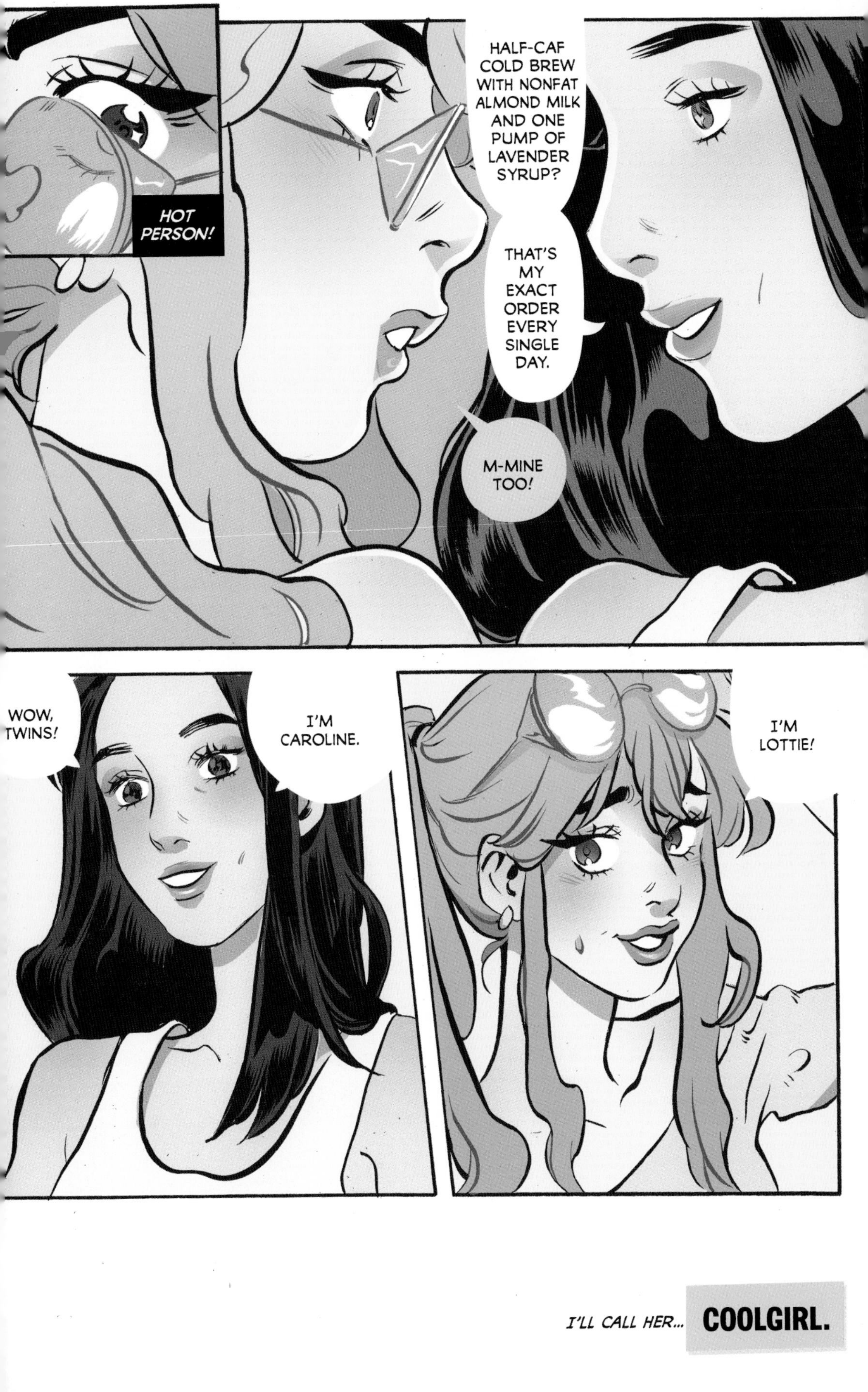
HOT PERSON!
HALF-CAF COLD BREW WITH NONFAT ALMOND MILK AND ONE PUMP OF LAVENDER SYRUP?
THAT'S MY EXACT ORDER EVERY SINGLE DAY.
M-MINE TOO!
WOW, TWINS!
I'M CAROLINE.
I'M LOTTIE!
I'LL CALL HER... COOLGIRL.

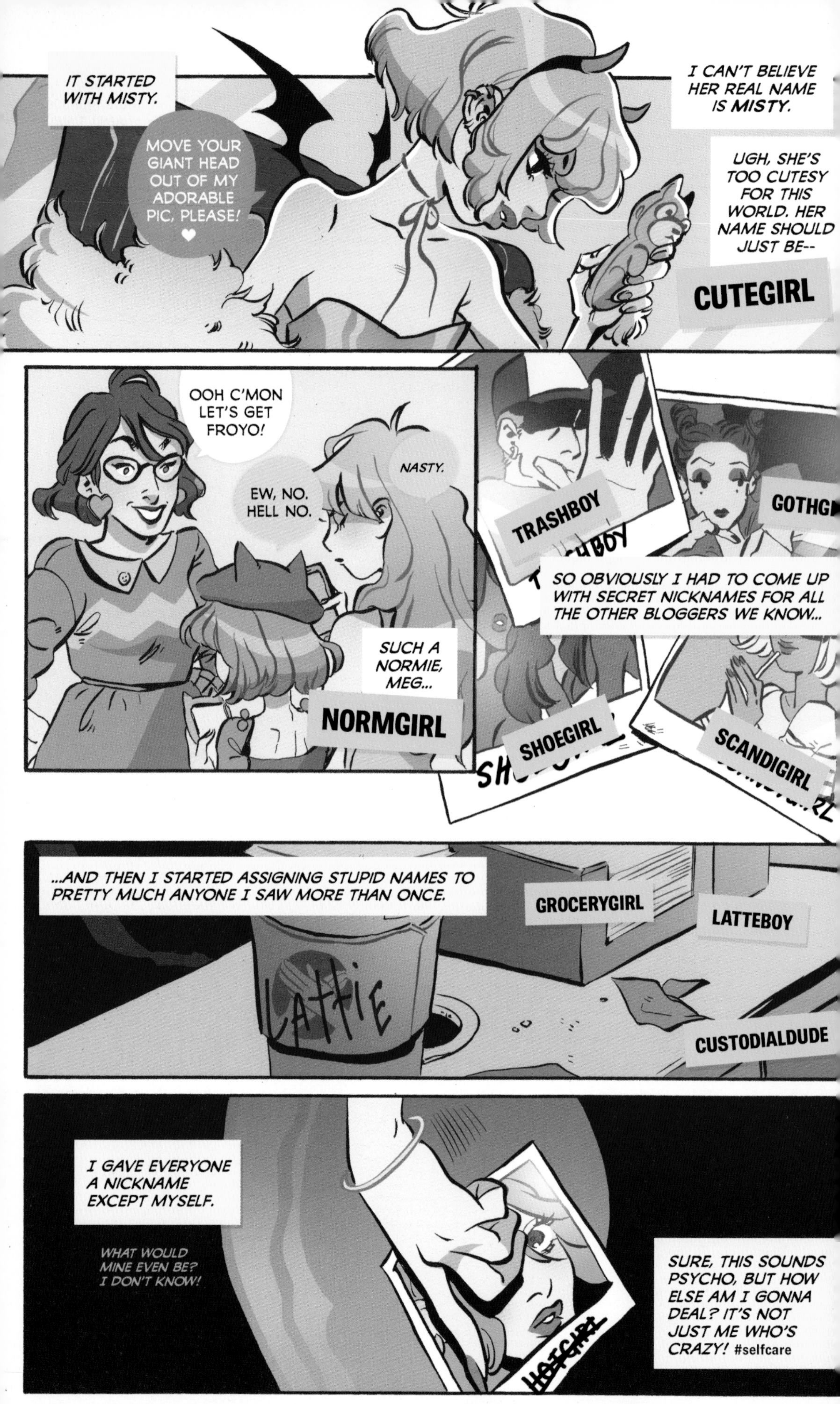

IT STARTED WITH MISTY.
MOVE YOUR GIANT HEAD OUT OF MY ADORABLE PIC, PLEASE! ♥
I CAN'T BELIEVE HER REAL NAME IS **MISTY.**
UGH, SHE'S TOO CUTESY FOR THIS WORLD. HER NAME SHOULD JUST BE--
CUTEGIRL
OOH C'MON LET'S GET FROYO!
EW, NO. HELL NO.
NASTY.
SUCH A NORMIE, MEG...
NORMGIRL
TRASHBOY
GOTHG
SO OBVIOUSLY I HAD TO COME UP WITH SECRET NICKNAMES FOR ALL THE OTHER BLOGGERS WE KNOW...
SHOEGIRL
SCANDIGIRL
...AND THEN I STARTED ASSIGNING STUPID NAMES TO PRETTY MUCH ANYONE I SAW MORE THAN ONCE.
GROCERYGIRL
LATTEBOY
Lattie
CUSTODIALDUDE
I GAVE EVERYONE A NICKNAME EXCEPT MYSELF.
WHAT WOULD MINE EVEN BE? I DON'T KNOW!
SURE, THIS SOUNDS PSYCHO, BUT HOW ELSE AM I GONNA DEAL? IT'S NOT JUST ME WHO'S CRAZY! #selfcare
HOTGIRL

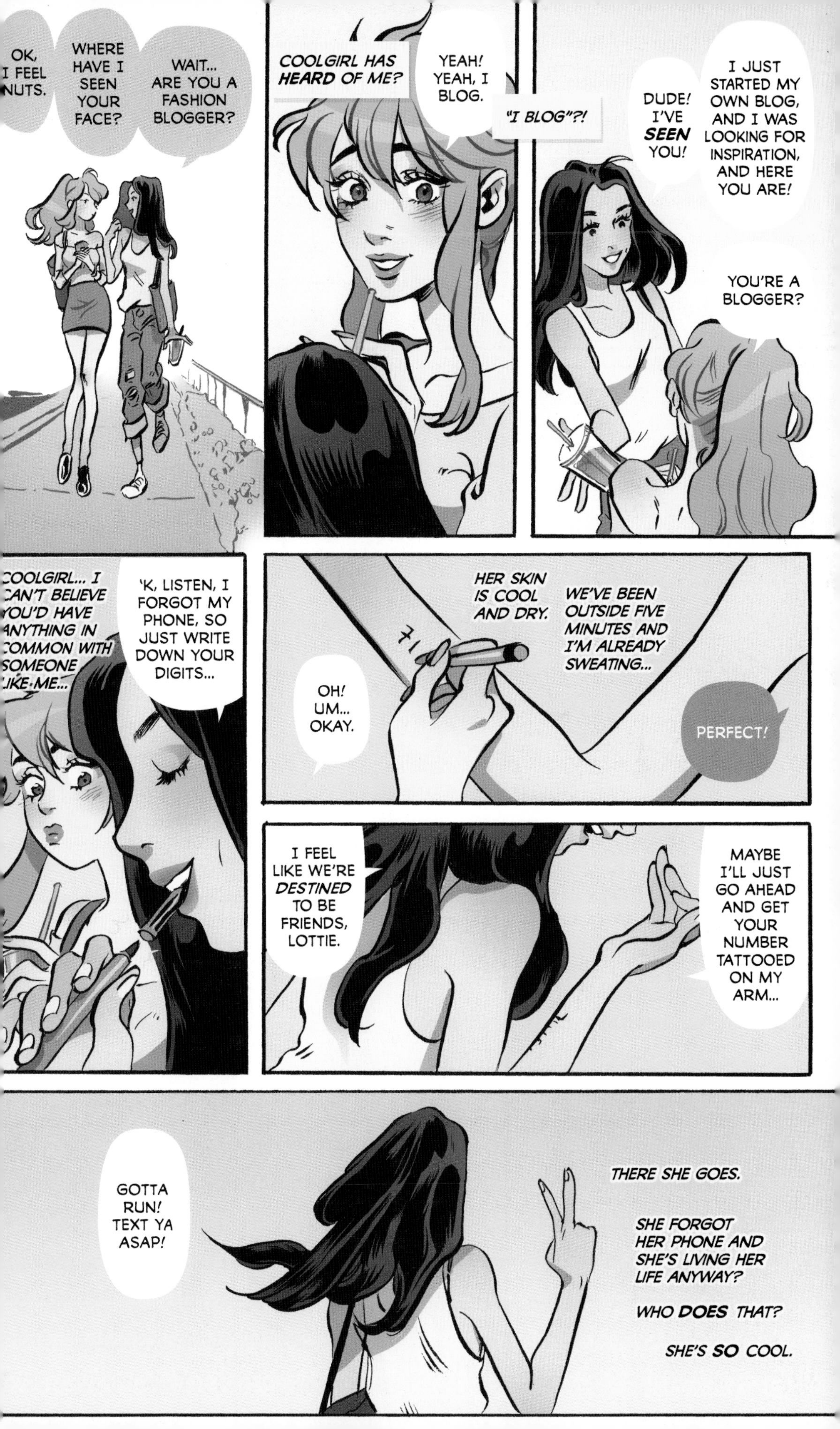
OK, I FEEL NUTS.
WHERE HAVE I SEEN YOUR FACE?
WAIT... ARE YOU A FASHION BLOGGER?
COOLGIRL HAS HEARD OF ME?
YEAH! YEAH, I BLOG.
"I BLOG"?!
DUDE! I'VE SEEN YOU!
I JUST STARTED MY OWN BLOG, AND I WAS LOOKING FOR INSPIRATION, AND HERE YOU ARE!
YOU'RE A BLOGGER?
COOLGIRL... I CAN'T BELIEVE YOU'D HAVE ANYTHING IN COMMON WITH SOMEONE LIKE ME...
'K, LISTEN, I FORGOT MY PHONE, SO JUST WRITE DOWN YOUR DIGITS...
HER SKIN IS COOL AND DRY.
WE'VE BEEN OUTSIDE FIVE MINUTES AND I'M ALREADY SWEATING...
OH! UM... OKAY.
PERFECT!
I FEEL LIKE WE'RE DESTINED TO BE FRIENDS, LOTTIE.
MAYBE I'LL JUST GO AHEAD AND GET YOUR NUMBER TATTOOED ON MY ARM...
GOTTA RUN! TEXT YA ASAP!
THERE SHE GOES.
SHE FORGOT HER PHONE AND SHE'S LIVING HER LIFE ANYWAY?
WHO DOES THAT?
SHE'S SO COOL.

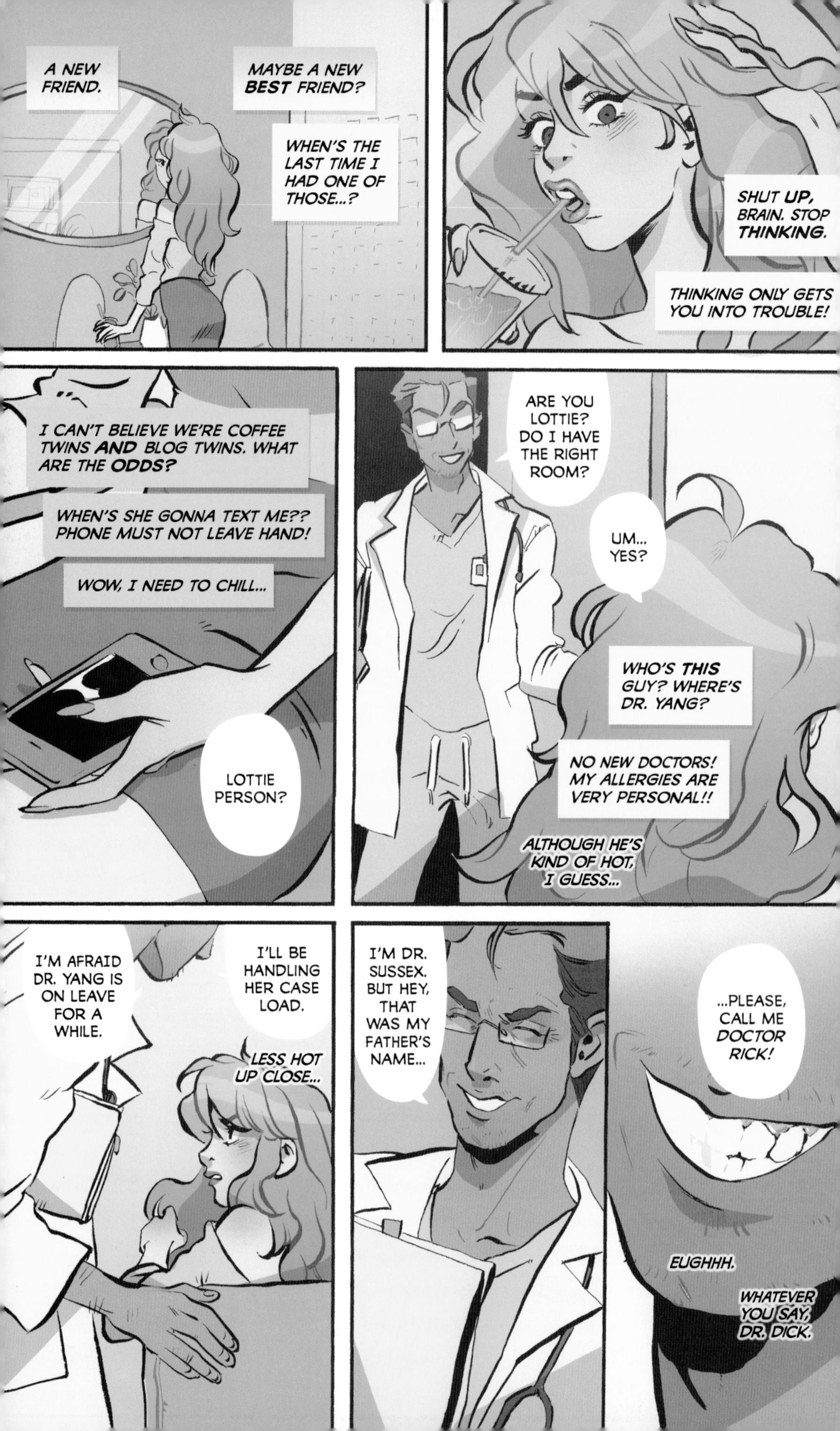
A NEW FRIEND.
MAYBE A NEW BEST FRIEND?
WHEN'S THE LAST TIME I HAD ONE OF THOSE...?
SHUT UP, BRAIN. STOP THINKING.
THINKING ONLY GETS YOU INTO TROUBLE!
I CAN'T BELIEVE WE'RE COFFEE TWINS AND BLOG TWINS. WHAT ARE THE ODDS?
WHEN'S SHE GONNA TEXT ME?? PHONE MUST NOT LEAVE HAND!
WOW, I NEED TO CHILL...
LOTTIE PERSON?
ARE YOU LOTTIE? DO I HAVE THE RIGHT ROOM?
UM... YES?
WHO'S THIS GUY? WHERE'S DR. YANG?
NO NEW DOCTORS! MY ALLERGIES ARE VERY PERSONAL!!
ALTHOUGH HE'S KIND OF HOT, I GUESS...
I'M AFRAID DR. YANG IS ON LEAVE FOR A WHILE.
I'LL BE HANDLING HER CASE LOAD.
LESS HOT UP CLOSE...
I'M DR. SUSSEX. BUT HEY, THAT WAS MY FATHER'S NAME...
...PLEASE, CALL ME DOCTOR RICK!
EUGHHH.
WHATEVER YOU SAY, DR. DICK.

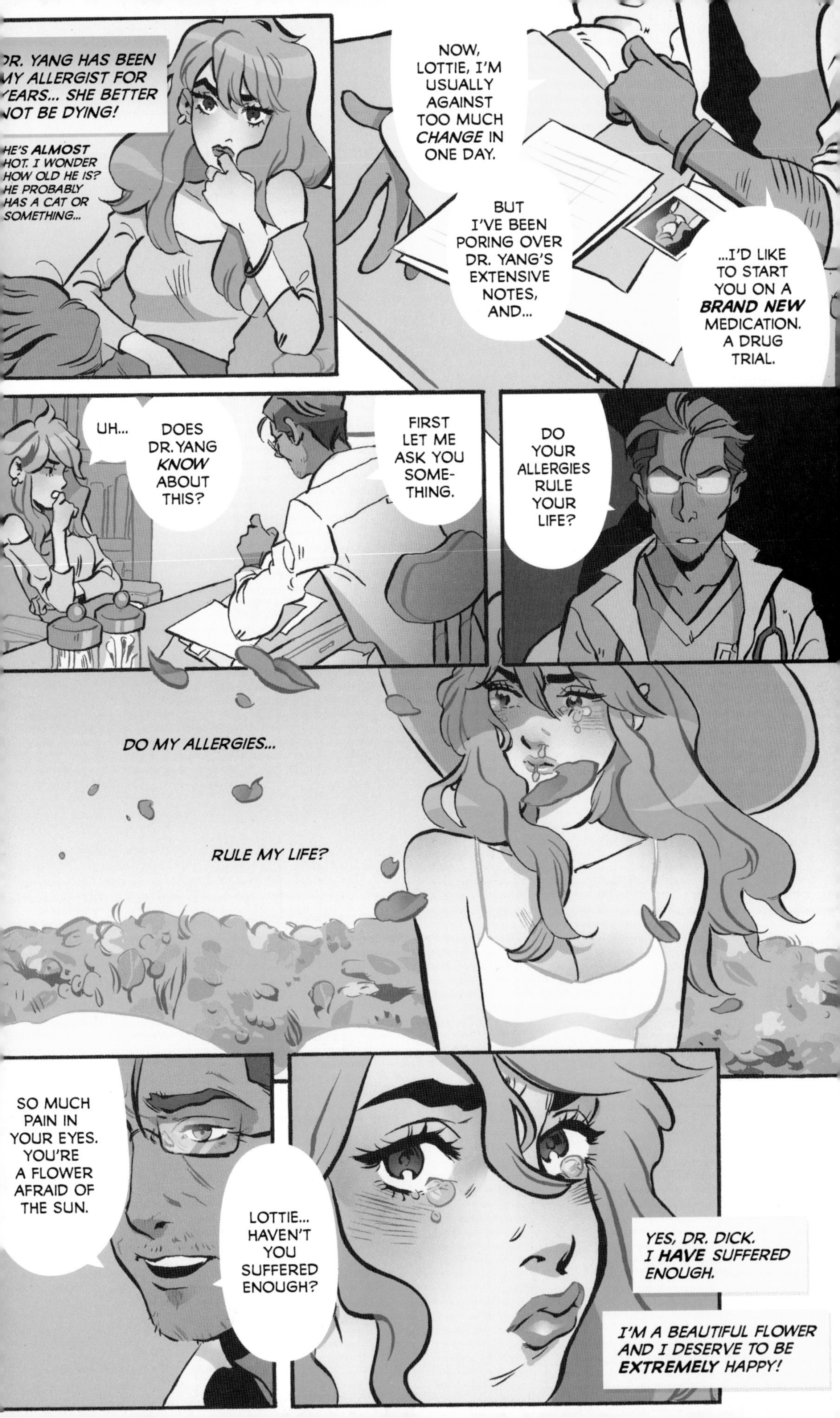
DR. YANG HAS BEEN MY ALLERGIST FOR YEARS... SHE BETTER NOT BE DYING!
HE'S ALMOST HOT. I WONDER HOW OLD HE IS? HE PROBABLY HAS A CAT OR SOMETHING...
NOW, LOTTIE, I'M USUALLY AGAINST TOO MUCH CHANGE IN ONE DAY.
BUT I'VE BEEN PORING OVER DR. YANG'S EXTENSIVE NOTES, AND...
...I'D LIKE TO START YOU ON A BRAND NEW MEDICATION. A DRUG TRIAL.
UH...
DOES DR. YANG KNOW ABOUT THIS?
FIRST LET ME ASK YOU SOME-THING.
DO YOUR ALLERGIES RULE YOUR LIFE?
DO MY ALLERGIES...
RULE MY LIFE?
SO MUCH PAIN IN YOUR EYES. YOU'RE A FLOWER AFRAID OF THE SUN.
LOTTIE... HAVEN'T YOU SUFFERED ENOUGH?
YES, DR. DICK. I HAVE SUFFERED ENOUGH.
I'M A BEAUTIFUL FLOWER AND I DESERVE TO BE EXTREMELY HAPPY!

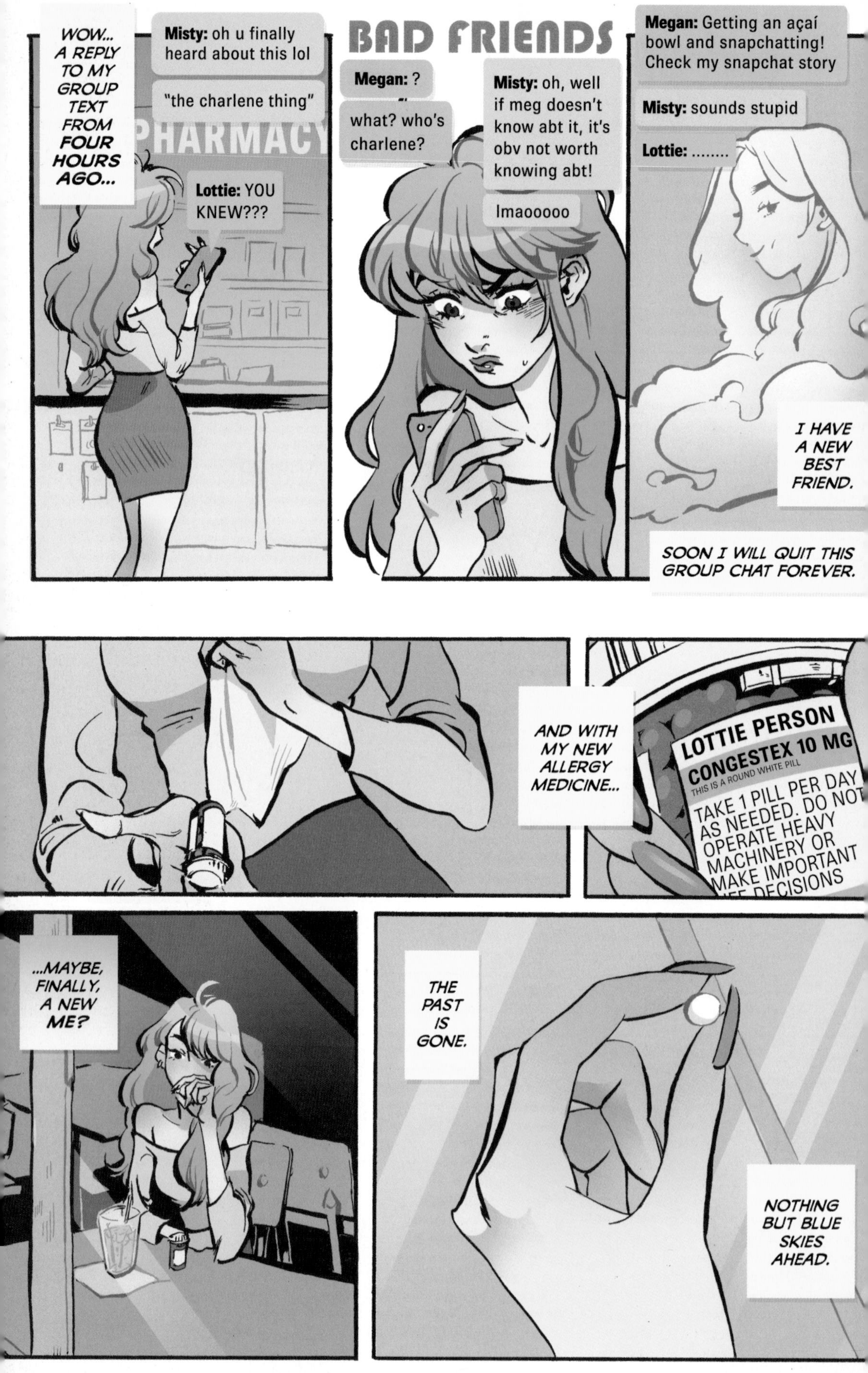
WOW... A REPLY TO MY GROUP TEXT FROM FOUR HOURS AGO...
Misty: oh u finally heard about this lol
"the charlene thing"
PHARMACY
Lottie: YOU KNEW???
BAD FRIENDS
Megan: ?
what? who's charlene?
Misty: oh, well if meg doesn't know abt it, it's obv not worth knowing abt!
lmaooooo
Megan: Getting an açaí bowl and snapchatting! Check my snapchat story
Misty: sounds stupid
Lottie: ....
I HAVE A NEW BEST FRIEND.
SOON I WILL QUIT THIS GROUP CHAT FOREVER.
AND WITH MY NEW ALLERGY MEDICINE...
LOTTIE PERSON
CONGESTEX 10 MG
THIS IS A ROUND WHITE PILL
TAKE 1 PILL PER DAY AS NEEDED. DO NOT OPERATE HEAVY MACHINERY OR MAKE IMPORTANT
...MAYBE, FINALLY, A NEW ME?
THE PAST IS GONE.
NOTHING BUT BLUE SKIES AHEAD.

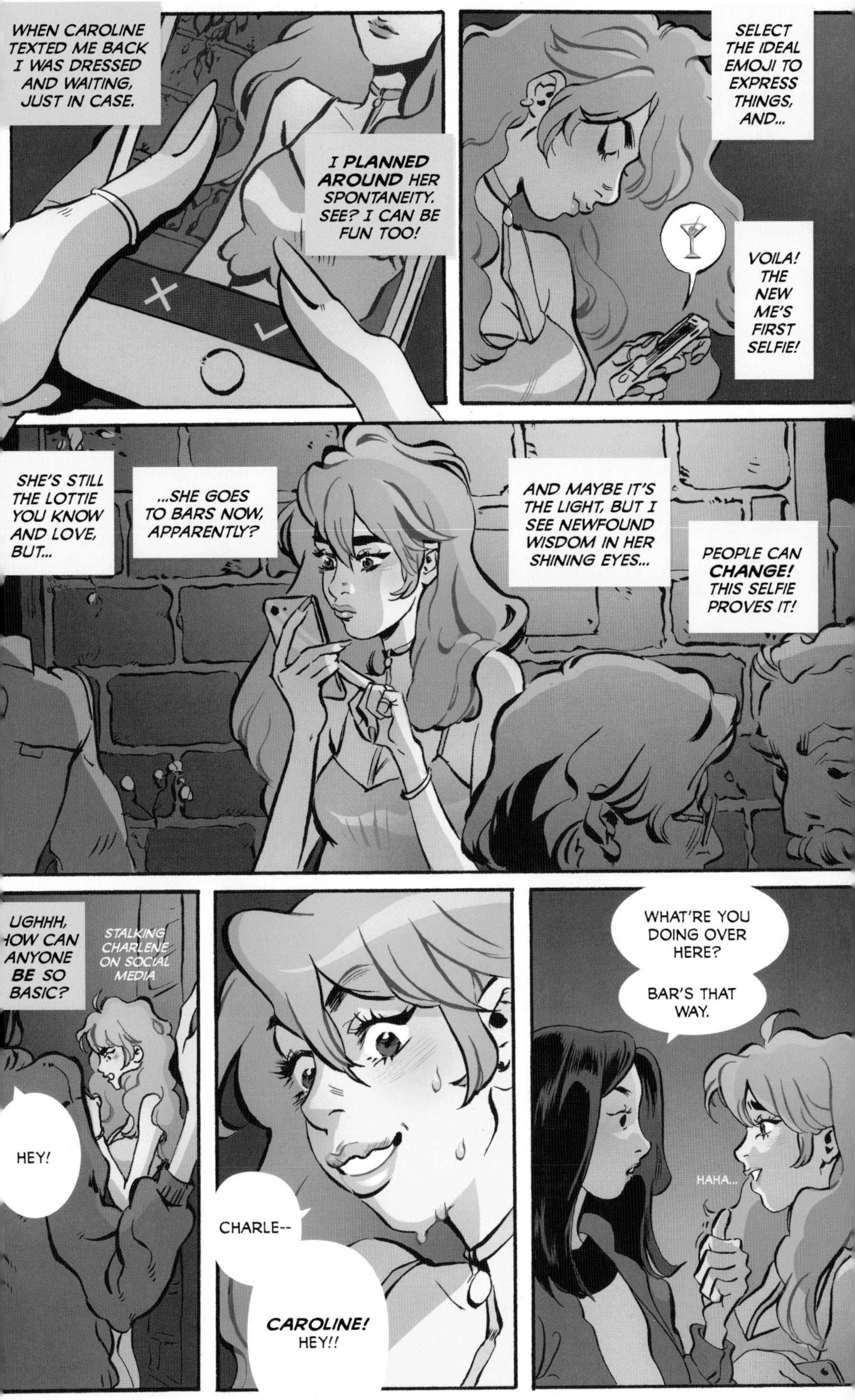
WHEN CAROLINE TEXTED ME BACK I WAS DRESSED AND WAITING, JUST IN CASE.
I PLANNED AROUND HER SPONTANEITY. SEE? I CAN BE FUN TOO!
SELECT THE IDEAL EMOJI TO EXPRESS THINGS, AND...
VOILA! THE NEW ME'S FIRST SELFIE!
SHE'S STILL THE LOTTIE YOU KNOW AND LOVE, BUT...
...SHE GOES TO BARS NOW, APPARENTLY?
AND MAYBE IT'S THE LIGHT, BUT I SEE NEWFOUND WISDOM IN HER SHINING EYES...
PEOPLE CAN CHANGE! THIS SELFIE PROVES IT!
UGHHH, HOW CAN ANYONE BE SO BASIC?
STALKING CHARLENE ON SOCIAL MEDIA
HEY!
CHARLE--
CAROLINE! HEY!!
WHAT'RE YOU DOING OVER HERE?
BAR'S THAT WAY.
HAHA...

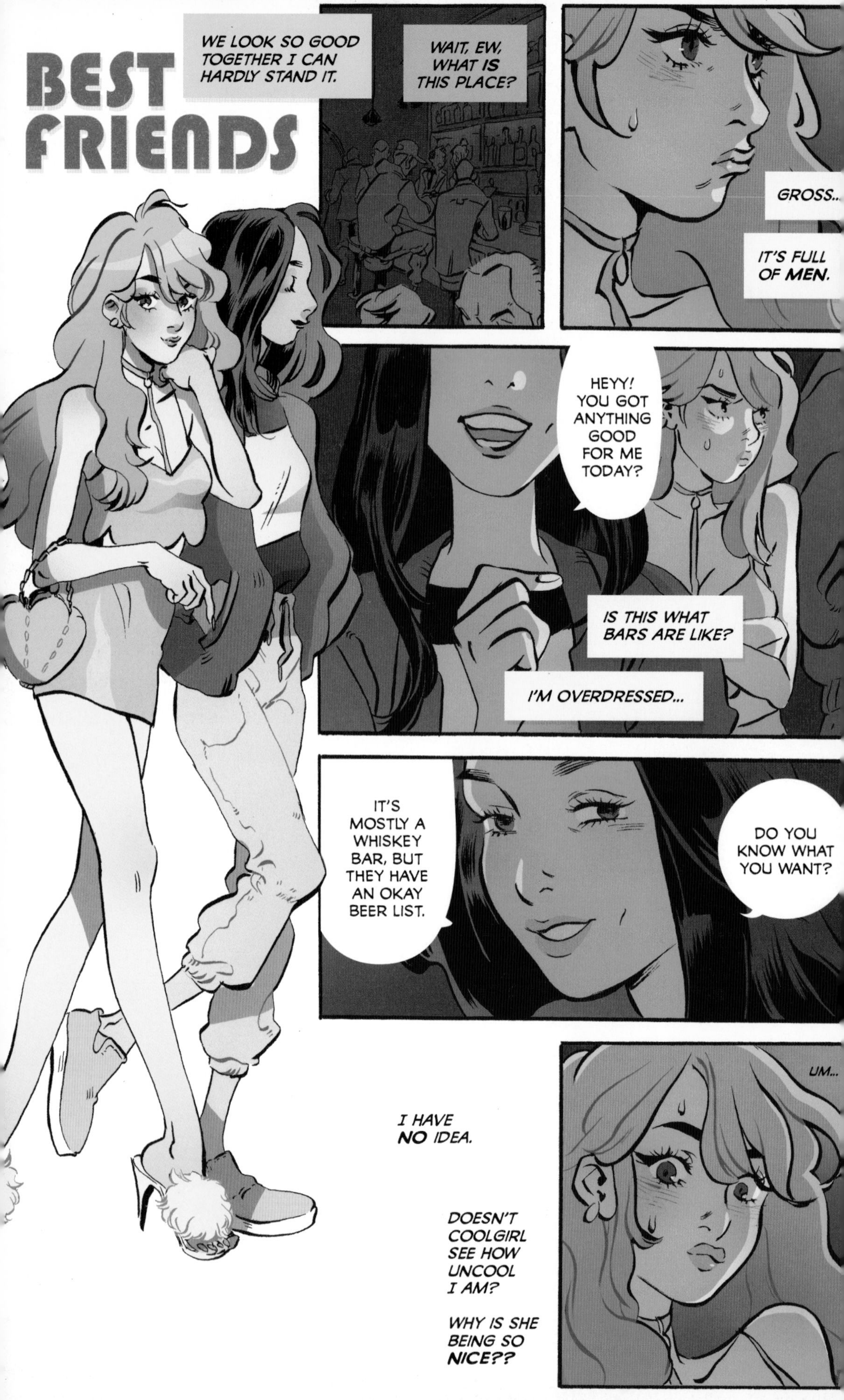
BEST FRIENDS
WE LOOK SO GOOD TOGETHER I CAN HARDLY STAND IT.
WAIT, EW, WHAT IS THIS PLACE?
GROSS...
IT'S FULL OF MEN.
HEYY! YOU GOT ANYTHING GOOD FOR ME TODAY?
IS THIS WHAT BARS ARE LIKE?
I'M OVERDRESSED...
IT'S MOSTLY A WHISKEY BAR, BUT THEY HAVE AN OKAY BEER LIST.
DO YOU KNOW WHAT YOU WANT?
UM...
I HAVE NO IDEA.
DOESN'T COOLGIRL SEE HOW UNCOOL I AM?
WHY IS SHE BEING SO NICE??

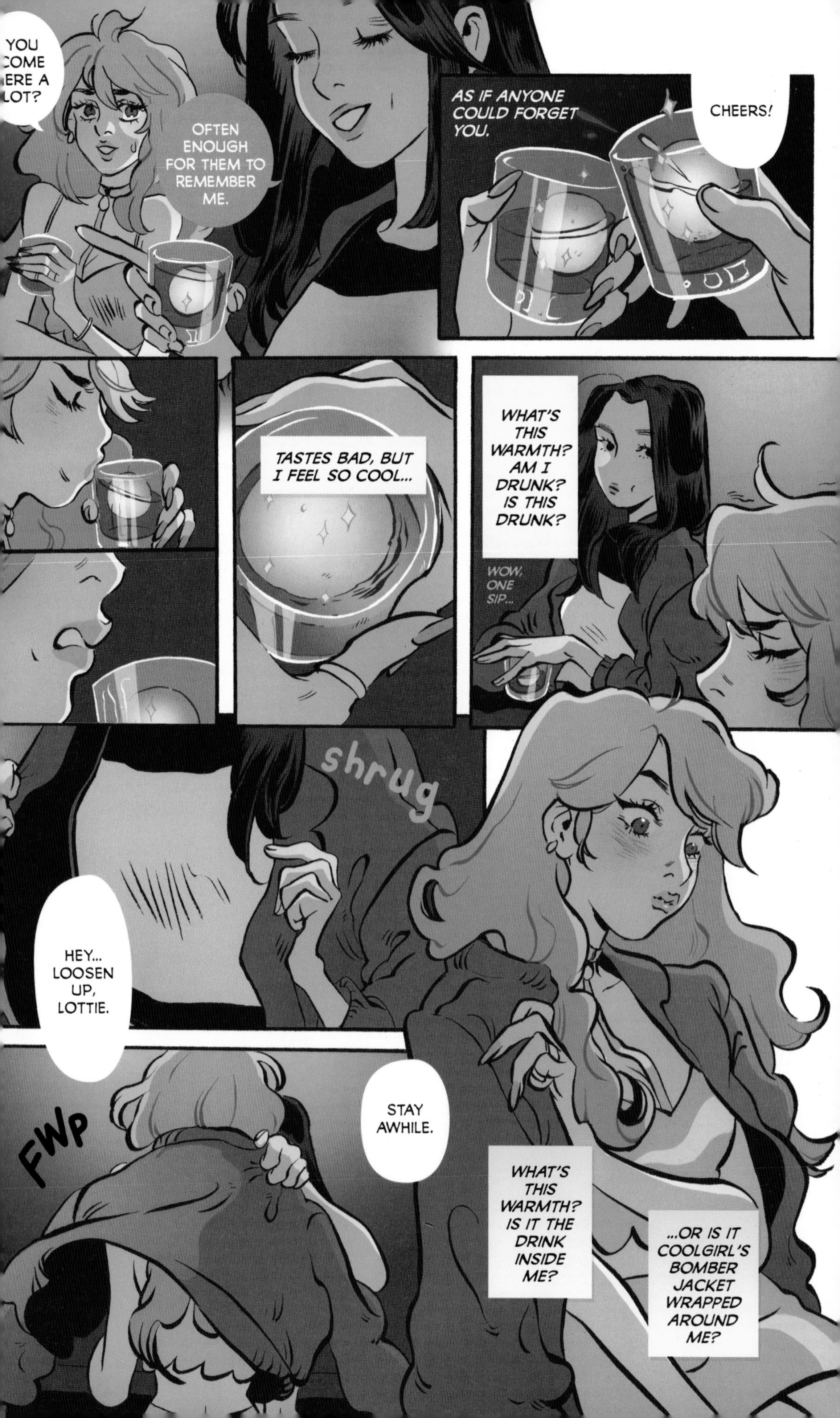
YOU COME ERE A LOT?
OFTEN ENOUGH FOR THEM TO REMEMBER ME.
AS IF ANYONE COULD FORGET YOU.
CHEERS!
TASTES BAD, BUT I FEEL SO COOL...
WHAT'S THIS WARMTH? AM I DRUNK? IS THIS DRUNK?
WOW, ONE SIP...
shrug
HEY... LOOSEN UP, LOTTIE.
FWP
STAY AWHILE.
WHAT'S THIS WARMTH? IS IT THE DRINK INSIDE ME?
...OR IS IT COOLGIRL'S BOMBER JACKET WRAPPED AROUND ME?

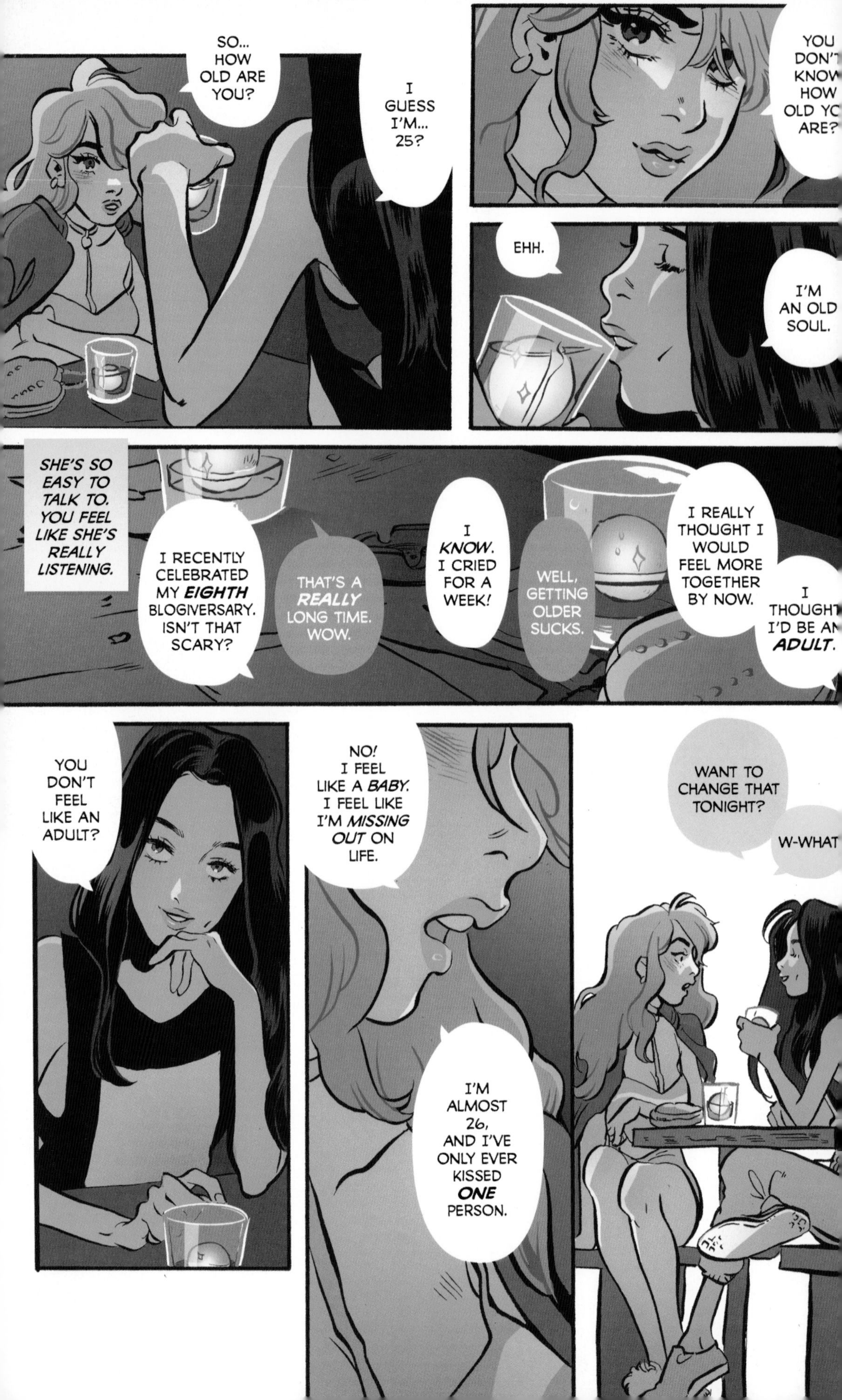
SO... HOW OLD ARE YOU?
I GUESS I'M... 25?
YOU DON'T KNOW HOW OLD YO ARE?
EHH.
I'M AN OLD SOUL.
SHE'S SO EASY TO TALK TO. YOU FEEL LIKE SHE'S REALLY LISTENING.
I RECENTLY CELEBRATED MY EIGHTH BLOGIVERSARY. ISN'T THAT SCARY?
THAT'S A REALLY LONG TIME. WOW.
I KNOW. I CRIED FOR A WEEK!
WELL, GETTING OLDER SUCKS.
I REALLY THOUGHT I WOULD FEEL MORE TOGETHER BY NOW.
I THOUGHT I'D BE AN ADULT.
YOU DON'T FEEL LIKE AN ADULT?
NO! I FEEL LIKE A BABY. I FEEL LIKE I'M MISSING OUT ON LIFE.
I'M ALMOST 26, AND I'VE ONLY EVER KISSED ONE PERSON.
WANT TO CHANGE THAT TONIGHT?
W-WHAT

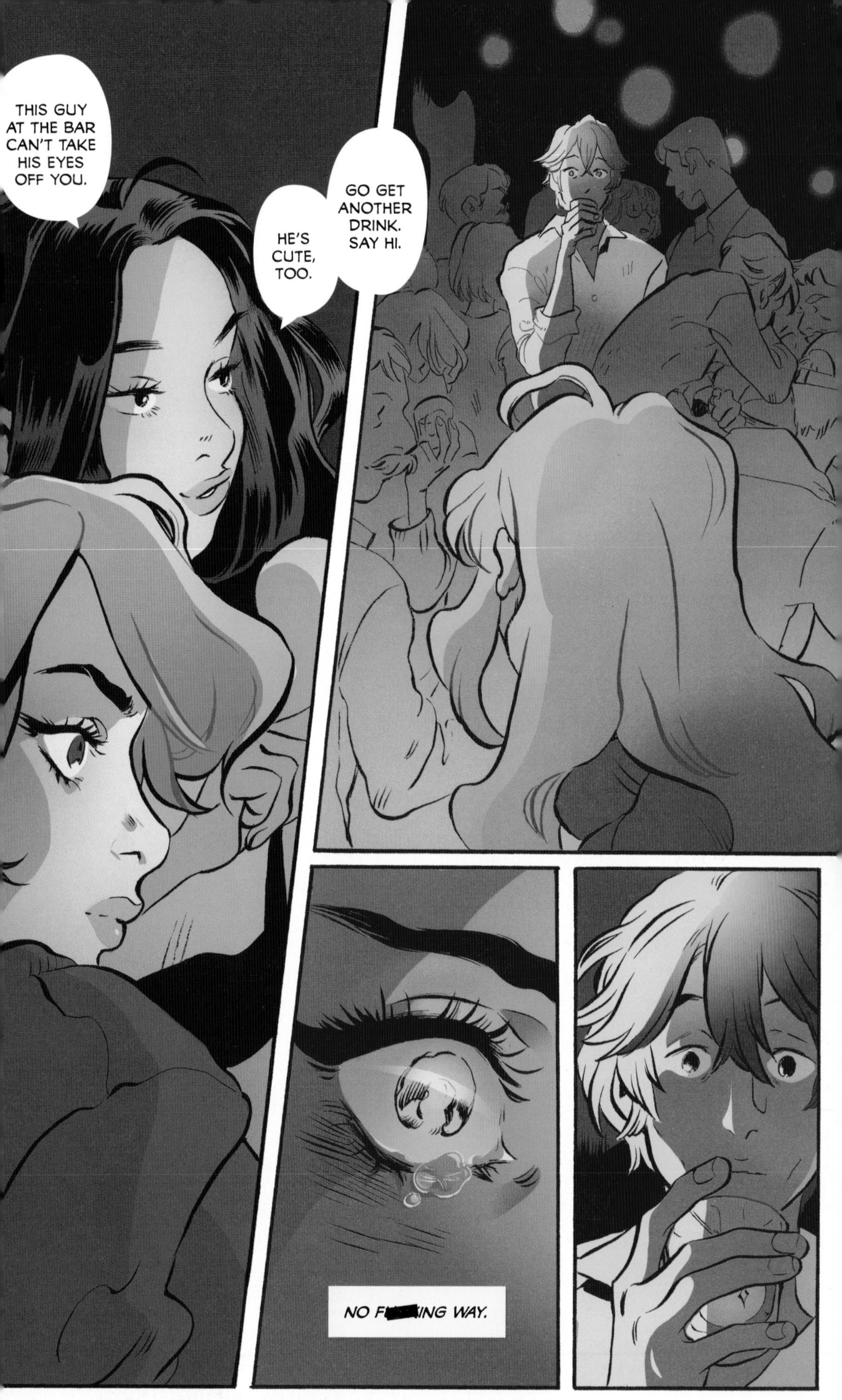
THIS GUY AT THE BAR CAN'T TAKE HIS EYES OFF YOU.
HE'S CUTE, TOO.
GO GET ANOTHER DRINK. SAY HI.
NO F[redacted]ING WAY.

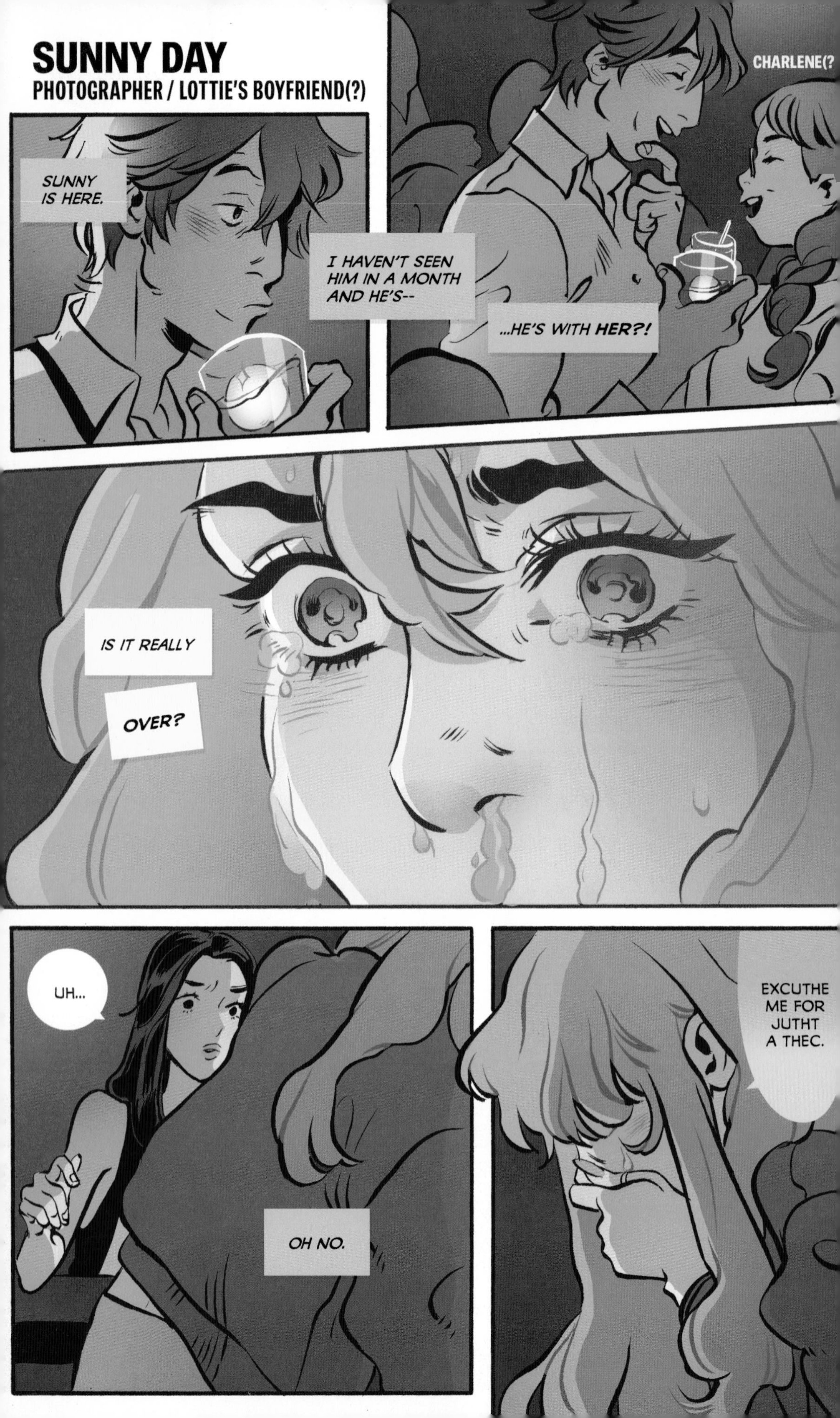
SUNNY DAY
PHOTOGRAPHER / LOTTIE'S BOYFRIEND(?)
SUNNY IS HERE.
I HAVEN'T SEEN HIM IN A MONTH AND HE'S--
CHARLENE(?
...HE'S WITH HER?!
IS IT REALLY
OVER?
UH...
OH NO.
EXCUTHE ME FOR JUTHT A THEC.

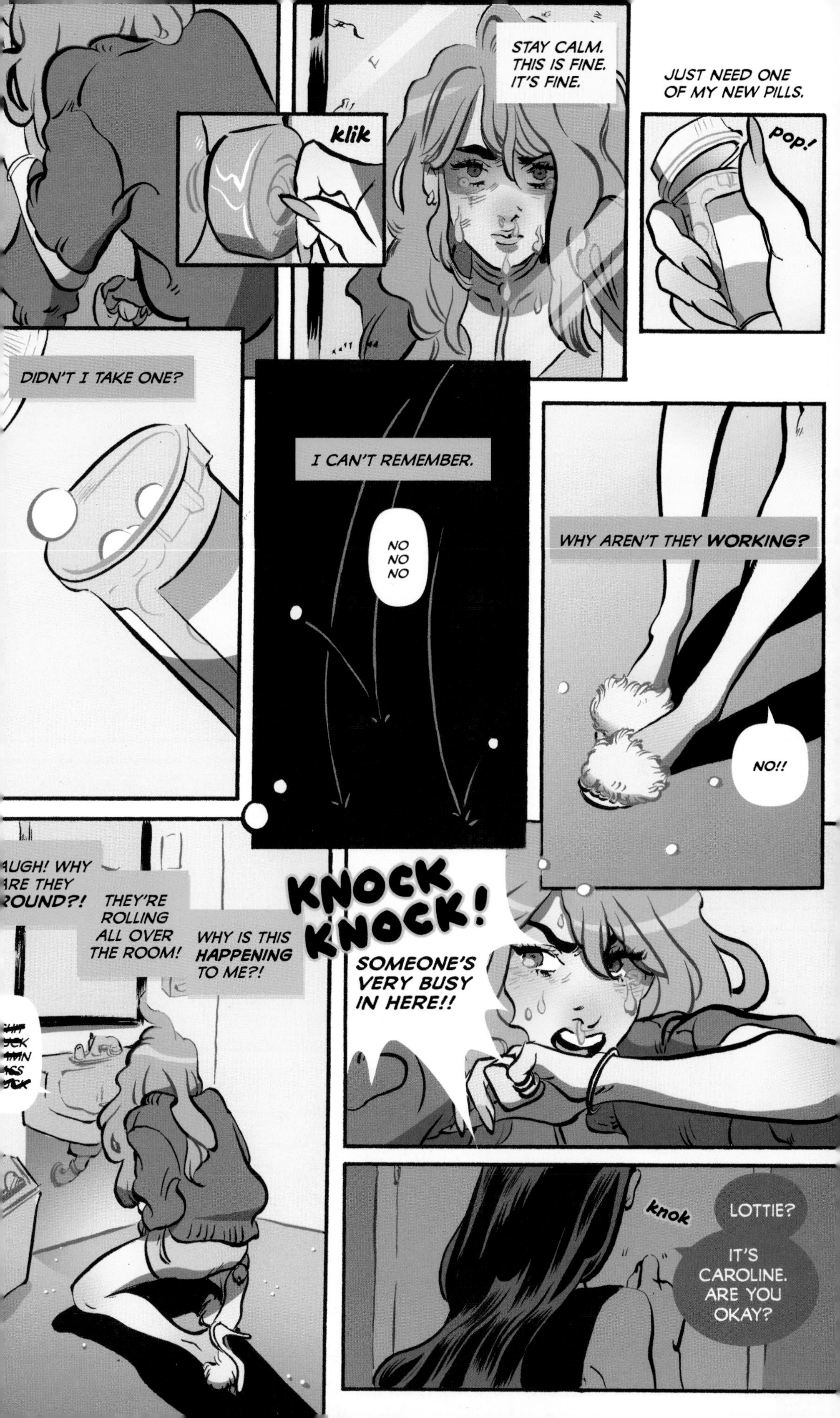

klik
STAY CALM. THIS IS FINE. IT'S FINE.
JUST NEED ONE OF MY NEW PILLS.
pop!
DIDN'T I TAKE ONE?
I CAN'T REMEMBER.
NO NO NO
WHY AREN'T THEY WORKING?
NO!!
UGH! WHY RE THEY ROUND?!
THEY'RE ROLLING ALL OVER THE ROOM!
WHY IS THIS HAPPENING TO ME?!
KNOCK KNOCK!
SOMEONE'S VERY BUSY IN HERE!!
knok
LOTTIE?
IT'S CAROLINE. ARE YOU OKAY?

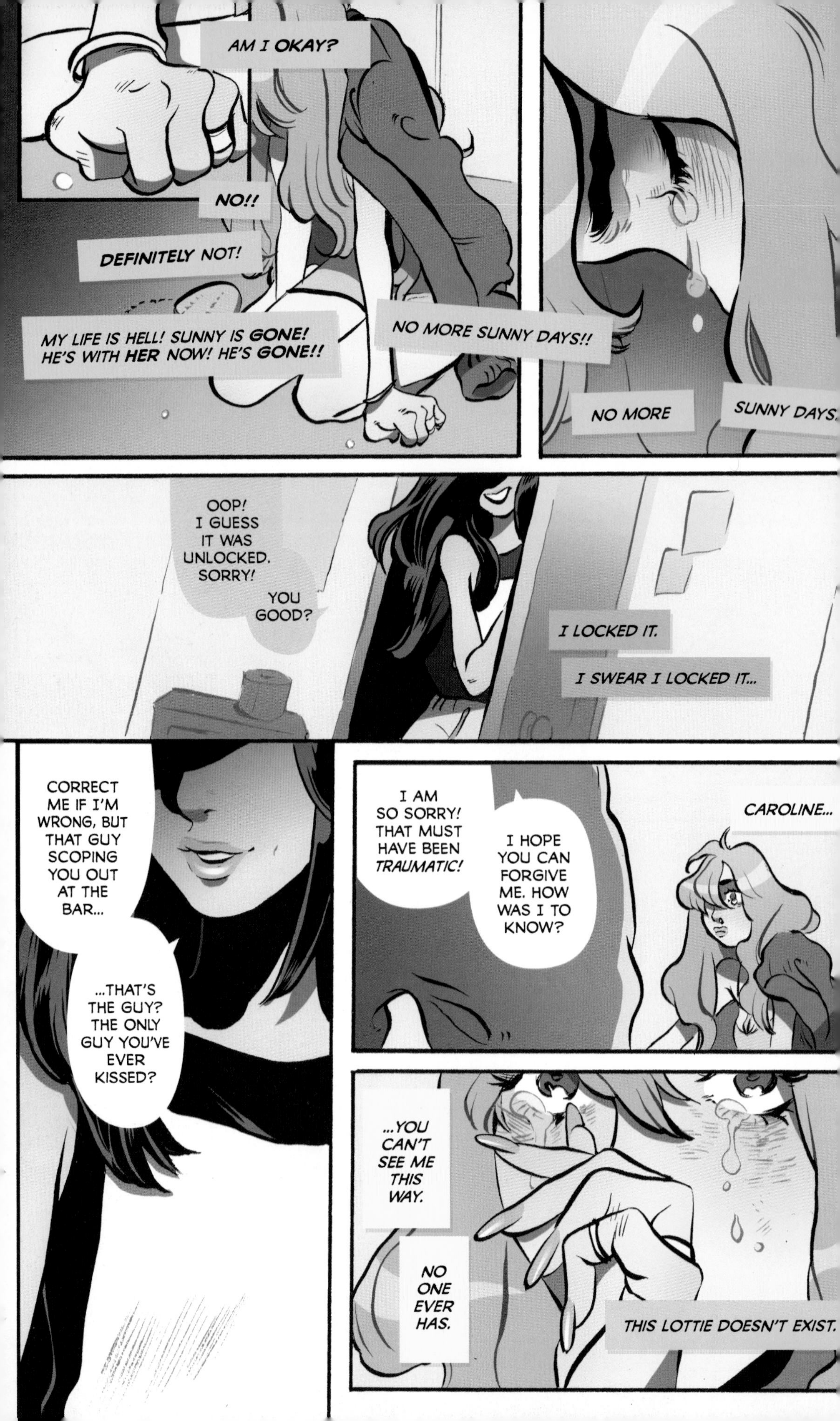
AM I OKAY?
NO!!
DEFINITELY NOT!
MY LIFE IS HELL! SUNNY IS GONE! HE'S WITH HER NOW! HE'S GONE!!
NO MORE SUNNY DAYS!!
NO MORE
SUNNY DAYS.
OOP! I GUESS IT WAS UNLOCKED. SORRY!
YOU GOOD?
I LOCKED IT.
I SWEAR I LOCKED IT...
CORRECT ME IF I'M WRONG, BUT THAT GUY SCOPING YOU OUT AT THE BAR...
...THAT'S THE GUY? THE ONLY GUY YOU'VE EVER KISSED?
I AM SO SORRY! THAT MUST HAVE BEEN TRAUMATIC!
I HOPE YOU CAN FORGIVE ME. HOW WAS I TO KNOW?
CAROLINE...
...YOU CAN'T SEE ME THIS WAY.
NO ONE EVER HAS.
THIS LOTTIE DOESN'T EXIST.

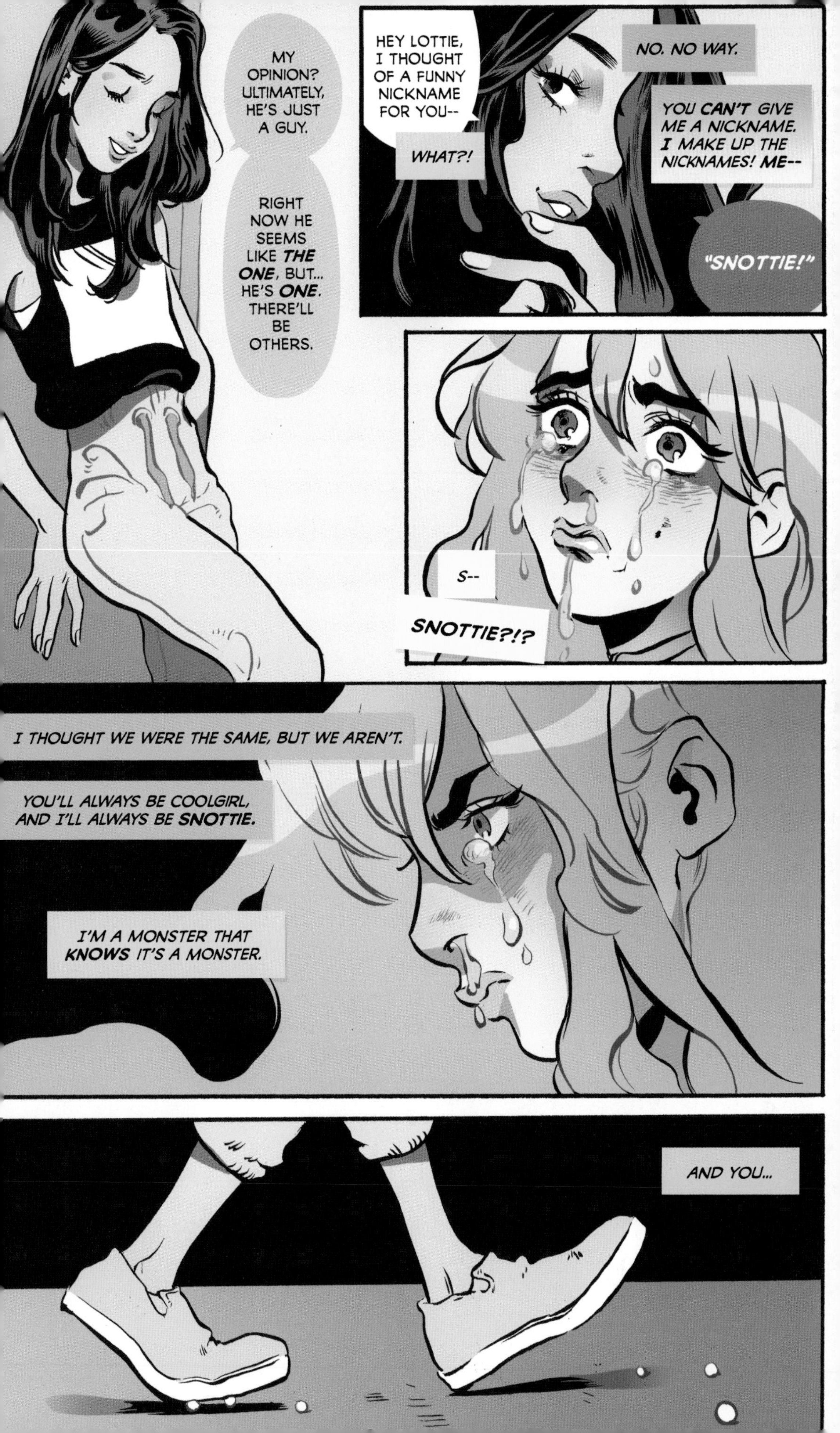
MY OPINION? ULTIMATELY, HE'S JUST A GUY.
RIGHT NOW HE SEEMS LIKE ***THE ONE***, BUT... HE'S ***ONE***. THERE'LL BE OTHERS.
HEY LOTTIE, I THOUGHT OF A FUNNY NICKNAME FOR YOU--
WHAT?!
NO. NO WAY.
YOU **CAN'T** GIVE ME A NICKNAME. **I** MAKE UP THE NICKNAMES! **ME--**
"SNOTTIE!"
S--
SNOTTIE?!?
I THOUGHT WE WERE THE SAME, BUT WE AREN'T.
YOU'LL ALWAYS BE COOLGIRL, AND I'LL ALWAYS BE **SNOTTIE**.
I'M A MONSTER THAT **KNOWS** IT'S A MONSTER.
AND YOU...

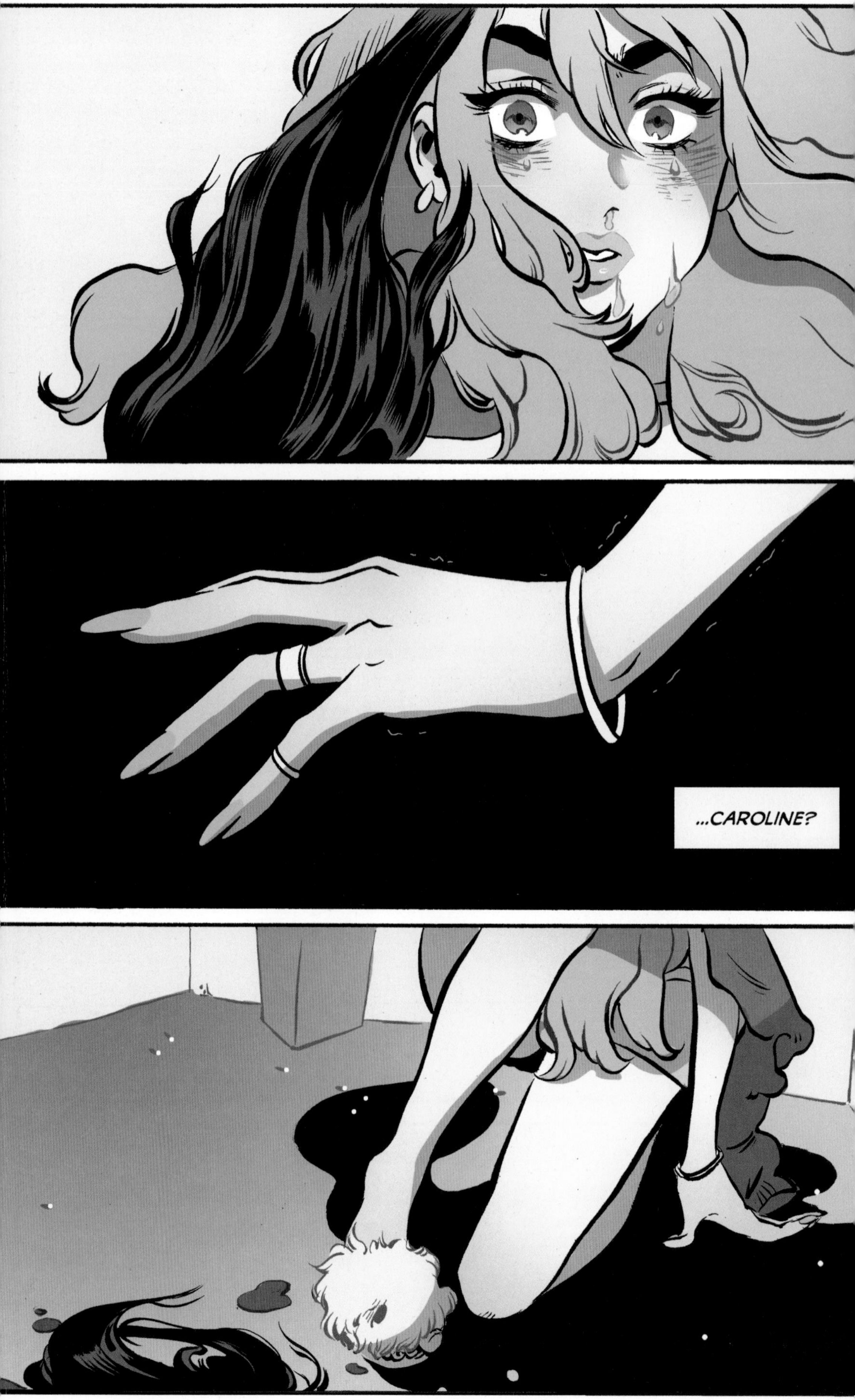
...CAROLINE?

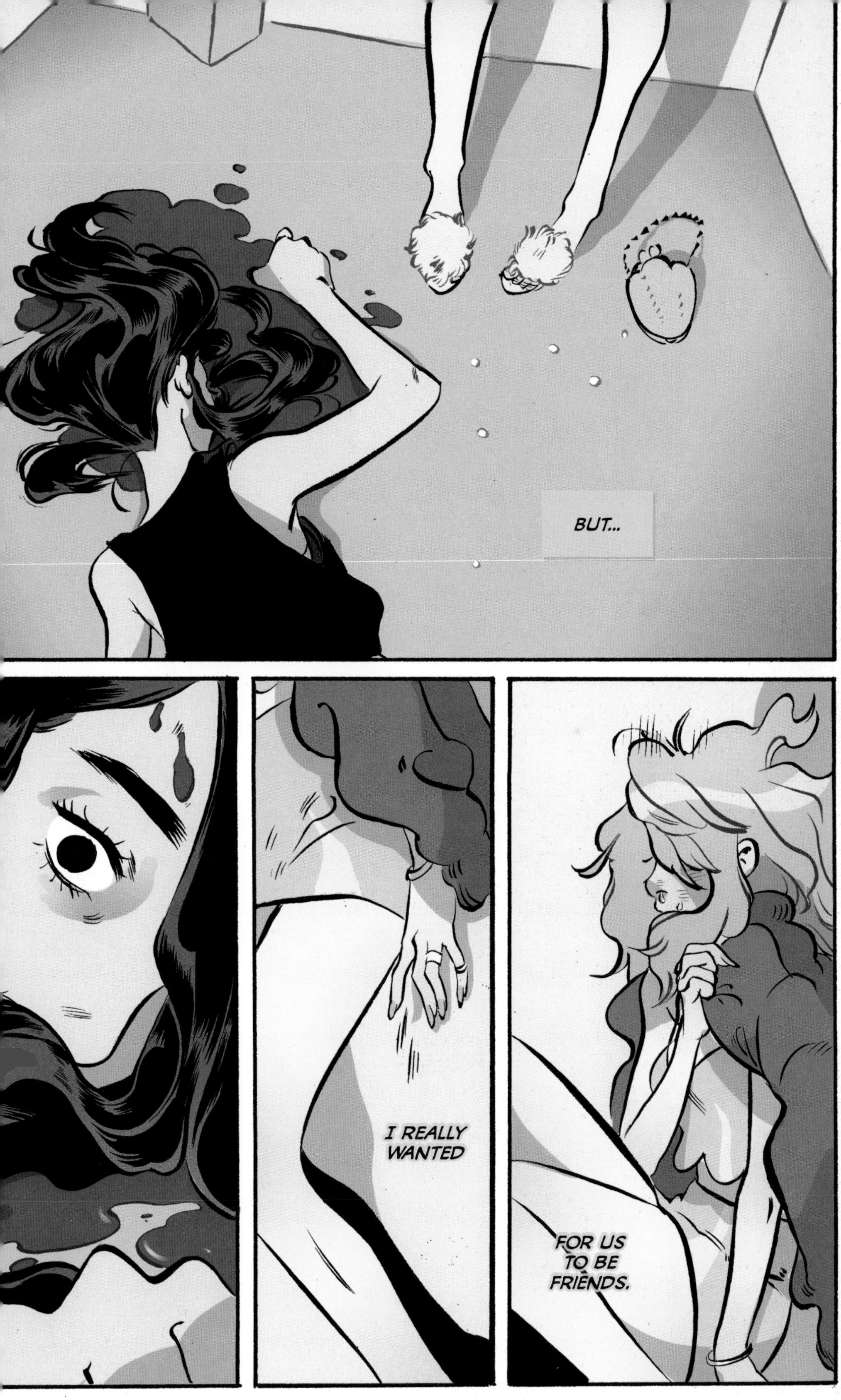
BUT...
I REALLY WANTED
FOR US TO BE FRIENDS.

Browser

Inbox (993 | Melt Cosme | ASOS | Shop | Victoria's Se | Opening (| Lottie Person - Fashion Blogger

Lottie Person

PHOTOS • TIPS • PRODUCTS • ABOUT • ARCHIVE • CONTACT

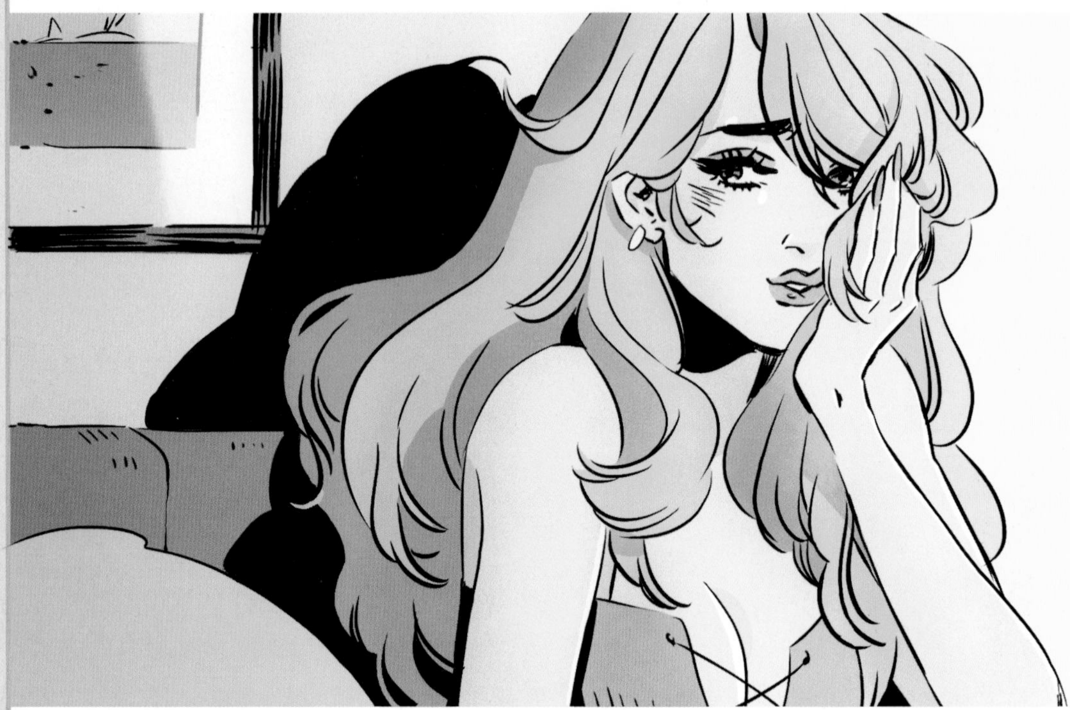

July 22, 2016 #LOTTIEPERSONAL

I'm Lottie Person, a 25-year-old girl living in downtown Los Angeles.

I've been a fashion blogger since 2008!

Stalk me on social media - I'll make it easy for you!

@lottieperson

Oh boy! It's really been a while, hasn't it? But it's like they say: life is what happens between blog posts. Right??

So, it's summer again and LA is an oven. And who wants to squeeze into a pair of high-waisted jeans when it's 90 out? Yeah, that's right - me! I can't get enough of these new skinnies from [redacted], and pairing them with an ankle boot isn't basic, it's CLASSIC.

Oh right! My birthday is coming up (scream!) and the lovely people at [redacted] Cosmetics are helping me host another giveaway! All you have to do is:

Lottie Person's Person-al Details!

Date of Birth: 8/6/1990 *(Leo!)*
Place of Birth: Fountain Valley, CA
Blood Type: AB+
Eye Color: Brown
Hair Color: Green

Height: 5'9"
Weight: Now that's TOO personal!!
Shoe Size: 8 US
Dress Size: 2 *(sometimes 4)*
Bra size: 30DDD

FAVORITE...
Color: Pink
Food: Croque Monsieur
Flower: Fake
Cats or Dogs? Neither! No offense!

02. WORSE PROBLEMS THAN BOY PROBLEMS

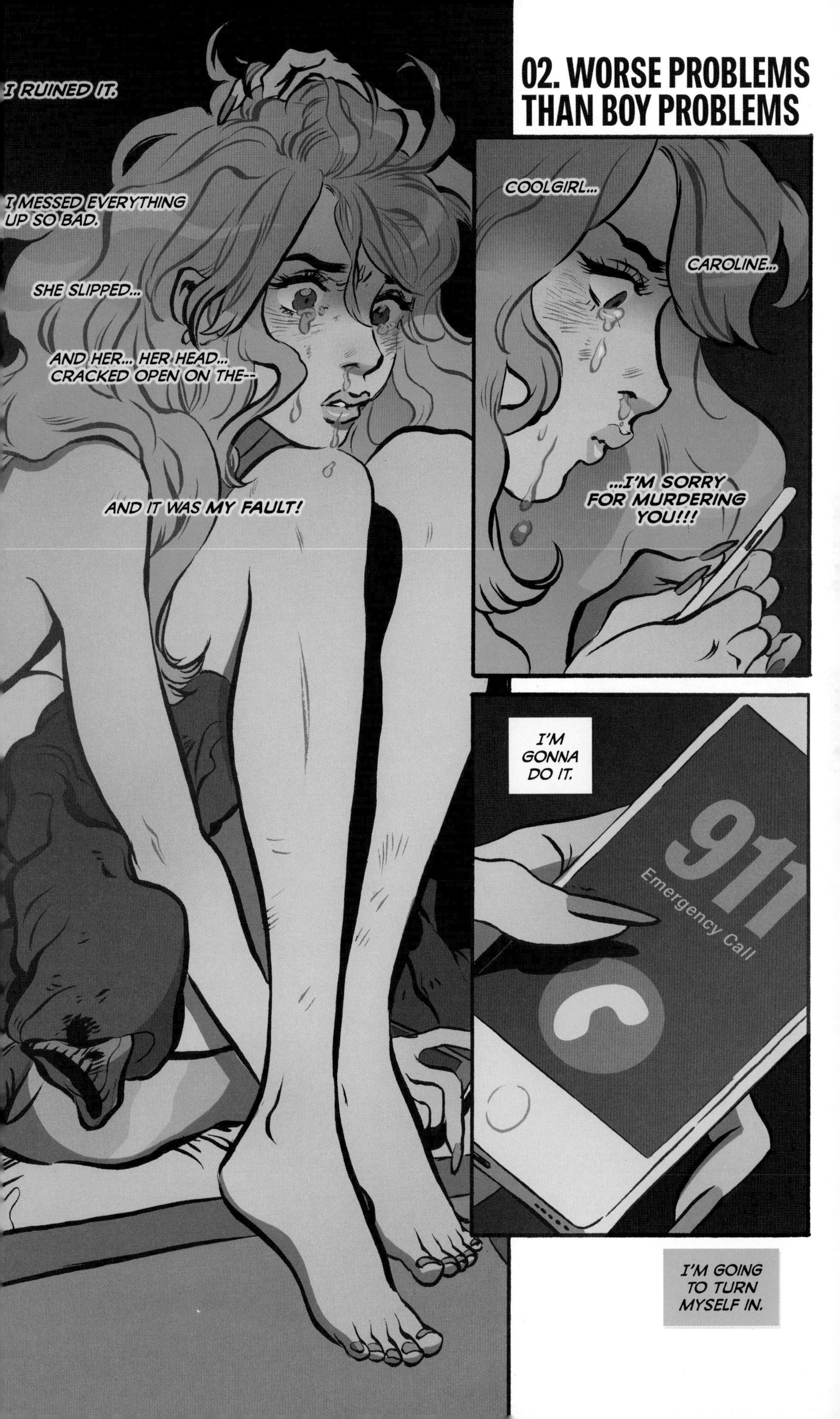
I RUINED IT.
I MESSED EVERYTHING UP SO BAD.
SHE SLIPPED...
AND HER... HER HEAD... CRACKED OPEN ON THE--
AND IT WAS MY FAULT!
COOLGIRL...
CAROLINE...
...I'M SORRY FOR MURDERING YOU!!!
I'M GONNA DO IT.
911
Emergency Call
I'M GOING TO TURN MYSELF IN.

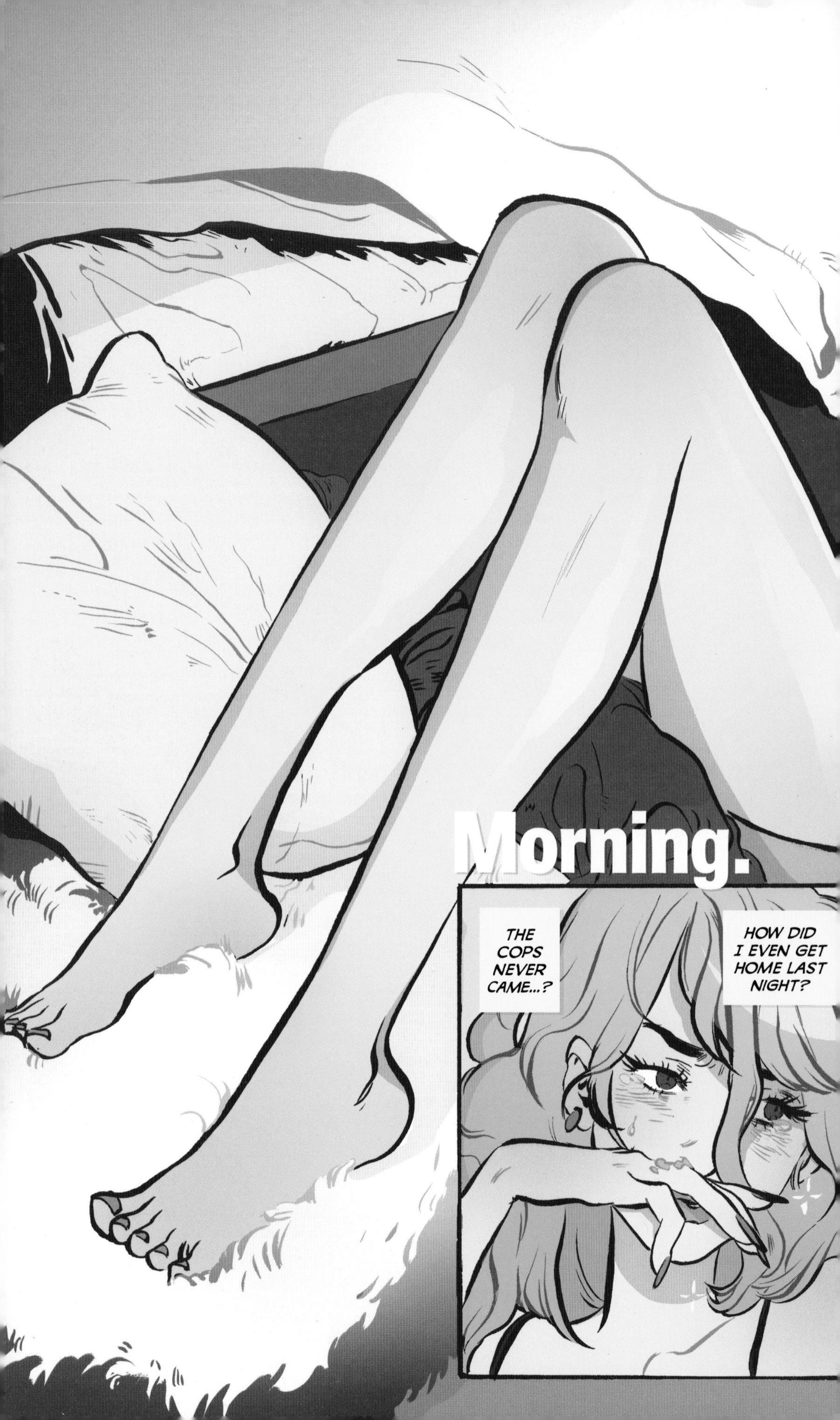
Morning.
THE COPS NEVER CAME...?
HOW DID I EVEN GET HOME LAST NIGHT?

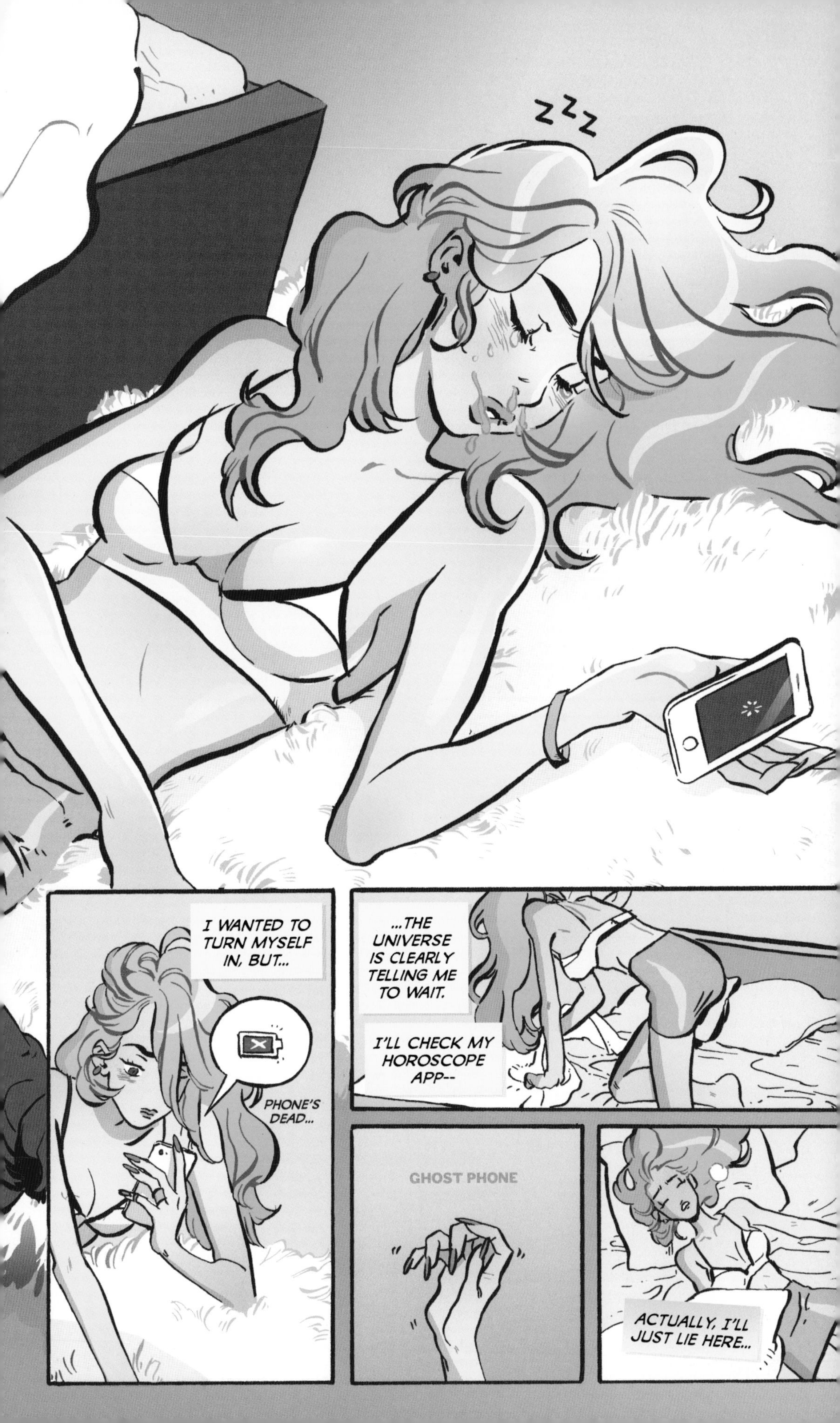
ZZZ
I WANTED TO TURN MYSELF IN, BUT...
PHONE'S DEAD...
...THE UNIVERSE IS CLEARLY TELLING ME TO WAIT.
I'LL CHECK MY HOROSCOPE APP--
GHOST PHONE
ACTUALLY, I'LL JUST LIE HERE...

HAVEN'T TURNED ON MY PHONE IN 72 HOURS. GOING CRAZY. ...CRAZIER THAN USUAL.

BUT THE COPS OR WHOEVER COULD TRACE MY PHONE OR WHATEVER, SO I'M AT

the Los Angeles Central Library.

(SAW THIS PLACE IN A MOVIE ONCE. NEVER ACTUALLY BEEN HERE.)

SHOOTING, STABBING, ROBBERY, HIGH-SPEED CHASE...

UGH, THE NEWS IS SO BORING!

ZERO ARTICLES ABOUT A FASHION BLOGGER GETTING BRAINED IN A WHISKEY BAR BATHROOM?!

WHEN DID L.A. GROW SO COLD TO HER HOT PEOPLE?

ALSO, 40% OFF AT OPENING CEREMONY??

WAIT!

D-DEAD GIRL FOUND...?

Dead girl found

NAIL

AUGUST 1, 2016, 10:34 AM

It was a random yet macabre discovery. The body [of a] young wo[man] in a local nail salon late last night. Law enforcement [ha]s identifie[d] as Excuse Mia, a 24-year-old economics chair from Queens, New [York,] in the wrong place at the wrong time! Someone 'nailed' her. Tune [in...]

...IN A NAIL SALON? FALSE ALARM! WRONG DEAD BODY.

phew!

THAT GIVES ME A REALLY GOOD IDEA, THOUGH...

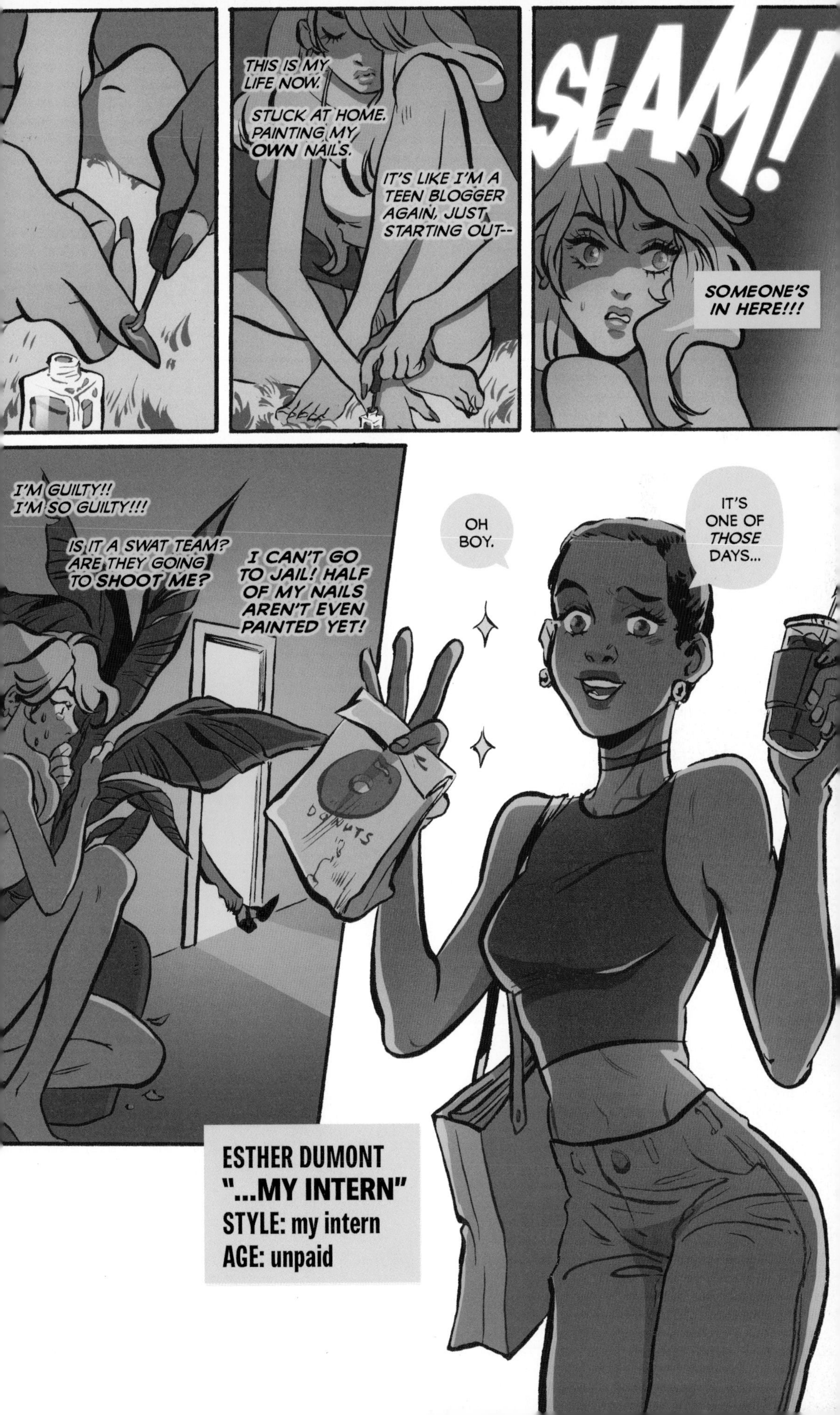
THIS IS MY LIFE NOW.
STUCK AT HOME. PAINTING MY OWN NAILS.
IT'S LIKE I'M A TEEN BLOGGER AGAIN, JUST STARTING OUT--
SLAM!
SOMEONE'S IN HERE!!!
I'M GUILTY!! I'M SO GUILTY!!!
IS IT A SWAT TEAM? ARE THEY GOING TO SHOOT ME?
I CAN'T GO TO JAIL! HALF OF MY NAILS AREN'T EVEN PAINTED YET!
OH BOY.
IT'S ONE OF THOSE DAYS...
DONUTS
ESTHER DUMONT
"...MY INTERN"
STYLE: my intern
AGE: unpaid

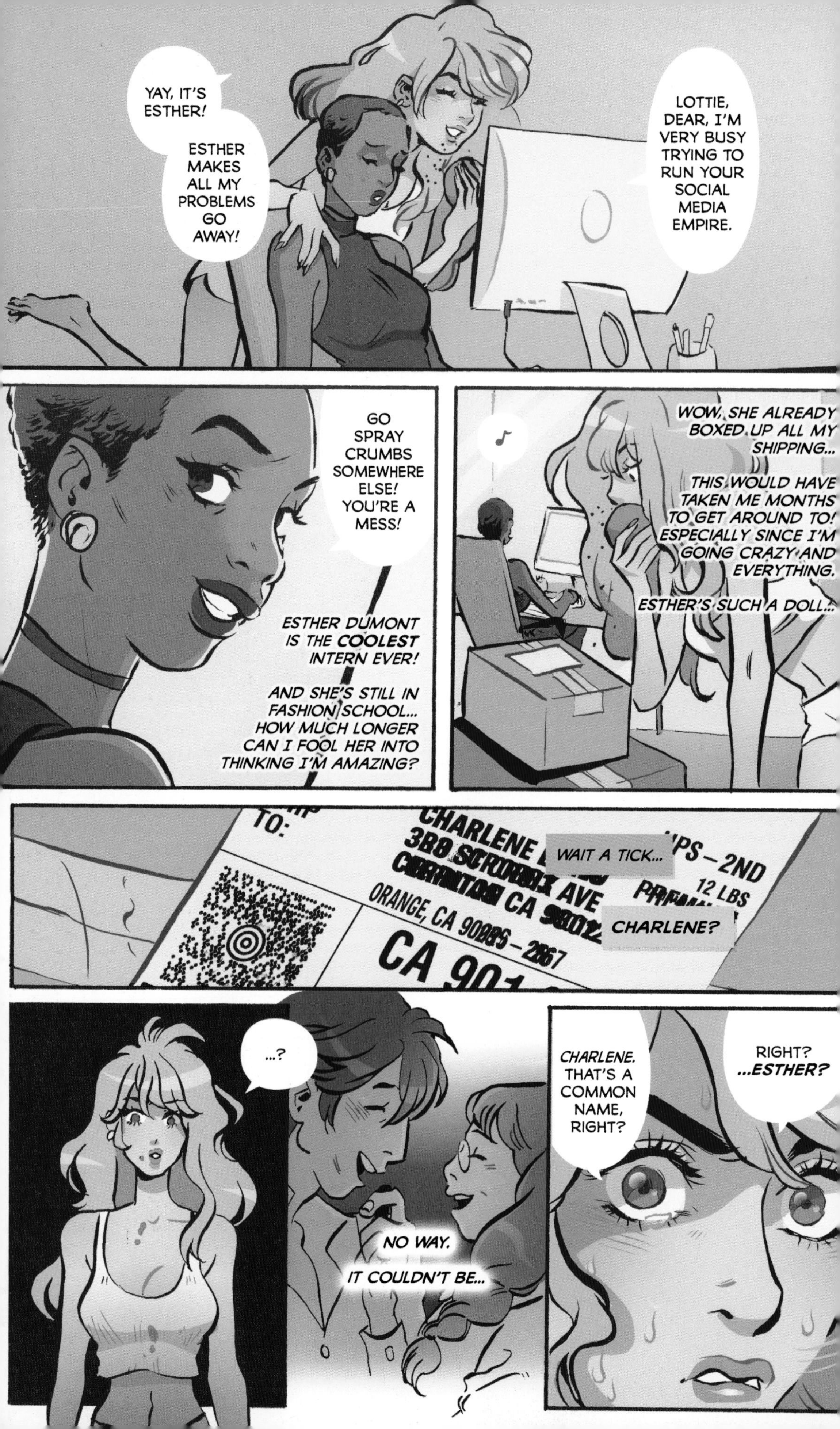
YAY, IT'S ESTHER!
ESTHER MAKES ALL MY PROBLEMS GO AWAY!
LOTTIE, DEAR, I'M VERY BUSY TRYING TO RUN YOUR SOCIAL MEDIA EMPIRE.
GO SPRAY CRUMBS SOMEWHERE ELSE! YOU'RE A MESS!
ESTHER DUMONT IS THE **COOLEST** INTERN EVER!
AND SHE'S STILL IN FASHION SCHOOL... HOW MUCH LONGER CAN I FOOL HER INTO THINKING I'M AMAZING?
♪
WOW, SHE ALREADY BOXED UP ALL MY SHIPPING...
THIS WOULD HAVE TAKEN ME MONTHS TO GET AROUND TO! ESPECIALLY SINCE I'M GOING CRAZY AND EVERYTHING.
ESTHER'S SUCH A DOLL...
TO:
CHARLENE
12 LBS
WAIT A TICK...
CHARLENE?
...?
NO WAY.
IT COULDN'T BE...
CHARLENE. THAT'S A COMMON NAME, RIGHT?
RIGHT? ***...ESTHER?***

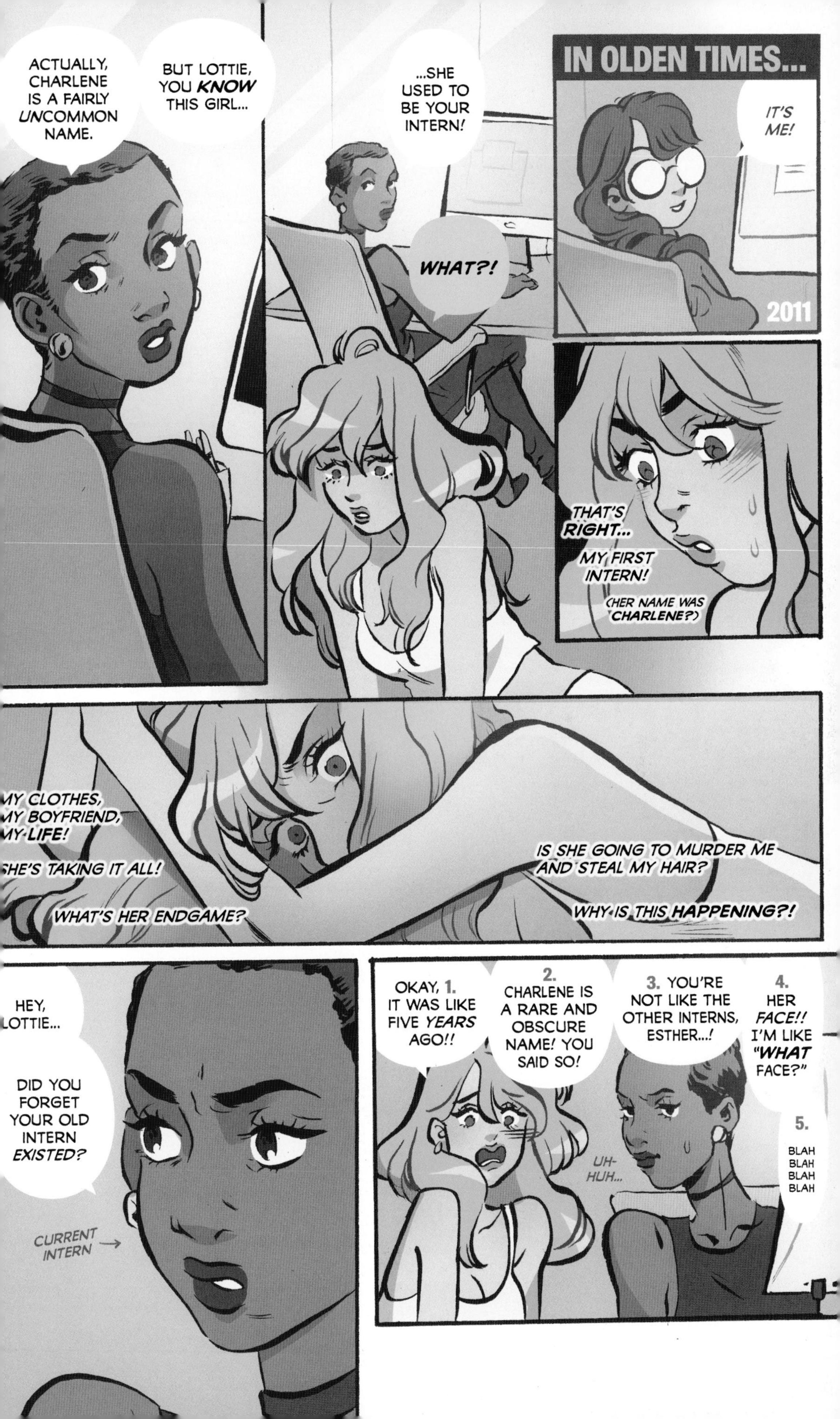

ACTUALLY, CHARLENE IS A FAIRLY *UNCOMMON* NAME.
BUT LOTTIE, YOU ***KNOW*** THIS GIRL...
...SHE USED TO BE YOUR INTERN!
WHAT?!
IN OLDEN TIMES...
IT'S ME!
2011
THAT'S ***RIGHT...***
MY FIRST INTERN!
(HER NAME WAS ***CHARLENE?)***
MY CLOTHES, MY BOYFRIEND, MY ***LIFE!***
SHE'S TAKING IT ALL!
WHAT'S HER ENDGAME?
IS SHE GOING TO MURDER ME AND STEAL MY HAIR?
WHY IS THIS ***HAPPENING?!***
HEY, LOTTIE...
DID YOU FORGET YOUR OLD INTERN *EXISTED?*
CURRENT INTERN →
OKAY, 1. IT WAS LIKE FIVE *YEARS* AGO!!
2. CHARLENE IS A RARE AND OBSCURE NAME! YOU SAID SO!
3. YOU'RE NOT LIKE THE OTHER INTERNS, ESTHER...!
4. HER *FACE!!* I'M LIKE ***"WHAT*** FACE?"
5.
BLAH BLAH BLAH BLAH
UH-HUH...

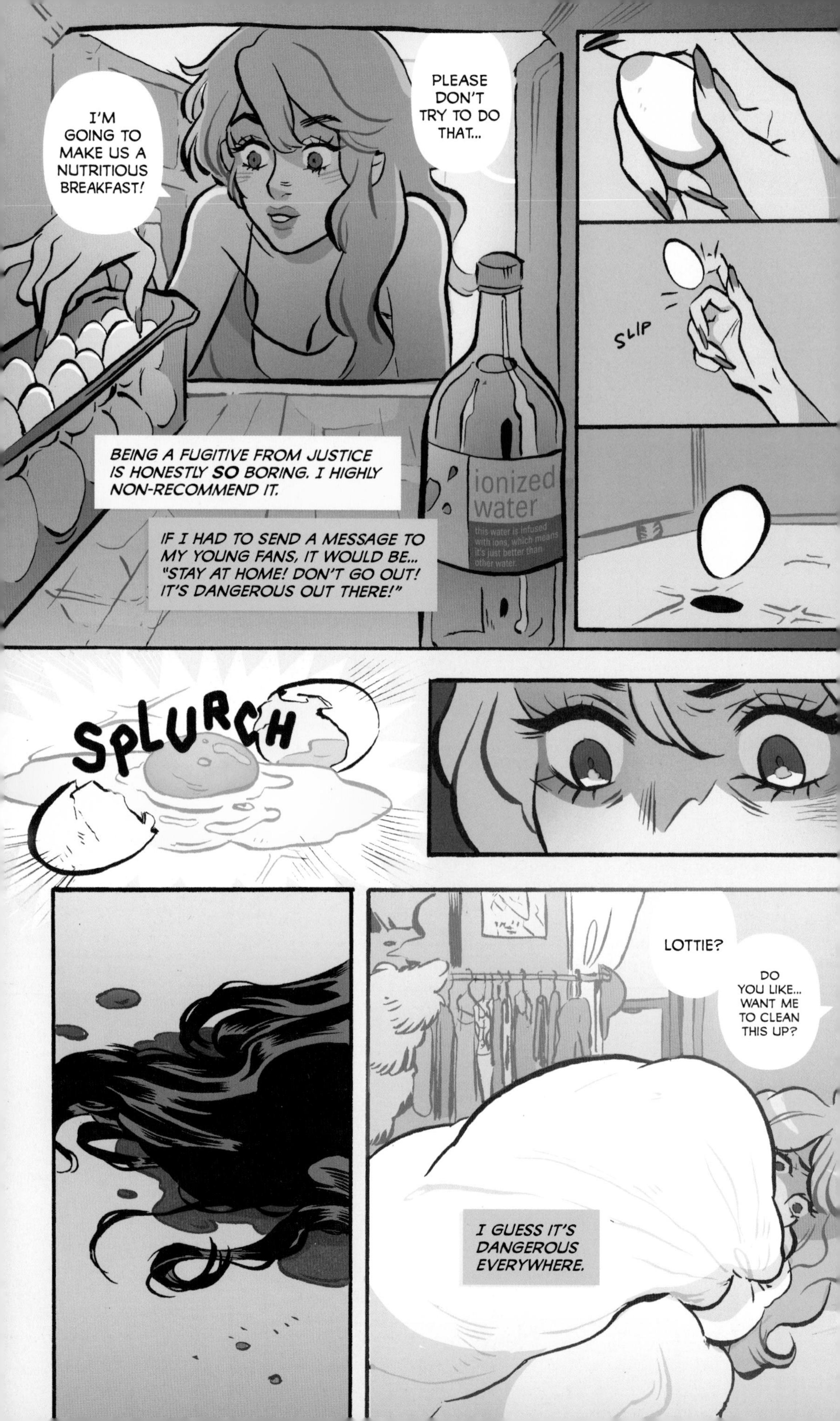
I'M GOING TO MAKE US A NUTRITIOUS BREAKFAST!
PLEASE DON'T TRY TO DO THAT...
BEING A FUGITIVE FROM JUSTICE IS HONESTLY SO BORING. I HIGHLY NON-RECOMMEND IT.
IF I HAD TO SEND A MESSAGE TO MY YOUNG FANS, IT WOULD BE... "STAY AT HOME! DON'T GO OUT! IT'S DANGEROUS OUT THERE!"
ionized water
this water is infused with ions, which means it's just better than other water.
SLIP
SPLURCH
LOTTIE?
DO YOU LIKE... WANT ME TO CLEAN THIS UP?
I GUESS IT'S DANGEROUS EVERYWHERE.

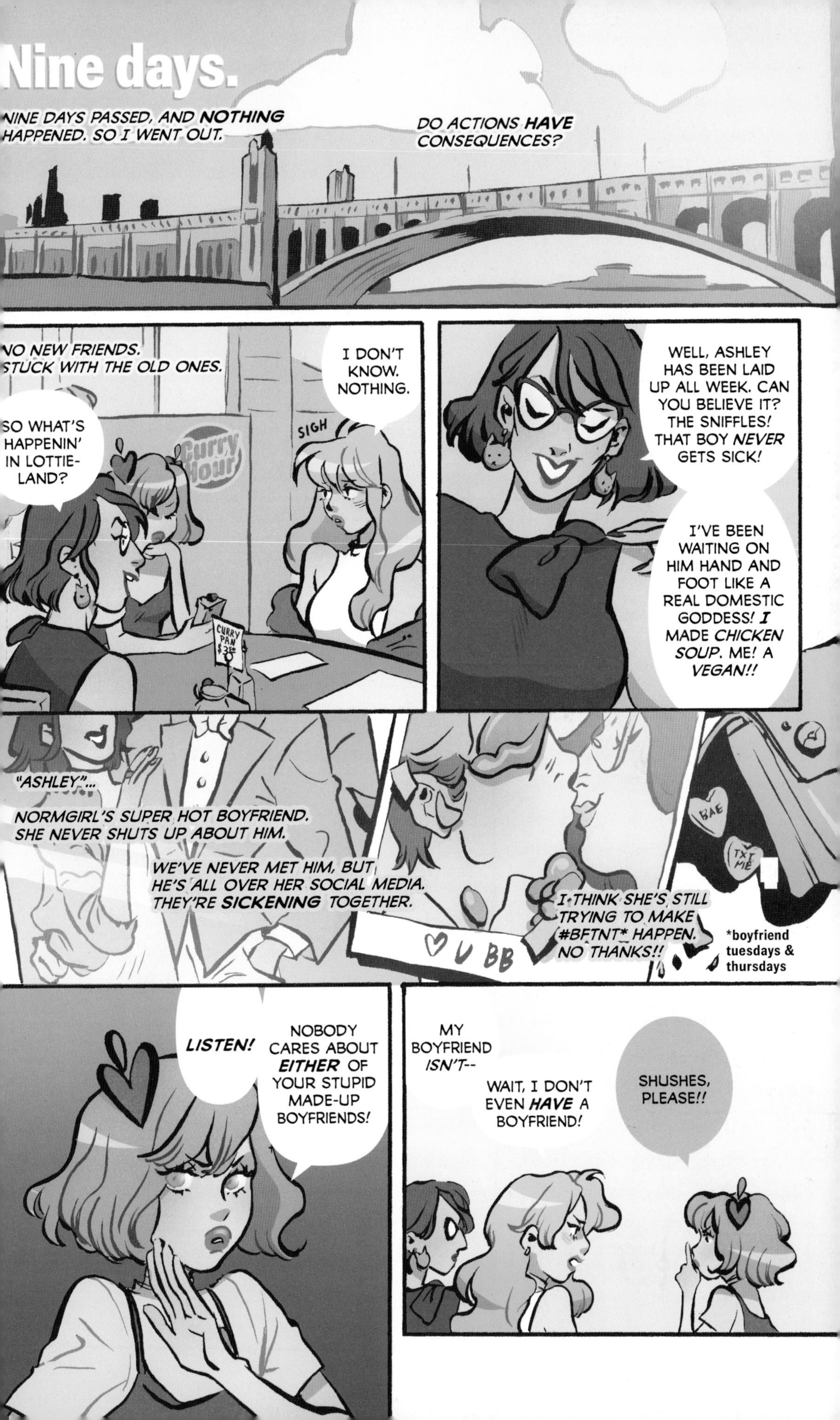
Nine days.
NINE DAYS PASSED, AND NOTHING HAPPENED. SO I WENT OUT.
DO ACTIONS HAVE CONSEQUENCES?
NO NEW FRIENDS. STUCK WITH THE OLD ONES.
SO WHAT'S HAPPENIN' IN LOTTIE-LAND?
Curry Hour
CURRY PAN
SIGH
I DON'T KNOW. NOTHING.
WELL, ASHLEY HAS BEEN LAID UP ALL WEEK. CAN YOU BELIEVE IT? THE SNIFFLES! THAT BOY NEVER GETS SICK!
I'VE BEEN WAITING ON HIM HAND AND FOOT LIKE A REAL DOMESTIC GODDESS! I MADE CHICKEN SOUP. ME! A VEGAN!!
"ASHLEY"...
NORMGIRL'S SUPER HOT BOYFRIEND. SHE NEVER SHUTS UP ABOUT HIM.
WE'VE NEVER MET HIM, BUT HE'S ALL OVER HER SOCIAL MEDIA. THEY'RE SICKENING TOGETHER.
♡ U BB
BAE
TXT ME
I THINK SHE'S STILL TRYING TO MAKE #BFTNT* HAPPEN. NO THANKS!!
*boyfriend tuesdays & thursdays
LISTEN!
NOBODY CARES ABOUT EITHER OF YOUR STUPID MADE-UP BOYFRIENDS!
MY BOYFRIEND ISN'T--
WAIT, I DON'T EVEN HAVE A BOYFRIEND!
SHUSHES, PLEASE!!

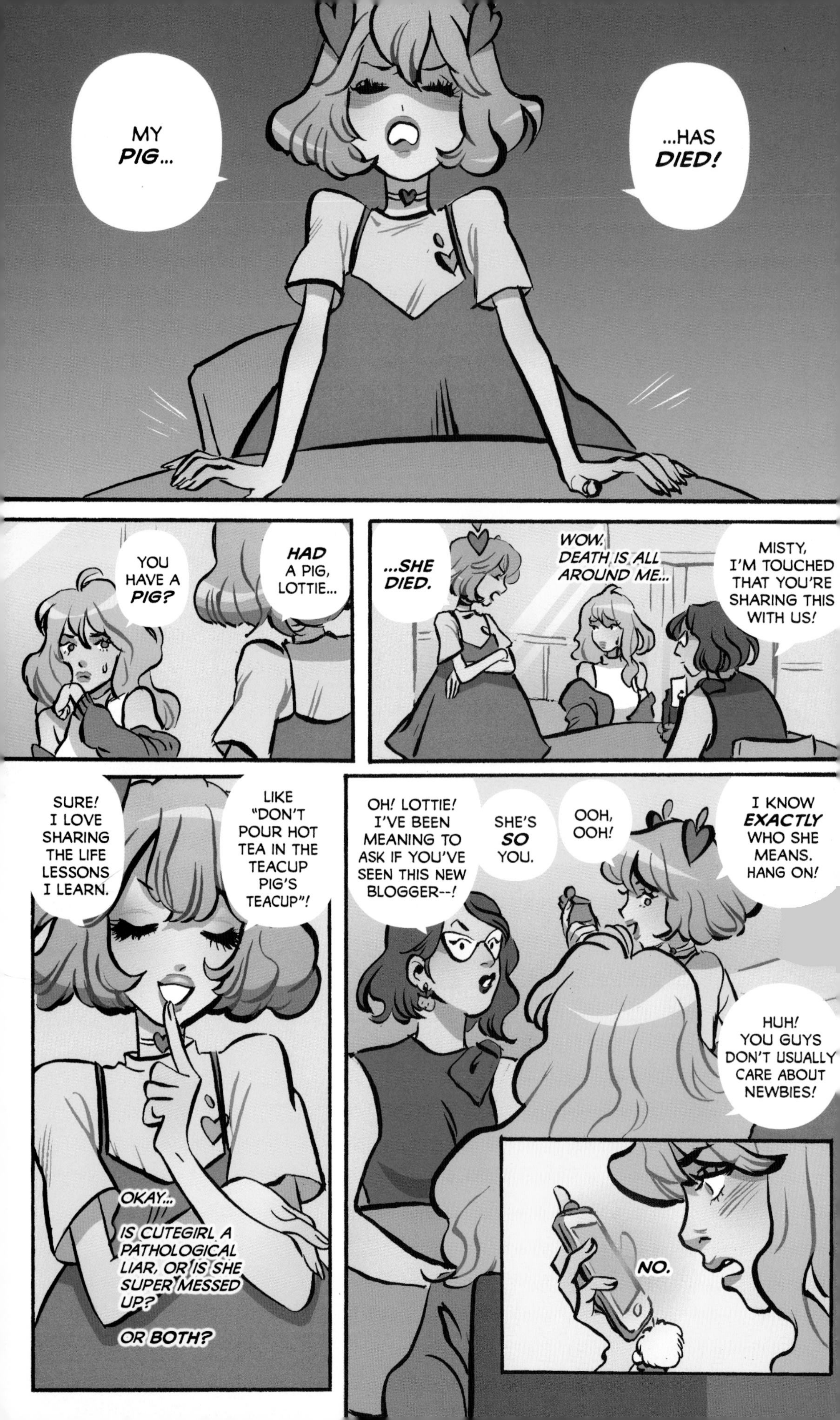
MY PIG...
...HAS DIED!
YOU HAVE A PIG?
HAD A PIG, LOTTIE...
...SHE DIED.
WOW. DEATH IS ALL AROUND ME...
MISTY, I'M TOUCHED THAT YOU'RE SHARING THIS WITH US!
SURE! I LOVE SHARING THE LIFE LESSONS I LEARN.
LIKE "DON'T POUR HOT TEA IN THE TEACUP PIG'S TEACUP"!
OKAY...
IS CUTEGIRL A PATHOLOGICAL LIAR, OR IS SHE SUPER MESSED UP?
OR BOTH?
OH! LOTTIE! I'VE BEEN MEANING TO ASK IF YOU'VE SEEN THIS NEW BLOGGER--!
SHE'S SO YOU.
OOH, OOH!
I KNOW EXACTLY WHO SHE MEANS. HANG ON!
HUH! YOU GUYS DON'T USUALLY CARE ABOUT NEWBIES!
NO.

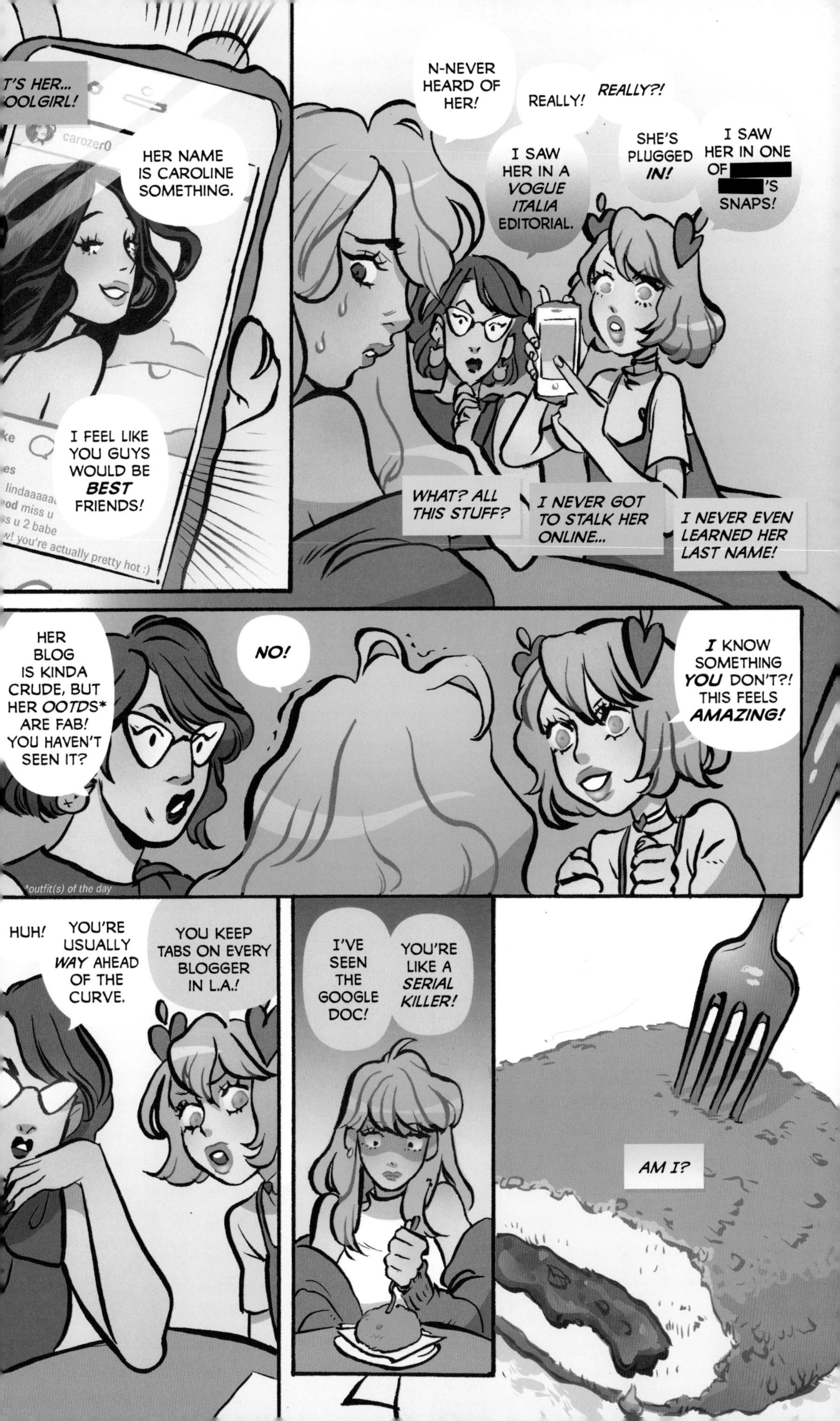
T'S HER... OOLGIRL!
carozer0
HER NAME IS CAROLINE SOMETHING.
I FEEL LIKE YOU GUYS WOULD BE **BEST** FRIENDS!
lindaaaaa
od miss u
ss u 2 babe
w! you're actually pretty hot :)
N-NEVER HEARD OF HER!
REALLY!
REALLY?!
I SAW HER IN A *VOGUE ITALIA* EDITORIAL.
SHE'S PLUGGED ***IN!***
I SAW HER IN ONE OF [redacted] [redacted]'S SNAPS!
WHAT? ALL THIS STUFF?
I NEVER GOT TO STALK HER ONLINE...
I NEVER EVEN LEARNED HER LAST NAME!
HER BLOG IS KINDA CRUDE, BUT HER *OOTDS** ARE FAB! YOU HAVEN'T SEEN IT?
NO!
I KNOW SOMETHING ***YOU*** DON'T?! THIS FEELS ***AMAZING!***
*outfit(s) of the day
HUH!
YOU'RE USUALLY *WAY* AHEAD OF THE CURVE.
YOU KEEP TABS ON EVERY BLOGGER IN L.A.!
I'VE SEEN THE GOOGLE DOC!
YOU'RE LIKE A *SERIAL KILLER!*
AM I?

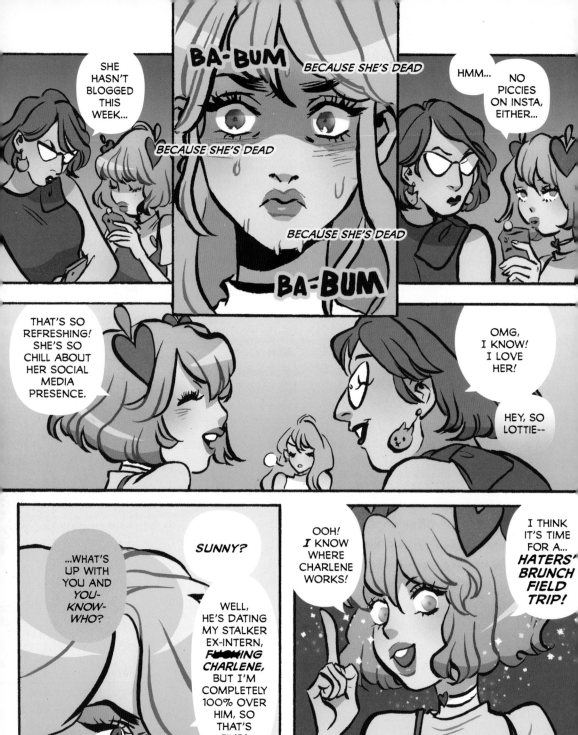

SHE HASN'T BLOGGED THIS WEEK...

BA-BUM

BECAUSE SHE'S DEAD

BECAUSE SHE'S DEAD

BECAUSE SHE'S DEAD

BA-BUM

HMM... NO PICCIES ON INSTA, EITHER...

THAT'S SO REFRESHING! SHE'S SO CHILL ABOUT HER SOCIAL MEDIA PRESENCE.

OMG, I KNOW! I LOVE HER!

HEY, SO LOTTIE--

...WHAT'S UP WITH YOU AND YOU-KNOW-WHO?

SUNNY?

WELL, HE'S DATING MY STALKER EX-INTERN, F̶U̶C̶K̶I̶N̶G̶ CHARLENE, BUT I'M COMPLETELY 100% OVER HIM, SO THAT'S FINE!

OOH! I KNOW WHERE CHARLENE WORKS!

I THINK IT'S TIME FOR A... HATERS' BRUNCH FIELD TRIP!

WHAT? NO!

HELL NO!

NO.

NO.

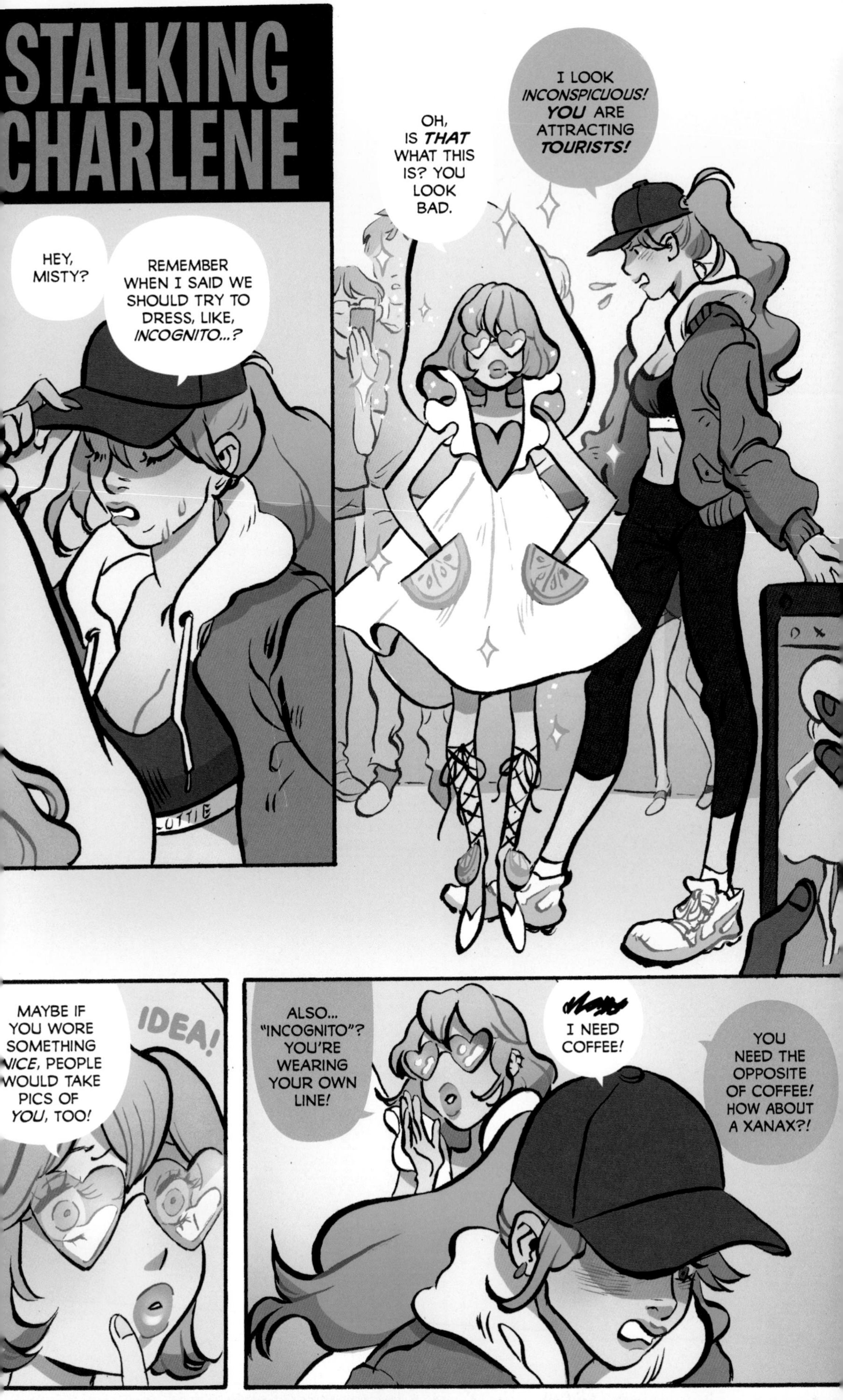
STALKING CHARLENE
HEY, MISTY?
REMEMBER WHEN I SAID WE SHOULD TRY TO DRESS, LIKE, *INCOGNITO...?*
OH, IS ***THAT*** WHAT THIS IS? YOU LOOK BAD.
I LOOK *INCONSPICUOUS!* ***YOU*** ARE ATTRACTING ***TOURISTS!***
MAYBE IF YOU WORE SOMETHING *VICE*, PEOPLE WOULD TAKE PICS OF *YOU*, TOO!
IDEA!
ALSO... "INCOGNITO"? YOU'RE WEARING YOUR OWN LINE!
I NEED COFFEE!
YOU NEED THE OPPOSITE OF COFFEE! HOW ABOUT A XANAX?!

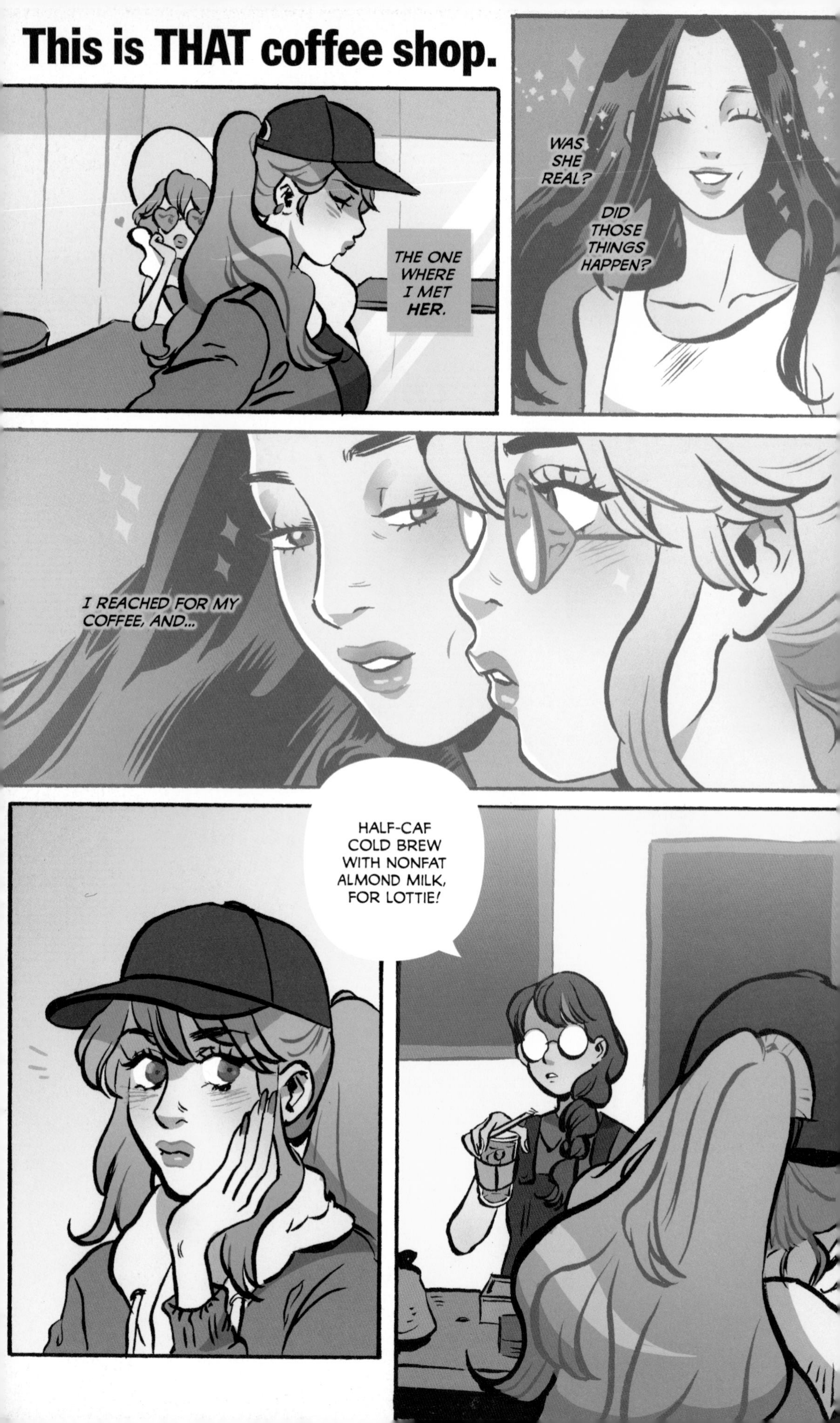
This is THAT coffee shop.
THE ONE WHERE I MET HER.
WAS SHE REAL?
DID THOSE THINGS HAPPEN?
I REACHED FOR MY COFFEE, AND...
HALF-CAF COLD BREW WITH NONFAT ALMOND MILK, FOR LOTTIE!

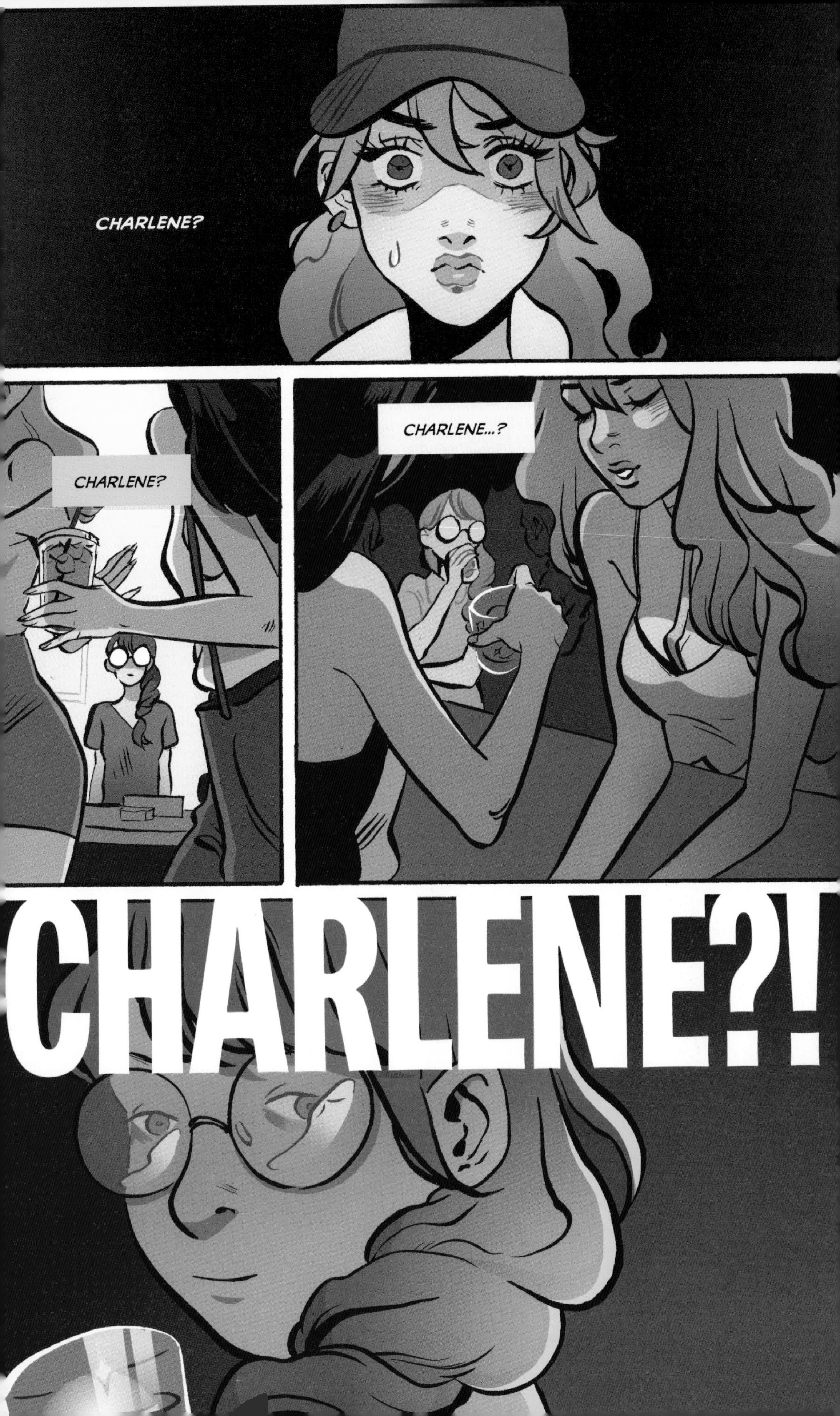
CHARLENE?
CHARLENE?
CHARLENE...?
CHARLENE?!

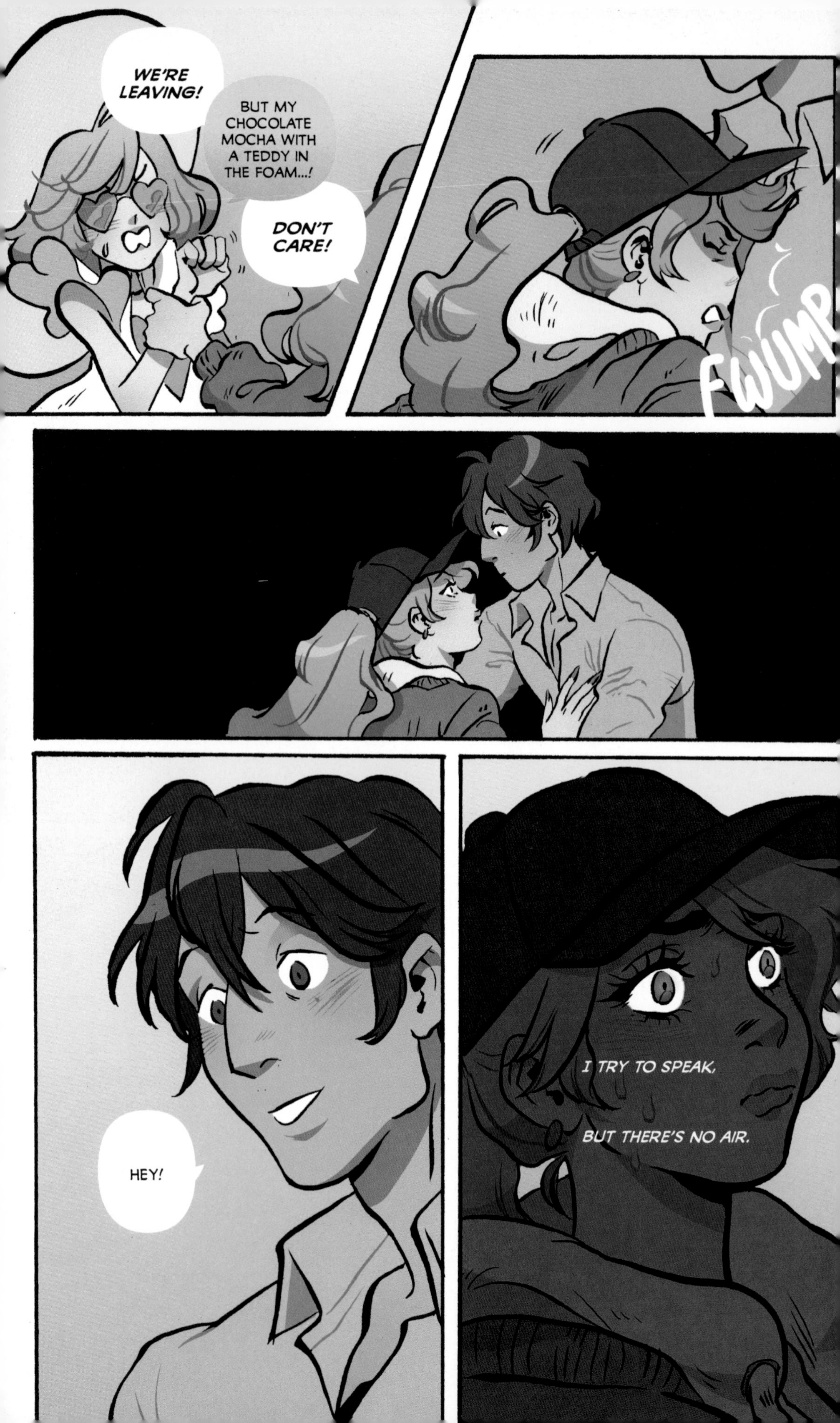
WE'RE LEAVING!
BUT MY CHOCOLATE MOCHA WITH A TEDDY IN THE FOAM...!
DON'T CARE!
FWUMP
HEY!
I TRY TO SPEAK,
BUT THERE'S NO AIR.

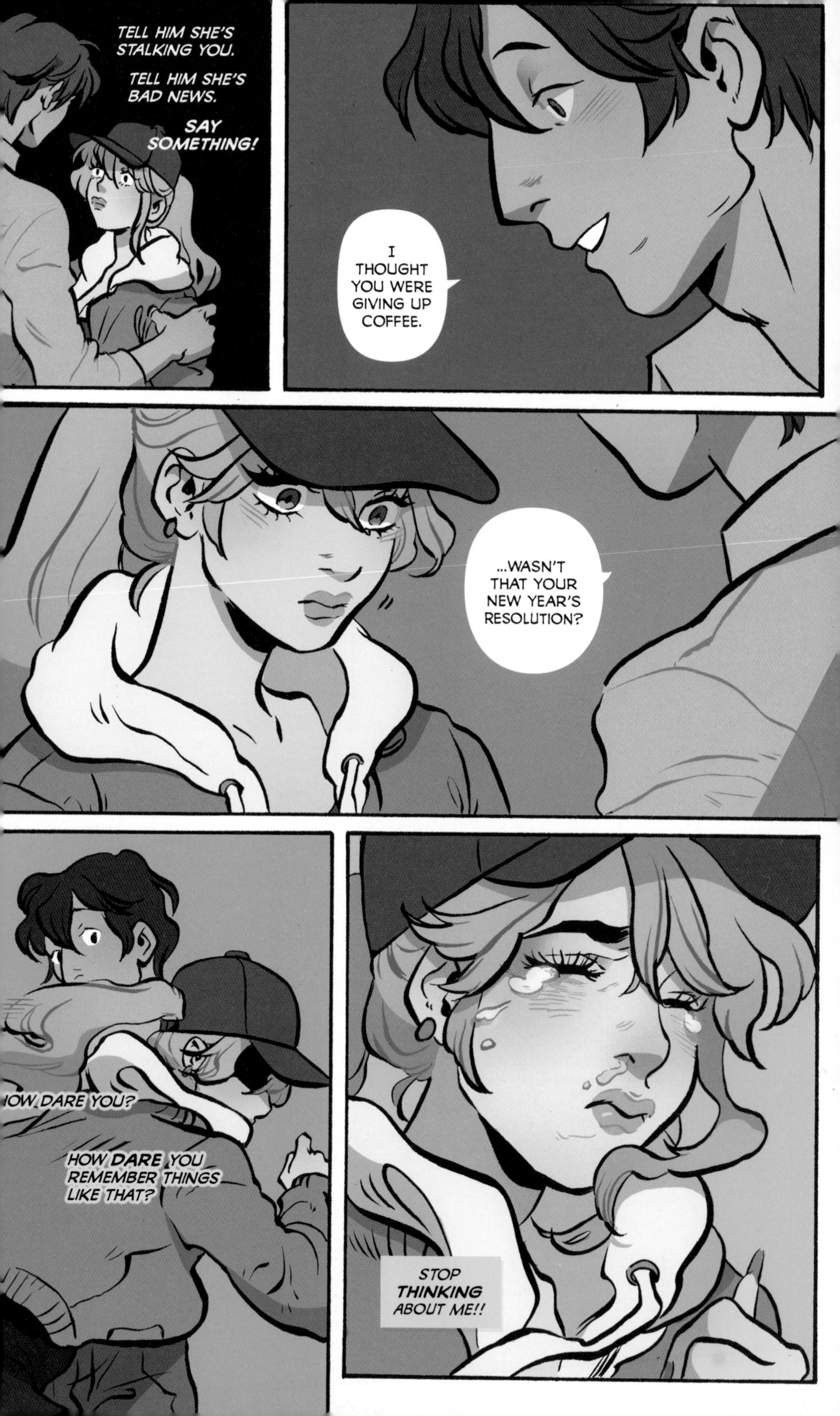
TELL HIM SHE'S STALKING YOU.
TELL HIM SHE'S BAD NEWS.
SAY SOMETHING!
I THOUGHT YOU WERE GIVING UP COFFEE.
...WASN'T THAT YOUR NEW YEAR'S RESOLUTION?
HOW DARE YOU?
HOW DARE YOU REMEMBER THINGS LIKE THAT?
STOP THINKING ABOUT ME!!

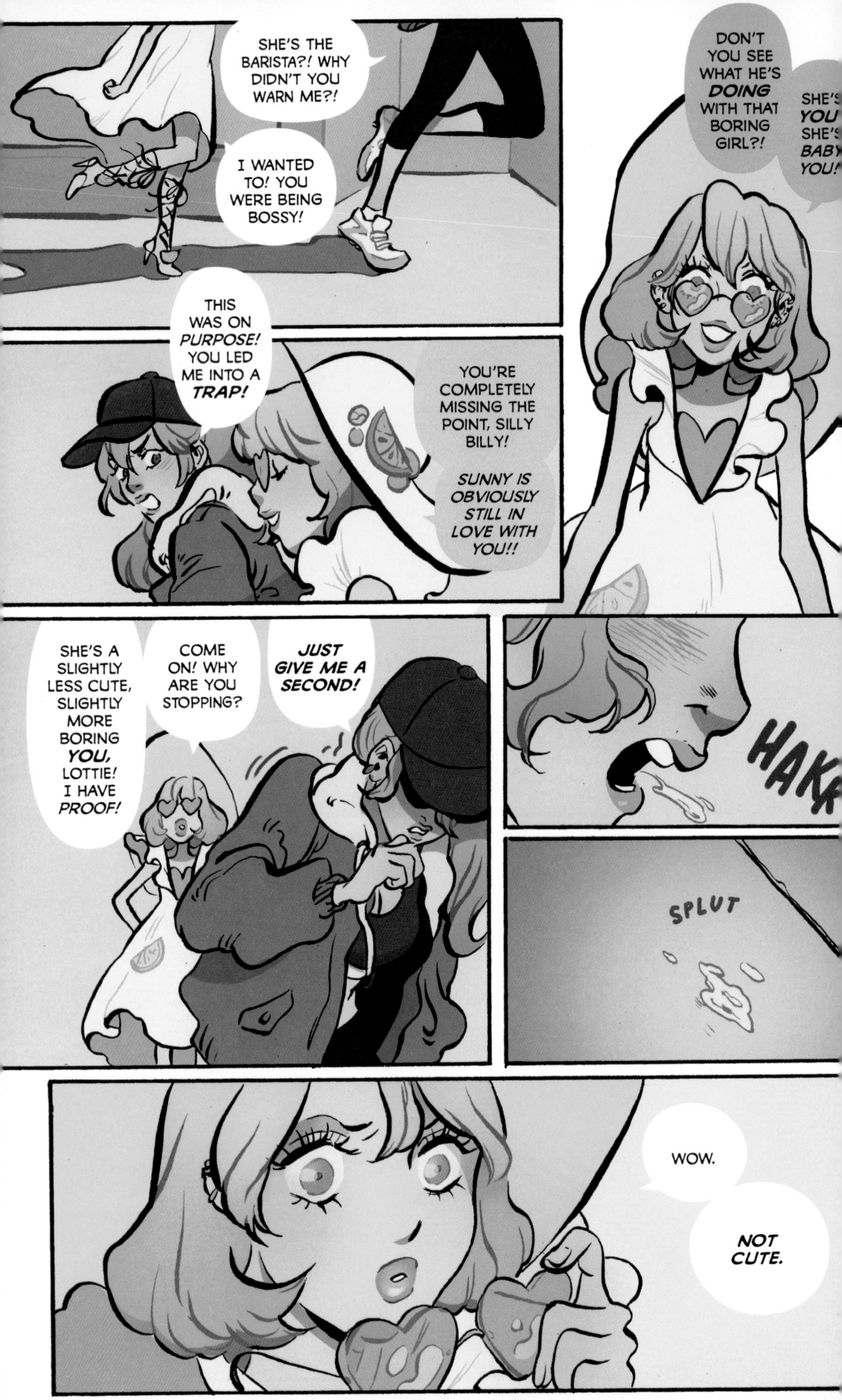

SHE'S THE BARISTA?! WHY DIDN'T YOU WARN ME?!
I WANTED TO! YOU WERE BEING BOSSY!
DON'T YOU SEE WHAT HE'S DOING WITH THAT BORING GIRL?!
THIS WAS ON PURPOSE! YOU LED ME INTO A TRAP!
YOU'RE COMPLETELY MISSING THE POINT, SILLY BILLY!
SUNNY IS OBVIOUSLY STILL IN LOVE WITH YOU!!
SHE'S A SLIGHTLY LESS CUTE, SLIGHTLY MORE BORING YOU, LOTTIE! I HAVE PROOF!
COME ON! WHY ARE YOU STOPPING?
JUST GIVE ME A SECOND!
SPLUT
WOW.
NOT CUTE.

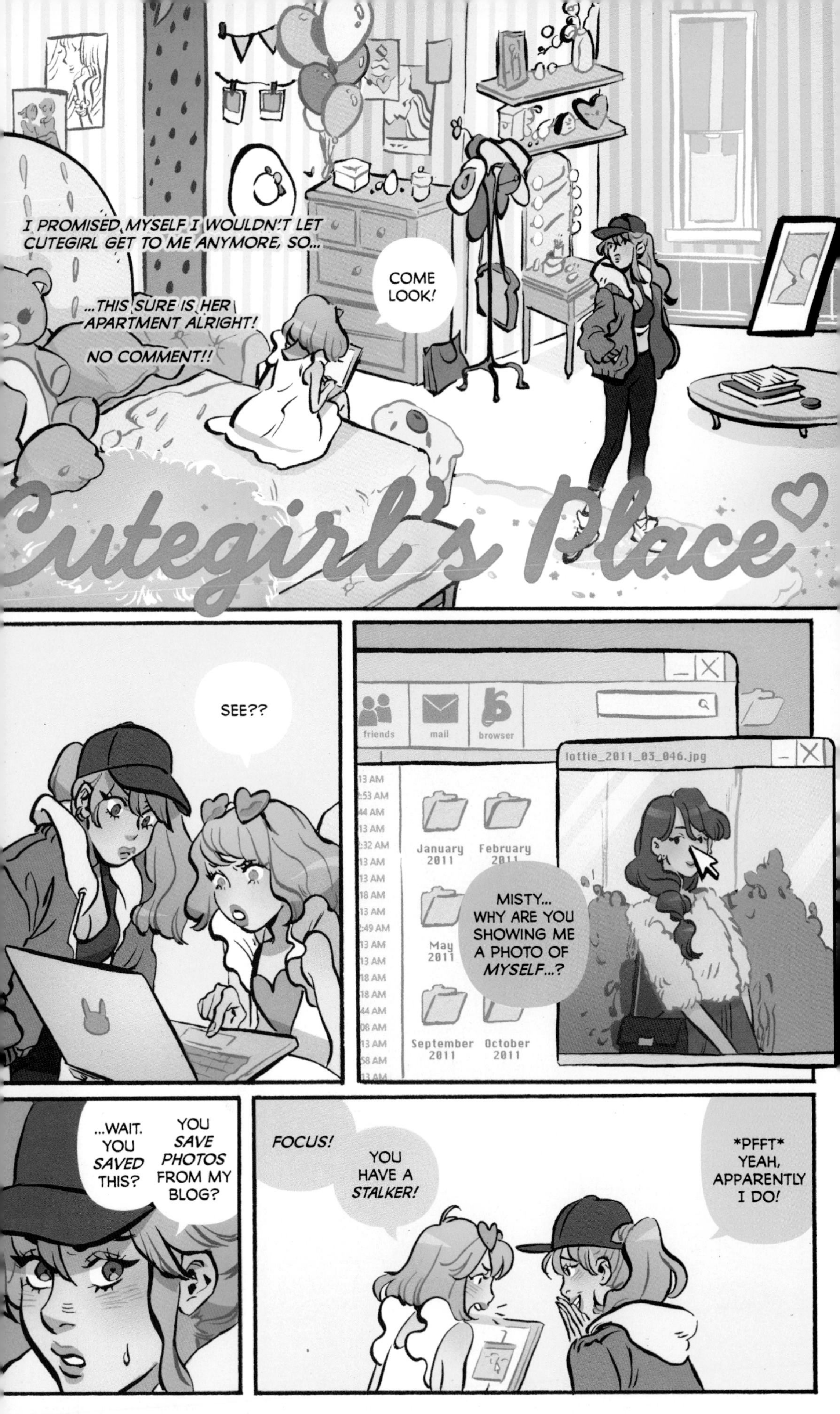

I PROMISED MYSELF I WOULDN'T LET CUTEGIRL GET TO ME ANYMORE, SO...
...THIS SURE IS HER APARTMENT ALRIGHT!
NO COMMENT!!
COME LOOK!
Cutegirl's Place
SEE??
friends
mail
browser
lottie_2011_03_046.jpg
January 2011
February 2011
May 2011
September 2011
October 2011
MISTY... WHY ARE YOU SHOWING ME A PHOTO OF *MYSELF*...?
...WAIT. YOU *SAVED* THIS?
YOU *SAVE PHOTOS* FROM MY BLOG?
FOCUS!
YOU HAVE A *STALKER!*
PFFT YEAH, APPARENTLY I DO!

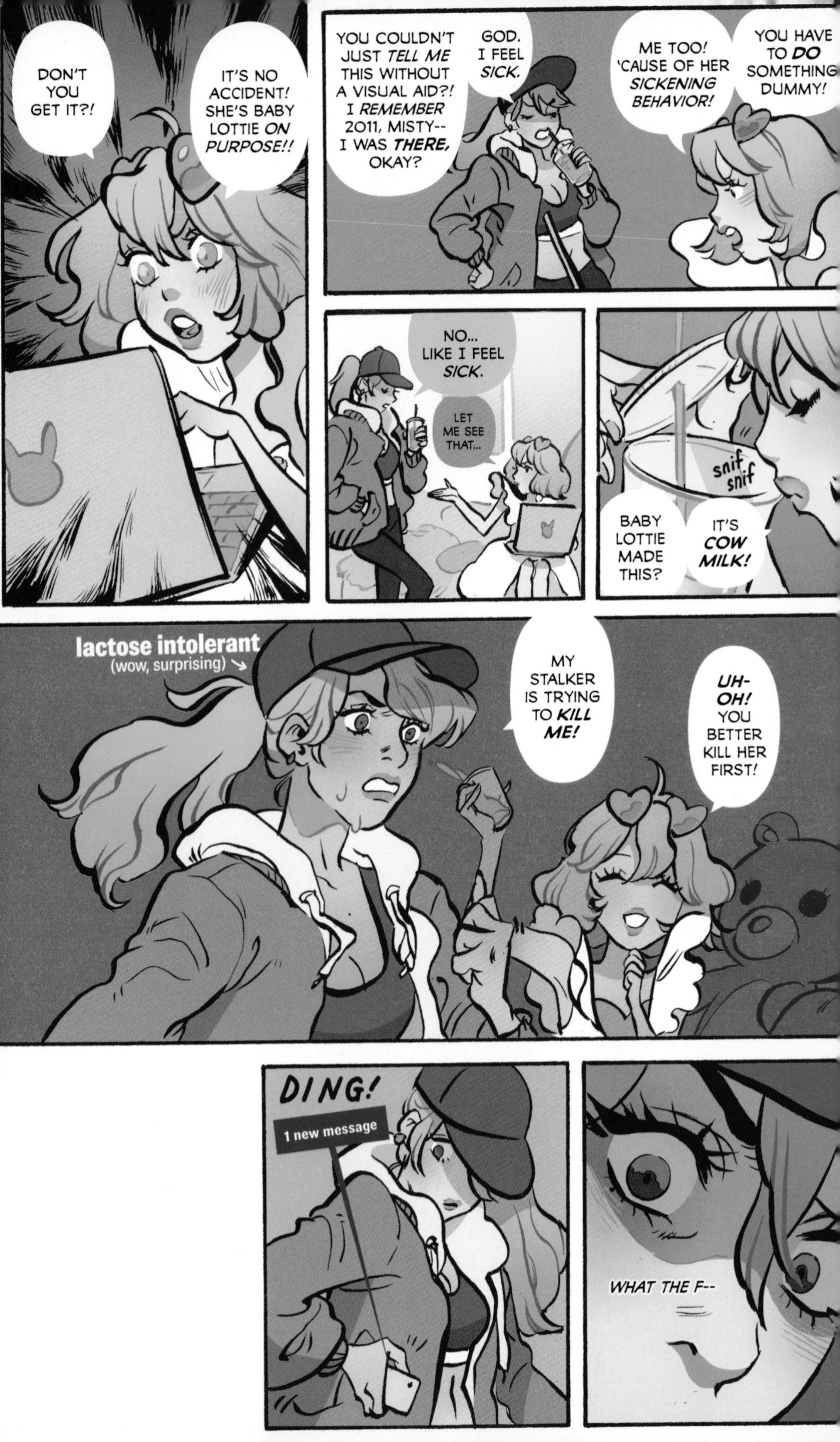
DON'T YOU GET IT?!
IT'S NO ACCIDENT! SHE'S BABY LOTTIE ON PURPOSE!!
YOU COULDN'T JUST TELL ME THIS WITHOUT A VISUAL AID?! I REMEMBER 2011, MISTY-- I WAS THERE, OKAY?
GOD. I FEEL SICK.
ME TOO! 'CAUSE OF HER SICKENING BEHAVIOR!
YOU HAVE TO DO SOMETHING DUMMY!
NO... LIKE I FEEL SICK.
LET ME SEE THAT...
snif snif
BABY LOTTIE MADE THIS?
IT'S COW MILK!
lactose intolerant
(wow, surprising)
MY STALKER IS TRYING TO KILL ME!
UH-OH! YOU BETTER KILL HER FIRST!
DING!
1 new message
WHAT THE F--

THIS IS...

IMPOSSIBLE.

DING!

coolgirl ⭐

yoooooooooo

Miss ya snottie!

That was fun the other night, jets do it again!

DING!

night, jets do it

*let's

DING!

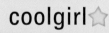

coolgirl ⭐

WHEN DID WE TAKE THIS? I DON'T REMEMBER THIS!

THIS IS FAKE, RIGHT? SHE **CAN'T** BE TEXTING ME.

SHE **CAN'T** BE ALIVE... NOT AFTER WHAT I SAW...

SO WHAT IS THIS? SOME KIND OF SICK JOKE? SOME KIND OF **TRAP**?

DOES SOMEONE **KNOW**?!

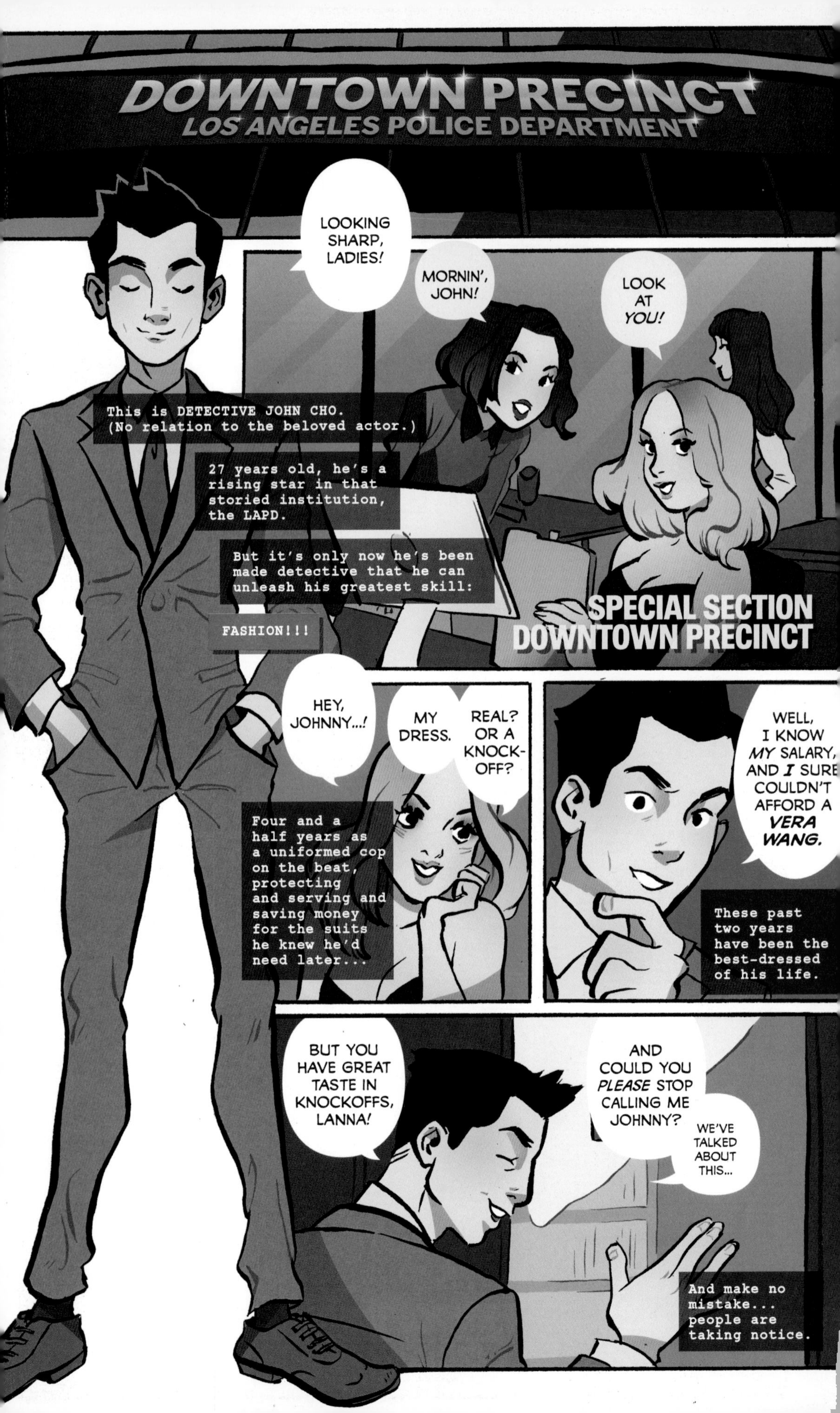
DOWNTOWN PRECINCT
LOS ANGELES POLICE DEPARTMENT
LOOKING SHARP, LADIES!
MORNIN', JOHN!
LOOK AT YOU!
This is DETECTIVE JOHN CHO. (No relation to the beloved actor.)
27 years old, he's a rising star in that storied institution, the LAPD.
But it's only now he's been made detective that he can unleash his greatest skill:
FASHION!!!
SPECIAL SECTION DOWNTOWN PRECINCT
HEY, JOHNNY...!
MY DRESS.
REAL? OR A KNOCK-OFF?
Four and a half years as a uniformed cop on the beat, protecting and serving and saving money for the suits he knew he'd need later...
WELL, I KNOW MY SALARY, AND I SURE COULDN'T AFFORD A VERA WANG.
These past two years have been the best-dressed of his life.
BUT YOU HAVE GREAT TASTE IN KNOCKOFFS, LANNA!
AND COULD YOU PLEASE STOP CALLING ME JOHNNY?
WE'VE TALKED ABOUT THIS...
And make no mistake... people are taking notice.

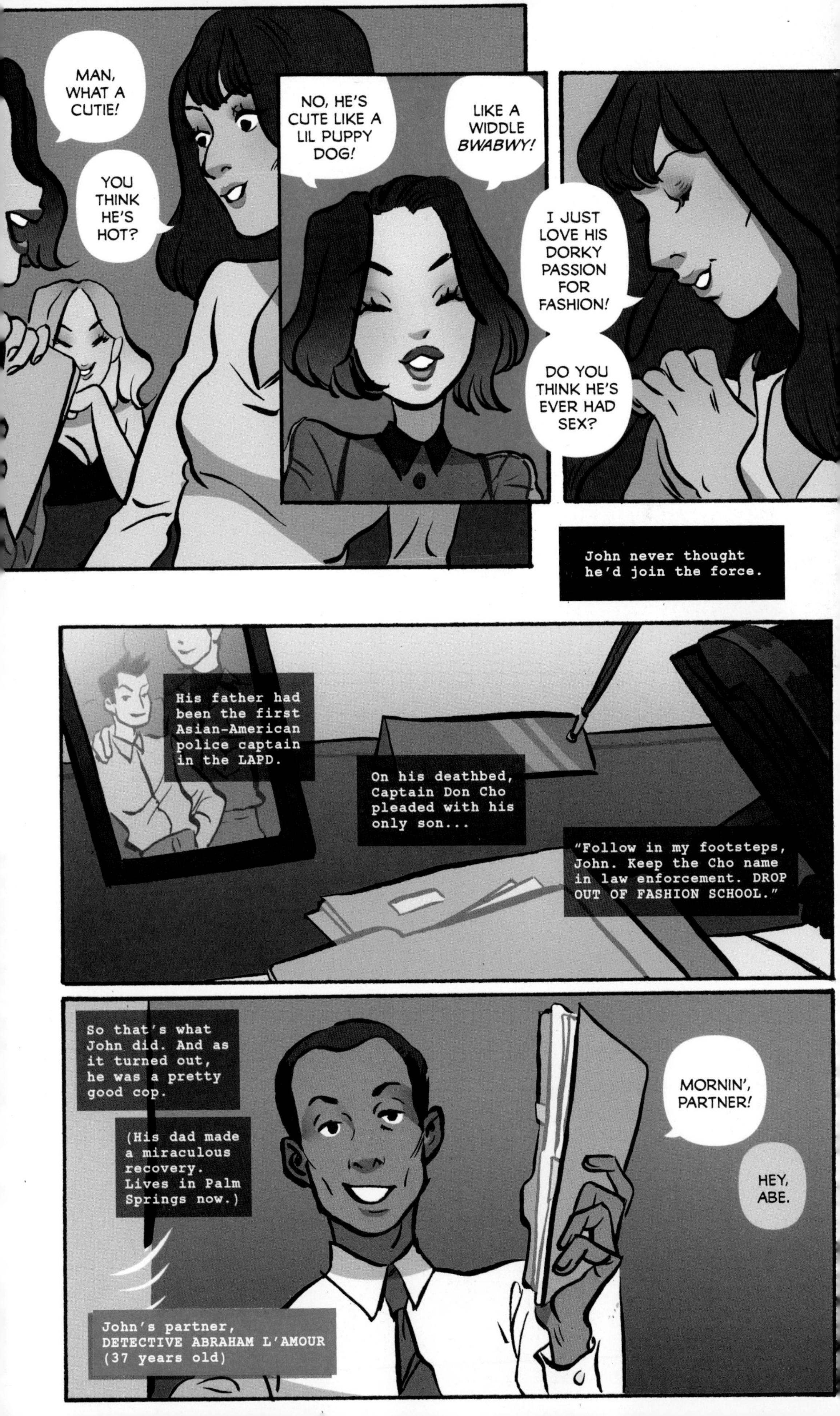
MAN, WHAT A CUTIE!
YOU THINK HE'S HOT?
NO, HE'S CUTE LIKE A LIL PUPPY DOG!
LIKE A WIDDLE *BWABWY!*
I JUST LOVE HIS DORKY PASSION FOR FASHION!
DO YOU THINK HE'S EVER HAD SEX?
John never thought he'd join the force.
His father had been the first Asian-American police captain in the LAPD.
On his deathbed, Captain Don Cho pleaded with his only son...
"Follow in my footsteps, John. Keep the Cho name in law enforcement. DROP OUT OF FASHION SCHOOL."
So that's what John did. And as it turned out, he was a pretty good cop.
(His dad made a miraculous recovery. Lives in Palm Springs now.)
MORNIN', PARTNER!
HEY, ABE.
John's partner, DETECTIVE ABRAHAM L'AMOUR (37 years old)

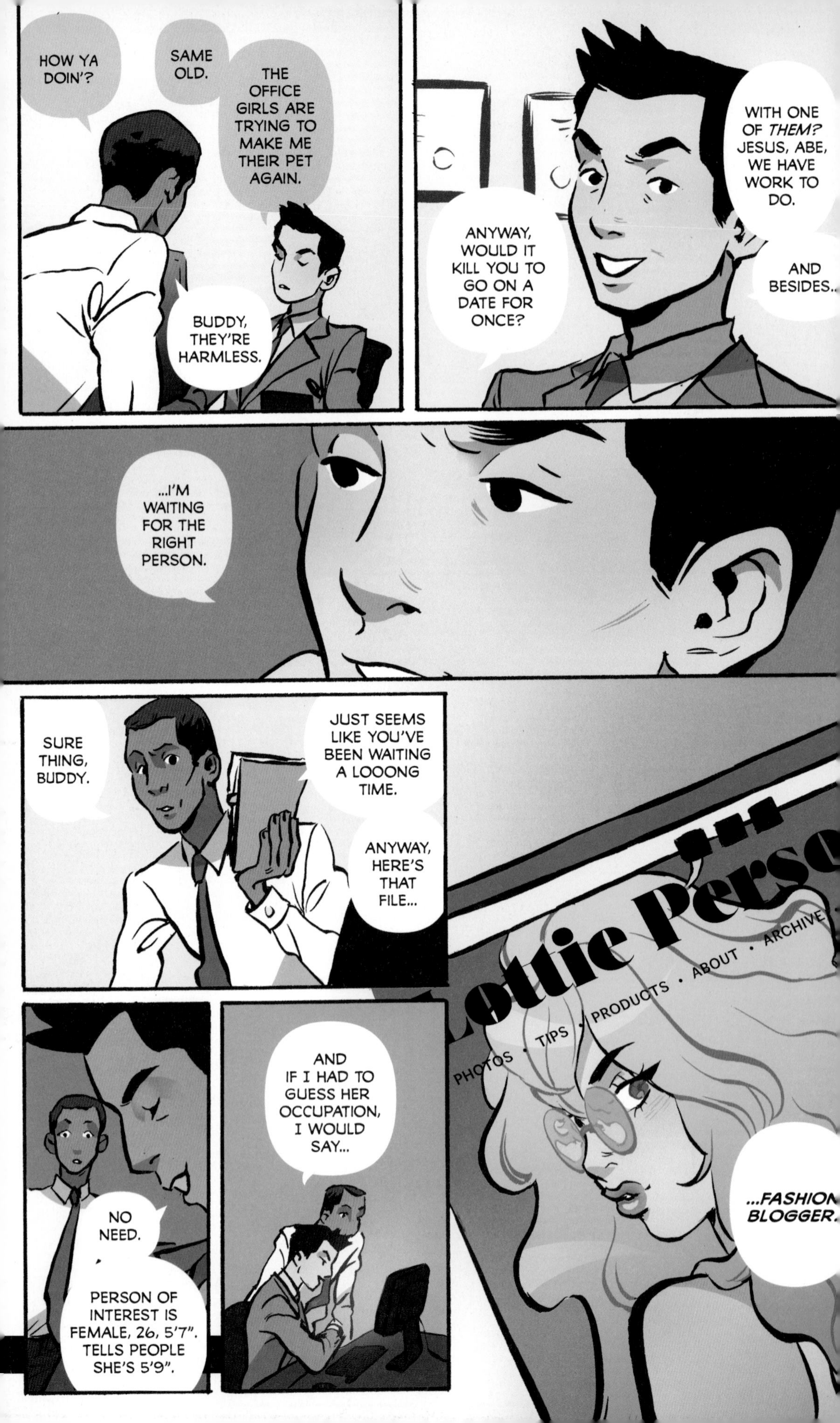
HOW YA DOIN'?
SAME OLD.
THE OFFICE GIRLS ARE TRYING TO MAKE ME THEIR PET AGAIN.
BUDDY, THEY'RE HARMLESS.
ANYWAY, WOULD IT KILL YOU TO GO ON A DATE FOR ONCE?
WITH ONE OF *THEM?* JESUS, ABE, WE HAVE WORK TO DO.
AND BESIDES...
...I'M WAITING FOR THE RIGHT PERSON.
SURE THING, BUDDY.
JUST SEEMS LIKE YOU'VE BEEN WAITING A LOOONG TIME.
ANYWAY, HERE'S THAT FILE...
NO NEED.
PERSON OF INTEREST IS FEMALE, 26, 5'7". TELLS PEOPLE SHE'S 5'9".
AND IF I HAD TO GUESS HER OCCUPATION, I WOULD SAY...
PHOTOS • TIPS • PRODUCTS • ABOUT • ARCHIVE
...FASHION BLOGGER.

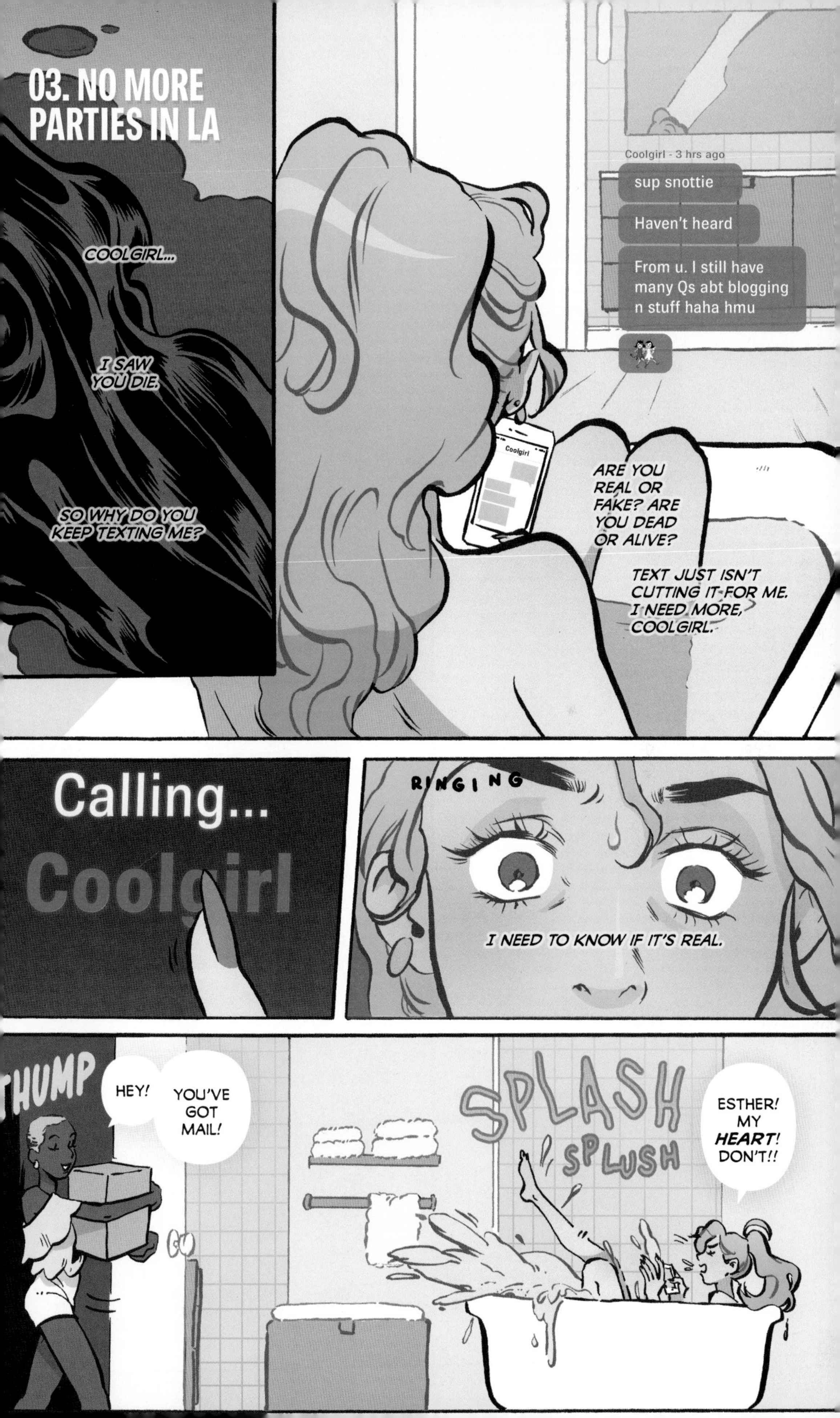
03. NO MORE PARTIES IN LA
COOLGIRL...
I SAW YOU DIE.
SO WHY DO YOU KEEP TEXTING ME?
Coolgirl - 3 hrs ago
sup snottie
Haven't heard
From u. I still have many Qs abt blogging n stuff haha hmu
Coolgirl
ARE YOU REAL OR FAKE? ARE YOU DEAD OR ALIVE?
TEXT JUST ISN'T CUTTING IT FOR ME. I NEED MORE, COOLGIRL.
Calling...
Coolgirl
RINGING
I NEED TO KNOW IF IT'S REAL.
THUMP
HEY!
YOU'VE GOT MAIL!
SPLASH
SPLUSH
ESTHER! MY HEART! DON'T!!

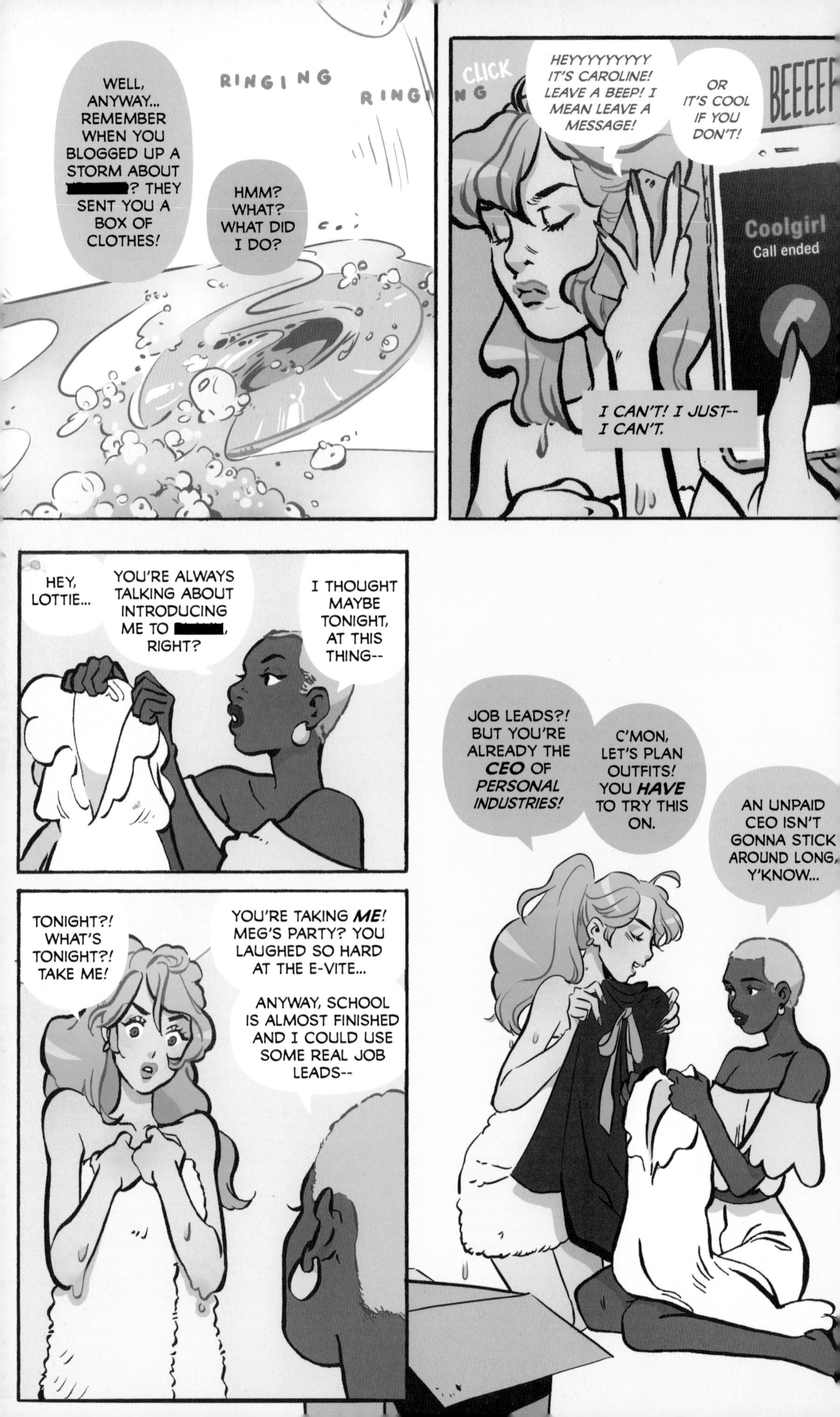
WELL, ANYWAY... REMEMBER WHEN YOU BLOGGED UP A STORM ABOUT [redacted]? THEY SENT YOU A BOX OF CLOTHES!
RINGING
RINGING
HMM? WHAT? WHAT DID I DO?
CLICK
HEYYYYYYYYY IT'S CAROLINE! LEAVE A BEEP! I MEAN LEAVE A MESSAGE!
OR IT'S COOL IF YOU DON'T!
BEEEEP
Coolgirl
Call ended
I CAN'T! I JUST-- I CAN'T.
HEY, LOTTIE...
YOU'RE ALWAYS TALKING ABOUT INTRODUCING ME TO [redacted], RIGHT?
I THOUGHT MAYBE TONIGHT, AT THIS THING--
TONIGHT?! WHAT'S TONIGHT?! TAKE ME!
YOU'RE TAKING *ME*! MEG'S PARTY? YOU LAUGHED SO HARD AT THE E-VITE...
ANYWAY, SCHOOL IS ALMOST FINISHED AND I COULD USE SOME REAL JOB LEADS--
JOB LEADS?! BUT YOU'RE ALREADY THE ***CEO*** OF *PERSONAL INDUSTRIES!*
C'MON, LET'S PLAN OUTFITS! YOU ***HAVE*** TO TRY THIS ON.
AN UNPAID CEO ISN'T GONNA STICK AROUND LONG, Y'KNOW...

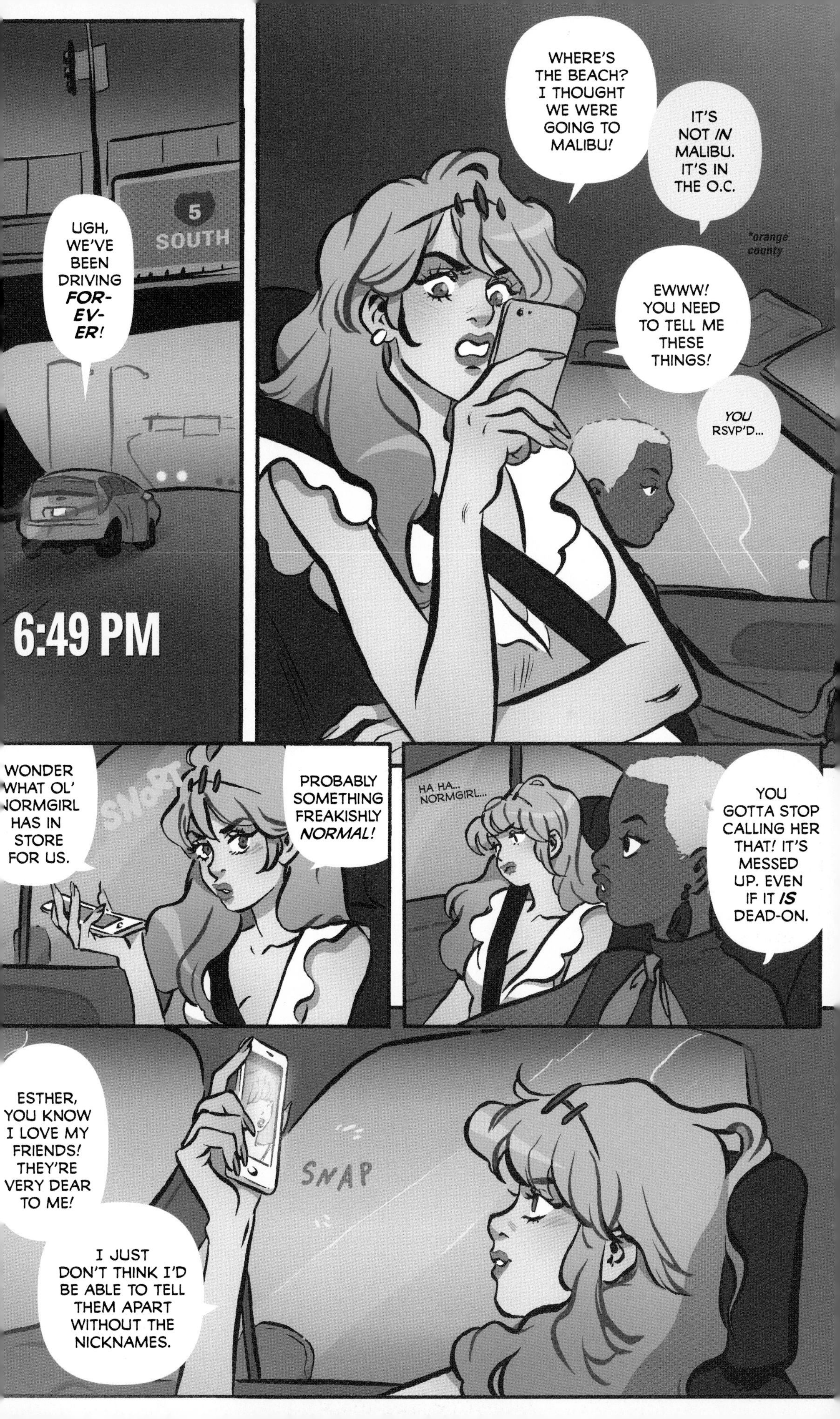

5
SOUTH
UGH, WE'VE BEEN DRIVING ***FOR-EV-ER!***
6:49 PM
WHERE'S THE BEACH? I THOUGHT WE WERE GOING TO MALIBU!
IT'S NOT *IN* MALIBU. IT'S IN THE O.C.
*orange county
EWWW! YOU NEED TO TELL ME THESE THINGS!
YOU RSVP'D...
WONDER WHAT OL' NORMGIRL HAS IN STORE FOR US.
SNORT
PROBABLY SOMETHING FREAKISHLY *NORMAL!*
HA HA... NORMGIRL...
YOU GOTTA STOP CALLING HER THAT! IT'S MESSED UP. EVEN IF IT ***IS*** DEAD-ON.
ESTHER, YOU KNOW I LOVE MY FRIENDS! THEY'RE VERY DEAR TO ME!
SNAP
I JUST DON'T THINK I'D BE ABLE TO TELL THEM APART WITHOUT THE NICKNAMES.

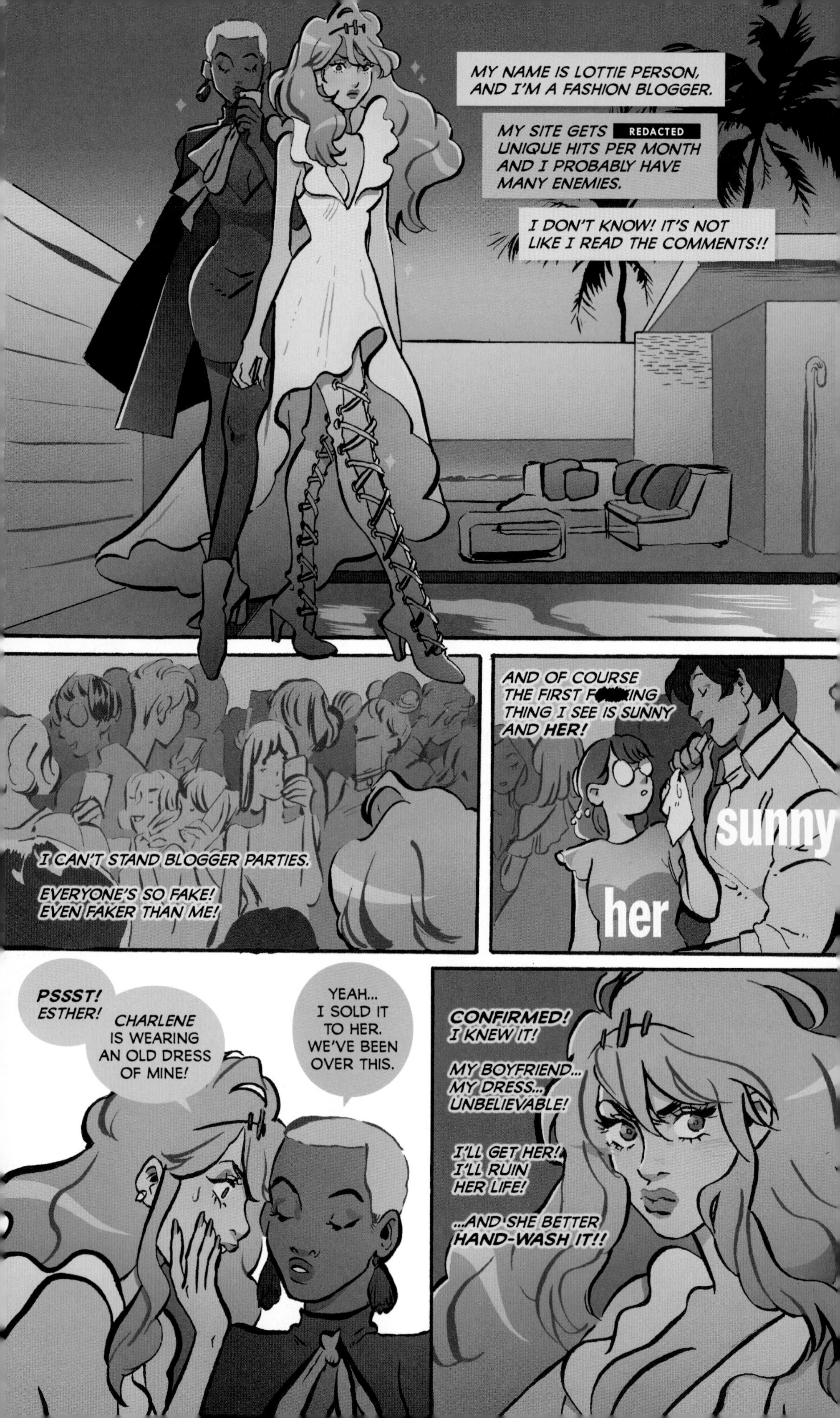
MY NAME IS LOTTIE PERSON, AND I'M A FASHION BLOGGER.
MY SITE GETS REDACTED UNIQUE HITS PER MONTH AND I PROBABLY HAVE MANY ENEMIES.
I DON'T KNOW! IT'S NOT LIKE I READ THE COMMENTS!!
I CAN'T STAND BLOGGER PARTIES.
EVERYONE'S SO FAKE! EVEN FAKER THAN ME!
AND OF COURSE THE FIRST F[redacted]ING THING I SEE IS SUNNY AND HER!
sunny
her
PSSST! ESTHER!
CHARLENE IS WEARING AN OLD DRESS OF MINE!
YEAH... I SOLD IT TO HER. WE'VE BEEN OVER THIS.
CONFIRMED! I KNEW IT!
MY BOYFRIEND... MY DRESS... UNBELIEVABLE!
I'LL GET HER! I'LL RUIN HER LIFE!
...AND SHE BETTER HAND-WASH IT!!

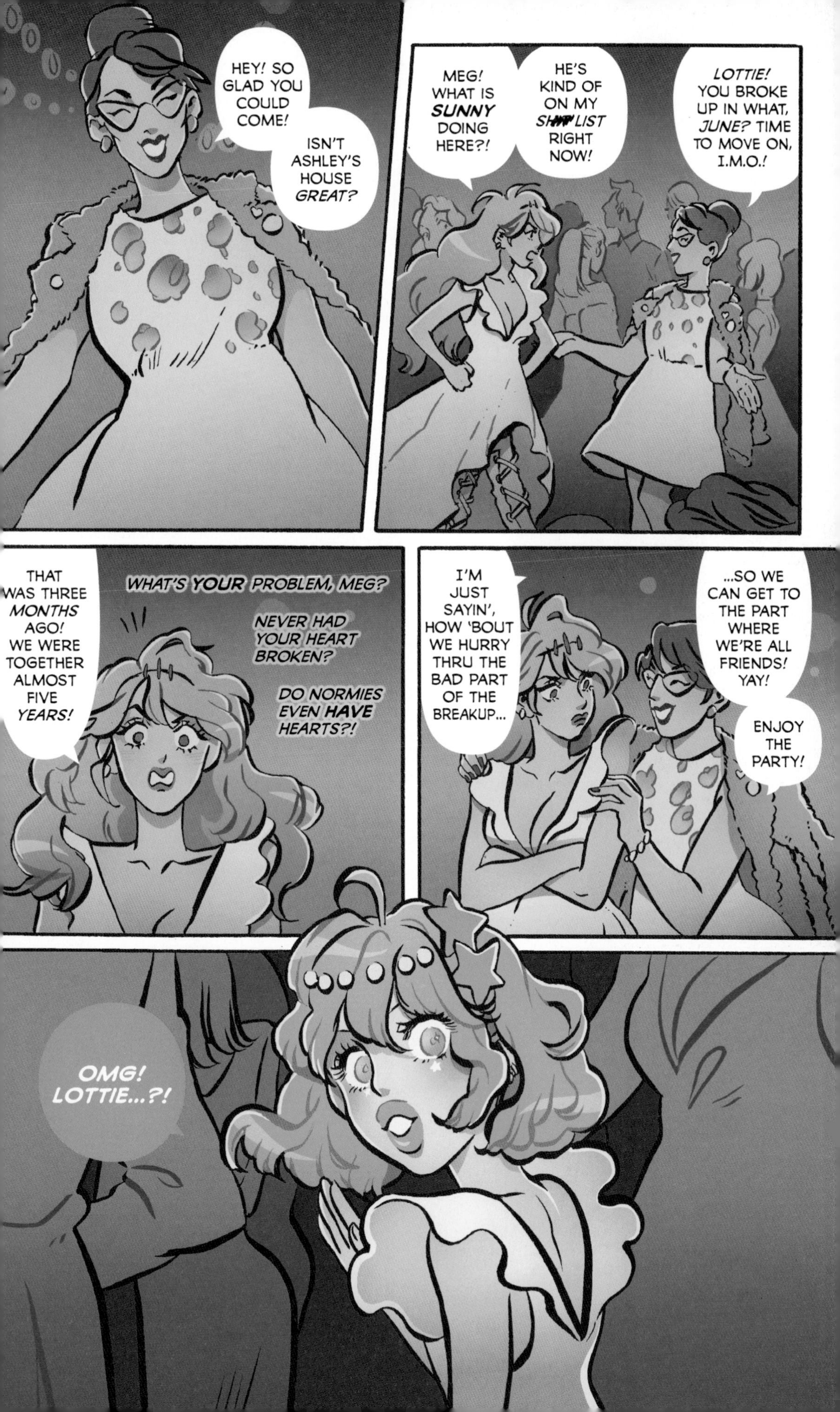
HEY! SO GLAD YOU COULD COME!
ISN'T ASHLEY'S HOUSE *GREAT?*
MEG! WHAT IS **SUNNY** DOING HERE?!
HE'S KIND OF ON MY *SH#!* LIST RIGHT NOW!
LOTTIE! YOU BROKE UP IN WHAT, *JUNE?* TIME TO MOVE ON, I.M.O.!
THAT WAS THREE *MONTHS* AGO! WE WERE TOGETHER ALMOST FIVE *YEARS!*
WHAT'S **YOUR** PROBLEM, MEG?
NEVER HAD YOUR HEART BROKEN?
DO NORMIES EVEN **HAVE** HEARTS?!
I'M JUST SAYIN', HOW 'BOUT WE HURRY THRU THE BAD PART OF THE BREAKUP...
...SO WE CAN GET TO THE PART WHERE WE'RE ALL FRIENDS! YAY!
ENJOY THE PARTY!
OMG! LOTTIE...?!

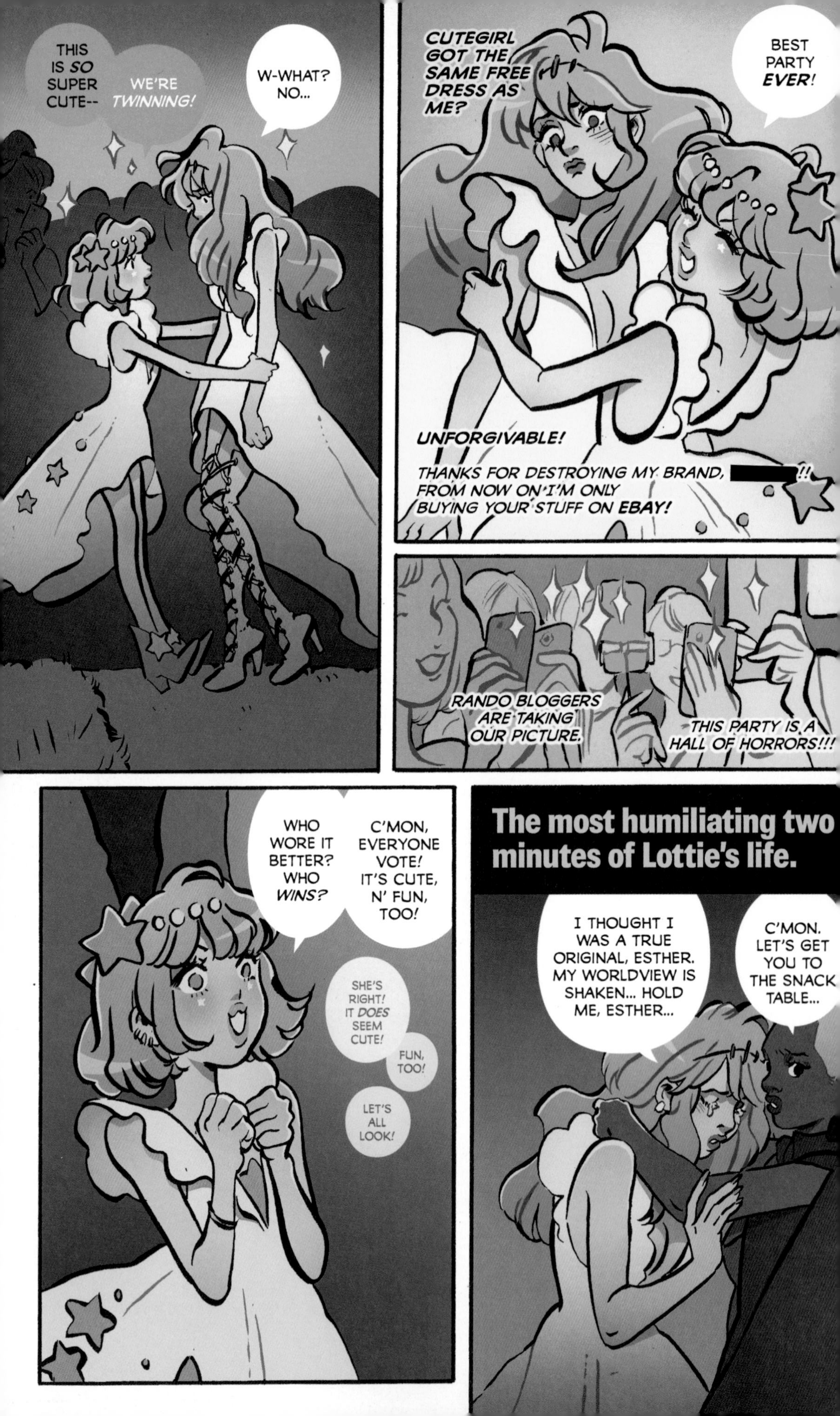
THIS IS *SO* SUPER CUTE--
WE'RE *TWINNING!*
W-WHAT? NO...
CUTEGIRL GOT THE SAME FREE DRESS AS ME?
BEST PARTY *EVER!*
UNFORGIVABLE!
THANKS FOR DESTROYING MY BRAND, [redacted]!! FROM NOW ON I'M ONLY BUYING YOUR STUFF ON EBAY!
RANDO BLOGGERS ARE TAKING OUR PICTURE.
THIS PARTY IS A HALL OF HORRORS!!!
WHO WORE IT BETTER? WHO *WINS?*
C'MON, EVERYONE VOTE! IT'S CUTE, N' FUN, TOO!
SHE'S RIGHT! IT *DOES* SEEM CUTE!
FUN, TOO!
LET'S ALL LOOK!
The most humiliating two minutes of Lottie's life.
I THOUGHT I WAS A TRUE ORIGINAL, ESTHER. MY WORLDVIEW IS SHAKEN... HOLD ME, ESTHER...
C'MON. LET'S GET YOU TO THE SNACK TABLE...

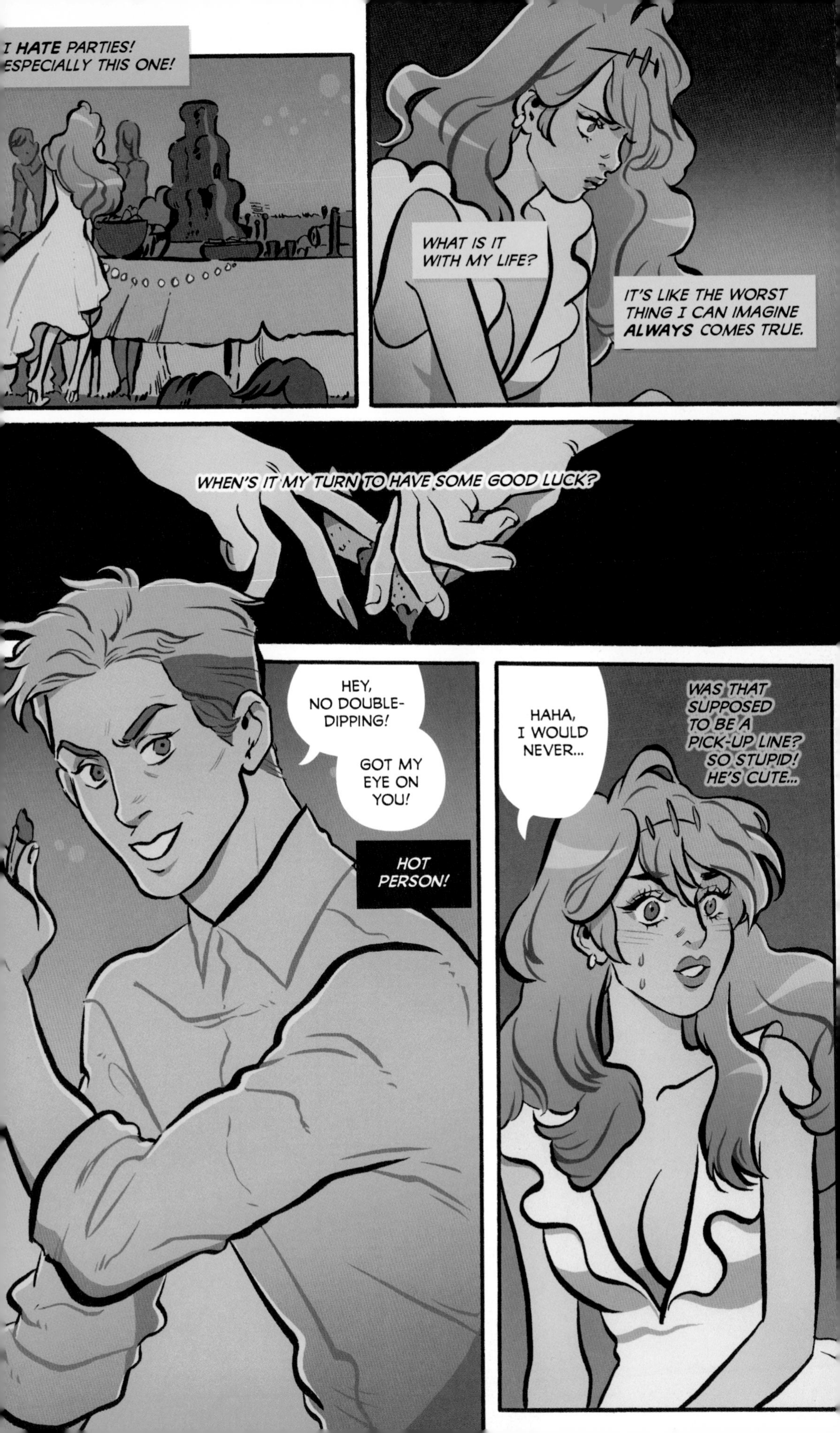
I **HATE** PARTIES! ESPECIALLY THIS ONE!
WHAT IS IT WITH MY LIFE?
IT'S LIKE THE WORST THING I CAN IMAGINE **ALWAYS** COMES TRUE.
WHEN'S IT MY TURN TO HAVE SOME GOOD LUCK?
HEY, NO DOUBLE-DIPPING!
GOT MY EYE ON YOU!
HOT PERSON!
HAHA, I WOULD NEVER...
WAS THAT SUPPOSED TO BE A PICK-UP LINE? SO STUPID! HE'S CUTE...

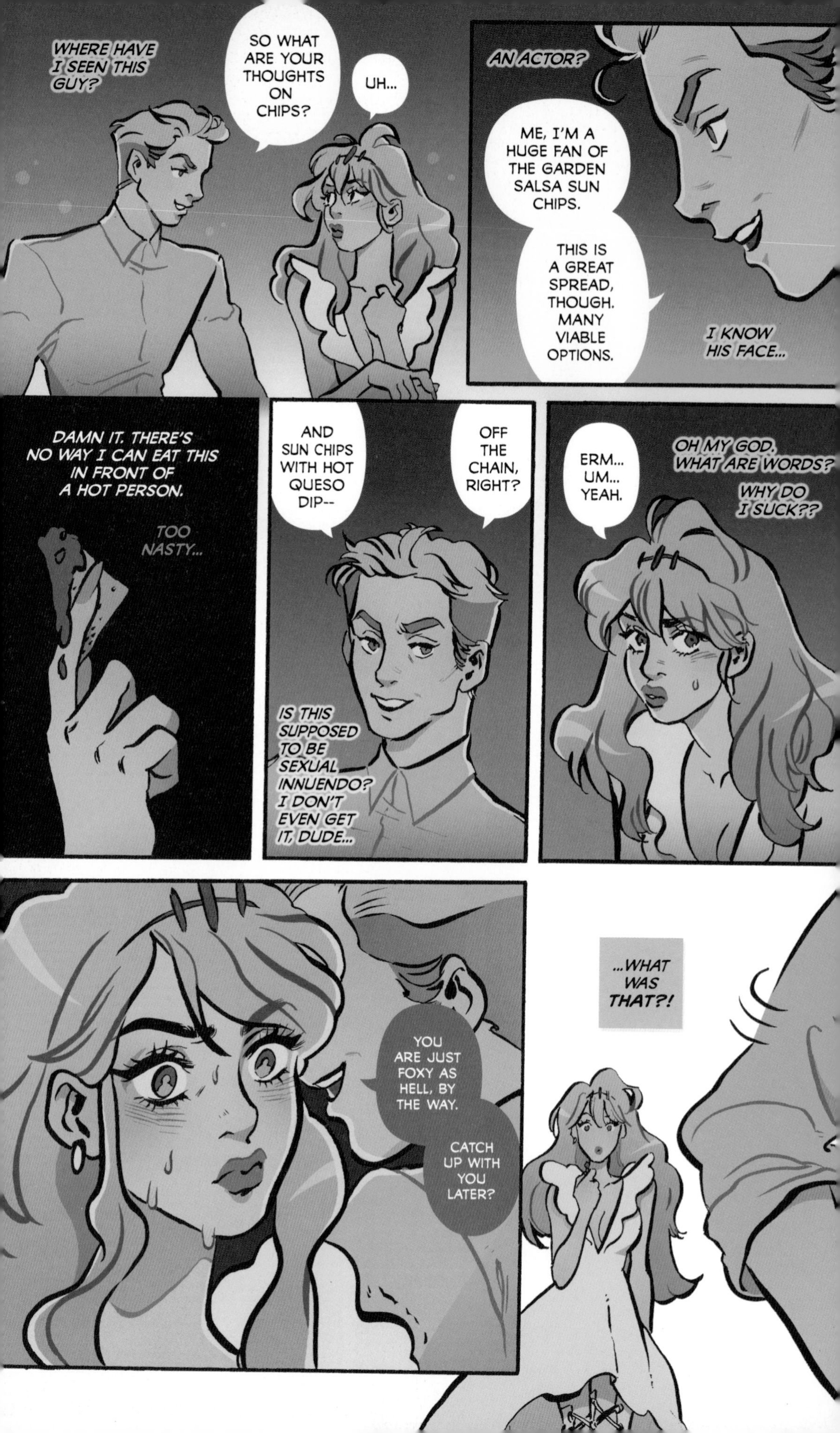

WHERE HAVE I SEEN THIS GUY?
SO WHAT ARE YOUR THOUGHTS ON CHIPS?
UH...
AN ACTOR?
ME, I'M A HUGE FAN OF THE GARDEN SALSA SUN CHIPS.
THIS IS A GREAT SPREAD, THOUGH. MANY VIABLE OPTIONS.
I KNOW HIS FACE...
DAMN IT. THERE'S NO WAY I CAN EAT THIS IN FRONT OF A HOT PERSON.
TOO NASTY...
AND SUN CHIPS WITH HOT QUESO DIP--
OFF THE CHAIN, RIGHT?
IS THIS SUPPOSED TO BE SEXUAL INNUENDO? I DON'T EVEN GET IT, DUDE...
ERM... UM... YEAH.
OH MY GOD. WHAT ARE WORDS?
WHY DO I SUCK??
YOU ARE JUST FOXY AS HELL, BY THE WAY.
CATCH UP WITH YOU LATER?
...WHAT WAS THAT?!

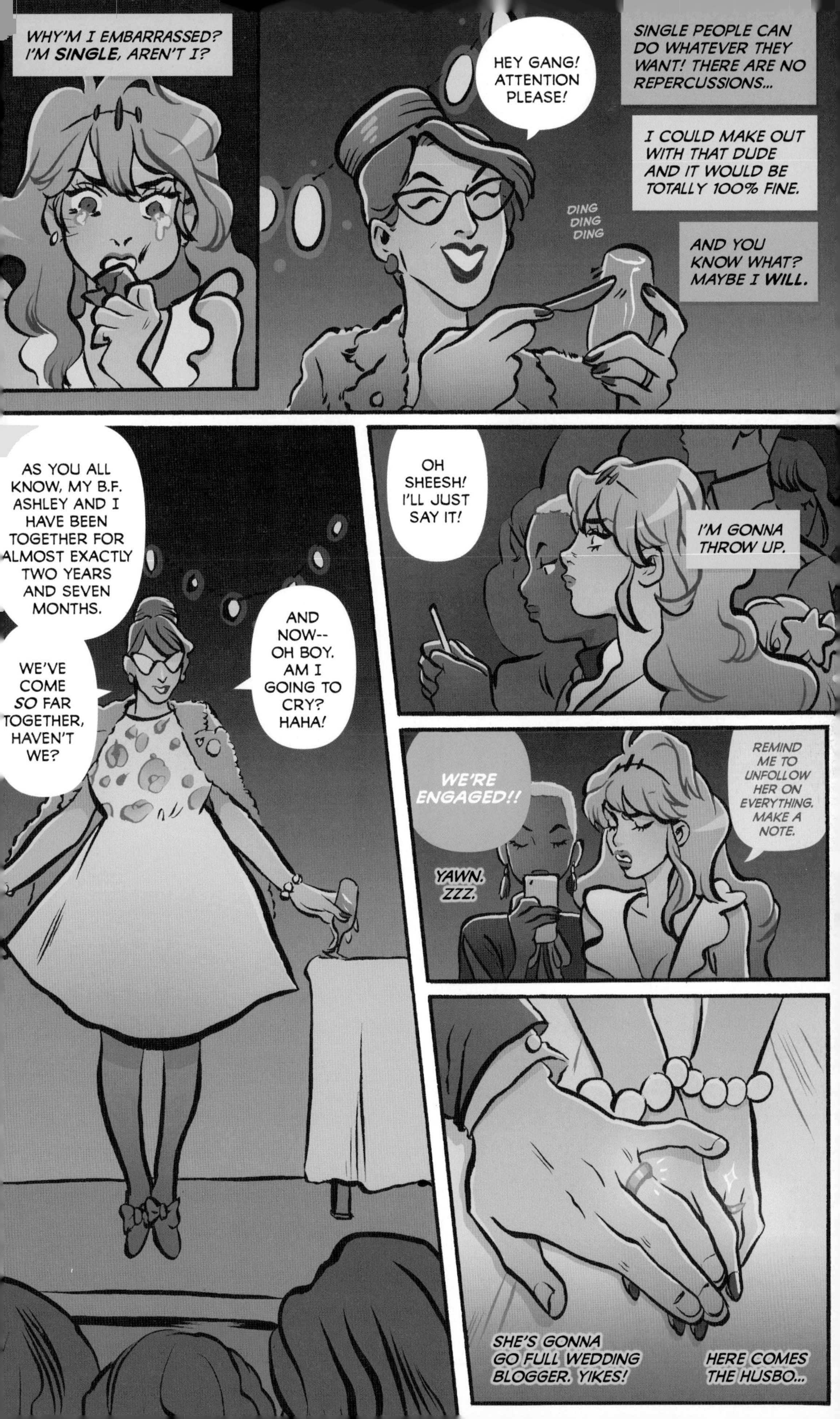
WHY'M I EMBARRASSED? I'M **SINGLE**, AREN'T I?
HEY GANG! ATTENTION PLEASE!
DING DING DING
SINGLE PEOPLE CAN DO WHATEVER THEY WANT! THERE ARE NO REPERCUSSIONS...
I COULD MAKE OUT WITH THAT DUDE AND IT WOULD BE TOTALLY 100% FINE.
AND YOU KNOW WHAT? MAYBE I **WILL**.
AS YOU ALL KNOW, MY B.F. ASHLEY AND I HAVE BEEN TOGETHER FOR ALMOST EXACTLY TWO YEARS AND SEVEN MONTHS.
WE'VE COME *SO* FAR TOGETHER, HAVEN'T WE?
AND NOW-- OH BOY. AM I GOING TO CRY? HAHA!
OH SHEESH! I'LL JUST SAY IT!
I'M GONNA THROW UP.
WE'RE ENGAGED!!
YAWN. ZZZ.
REMIND ME TO UNFOLLOW HER ON EVERYTHING. MAKE A NOTE.
SHE'S GONNA GO FULL WEDDING BLOGGER. YIKES!
HERE COMES THE HUSBO...

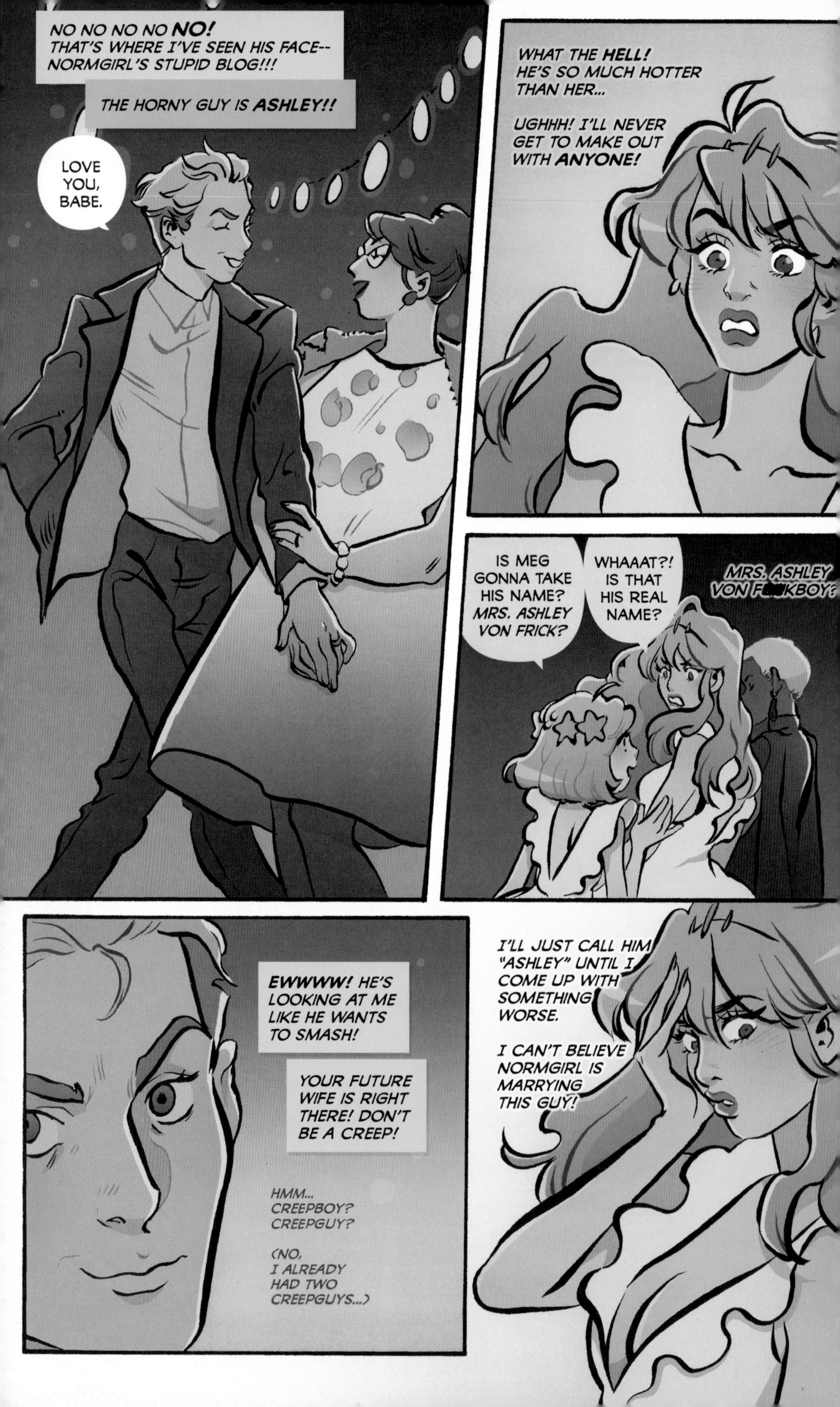

NO NO NO NO **NO!** THAT'S WHERE I'VE SEEN HIS FACE-- NORMGIRL'S STUPID BLOG!!!
THE HORNY GUY IS **ASHLEY!!**
LOVE YOU, BABE.
WHAT THE **HELL!** HE'S SO MUCH HOTTER THAN HER...
UGHHH! I'LL NEVER GET TO MAKE OUT WITH **ANYONE!**
IS MEG GONNA TAKE HIS NAME? *MRS. ASHLEY VON FRICK?*
WHAAAT?! IS THAT HIS REAL NAME?
MRS. ASHLEY VON F[redacted]KBOY?
EWWWW! HE'S LOOKING AT ME LIKE HE WANTS TO SMASH!
YOUR FUTURE WIFE IS RIGHT THERE! DON'T BE A CREEP!
HMM... CREEPBOY? CREEPGUY?
(NO, I ALREADY HAD TWO CREEPGUYS...)
I'LL JUST CALL HIM "ASHLEY" UNTIL I COME UP WITH SOMETHING WORSE.
I CAN'T BELIEVE NORMGIRL IS MARRYING THIS GUY!

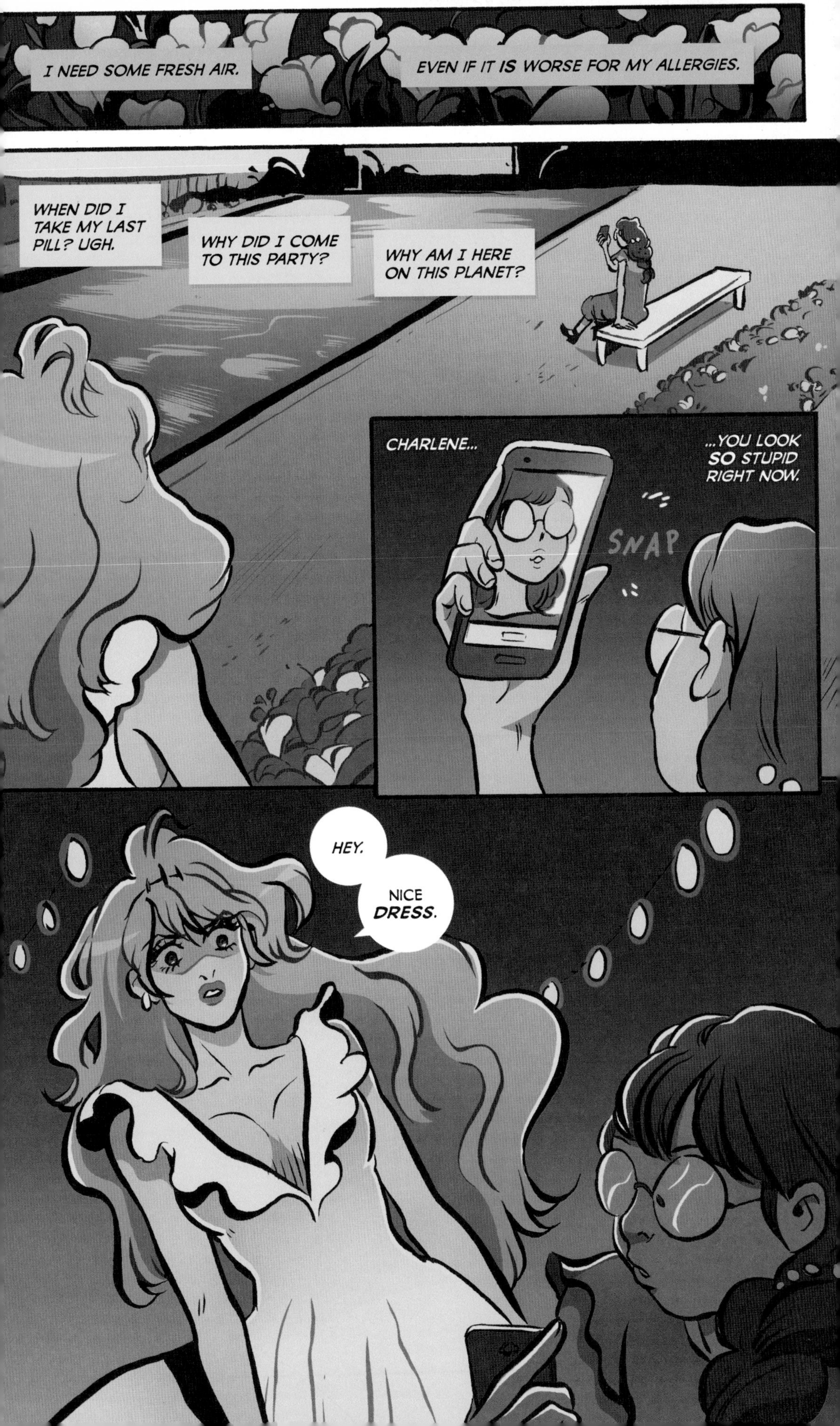
I NEED SOME FRESH AIR.
EVEN IF IT IS WORSE FOR MY ALLERGIES.
WHEN DID I TAKE MY LAST PILL? UGH.
WHY DID I COME TO THIS PARTY?
WHY AM I HERE ON THIS PLANET?
CHARLENE...
...YOU LOOK SO STUPID RIGHT NOW.
SNAP
HEY.
NICE DRESS.

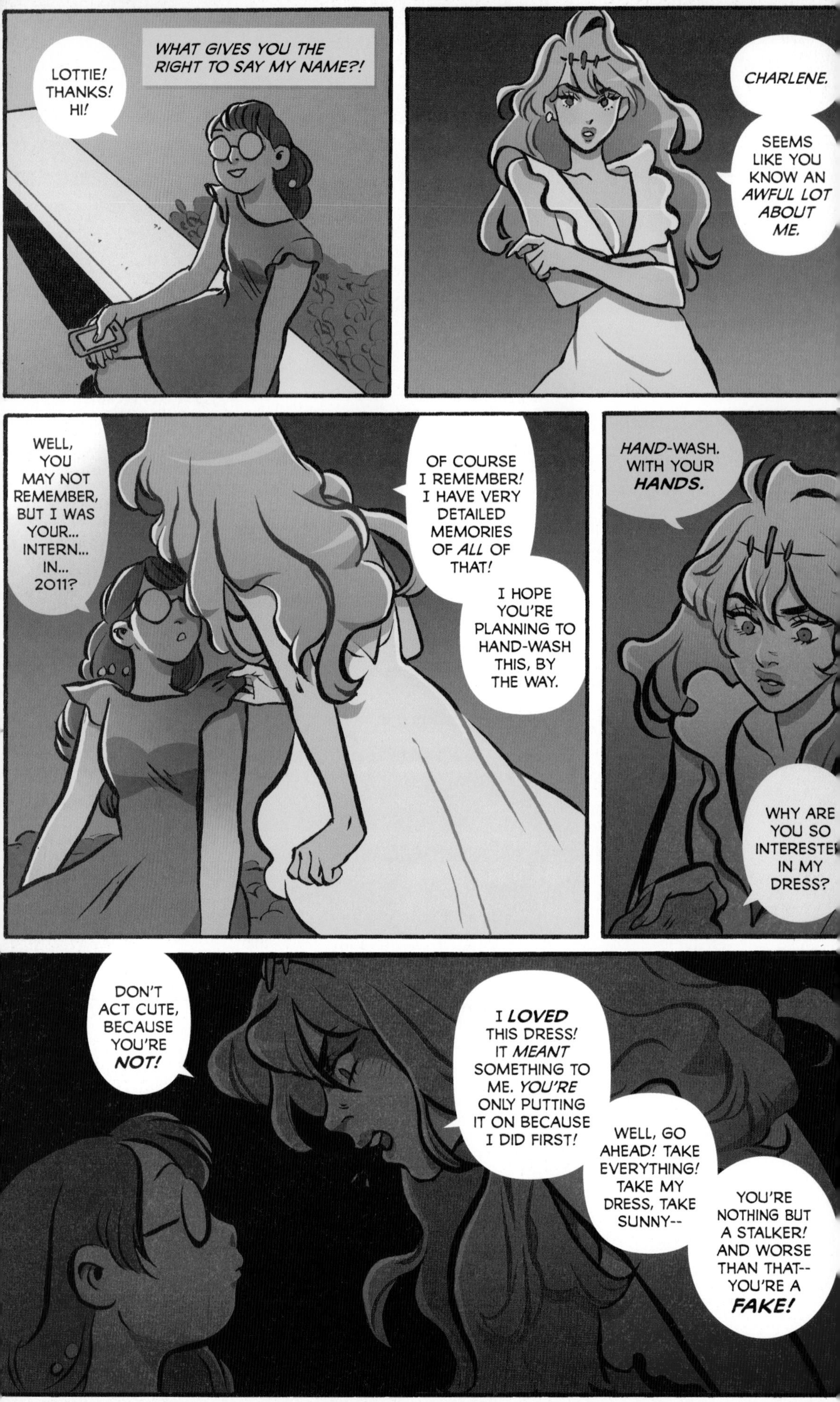
WHAT GIVES YOU THE RIGHT TO SAY MY NAME?!
LOTTIE! THANKS! HI!
CHARLENE.
SEEMS LIKE YOU KNOW AN AWFUL LOT ABOUT ME.
WELL, YOU MAY NOT REMEMBER, BUT I WAS YOUR... INTERN... IN... 2011?
OF COURSE I REMEMBER! I HAVE VERY DETAILED MEMORIES OF ALL OF THAT!
I HOPE YOU'RE PLANNING TO HAND-WASH THIS, BY THE WAY.
HAND-WASH. WITH YOUR HANDS.
WHY ARE YOU SO INTERESTE IN MY DRESS?
DON'T ACT CUTE, BECAUSE YOU'RE NOT!
I LOVED THIS DRESS! IT MEANT SOMETHING TO ME. YOU'RE ONLY PUTTING IT ON BECAUSE I DID FIRST!
WELL, GO AHEAD! TAKE EVERYTHING! TAKE MY DRESS, TAKE SUNNY--
YOU'RE NOTHING BUT A STALKER! AND WORSE THAN THAT-- YOU'RE A FAKE!

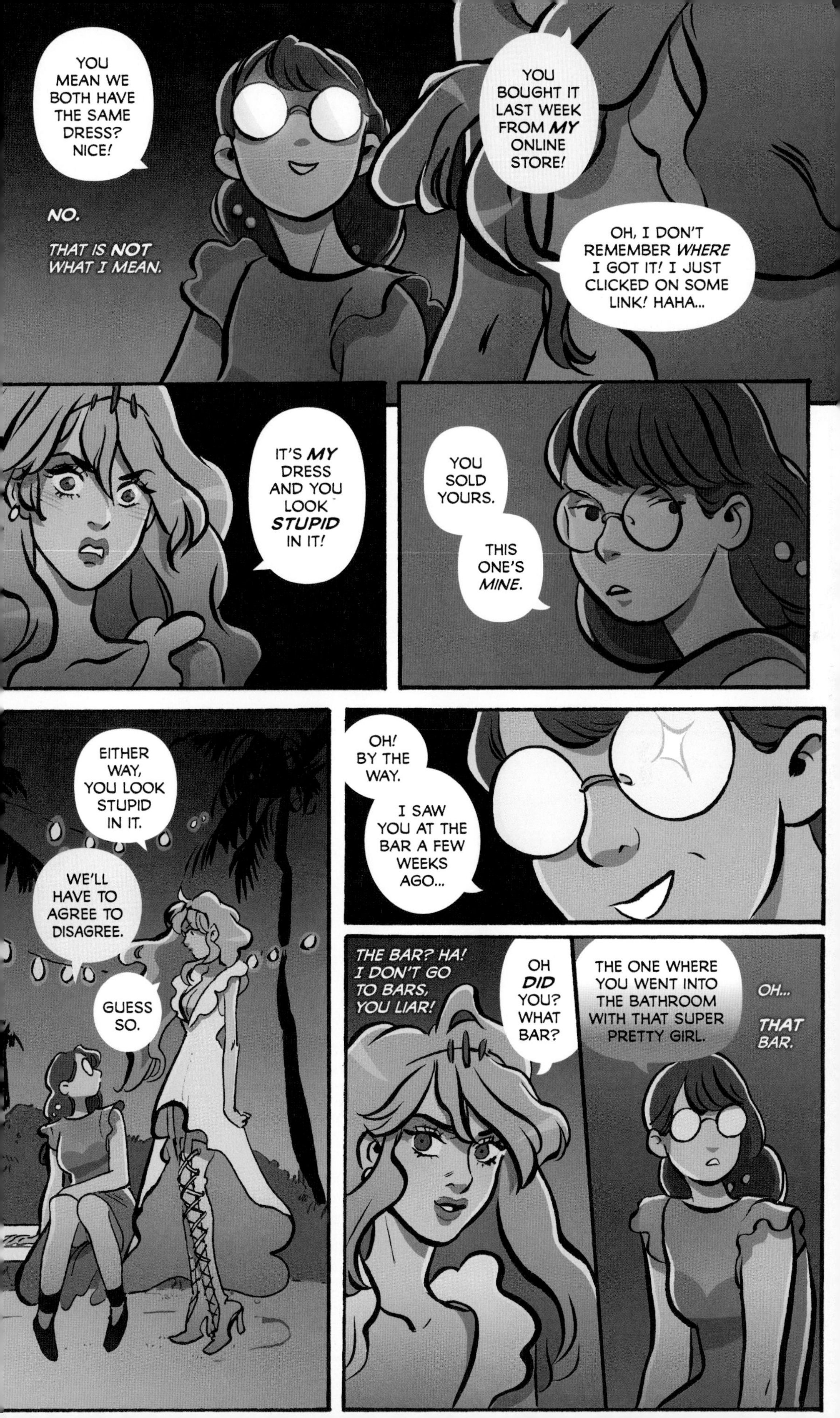

YOU MEAN WE BOTH HAVE THE SAME DRESS? NICE!
YOU BOUGHT IT LAST WEEK FROM *MY* ONLINE STORE!
NO.
THAT IS NOT WHAT I MEAN.
OH, I DON'T REMEMBER *WHERE* I GOT IT! I JUST CLICKED ON SOME LINK! HAHA...
IT'S *MY* DRESS AND YOU LOOK *STUPID* IN IT!
YOU SOLD YOURS.
THIS ONE'S *MINE.*
EITHER WAY, YOU LOOK STUPID IN IT.
WE'LL HAVE TO AGREE TO DISAGREE.
GUESS SO.
OH! BY THE WAY.
I SAW YOU AT THE BAR A FEW WEEKS AGO...
THE BAR? HA! I DON'T GO TO BARS, YOU LIAR!
OH *DID* YOU? WHAT BAR?
THE ONE WHERE YOU WENT INTO THE BATHROOM WITH THAT SUPER PRETTY GIRL.
OH...
THAT BAR.

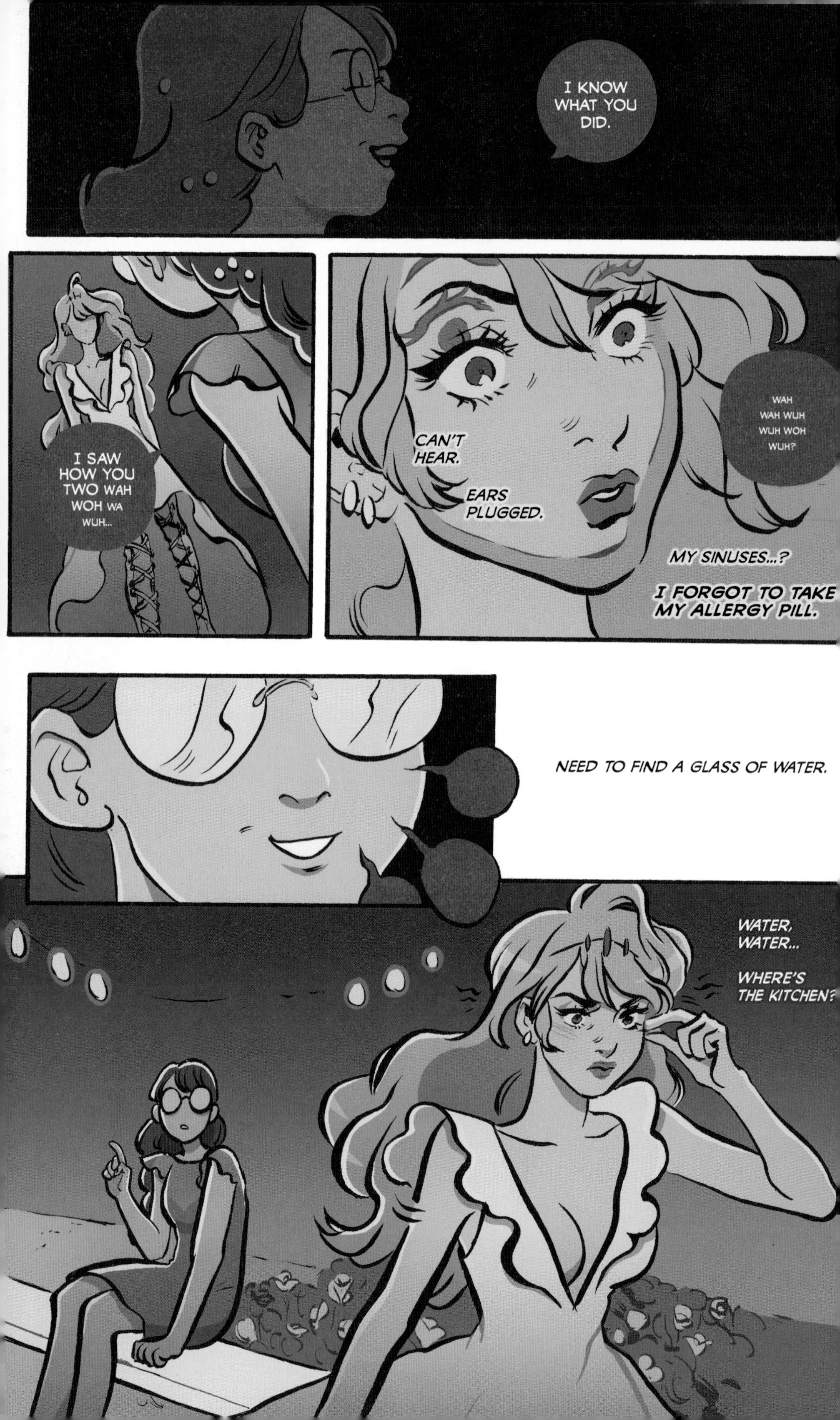
I KNOW WHAT YOU DID.
I SAW HOW YOU TWO WAH WOH WA WUH...
CAN'T HEAR.
EARS PLUGGED.
WAH WAH WUH WUH WOH WUH?
MY SINUSES...?
I FORGOT TO TAKE MY ALLERGY PILL.
NEED TO FIND A GLASS OF WATER.
WATER, WATER...
WHERE'S THE KITCHEN?

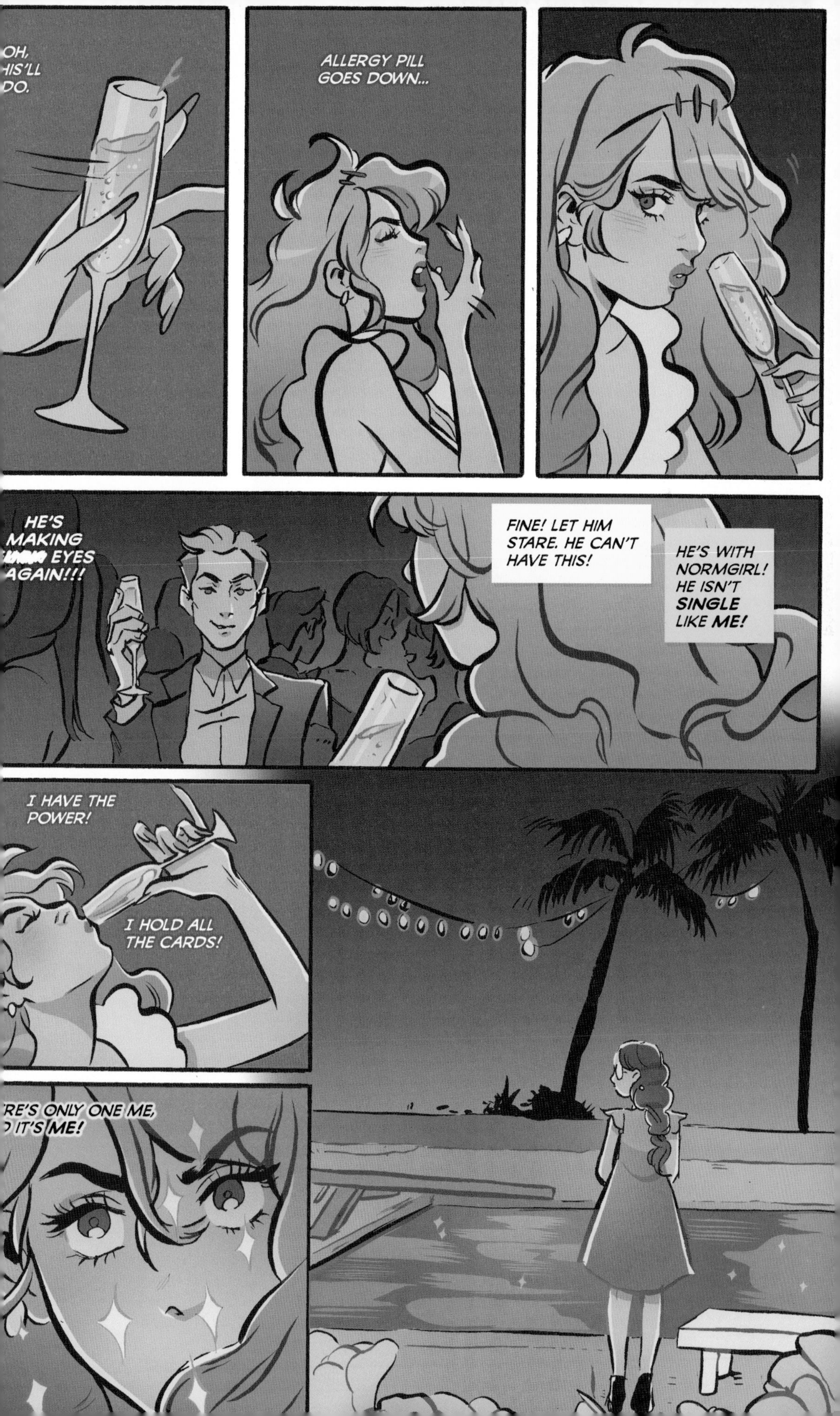

OH,
HIS'LL
DO.
ALLERGY PILL
GOES DOWN...
HE'S
MAKING
[redacted] EYES
AGAIN!!!
FINE! LET HIM
STARE. HE CAN'T
HAVE THIS!
HE'S WITH
NORMGIRL!
HE ISN'T
SINGLE
LIKE ME!
I HAVE THE
POWER!
I HOLD ALL
THE CARDS!
RE'S ONLY ONE ME,
D IT'S ME!

NOT YOU--

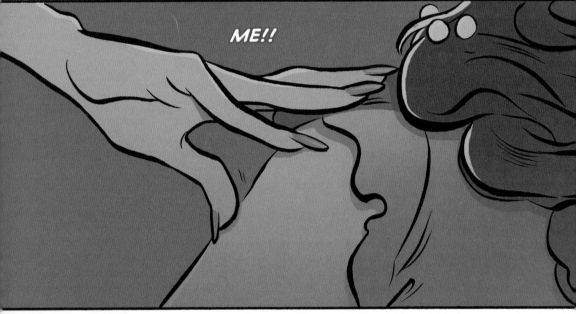

ME!!

SPLOOSH

OH *DANG.*

SAVAGE!

THAT WAS NOT *ME,* EVERYONE! THAT WAS MY *TWIN!*

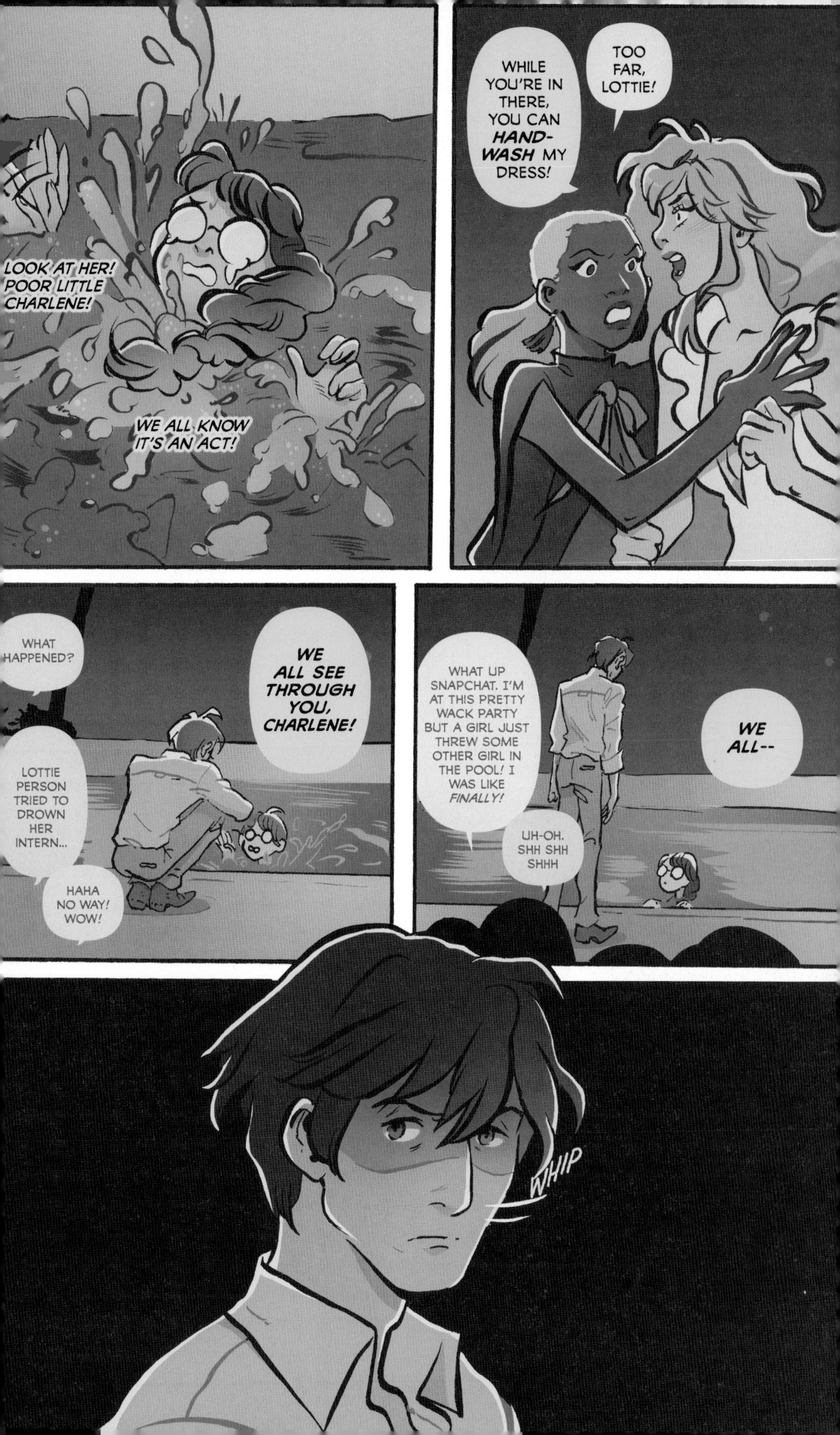
LOOK AT HER! POOR LITTLE CHARLENE!
WE ALL KNOW IT'S AN ACT!
WHILE YOU'RE IN THERE, YOU CAN **HAND-WASH** MY DRESS!
TOO FAR, LOTTIE!
WHAT HAPPENED?
LOTTIE PERSON TRIED TO DROWN HER INTERN...
HAHA NO WAY! WOW!
WE ALL SEE THROUGH YOU, CHARLENE!
WHAT UP SNAPCHAT. I'M AT THIS PRETTY WACK PARTY BUT A GIRL JUST THREW SOME OTHER GIRL IN THE POOL! I WAS LIKE *FINALLY!*
UH-OH. SHH SHH SHHH
WE ALL--
WHIP

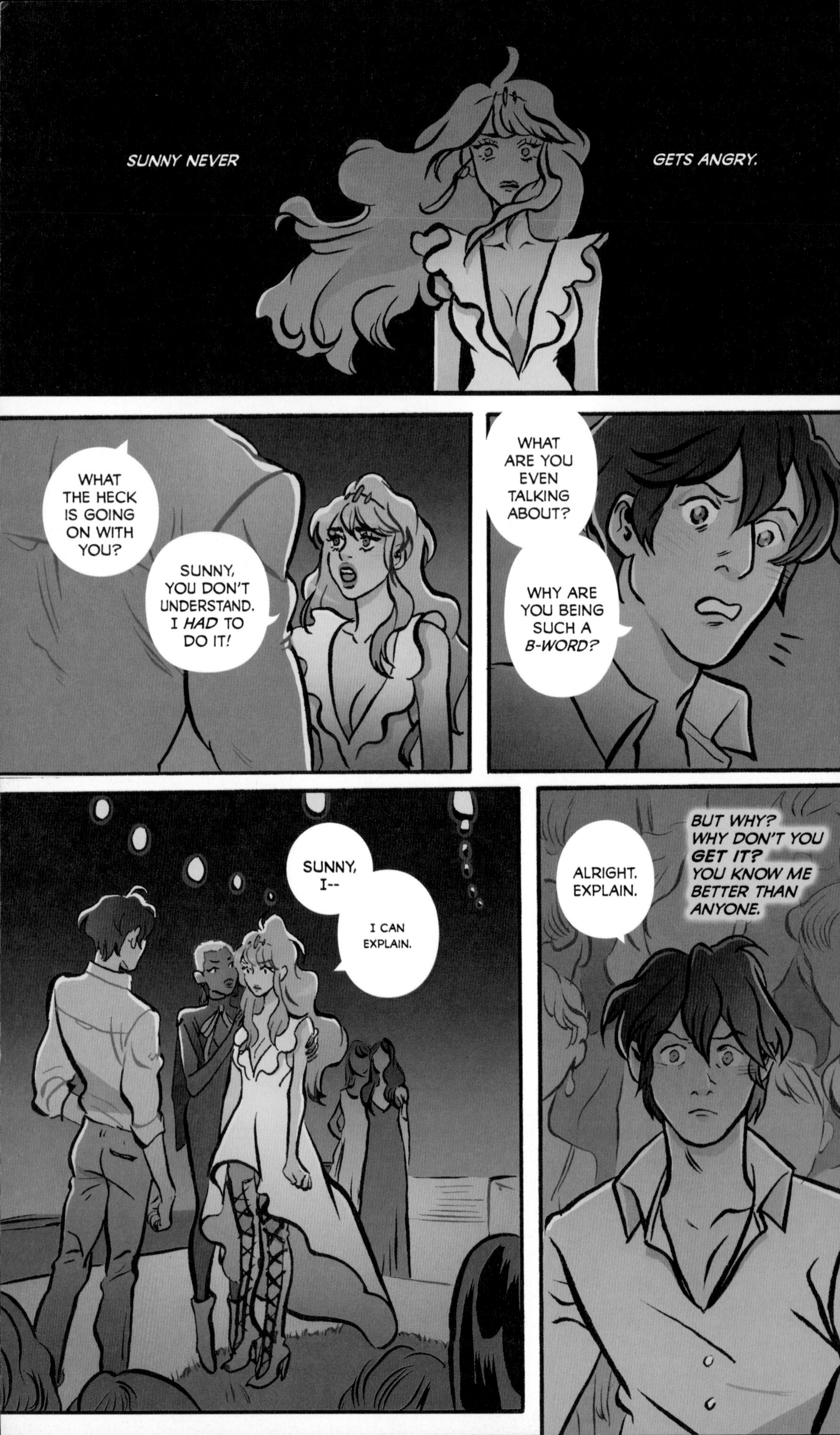
SUNNY NEVER
GETS ANGRY.
WHAT THE HECK IS GOING ON WITH YOU?
SUNNY, YOU DON'T UNDERSTAND. I *HAD* TO DO IT!
WHAT ARE YOU EVEN TALKING ABOUT?
WHY ARE YOU BEING SUCH A *B-WORD?*
SUNNY, I--
I CAN EXPLAIN.
ALRIGHT. EXPLAIN.
BUT WHY? WHY DON'T YOU ***GET IT?*** *YOU KNOW ME BETTER THAN ANYONE.*

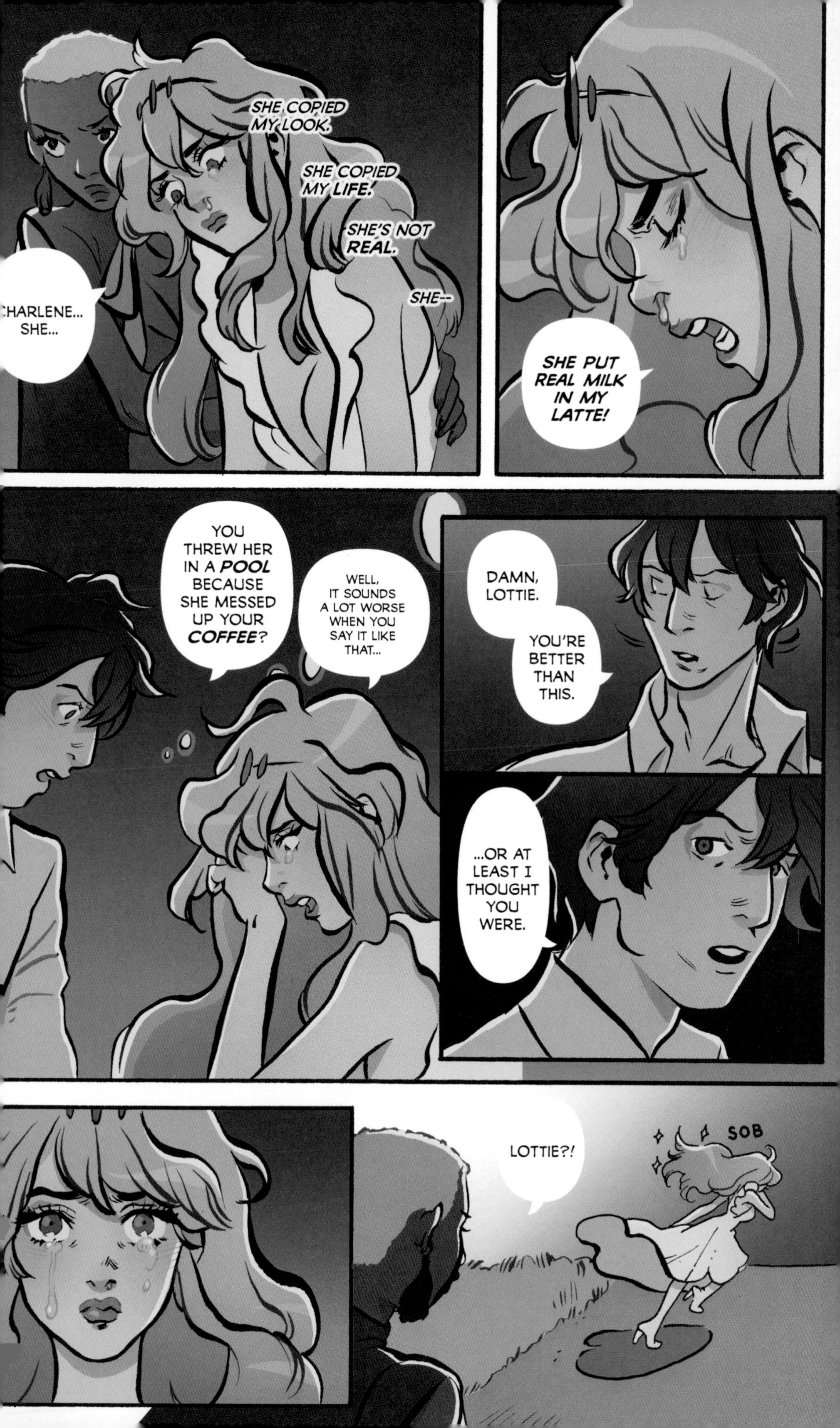
SHE COPIED MY LOOK.
SHE COPIED MY LIFE.
SHE'S NOT REAL.
SHE--
CHARLENE... SHE...
SHE PUT REAL MILK IN MY LATTE!
YOU THREW HER IN A POOL BECAUSE SHE MESSED UP YOUR COFFEE?
WELL, IT SOUNDS A LOT WORSE WHEN YOU SAY IT LIKE THAT...
DAMN, LOTTIE.
YOU'RE BETTER THAN THIS.
...OR AT LEAST I THOUGHT YOU WERE.
LOTTIE?!
SOB

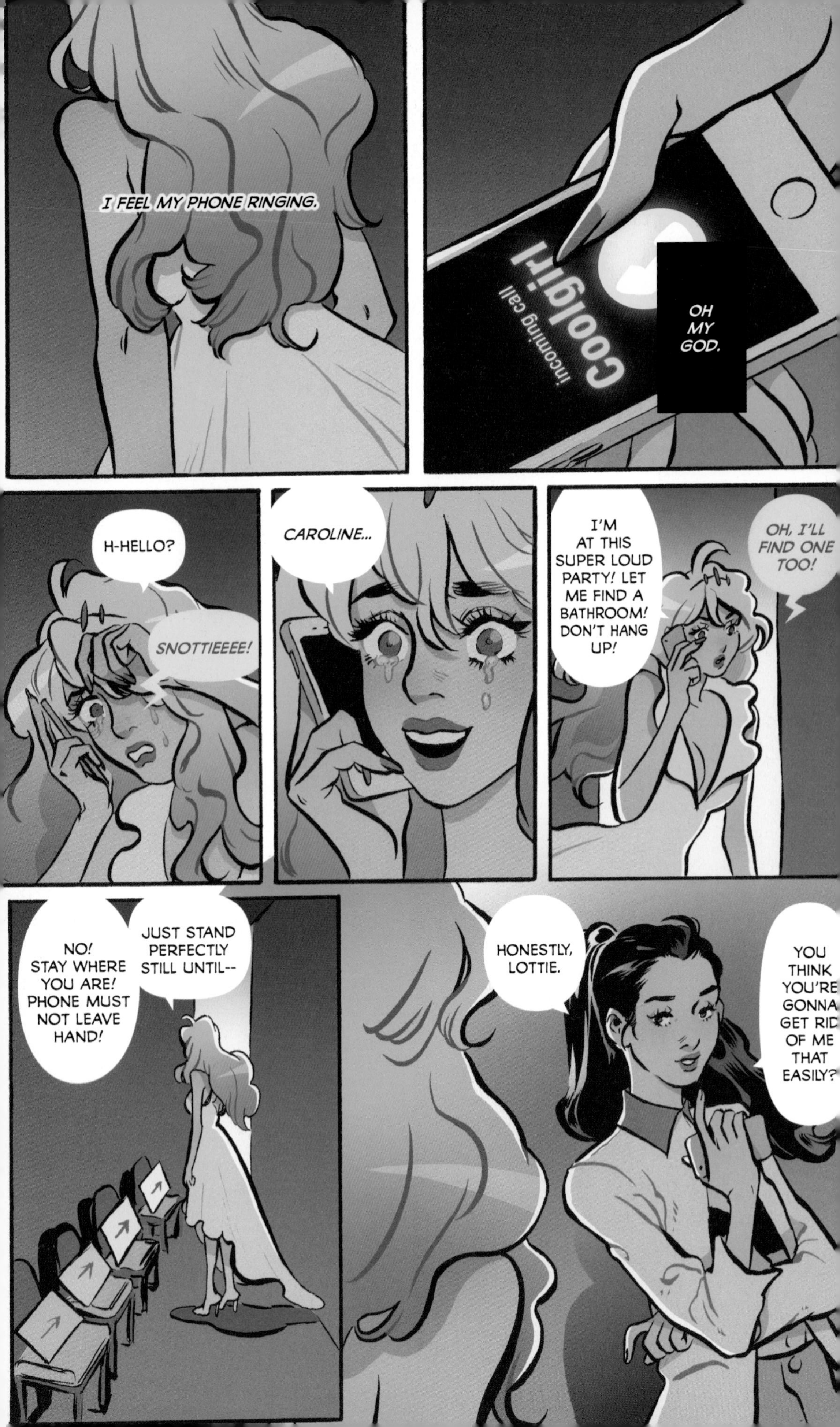
I FEEL MY PHONE RINGING.
Coolgirl
incoming call
OH MY GOD.
H-HELLO?
SNOTTIEEEE!
CAROLINE...
I'M AT THIS SUPER LOUD PARTY! LET ME FIND A BATHROOM! DON'T HANG UP!
OH, I'LL FIND ONE TOO!
NO! STAY WHERE YOU ARE! PHONE MUST NOT LEAVE HAND!
JUST STAND PERFECTLY STILL UNTIL--
HONESTLY, LOTTIE.
YOU THINK YOU'RE GONNA GET RID OF ME THAT EASILY?

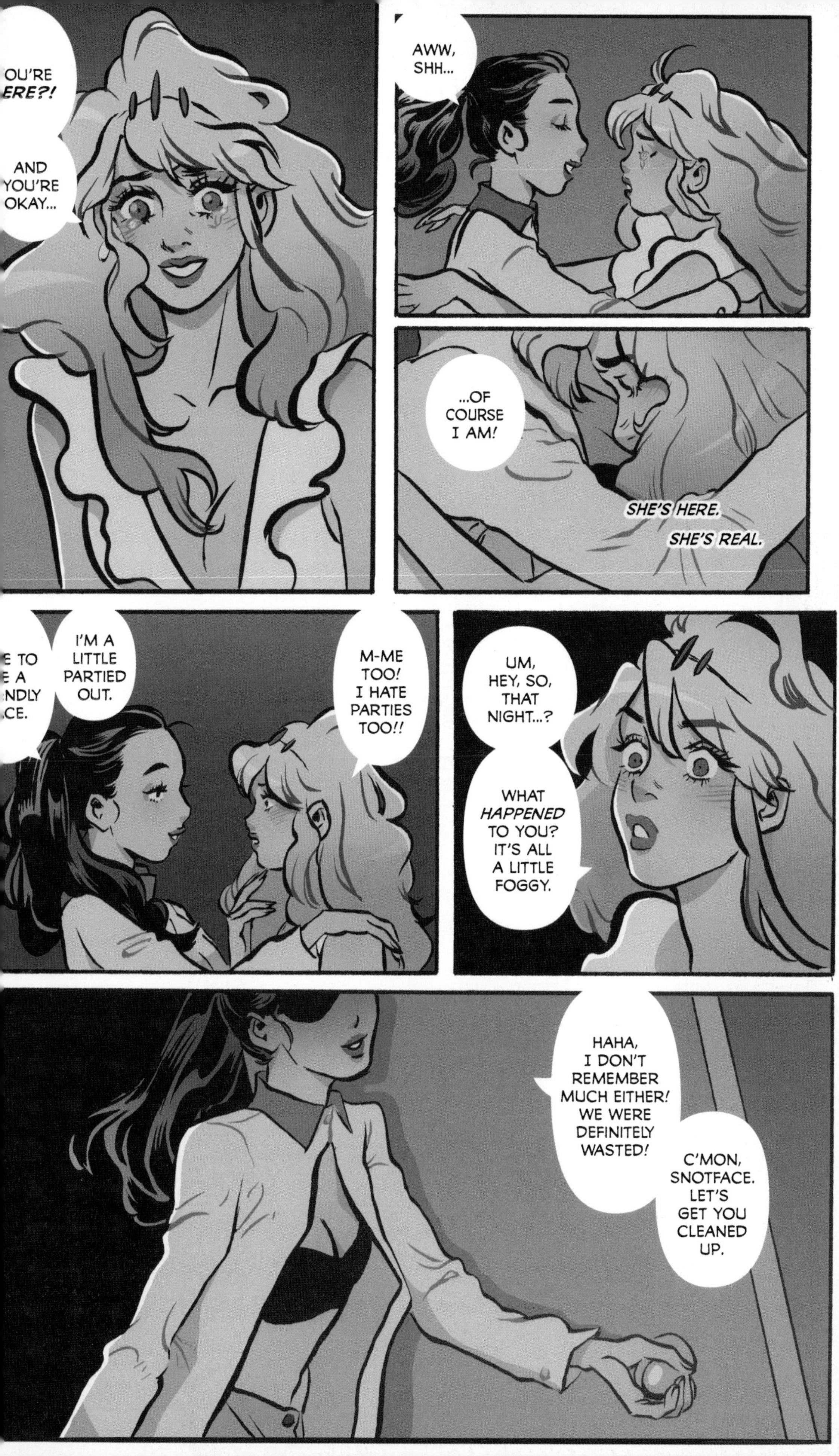

OU'RE ERE?!
AND YOU'RE OKAY...
AWW, SHH...
...OF COURSE I AM!
SHE'S HERE.
SHE'S REAL.
E TO E A NDLY CE.
I'M A LITTLE PARTIED OUT.
M-ME TOO! I HATE PARTIES TOO!!
UM, HEY, SO, THAT NIGHT...?
WHAT HAPPENED TO YOU? IT'S ALL A LITTLE FOGGY.
HAHA, I DON'T REMEMBER MUCH EITHER! WE WERE DEFINITELY WASTED!
C'MON, SNOTFACE. LET'S GET YOU CLEANED UP.

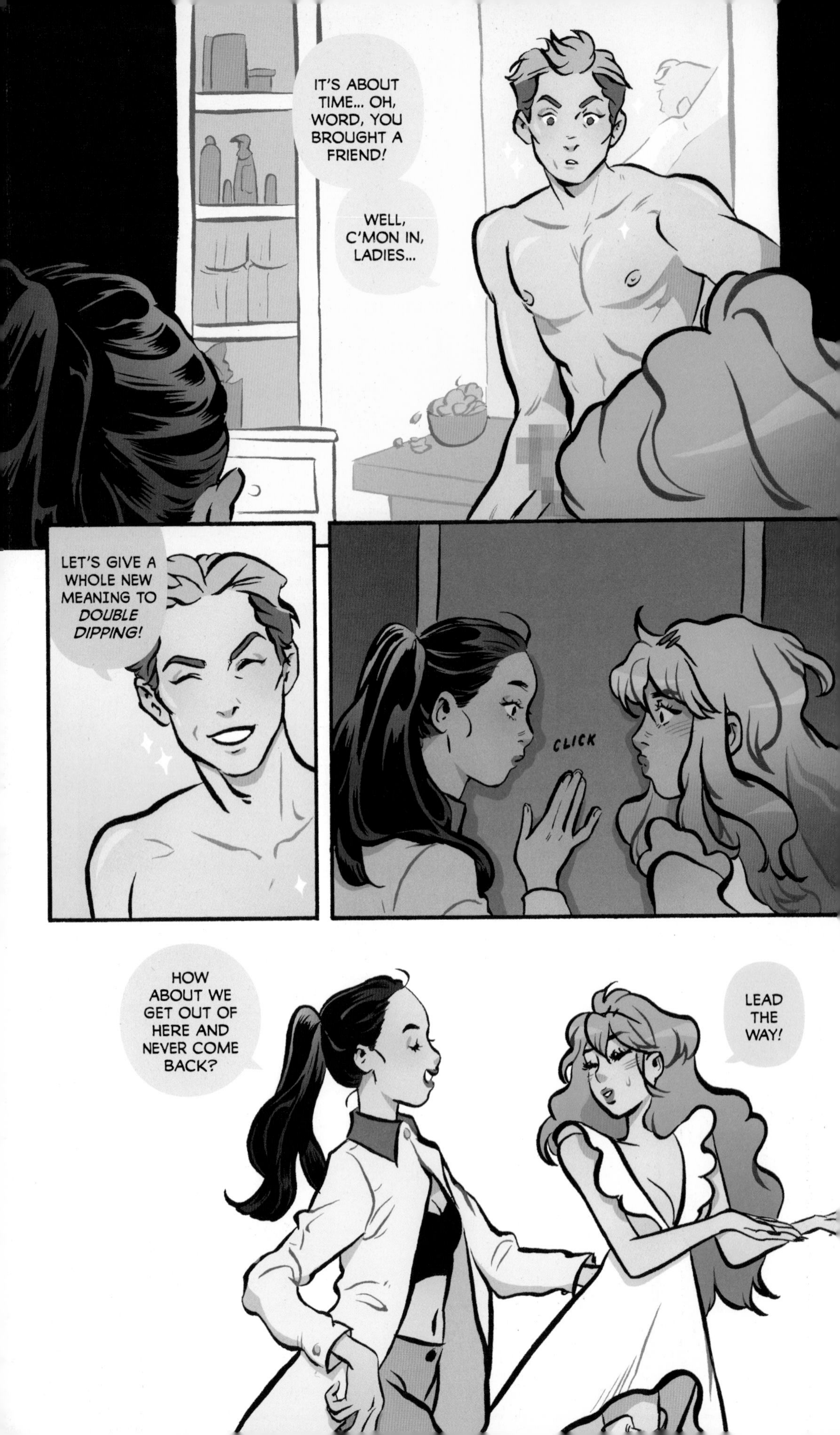
IT'S ABOUT TIME... OH, WORD, YOU BROUGHT A FRIEND!
WELL, C'MON IN, LADIES...
LET'S GIVE A WHOLE NEW MEANING TO *DOUBLE DIPPING!*
CLICK
HOW ABOUT WE GET OUT OF HERE AND NEVER COME BACK?
LEAD THE WAY!

SHE'S

SO

REAL.

SHE'S

FLAWLESS.

HER SOUL

IS LIKE A RIVER

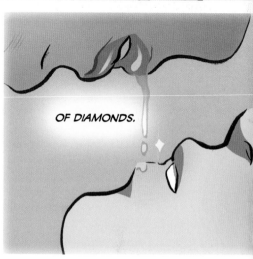

OF DIAMONDS.

E EVEN LOOKS GREAT

POOPING WITH THE DOOR OPEN...

BZZT

BZZT

BZZT

BZZT

5:15 AM

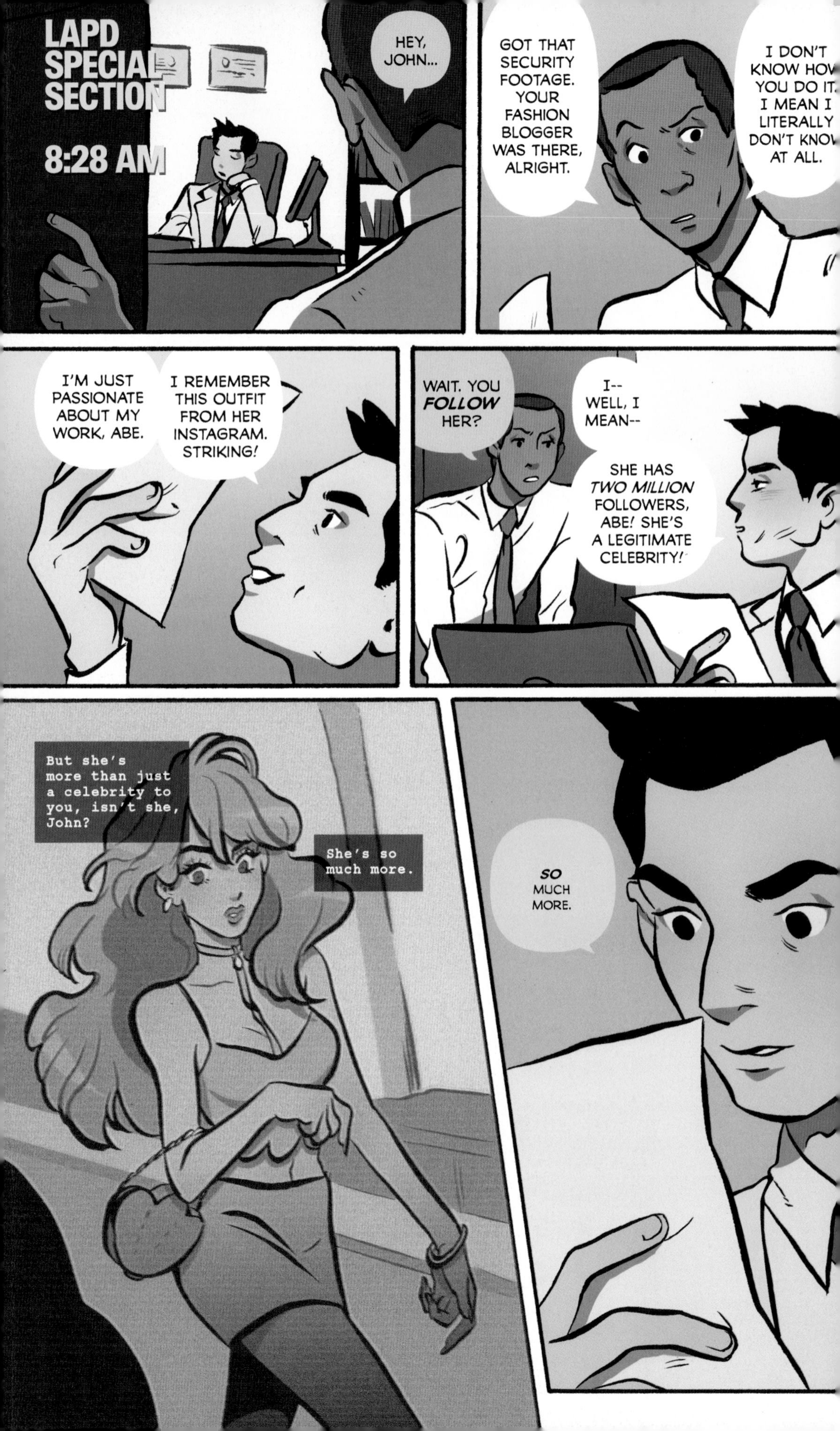
LAPD SPECIAL SECTION
8:28 AM
HEY, JOHN...
GOT THAT SECURITY FOOTAGE. YOUR FASHION BLOGGER WAS THERE, ALRIGHT.
I DON'T KNOW HOW YOU DO IT. I MEAN I LITERALLY DON'T KNOW AT ALL.
I'M JUST PASSIONATE ABOUT MY WORK, ABE.
I REMEMBER THIS OUTFIT FROM HER INSTAGRAM. STRIKING!
WAIT. YOU FOLLOW HER?
I-- WELL, I MEAN--
SHE HAS TWO MILLION FOLLOWERS, ABE! SHE'S A LEGITIMATE CELEBRITY!
But she's more than just a celebrity to you, isn't she, John?
She's so much more.
SO MUCH MORE.

04. NOW EVERYTHING'S EMBARRASSING

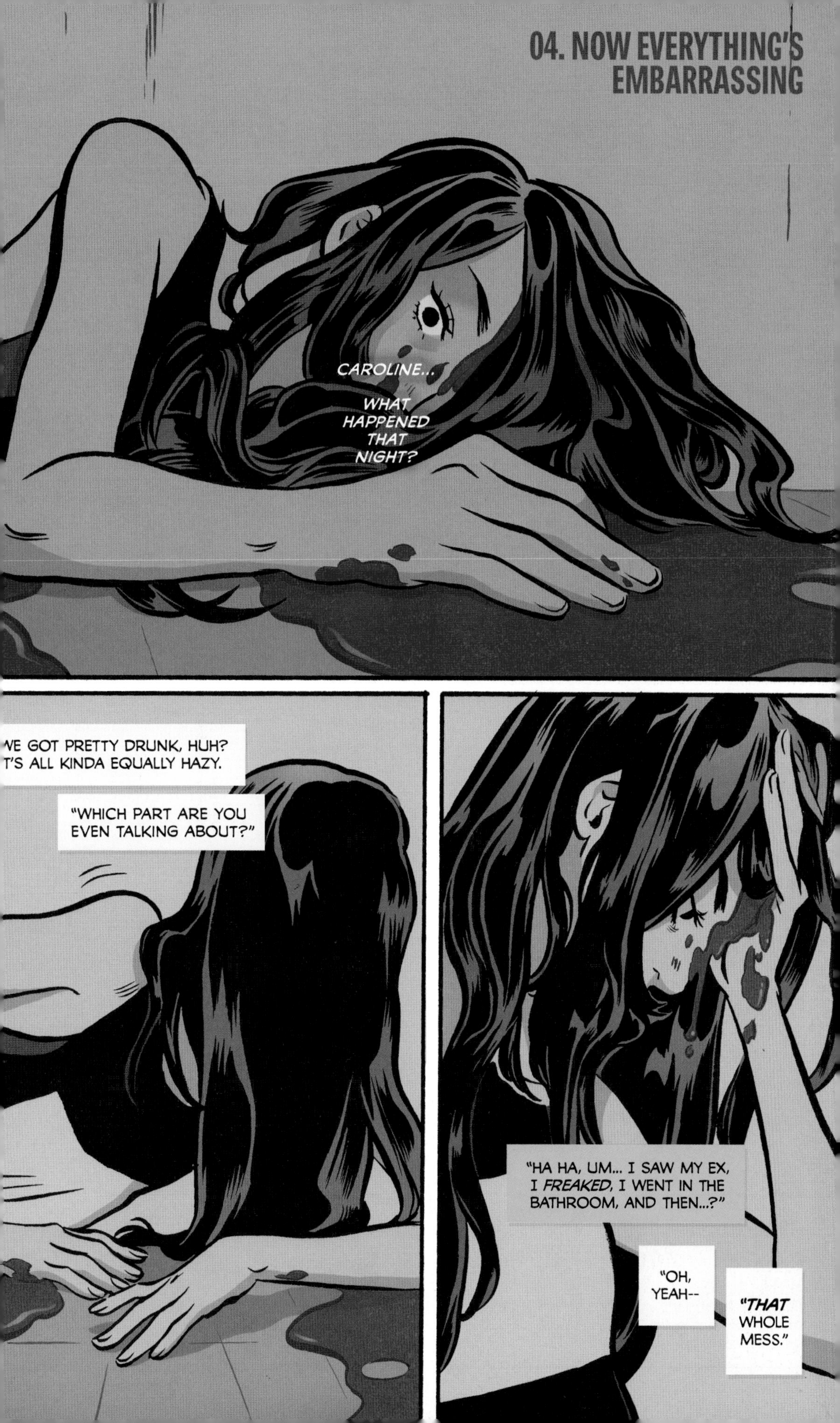

CAROLINE...
WHAT HAPPENED THAT NIGHT?
WE GOT PRETTY DRUNK, HUH? T'S ALL KINDA EQUALLY HAZY.
"WHICH PART ARE YOU EVEN TALKING ABOUT?"
"HA HA, UM... I SAW MY EX, I *FREAKED,* I WENT IN THE BATHROOM, AND THEN...?"
"OH, YEAH--
"*THAT* WHOLE MESS."

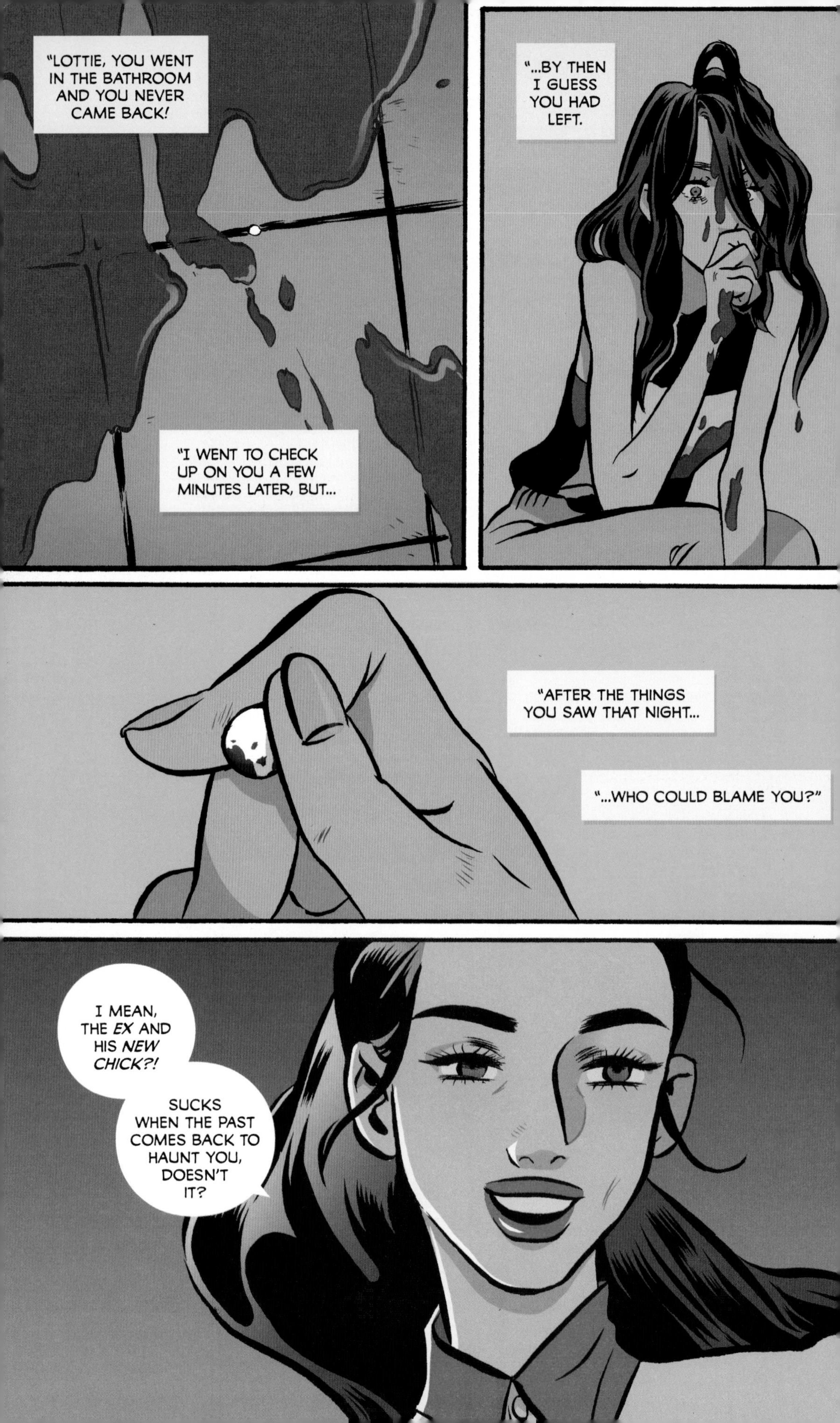
"LOTTIE, YOU WENT IN THE BATHROOM AND YOU NEVER CAME BACK!
"I WENT TO CHECK UP ON YOU A FEW MINUTES LATER, BUT...
"...BY THEN I GUESS YOU HAD LEFT.
"AFTER THE THINGS YOU SAW THAT NIGHT...
"...WHO COULD BLAME YOU?"
I MEAN, THE *EX* AND HIS *NEW CHICK?!*
SUCKS WHEN THE PAST COMES BACK TO HAUNT YOU, DOESN'T IT?

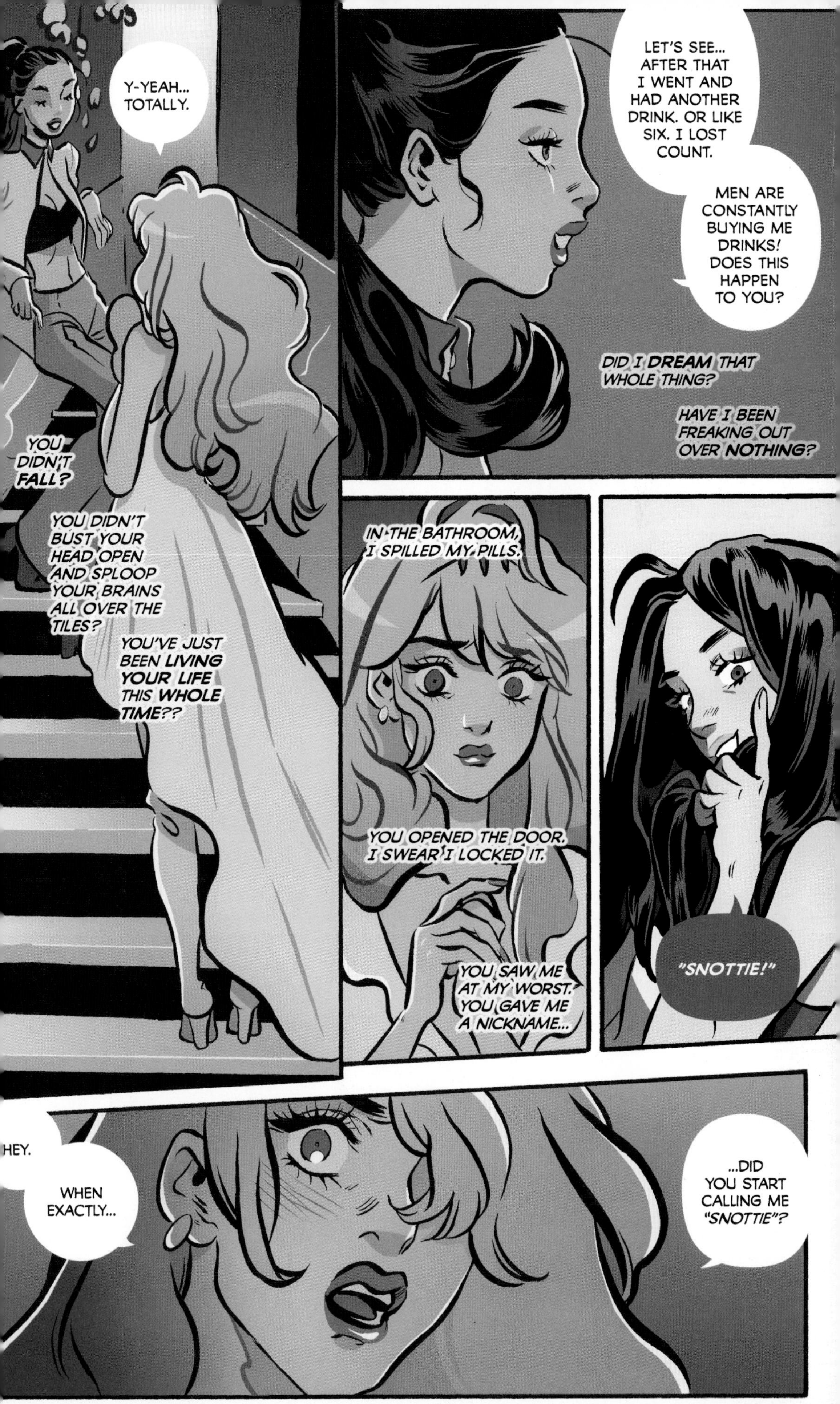
Y-YEAH... TOTALLY.
LET'S SEE... AFTER THAT I WENT AND HAD ANOTHER DRINK. OR LIKE SIX. I LOST COUNT.
MEN ARE CONSTANTLY BUYING ME DRINKS! DOES THIS HAPPEN TO YOU?
DID I DREAM THAT WHOLE THING?
HAVE I BEEN FREAKING OUT OVER NOTHING?
YOU DIDN'T FALL?
YOU DIDN'T BUST YOUR HEAD OPEN AND SPLOOP YOUR BRAINS ALL OVER THE TILES?
YOU'VE JUST BEEN LIVING YOUR LIFE THIS WHOLE TIME??
IN THE BATHROOM, I SPILLED MY PILLS.
YOU OPENED THE DOOR. I SWEAR I LOCKED IT.
YOU SAW ME AT MY WORST. YOU GAVE ME A NICKNAME...
"SNOTTIE!"
HEY.
WHEN EXACTLY...
...DID YOU START CALLING ME "SNOTTIE"?

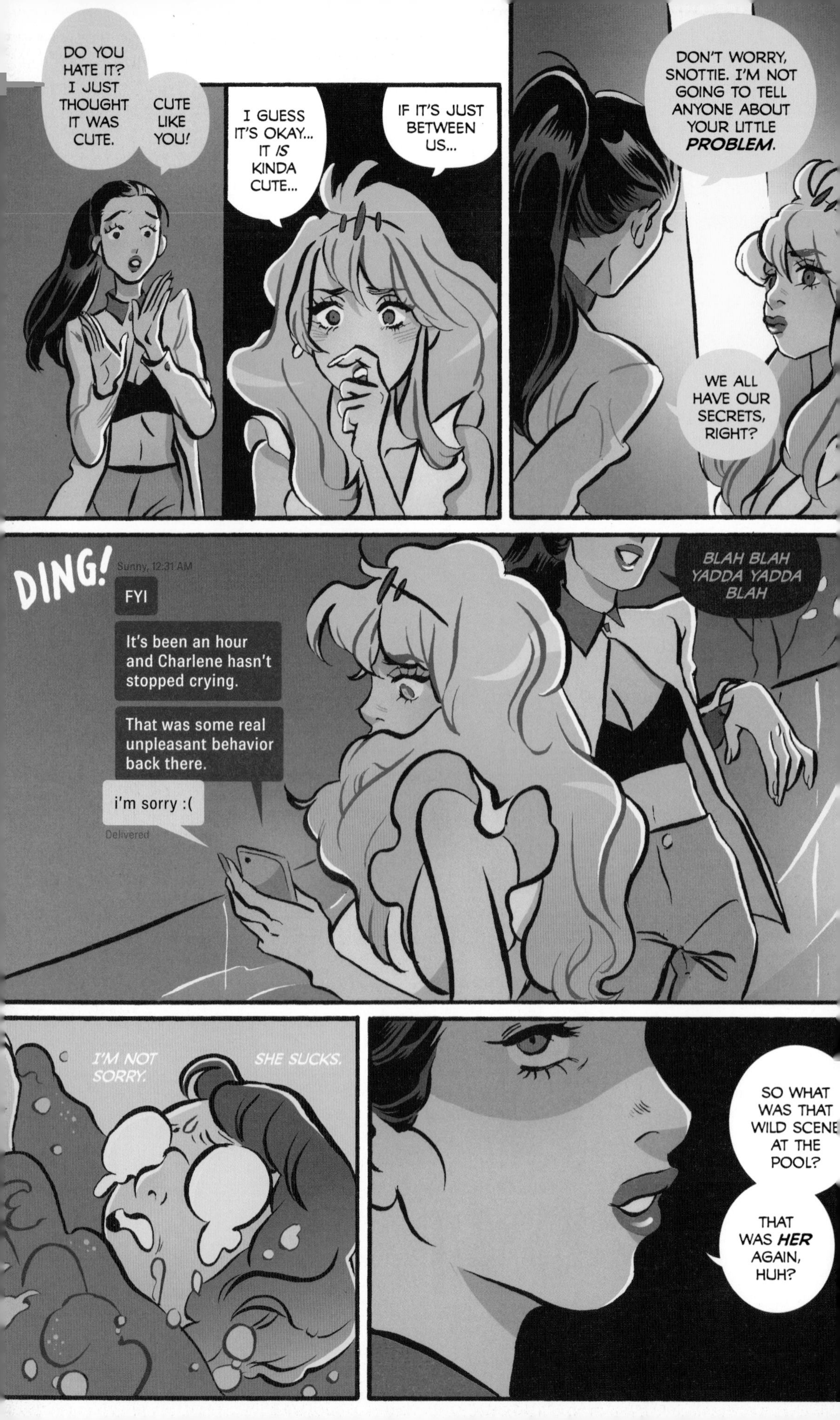
DO YOU HATE IT? I JUST THOUGHT IT WAS CUTE.
CUTE LIKE YOU!
I GUESS IT'S OKAY... IT *IS* KINDA CUTE...
IF IT'S JUST BETWEEN US...
DON'T WORRY, SNOTTIE. I'M NOT GOING TO TELL ANYONE ABOUT YOUR LITTLE ***PROBLEM***.
WE ALL HAVE OUR SECRETS, RIGHT?
DING!
Sunny, 12:31 AM
FYI
It's been an hour and Charlene hasn't stopped crying.
That was some real unpleasant behavior back there.
i'm sorry :(
Delivered
BLAH BLAH YADDA YADDA BLAH
I'M NOT SORRY.
SHE SUCKS.
SO WHAT WAS THAT WILD SCENE AT THE POOL?
THAT WAS ***HER*** AGAIN, HUH?

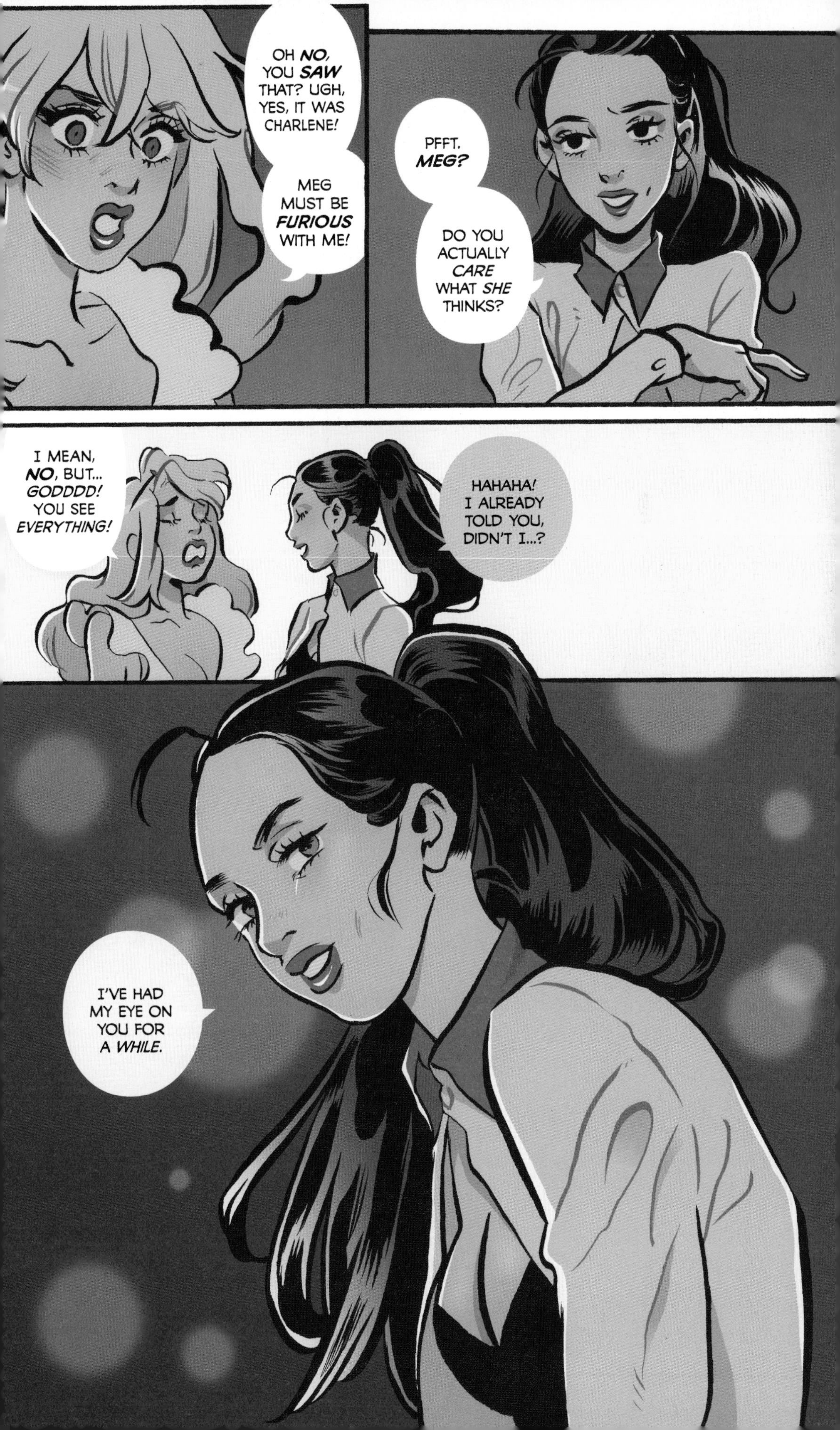
OH NO, YOU SAW THAT? UGH, YES, IT WAS CHARLENE!
MEG MUST BE FURIOUS WITH ME!
PFFT. MEG?
DO YOU ACTUALLY CARE WHAT SHE THINKS?
I MEAN, NO, BUT... GODDDD! YOU SEE EVERYTHING!
HAHAHA! I ALREADY TOLD YOU, DIDN'T I...?
I'VE HAD MY EYE ON YOU FOR A WHILE.

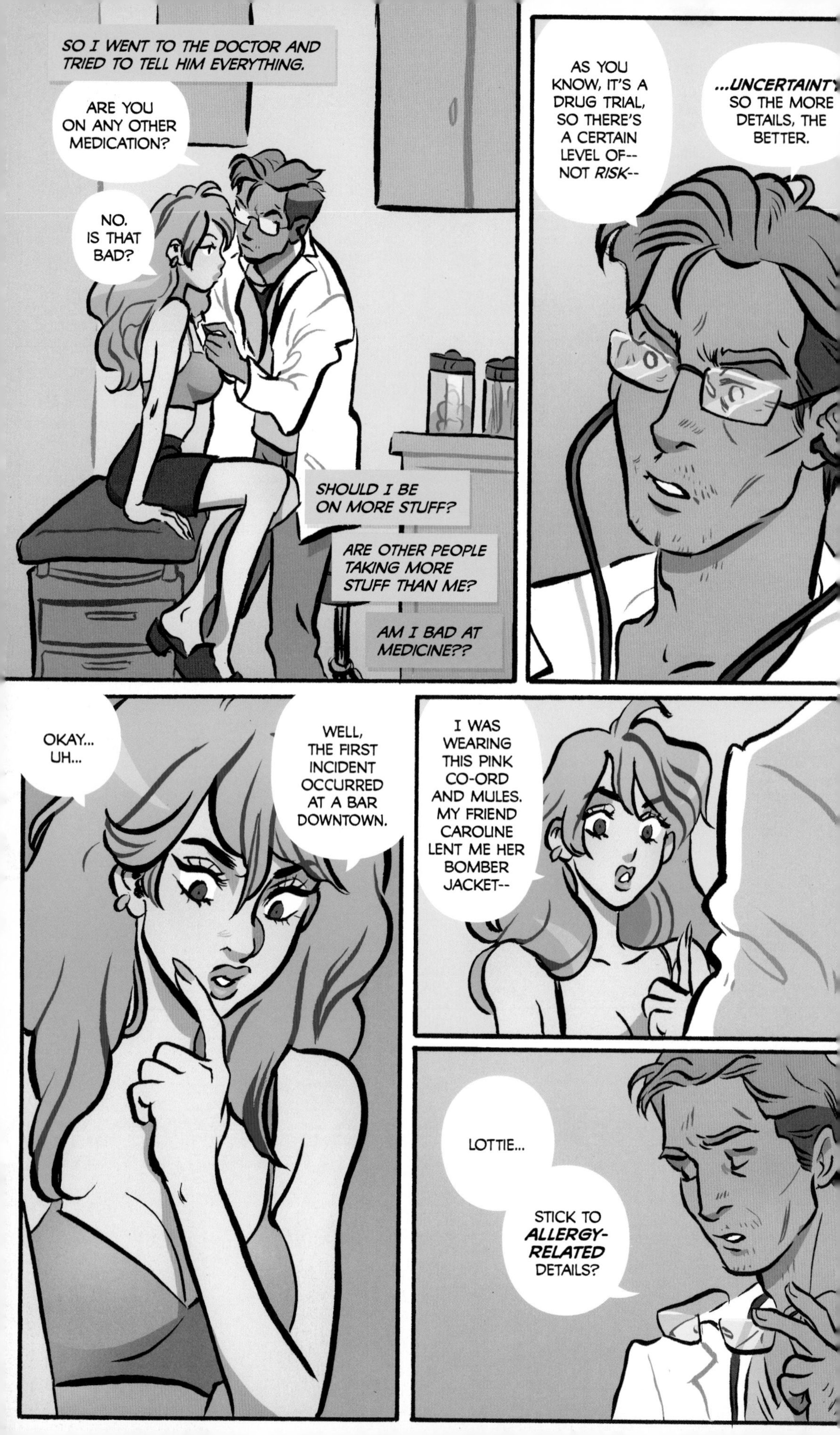

SO I WENT TO THE DOCTOR AND TRIED TO TELL HIM EVERYTHING.
ARE YOU ON ANY OTHER MEDICATION?
NO. IS THAT BAD?
SHOULD I BE ON MORE STUFF?
ARE OTHER PEOPLE TAKING MORE STUFF THAN ME?
AM I BAD AT MEDICINE??
AS YOU KNOW, IT'S A DRUG TRIAL, SO THERE'S A CERTAIN LEVEL OF-- NOT *RISK*--
...UNCERTAINTY. SO THE MORE DETAILS, THE BETTER.
OKAY... UH...
WELL, THE FIRST INCIDENT OCCURRED AT A BAR DOWNTOWN.
I WAS WEARING THIS PINK CO-ORD AND MULES. MY FRIEND CAROLINE LENT ME HER BOMBER JACKET--
LOTTIE...
STICK TO ***ALLERGY-RELATED*** DETAILS?

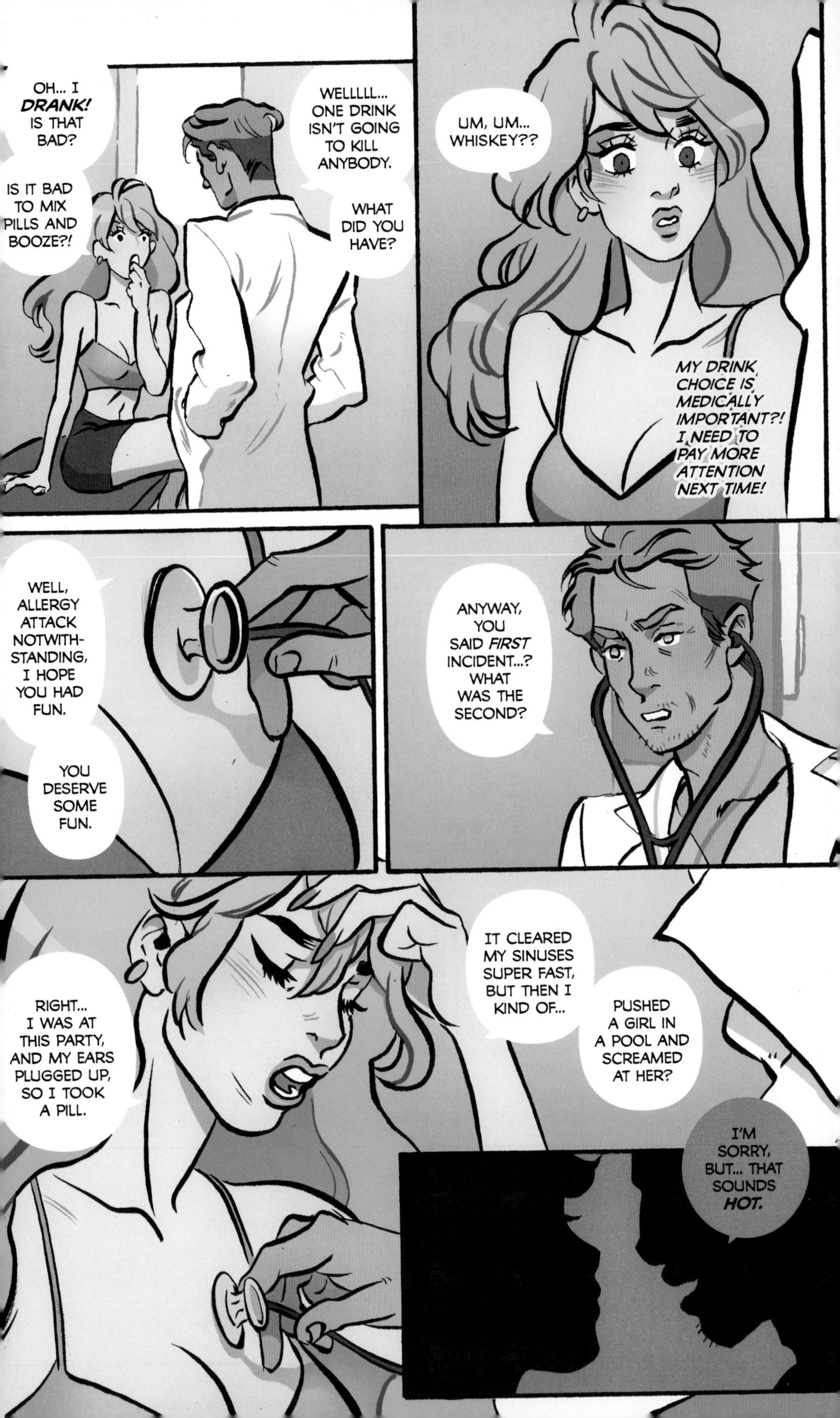
OH... I *DRANK!* IS THAT BAD?
IS IT BAD TO MIX PILLS AND BOOZE?!
WELLLLL... ONE DRINK ISN'T GOING TO KILL ANYBODY.
WHAT DID YOU HAVE?
UM, UM... WHISKEY??
MY DRINK CHOICE IS MEDICALLY IMPORTANT?! I NEED TO PAY MORE ATTENTION NEXT TIME!
WELL, ALLERGY ATTACK NOTWITH-STANDING, I HOPE YOU HAD FUN.
YOU DESERVE SOME FUN.
ANYWAY, YOU SAID *FIRST* INCIDENT...? WHAT WAS THE SECOND?
RIGHT... I WAS AT THIS PARTY, AND MY EARS PLUGGED UP, SO I TOOK A PILL.
IT CLEARED MY SINUSES SUPER FAST, BUT THEN I KIND OF...
PUSHED A GIRL IN A POOL AND SCREAMED AT HER?
I'M SORRY, BUT... THAT SOUNDS *HOT.*

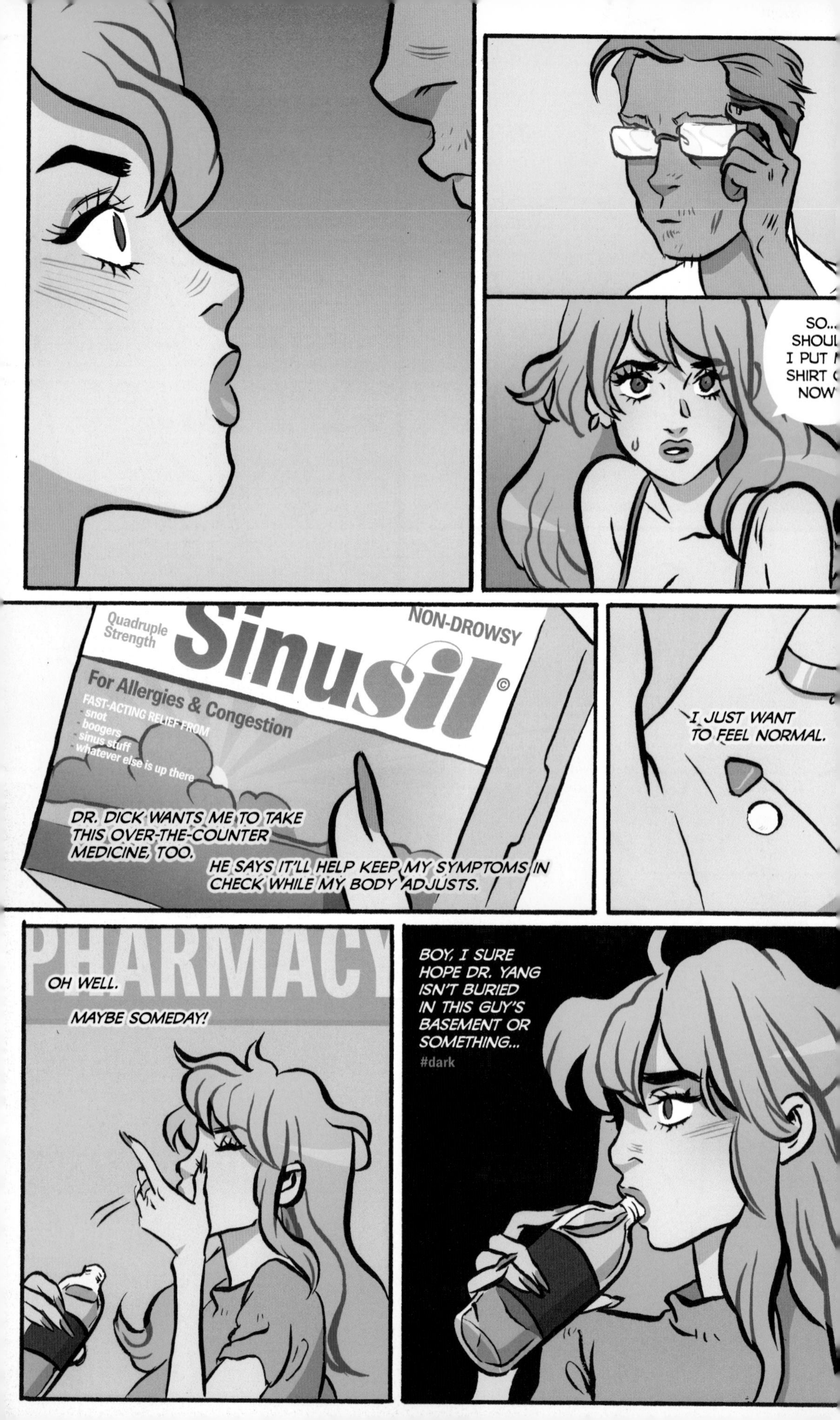

SO... SHOUL I PUT SHIRT NOW
Quadruple Strength
Sinusil ©
NON-DROWSY
For Allergies & Congestion
FAST-ACTING RELIEF FROM
- snot
- boogers
- sinus stuff
- whatever else is up there
DR. DICK WANTS ME TO TAKE THIS OVER-THE-COUNTER MEDICINE, TOO.
HE SAYS IT'LL HELP KEEP MY SYMPTOMS IN CHECK WHILE MY BODY ADJUSTS.
I JUST WANT TO FEEL NORMAL.
PHARMACY
OH WELL.
MAYBE SOMEDAY!
BOY, I SURE HOPE DR. YANG ISN'T BURIED IN THIS GUY'S BASEMENT OR SOMETHING...
#dark

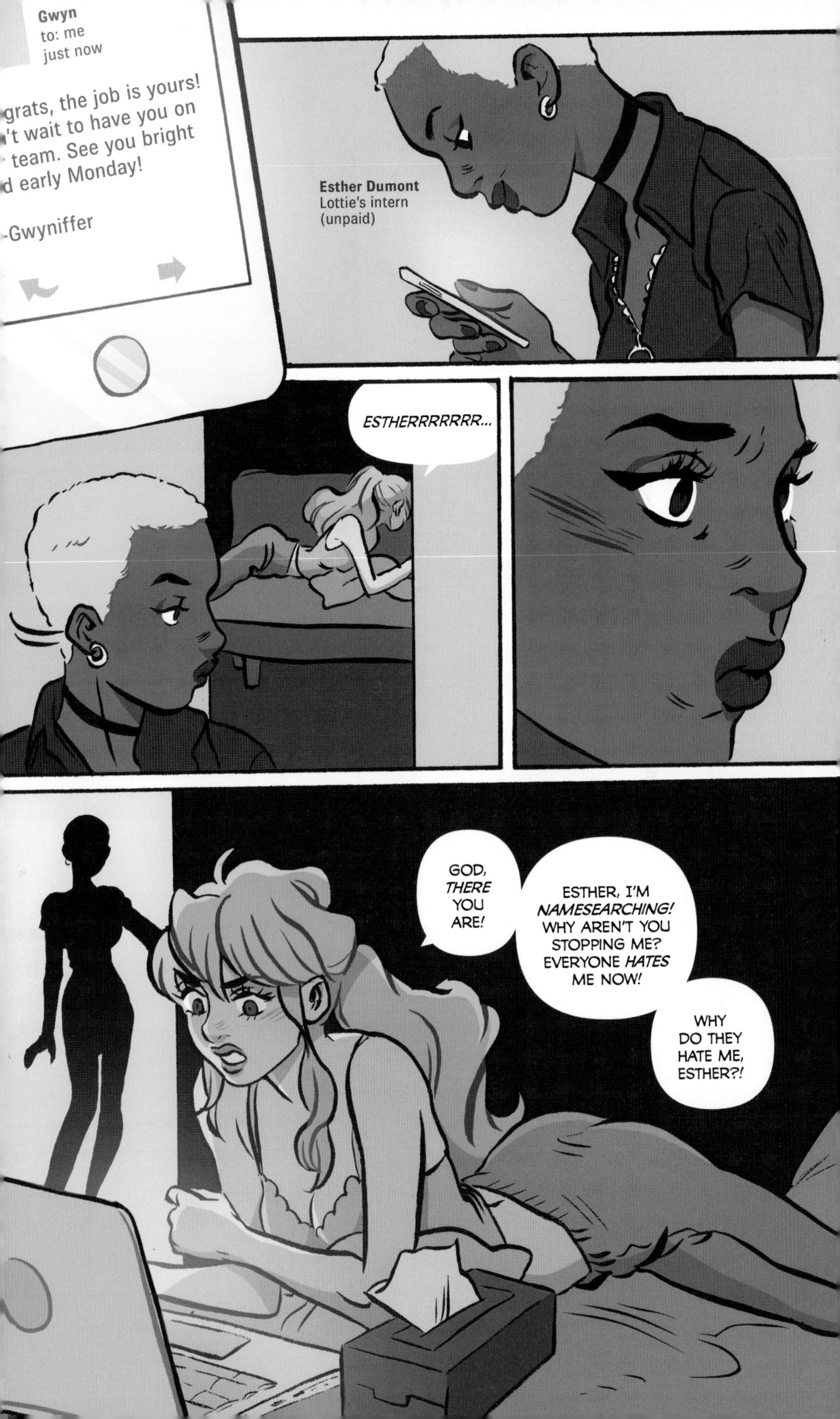
Gwyn
to: me
just now
grats, the job is yours!
't wait to have you on
team. See you bright
d early Monday!
-Gwyniffer
Esther Dumont
Lottie's intern
(unpaid)
ESTHERRRRRRR...
GOD, *THERE* YOU ARE!
ESTHER, I'M *NAMESEARCHING!* WHY AREN'T YOU STOPPING ME? EVERYONE *HATES* ME NOW!
WHY DO THEY HATE ME, ESTHER?!

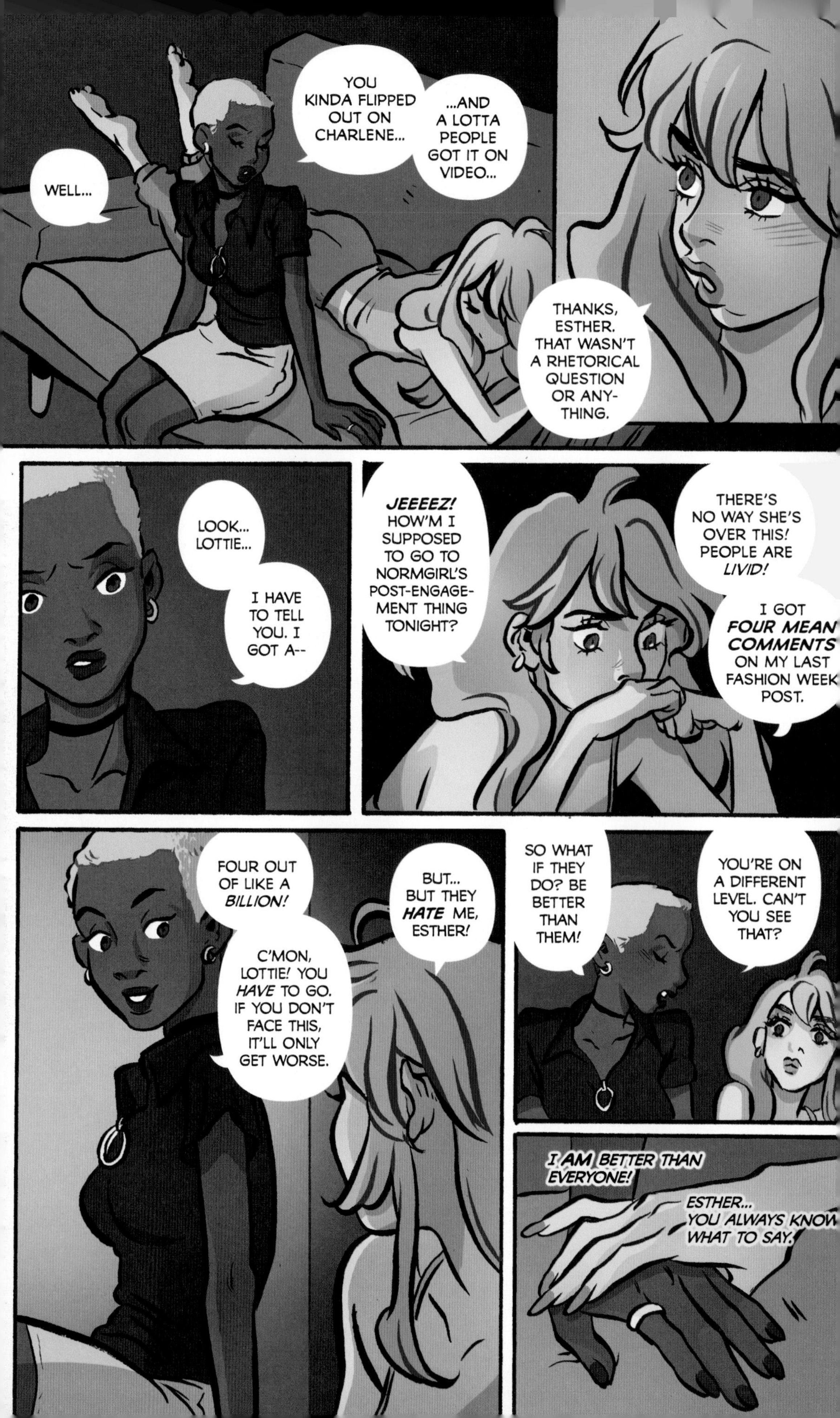
WELL...
YOU KINDA FLIPPED OUT ON CHARLENE...
...AND A LOTTA PEOPLE GOT IT ON VIDEO...
THANKS, ESTHER. THAT WASN'T A RHETORICAL QUESTION OR ANY-THING.
LOOK... LOTTIE...
I HAVE TO TELL YOU. I GOT A--
JEEEEZ! HOW'M I SUPPOSED TO GO TO NORMGIRL'S POST-ENGAGE-MENT THING TONIGHT?
THERE'S NO WAY SHE'S OVER THIS! PEOPLE ARE LIVID!
I GOT FOUR MEAN COMMENTS ON MY LAST FASHION WEEK POST.
FOUR OUT OF LIKE A BILLION!
BUT... BUT THEY HATE ME, ESTHER!
C'MON, LOTTIE! YOU HAVE TO GO. IF YOU DON'T FACE THIS, IT'LL ONLY GET WORSE.
SO WHAT IF THEY DO? BE BETTER THAN THEM!
YOU'RE ON A DIFFERENT LEVEL. CAN'T YOU SEE THAT?
I AM BETTER THAN EVERYONE!
ESTHER... YOU ALWAYS KNOW WHAT TO SAY.

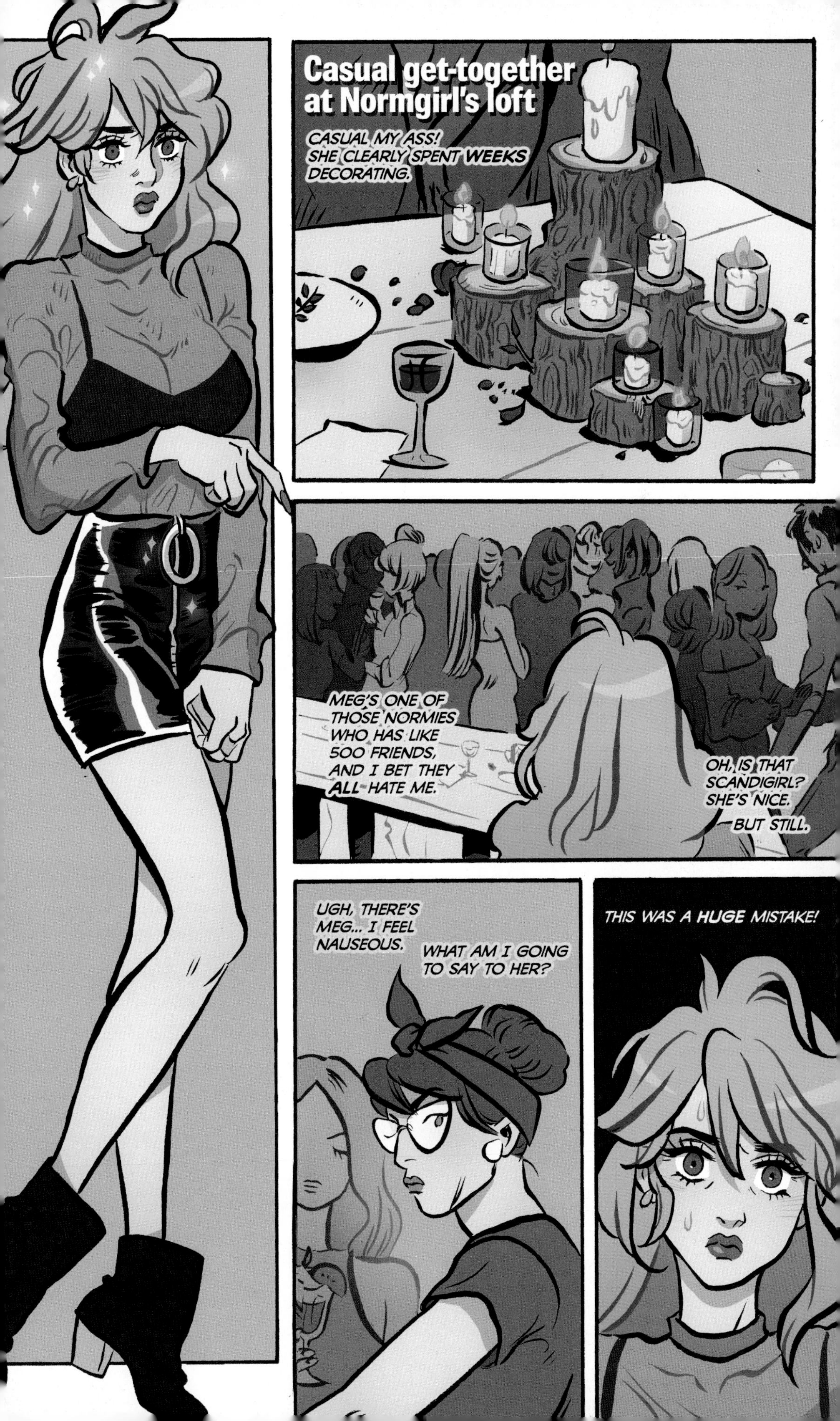
Casual get-together at Normgirl's loft
CASUAL MY ASS! SHE CLEARLY SPENT WEEKS DECORATING.
MEG'S ONE OF THOSE NORMIES WHO HAS LIKE 500 FRIENDS, AND I BET THEY ALL HATE ME.
OH, IS THAT SCANDIGIRL? SHE'S NICE.
BUT STILL.
UGH, THERE'S MEG... I FEEL NAUSEOUS.
WHAT AM I GOING TO SAY TO HER?
THIS WAS A HUGE MISTAKE!

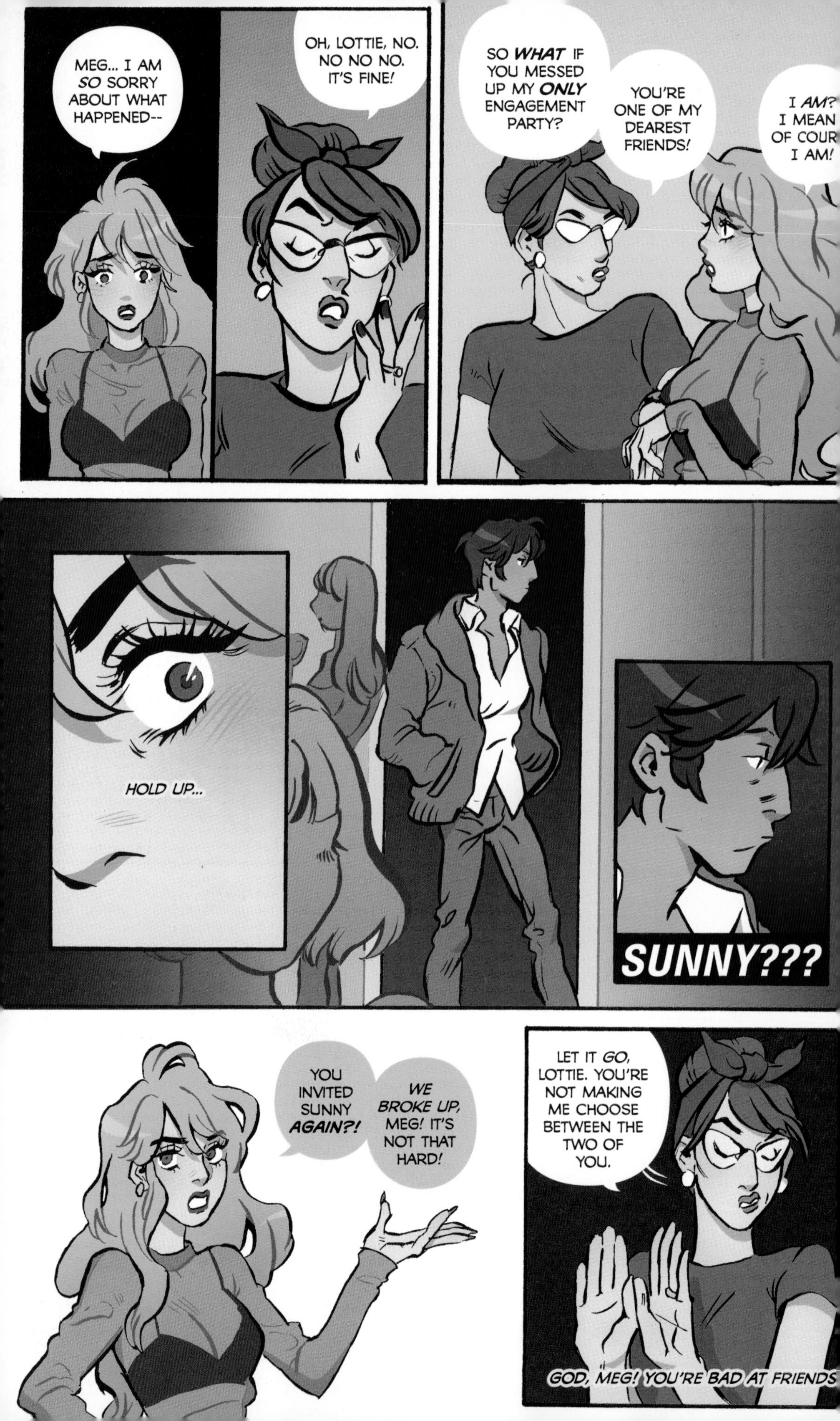

MEG... I AM *SO* SORRY ABOUT WHAT HAPPENED--
OH, LOTTIE, NO. NO NO NO. IT'S FINE!
SO ***WHAT*** IF YOU MESSED UP MY ***ONLY*** ENGAGEMENT PARTY?
YOU'RE ONE OF MY DEAREST FRIENDS!
I *AM*? I MEAN OF COUR I AM!
HOLD UP...
SUNNY???
YOU INVITED SUNNY ***AGAIN?!***
WE BROKE UP, MEG! IT'S NOT THAT HARD!
LET IT *GO,* LOTTIE. YOU'RE NOT MAKING ME CHOOSE BETWEEN THE TWO OF YOU.
GOD, MEG! YOU'RE BAD AT FRIENDS

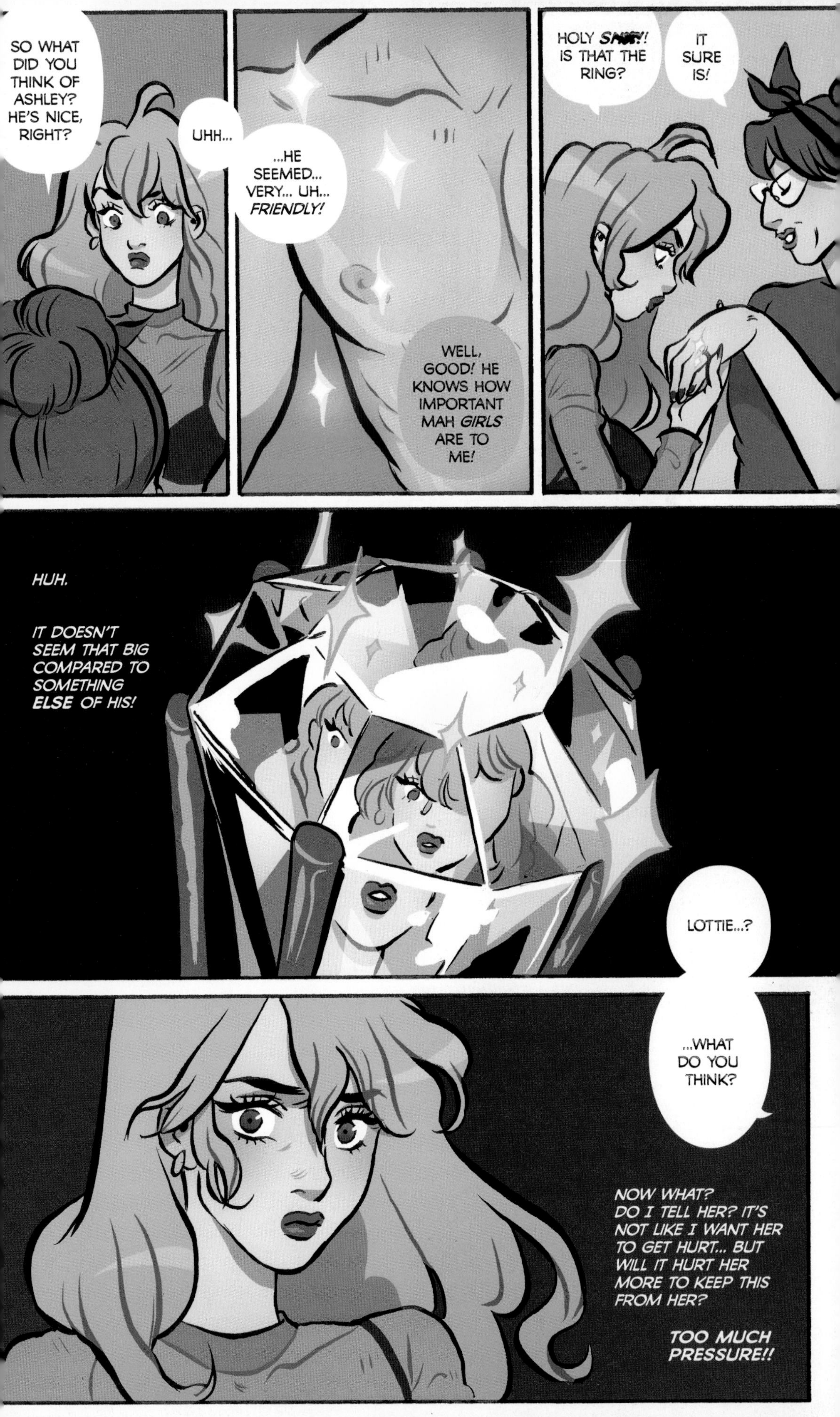
SO WHAT DID YOU THINK OF ASHLEY? HE'S NICE, RIGHT?
UHH...
...HE SEEMED... VERY... UH... *FRIENDLY!*
WELL, GOOD! HE KNOWS HOW IMPORTANT MAH *GIRLS* ARE TO ME!
HOLY *S*[redacted]! IS THAT THE RING?
IT SURE IS!
HUH.
IT DOESN'T SEEM THAT BIG COMPARED TO SOMETHING ***ELSE*** *OF HIS!*
LOTTIE...?
...WHAT DO YOU THINK?
NOW WHAT? DO I TELL HER? IT'S NOT LIKE I WANT HER TO GET HURT... BUT WILL IT HURT HER MORE TO KEEP THIS FROM HER?
TOO MUCH PRESSURE!!

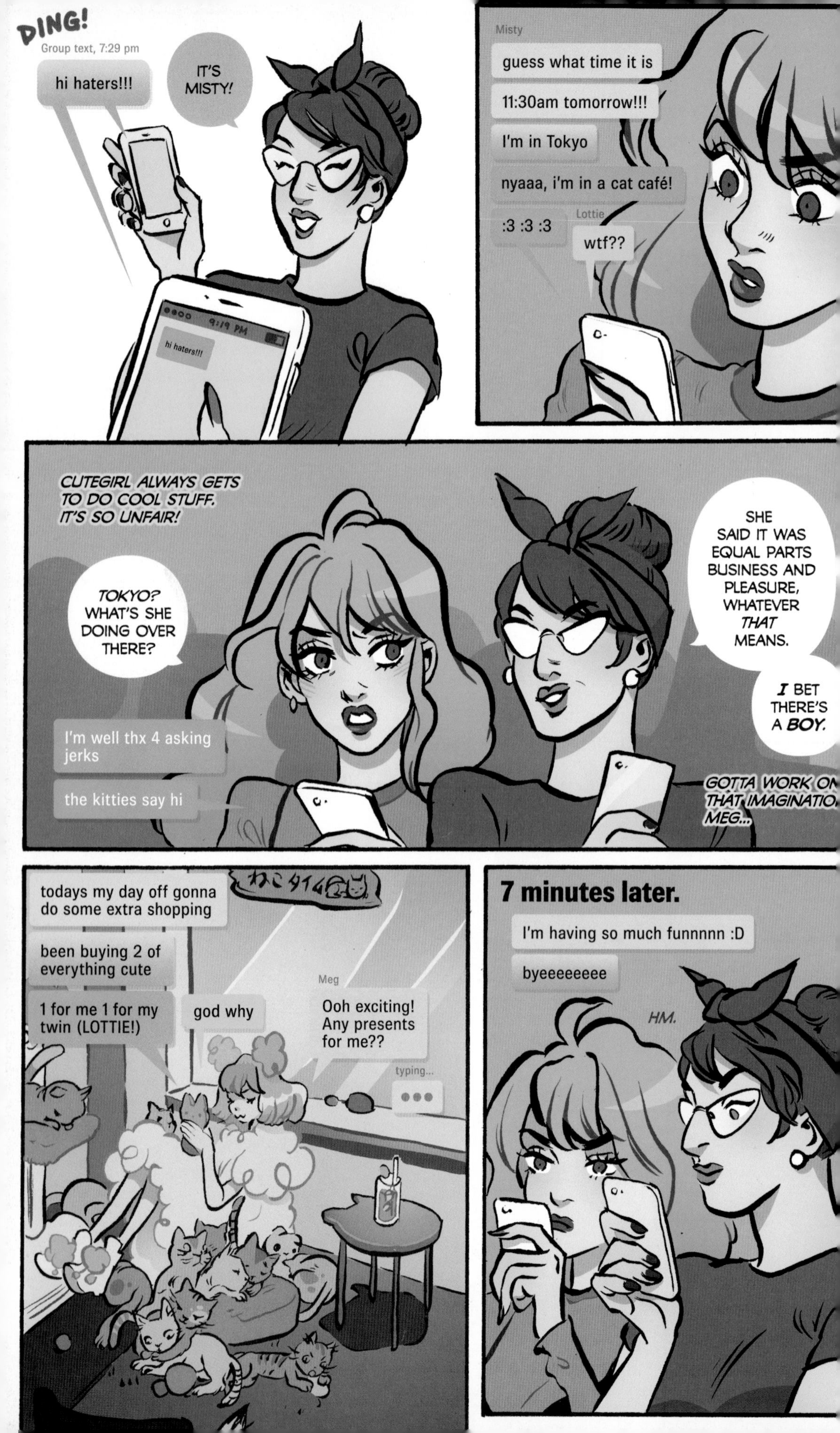
DING!
Group text, 7:29 pm
hi haters!!!
IT'S MISTY!
hi haters!!!
Misty
guess what time it is
11:30am tomorrow!!!
I'm in Tokyo
nyaaa, i'm in a cat café!
:3 :3 :3
Lottie
wtf??
CUTEGIRL ALWAYS GETS TO DO COOL STUFF. IT'S SO UNFAIR!
TOKYO? WHAT'S SHE DOING OVER THERE?
SHE SAID IT WAS EQUAL PARTS BUSINESS AND PLEASURE, WHATEVER THAT MEANS.
I BET THERE'S A BOY.
I'm well thx 4 asking jerks
the kitties say hi
GOTTA WORK ON THAT IMAGINATIO MEG...
todays my day off gonna do some extra shopping
been buying 2 of everything cute
1 for me 1 for my twin (LOTTIE!)
god why
Meg
Ooh exciting! Any presents for me??
typing...
7 minutes later.
I'm having so much funnnnn :D
byeeeeeeee
HM.

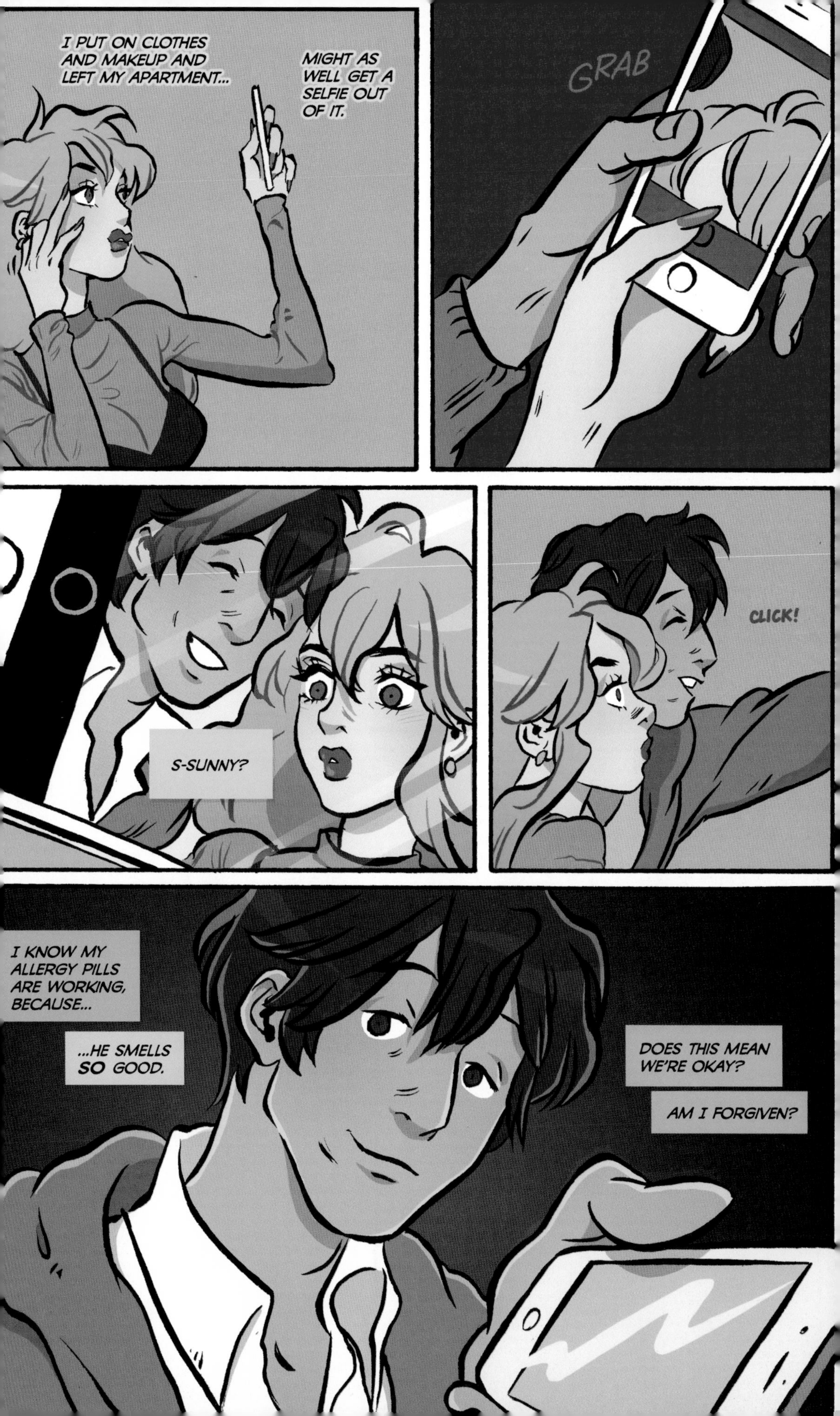
I PUT ON CLOTHES AND MAKEUP AND LEFT MY APARTMENT...
MIGHT AS WELL GET A SELFIE OUT OF IT.
GRAB
S-SUNNY?
CLICK!
I KNOW MY ALLERGY PILLS ARE WORKING, BECAUSE...
...HE SMELLS SO GOOD.
DOES THIS MEAN WE'RE OKAY?
AM I FORGIVEN?

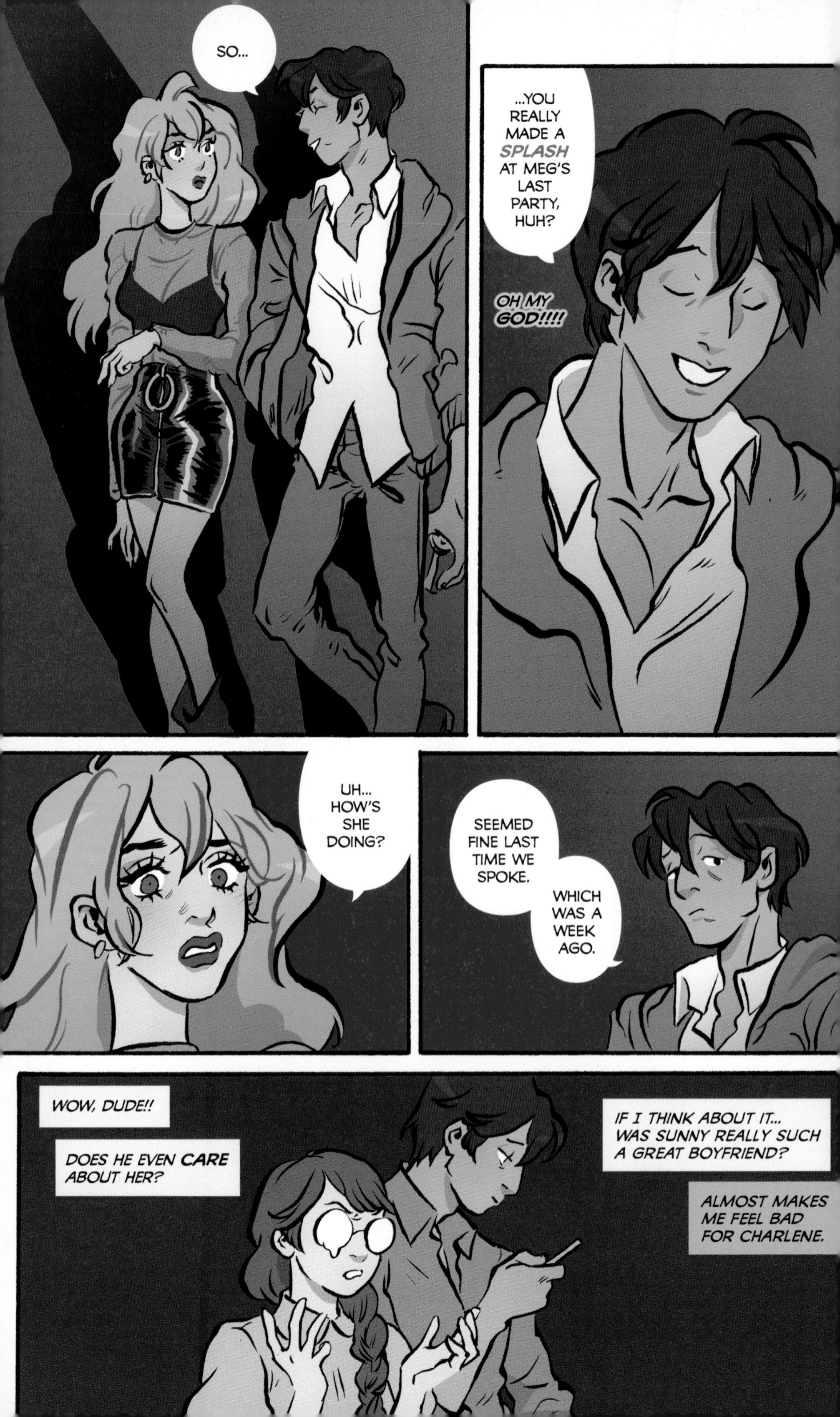
SO...
...YOU REALLY MADE A SPLASH AT MEG'S LAST PARTY, HUH?
OH MY GOD!!!!
UH... HOW'S SHE DOING?
SEEMED FINE LAST TIME WE SPOKE.
WHICH WAS A WEEK AGO.
WOW, DUDE!!
DOES HE EVEN CARE ABOUT HER?
IF I THINK ABOUT IT... WAS SUNNY REALLY SUCH A GREAT BOYFRIEND?
ALMOST MAKES ME FEEL BAD FOR CHARLENE.

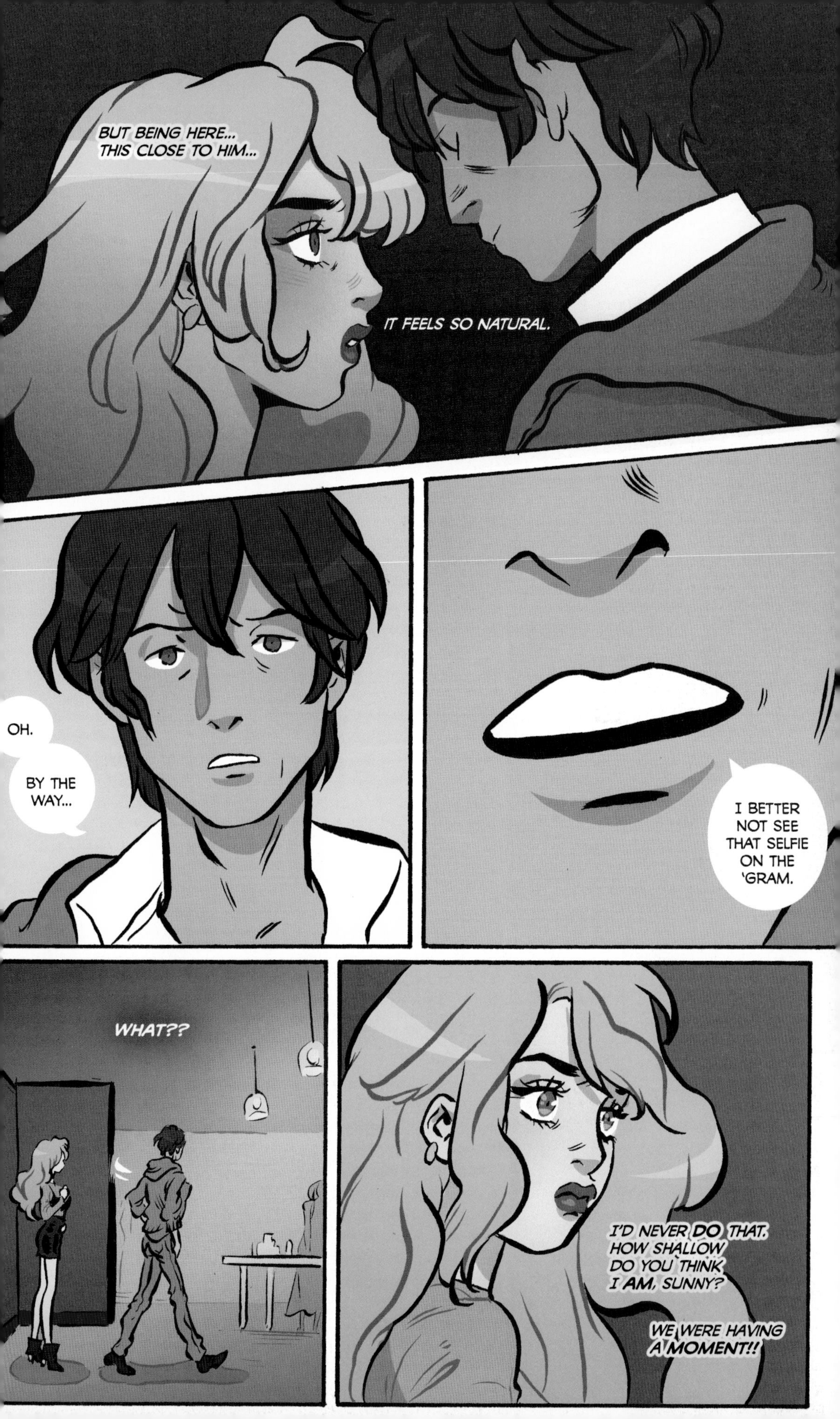
BUT BEING HERE... THIS CLOSE TO HIM...
IT FEELS SO NATURAL.
OH.
BY THE WAY...
I BETTER NOT SEE THAT SELFIE ON THE 'GRAM.
WHAT??
I'D NEVER DO THAT. HOW SHALLOW DO YOU THINK I AM, SUNNY?
WE WERE HAVING A MOMENT!!

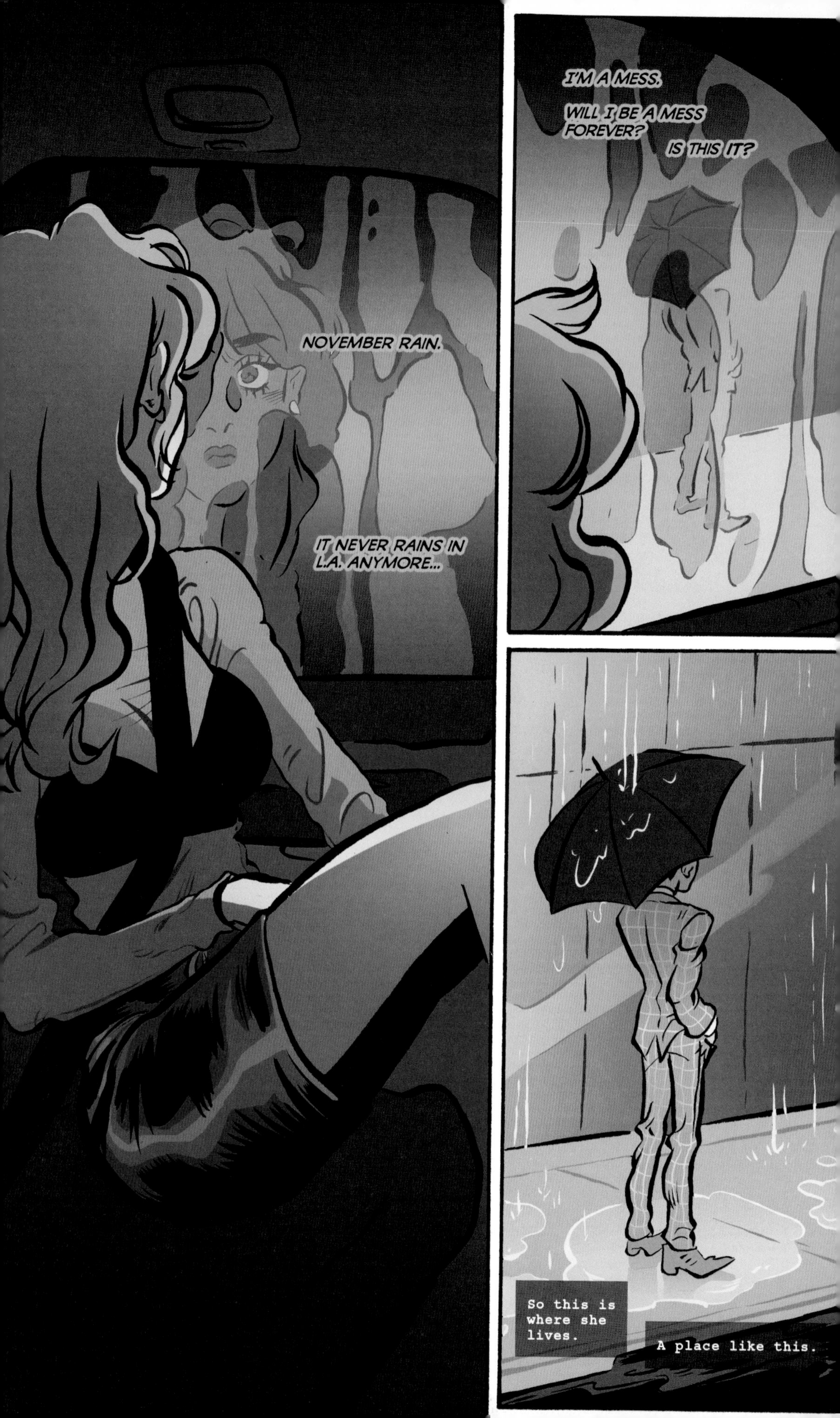
NOVEMBER RAIN.
IT NEVER RAINS IN L.A. ANYMORE...
I'M A MESS.
WILL I BE A MESS FOREVER?
IS THIS IT?
So this is where she lives.
A place like this.

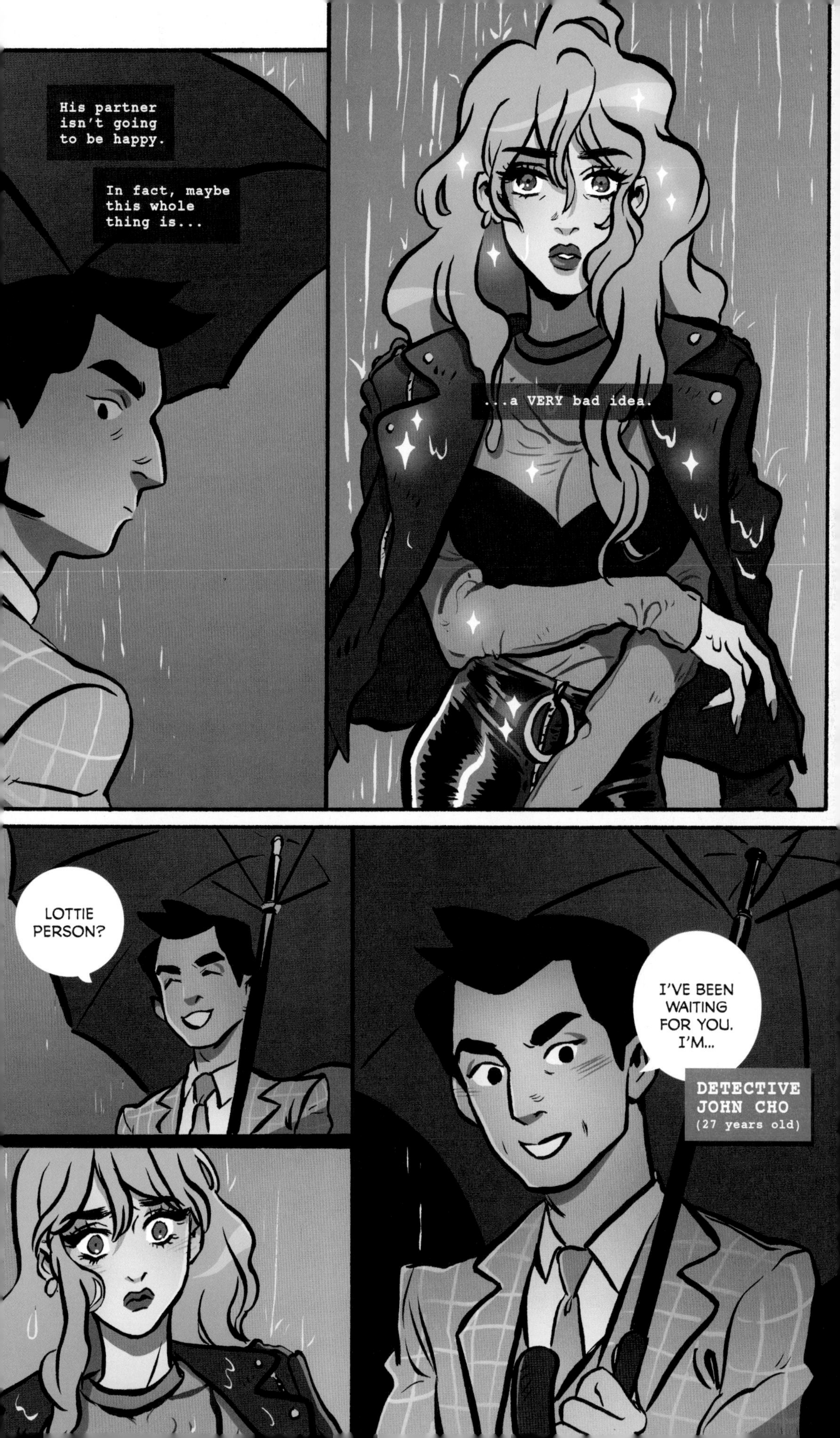

His partner isn't going to be happy.
In fact, maybe this whole thing is...
...a VERY bad idea.
LOTTIE PERSON?
I'VE BEEN WAITING FOR YOU. I'M...
DETECTIVE JOHN CHO (27 years old)

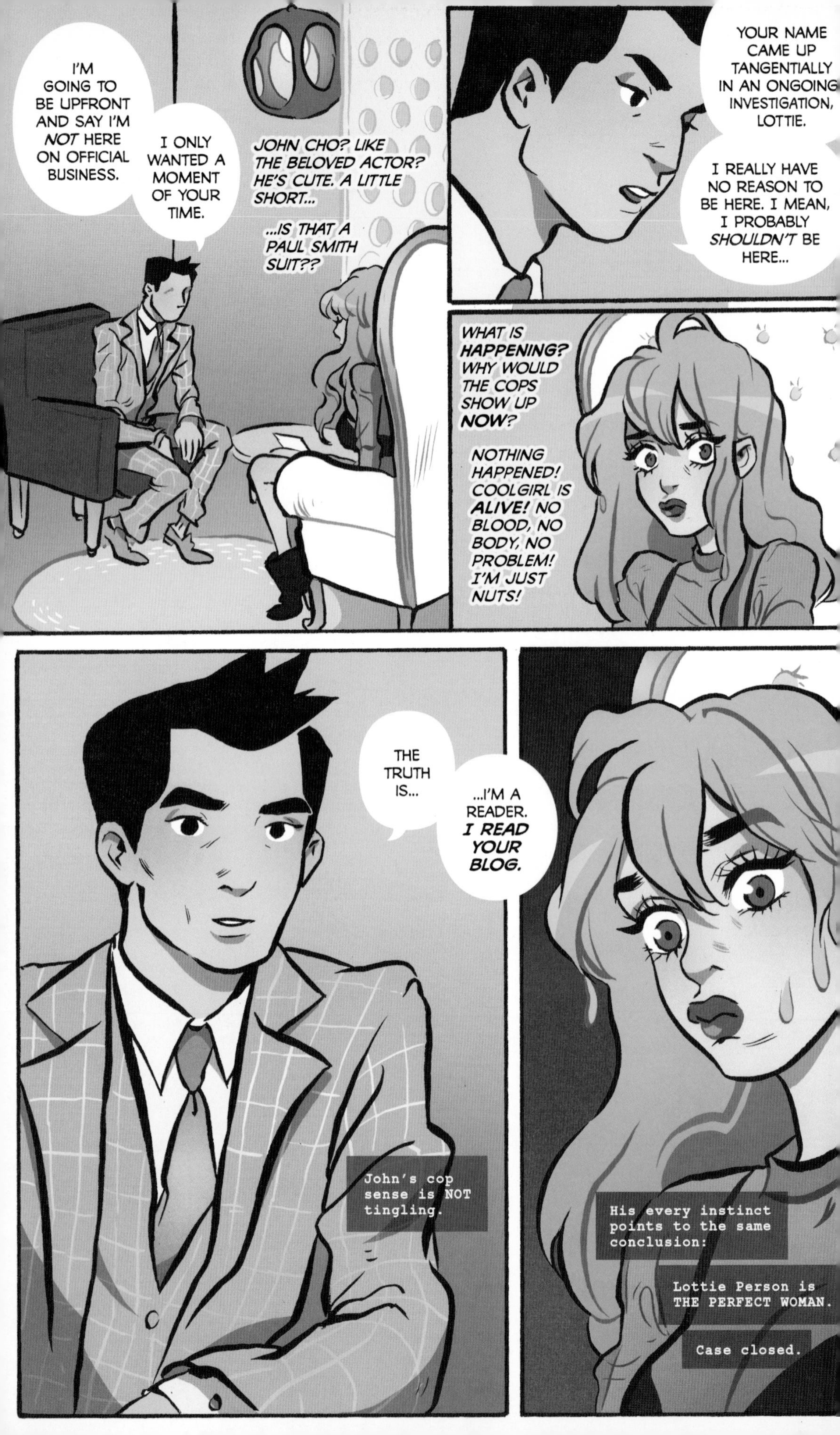
I'M GOING TO BE UPFRONT AND SAY I'M *NOT* HERE ON OFFICIAL BUSINESS.
I ONLY WANTED A MOMENT OF YOUR TIME.
JOHN CHO? LIKE THE BELOVED ACTOR? HE'S CUTE. A LITTLE SHORT...
...IS THAT A PAUL SMITH SUIT??
YOUR NAME CAME UP TANGENTIALLY IN AN ONGOING INVESTIGATION, LOTTIE.
I REALLY HAVE NO REASON TO BE HERE. I MEAN, I PROBABLY *SHOULDN'T* BE HERE...
*WHAT IS **HAPPENING?** WHY WOULD THE COPS SHOW UP **NOW?***
*NOTHING HAPPENED! COOLGIRL IS **ALIVE!** NO BLOOD, NO BODY, NO PROBLEM! I'M JUST NUTS!*
THE TRUTH IS...
...I'M A READER. ***I READ YOUR BLOG.***
John's cop sense is NOT tingling.
His every instinct points to the same conclusion:
Lottie Person is THE PERFECT WOMAN.
Case closed.

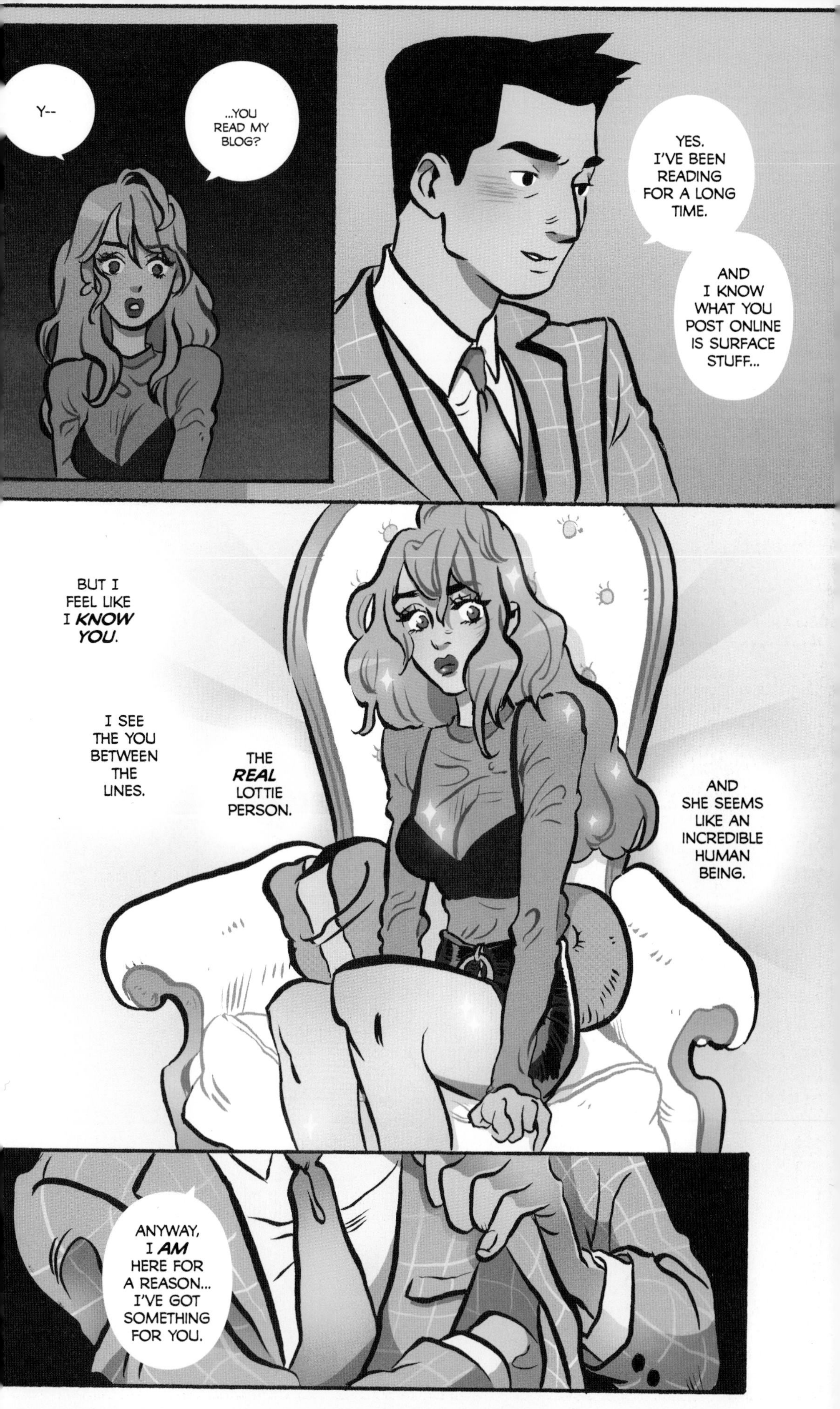
Y--
...YOU READ MY BLOG?
YES. I'VE BEEN READING FOR A LONG TIME.
AND I KNOW WHAT YOU POST ONLINE IS SURFACE STUFF...
BUT I FEEL LIKE I *KNOW YOU*.
I SEE THE YOU BETWEEN THE LINES.
THE *REAL* LOTTIE PERSON.
AND SHE SEEMS LIKE AN INCREDIBLE HUMAN BEING.
ANYWAY, I *AM* HERE FOR A REASON... I'VE GOT SOMETHING FOR YOU.

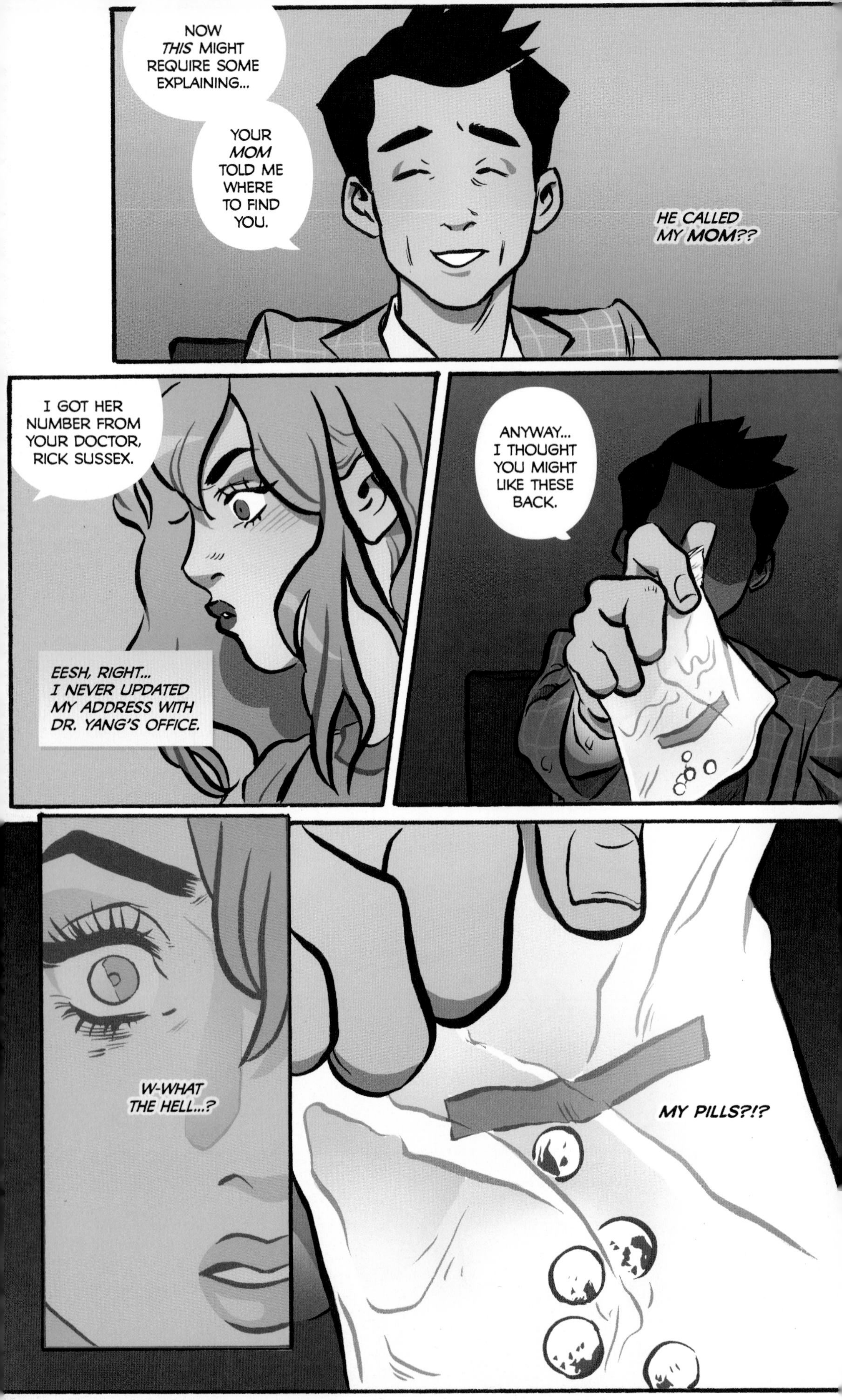
NOW *THIS* MIGHT REQUIRE SOME EXPLAINING...
YOUR *MOM* TOLD ME WHERE TO FIND YOU.
HE CALLED MY MOM??
I GOT HER NUMBER FROM YOUR DOCTOR, RICK SUSSEX.
EESH, RIGHT... I NEVER UPDATED MY ADDRESS WITH DR. YANG'S OFFICE.
ANYWAY... I THOUGHT YOU MIGHT LIKE THESE BACK.
W-WHAT THE HELL...?
MY PILLS?!?

05. SAME OL' MISTAKES

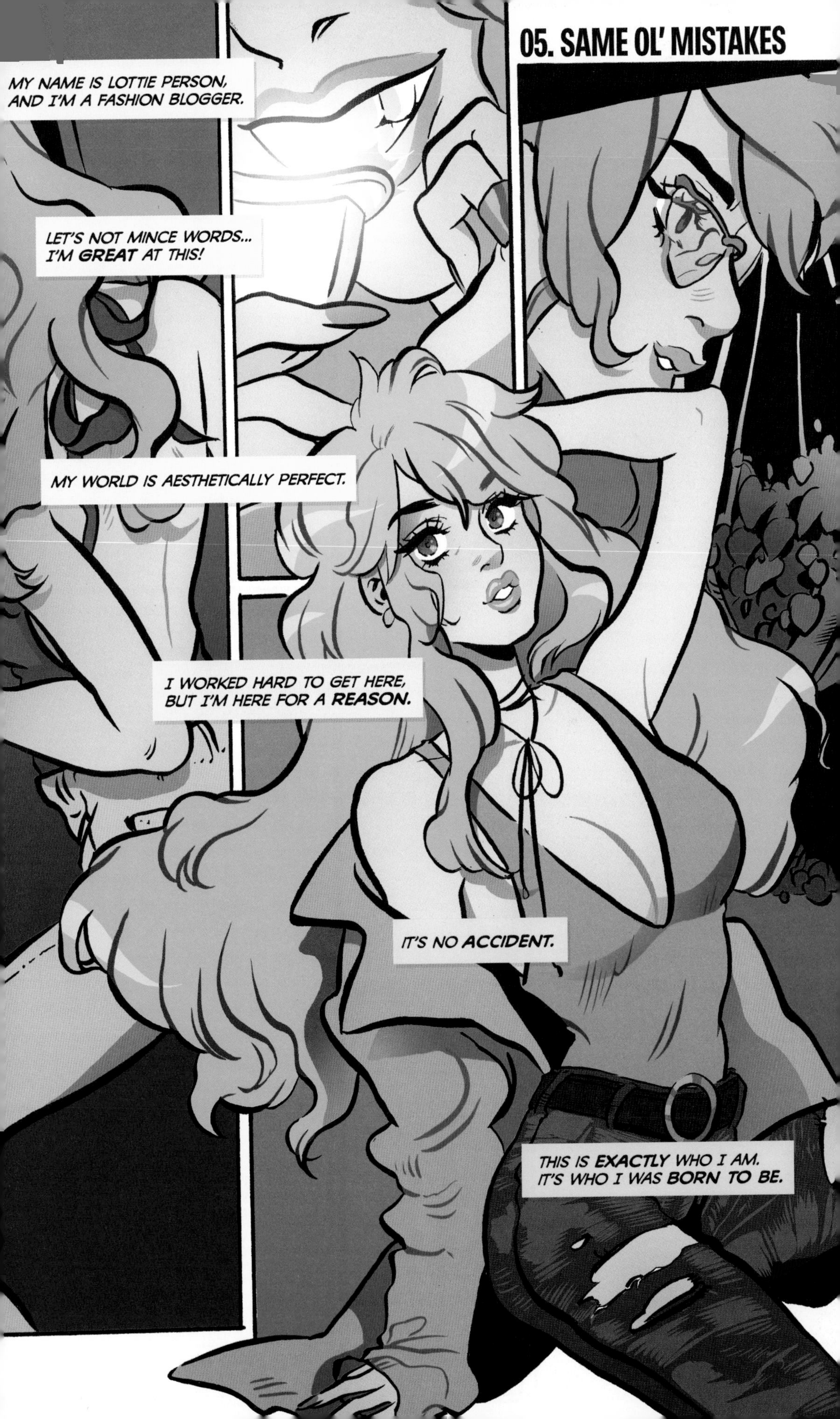
MY NAME IS LOTTIE PERSON, AND I'M A FASHION BLOGGER.
LET'S NOT MINCE WORDS... I'M GREAT AT THIS!
MY WORLD IS AESTHETICALLY PERFECT.
I WORKED HARD TO GET HERE, BUT I'M HERE FOR A REASON.
IT'S NO ACCIDENT.
THIS IS EXACTLY WHO I AM. IT'S WHO I WAS BORN TO BE.

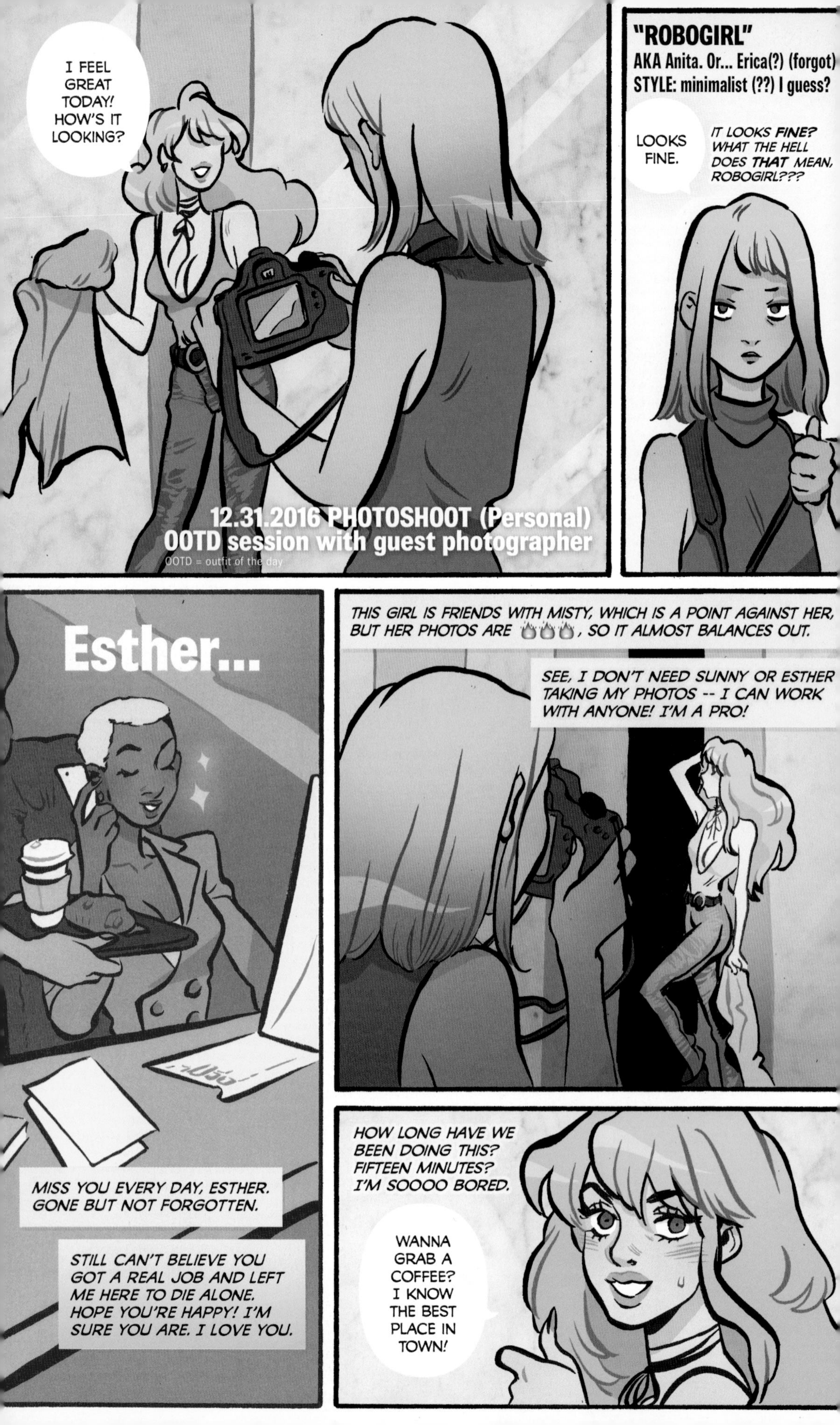
I FEEL GREAT TODAY! HOW'S IT LOOKING?
12.31.2016 PHOTOSHOOT (Personal)
OOTD session with guest photographer
OOTD = outfit of the day
"ROBOGIRL"
AKA Anita. Or... Erica(?) (forgot)
STYLE: minimalist (??) I guess?
LOOKS FINE.
IT LOOKS FINE? WHAT THE HELL DOES THAT MEAN, ROBOGIRL???
Esther...
MISS YOU EVERY DAY, ESTHER. GONE BUT NOT FORGOTTEN.
STILL CAN'T BELIEVE YOU GOT A REAL JOB AND LEFT ME HERE TO DIE ALONE. HOPE YOU'RE HAPPY! I'M SURE YOU ARE. I LOVE YOU.
THIS GIRL IS FRIENDS WITH MISTY, WHICH IS A POINT AGAINST HER, BUT HER PHOTOS ARE 🔥🔥🔥, SO IT ALMOST BALANCES OUT.
SEE, I DON'T NEED SUNNY OR ESTHER TAKING MY PHOTOS -- I CAN WORK WITH ANYONE! I'M A PRO!
HOW LONG HAVE WE BEEN DOING THIS? FIFTEEN MINUTES? I'M SOOOO BORED.
WANNA GRAB A COFFEE? I KNOW THE BEST PLACE IN TOWN!

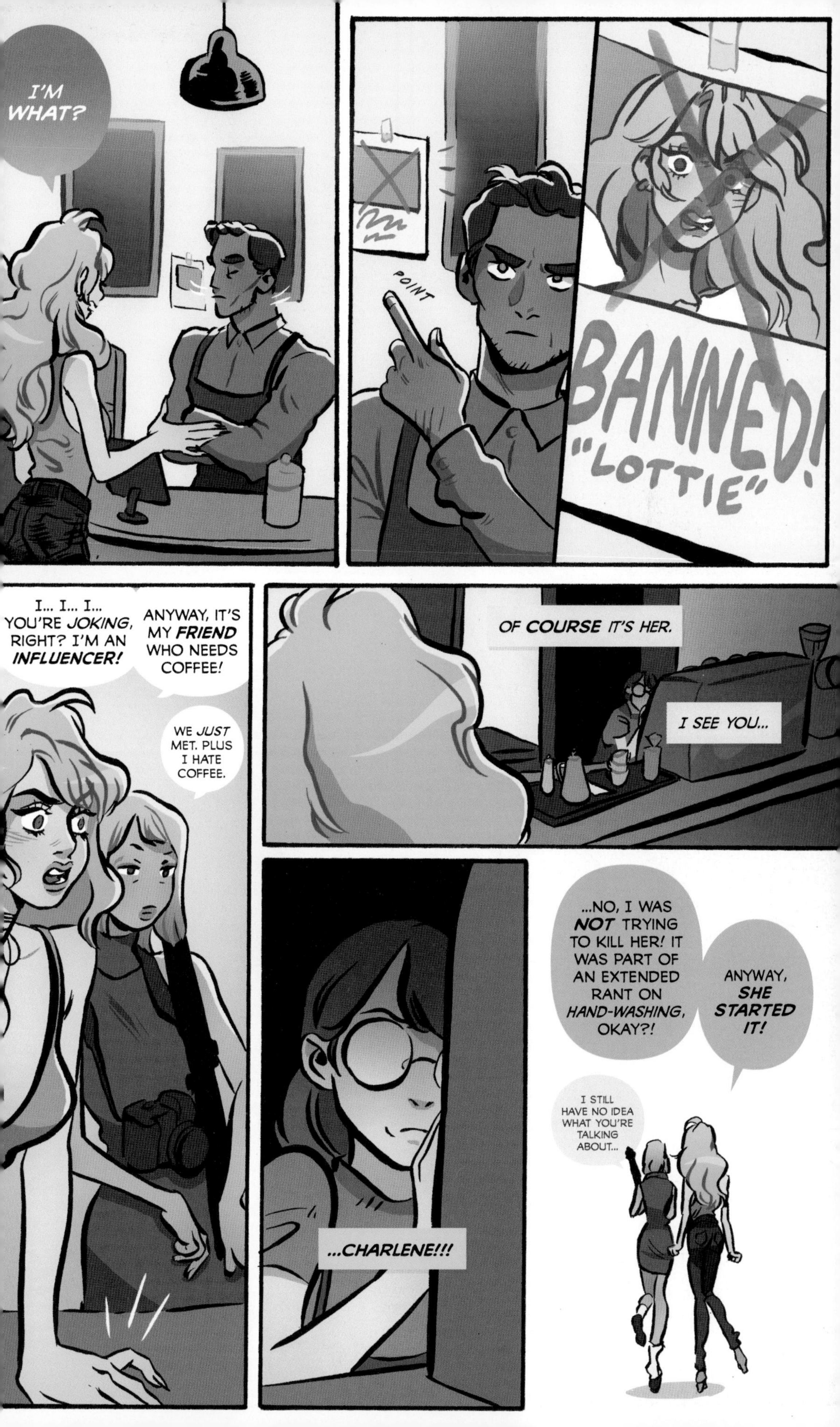
I'M WHAT?
POINT
BANNED! "LOTTIE"
I... I... I... YOU'RE JOKING, RIGHT? I'M AN INFLUENCER!
ANYWAY, IT'S MY FRIEND WHO NEEDS COFFEE!
WE JUST MET. PLUS I HATE COFFEE.
OF COURSE IT'S HER.
I SEE YOU...
...CHARLENE!!!
...NO, I WAS NOT TRYING TO KILL HER! IT WAS PART OF AN EXTENDED RANT ON HAND-WASHING, OKAY?!
ANYWAY, SHE STARTED IT!
I STILL HAVE NO IDEA WHAT YOU'RE TALKING ABOUT...

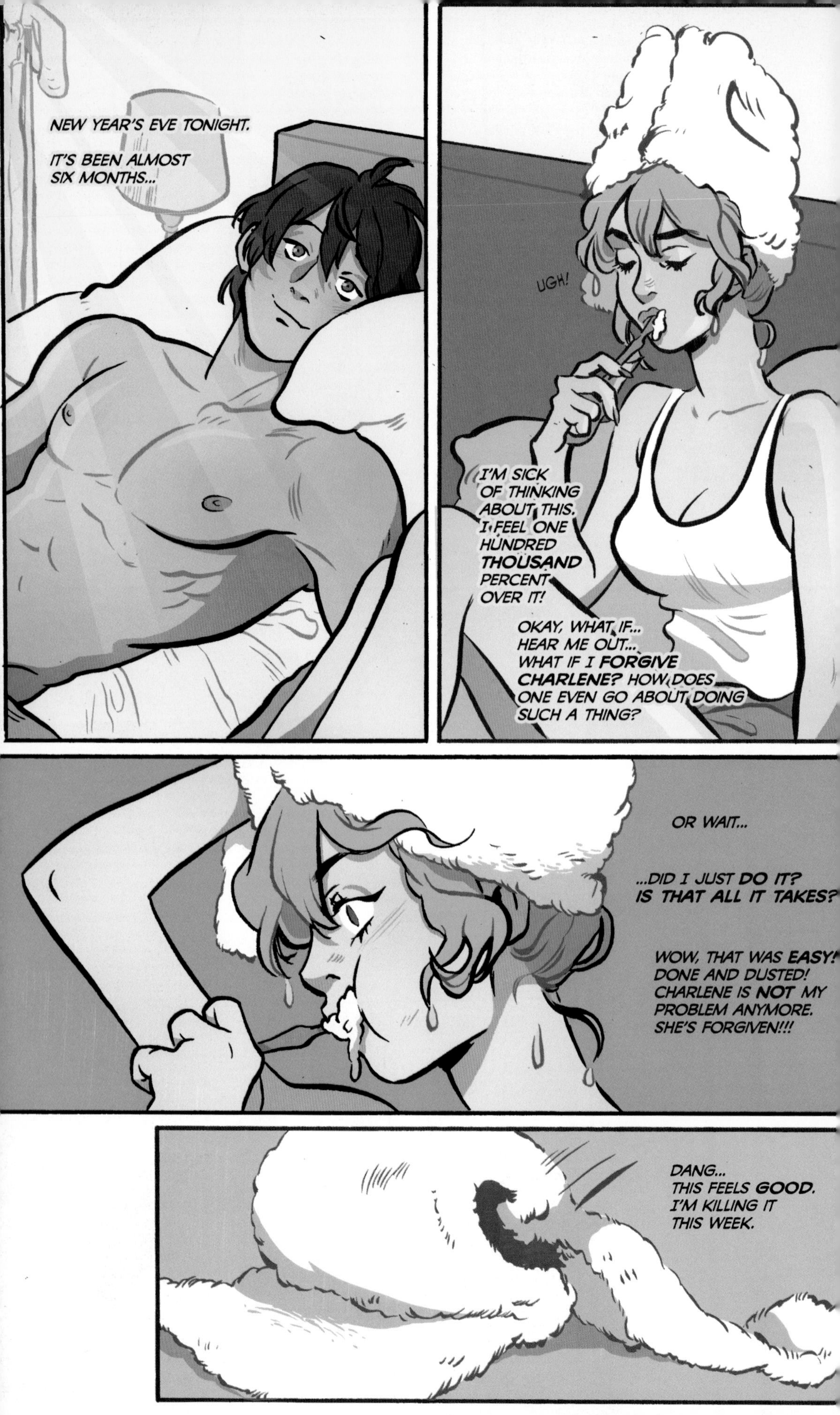

NEW YEAR'S EVE TONIGHT.
IT'S BEEN ALMOST SIX MONTHS...
UGH!
I'M SICK OF THINKING ABOUT THIS. I FEEL ONE HUNDRED **THOUSAND** PERCENT OVER IT!
OKAY, WHAT IF... HEAR ME OUT... WHAT IF I **FORGIVE CHARLENE?** HOW DOES ONE EVEN GO ABOUT DOING SUCH A THING?
OR WAIT...
...DID I JUST **DO IT? IS THAT ALL IT TAKES?**
WOW, THAT WAS **EASY!** DONE AND DUSTED! CHARLENE IS **NOT** MY PROBLEM ANYMORE. SHE'S FORGIVEN!!!
DANG... THIS FEELS **GOOD.** I'M KILLING IT THIS WEEK.

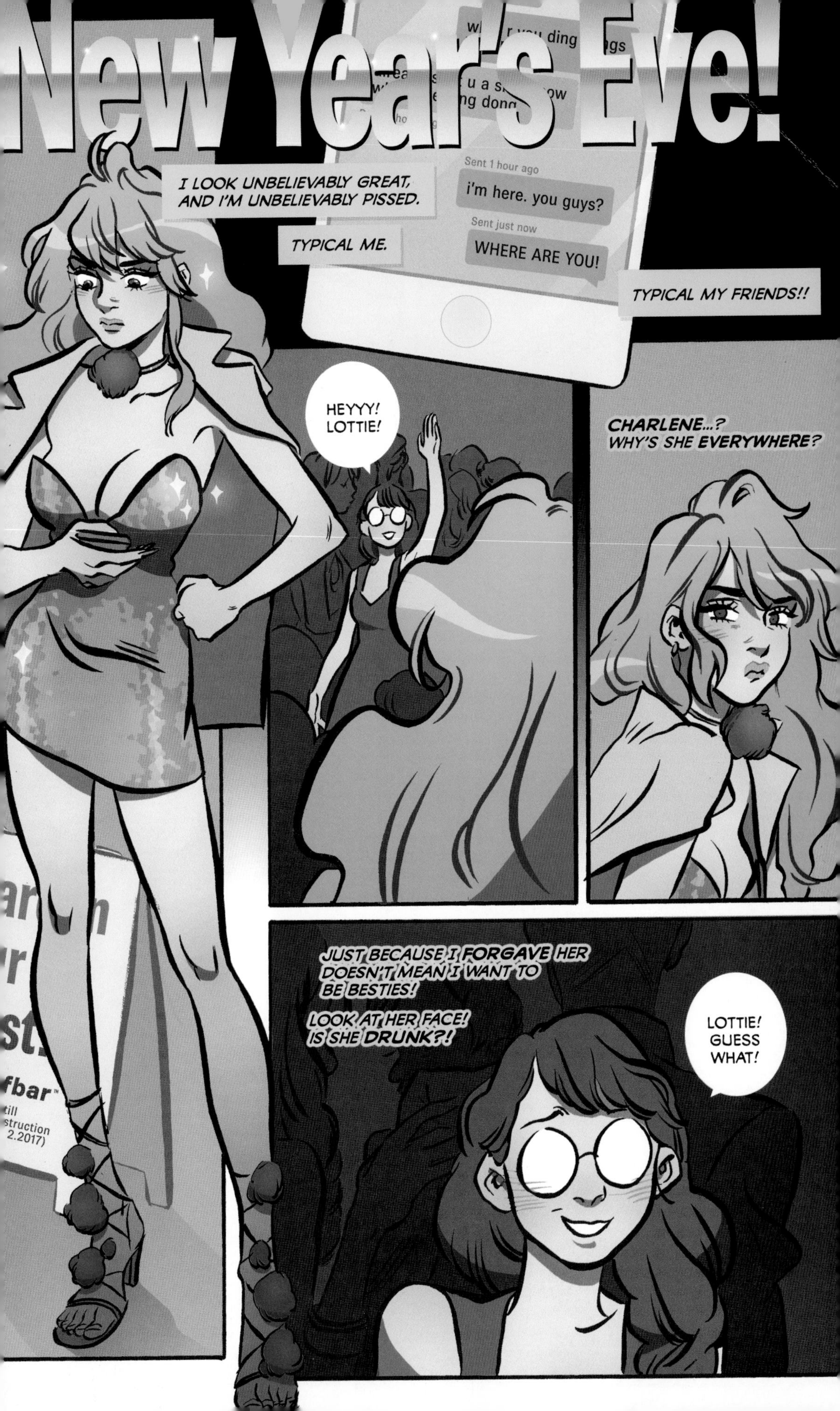

New Year's Eve!
I LOOK UNBELIEVABLY GREAT, AND I'M UNBELIEVABLY PISSED.
TYPICAL ME.
Sent 1 hour ago
i'm here. you guys?
Sent just now
WHERE ARE YOU!
TYPICAL MY FRIENDS!!
HEYYY! LOTTIE!
CHARLENE...? WHY'S SHE EVERYWHERE?
JUST BECAUSE I FORGAVE HER DOESN'T MEAN I WANT TO BE BESTIES!
LOOK AT HER FACE! IS SHE DRUNK?!
LOTTIE! GUESS WHAT!

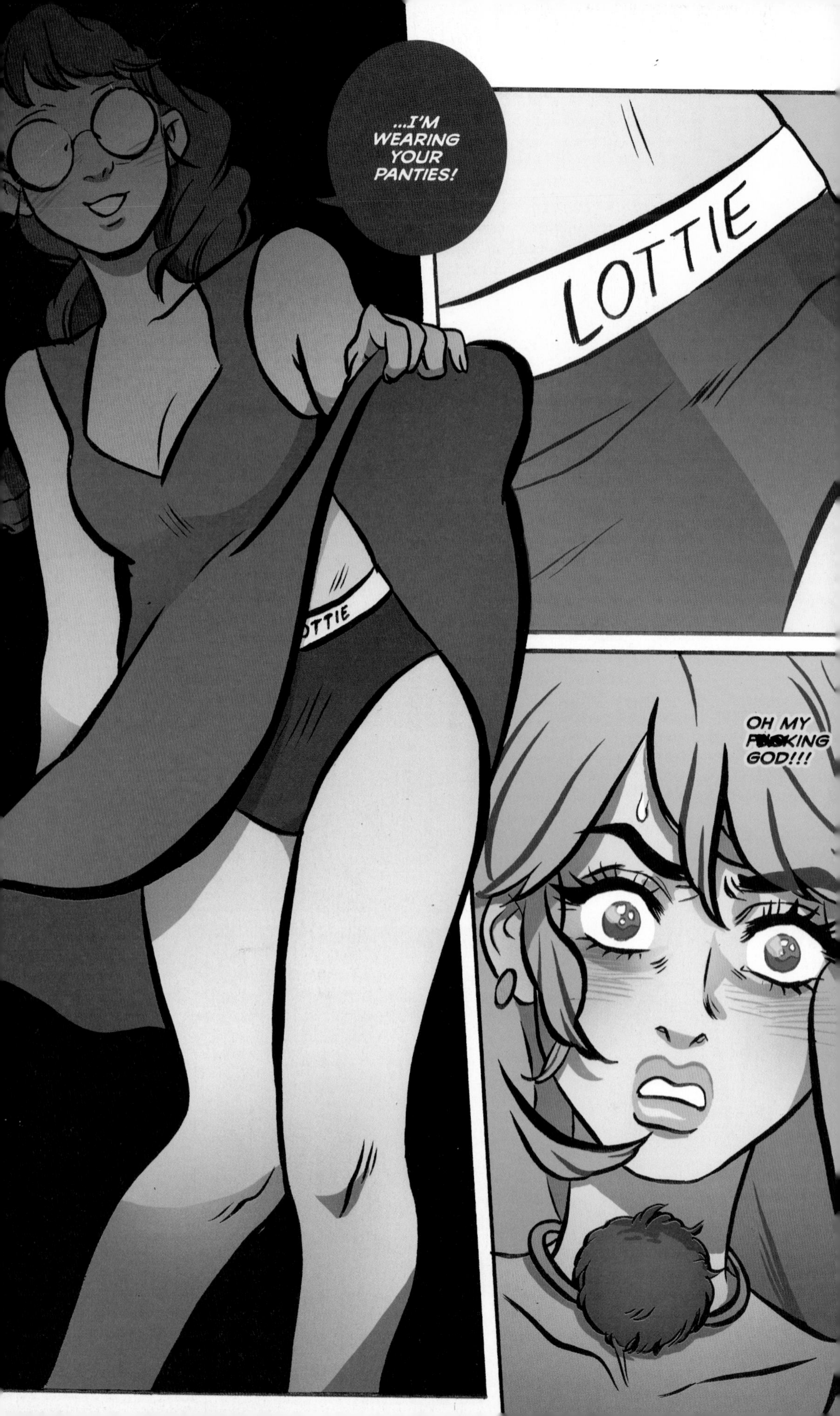
...I'M WEARING YOUR PANTIES!
OTTIE
LOTTIE
OH MY F[redacted]KING GOD!!!

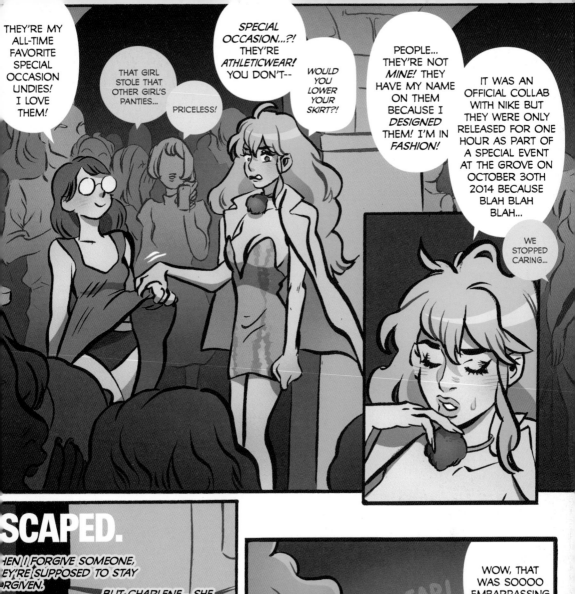

THEY'RE MY ALL-TIME FAVORITE SPECIAL OCCASION *UNDIES!* I LOVE THEM!

THAT GIRL STOLE THAT OTHER GIRL'S PANTIES...

PRICELESS!

SPECIAL OCCASION...?! THEY'RE *ATHLETICWEAR!* YOU DON'T--

WOULD YOU LOWER YOUR SKIRT?!

PEOPLE... THEY'RE NOT *MINE!* THEY HAVE MY NAME ON THEM BECAUSE I *DESIGNED* THEM! I'M IN *FASHION!*

IT WAS AN OFFICIAL COLLAB WITH NIKE BUT THEY WERE ONLY RELEASED FOR ONE HOUR AS PART OF A SPECIAL EVENT AT THE GROVE ON OCTOBER 30TH 2014 BECAUSE BLAH BLAH BLAH...

WE STOPPED CARING...

SCAPED.

HEN I FORGIVE SOMEONE, EY'RE SUPPOSED TO STAY RGIVEN.

BUT CHARLENE... SHE JUST KEEPS BEING THE WORST!

WHAT DO I HAVE TO DO, *KILL HER?*

APPEAR!

WOW, THAT WAS SOOOO EMBARRASSING FOR YOU!

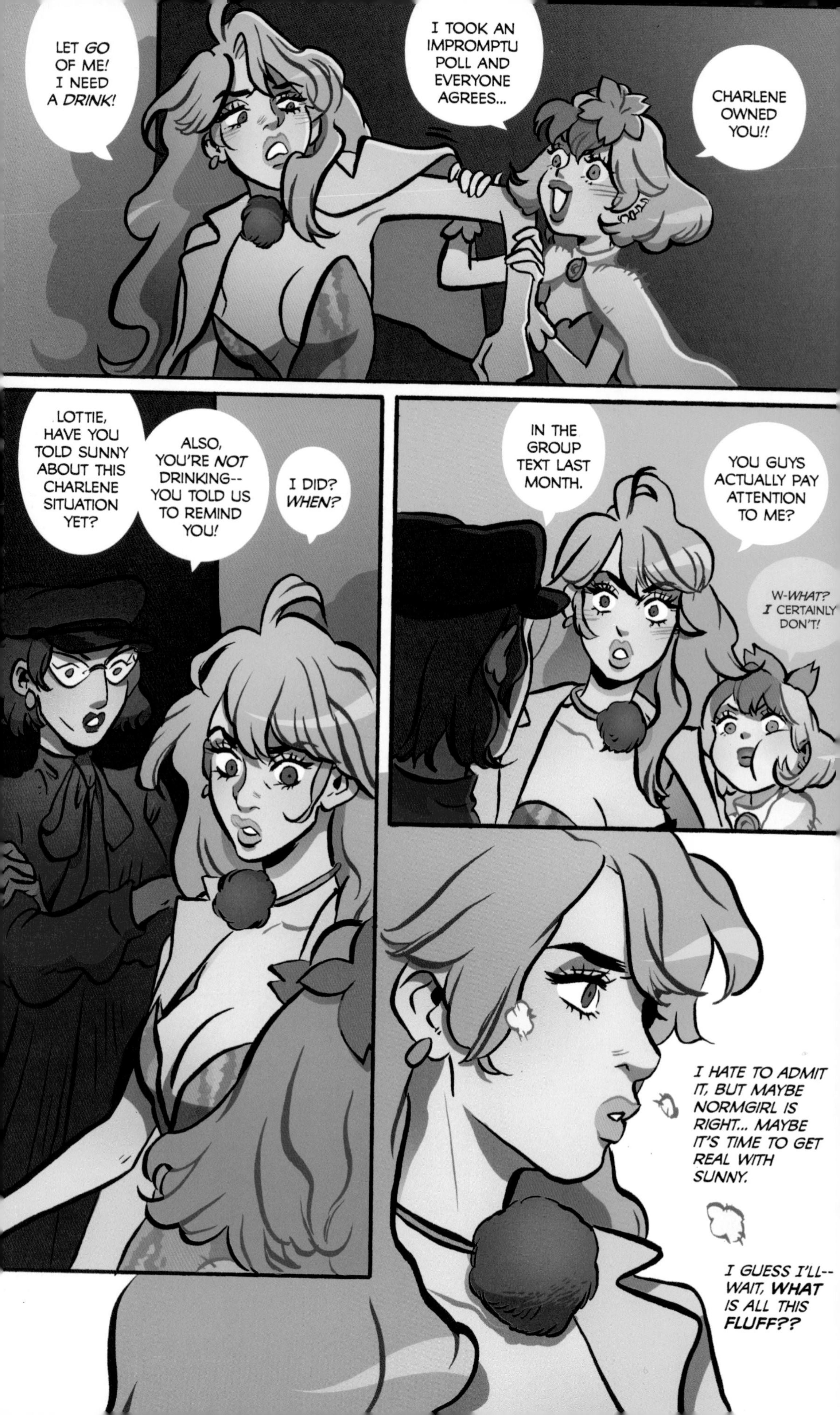
LET GO OF ME! I NEED A DRINK!
I TOOK AN IMPROMPTU POLL AND EVERYONE AGREES...
CHARLENE OWNED YOU!!
LOTTIE, HAVE YOU TOLD SUNNY ABOUT THIS CHARLENE SITUATION YET?
ALSO, YOU'RE NOT DRINKING-- YOU TOLD US TO REMIND YOU!
I DID? WHEN?
IN THE GROUP TEXT LAST MONTH.
YOU GUYS ACTUALLY PAY ATTENTION TO ME?
W-WHAT? I CERTAINLY DON'T!
I HATE TO ADMIT IT, BUT MAYBE NORMGIRL IS RIGHT... MAYBE IT'S TIME TO GET REAL WITH SUNNY.
I GUESS I'LL-- WAIT, WHAT IS ALL THIS FLUFF??

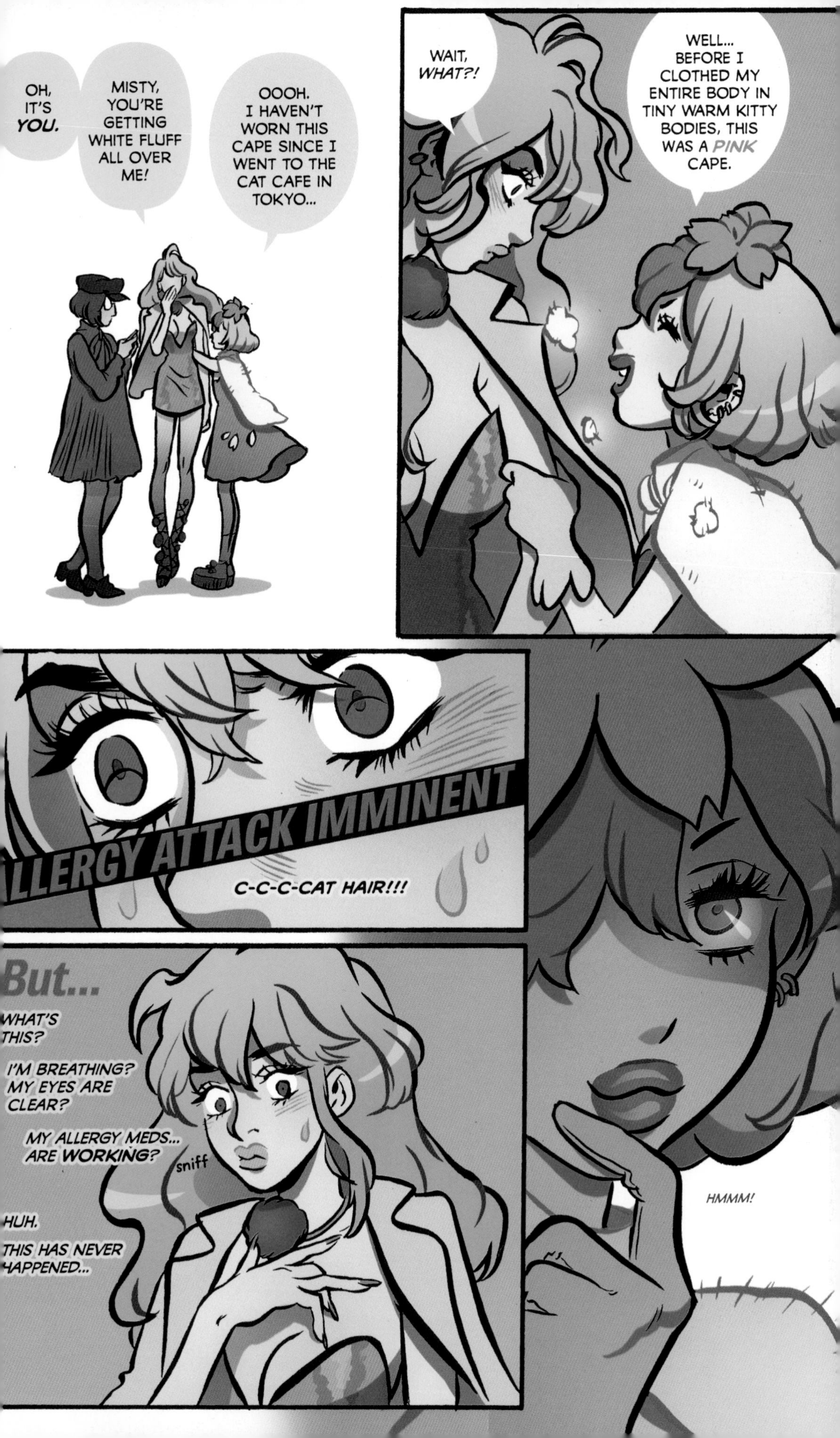
OH, IT'S **YOU.**
MISTY, YOU'RE GETTING WHITE FLUFF ALL OVER ME!
OOOH. I HAVEN'T WORN THIS CAPE SINCE I WENT TO THE CAT CAFE IN TOKYO...
WAIT, *WHAT?!*
WELL... BEFORE I CLOTHED MY ENTIRE BODY IN TINY WARM KITTY BODIES, THIS WAS A *PINK* CAPE.
ALLERGY ATTACK IMMINENT
C-C-C-CAT HAIR!!!
But...
WHAT'S THIS?
I'M BREATHING? MY EYES ARE CLEAR?
MY ALLERGY MEDS... ARE **WORKING?**
sniff
HUH.
THIS HAS NEVER HAPPENED...
HMMM!

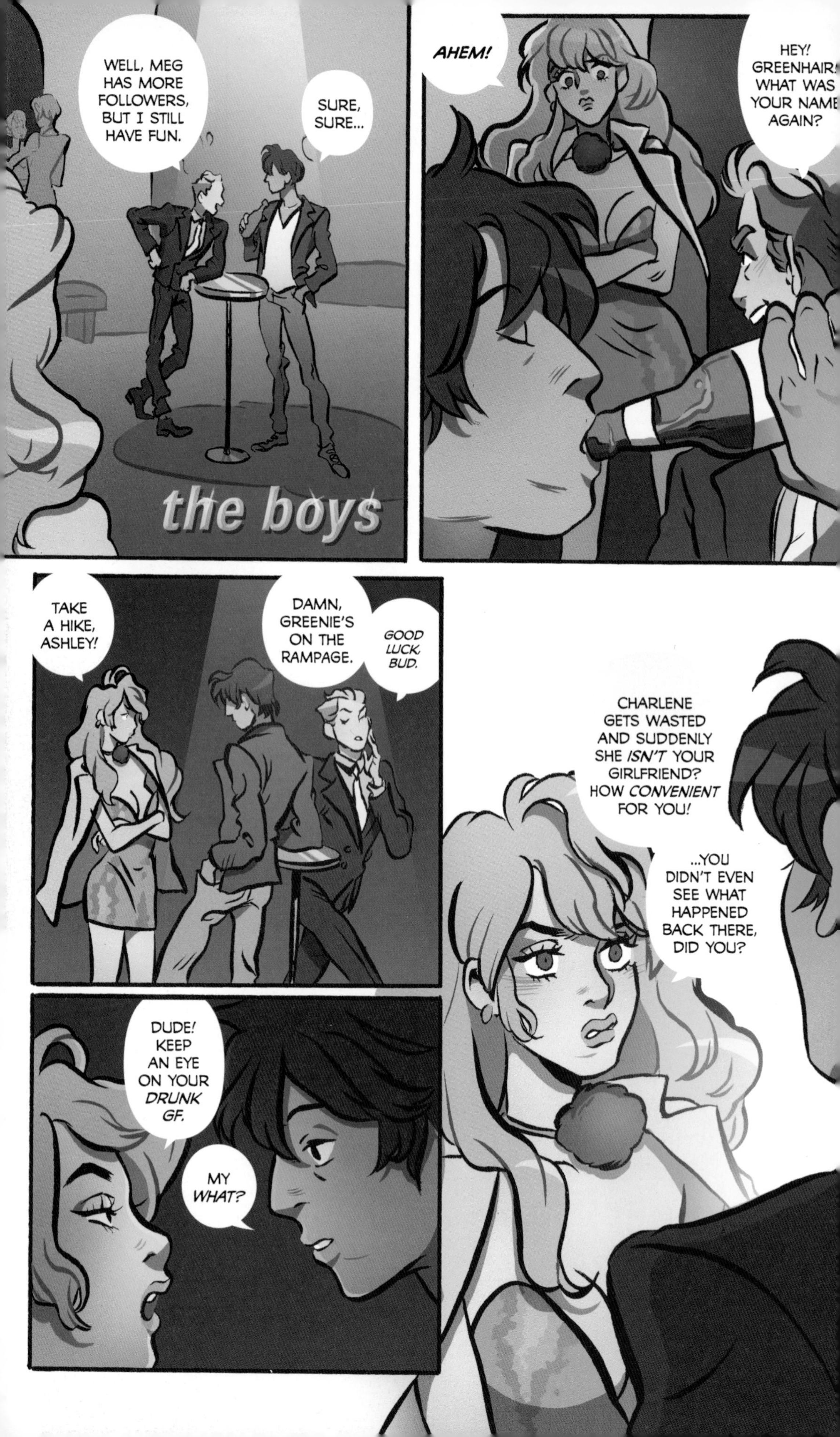
WELL, MEG HAS MORE FOLLOWERS, BUT I STILL HAVE FUN.
SURE, SURE...
the boys
AHEM!
HEY! GREENHAIR! WHAT WAS YOUR NAME AGAIN?
TAKE A HIKE, ASHLEY!
DAMN, GREENIE'S ON THE RAMPAGE.
GOOD LUCK, BUD.
DUDE! KEEP AN EYE ON YOUR DRUNK GF.
MY WHAT?
CHARLENE GETS WASTED AND SUDDENLY SHE ISN'T YOUR GIRLFRIEND? HOW CONVENIENT FOR YOU!
...YOU DIDN'T EVEN SEE WHAT HAPPENED BACK THERE, DID YOU?

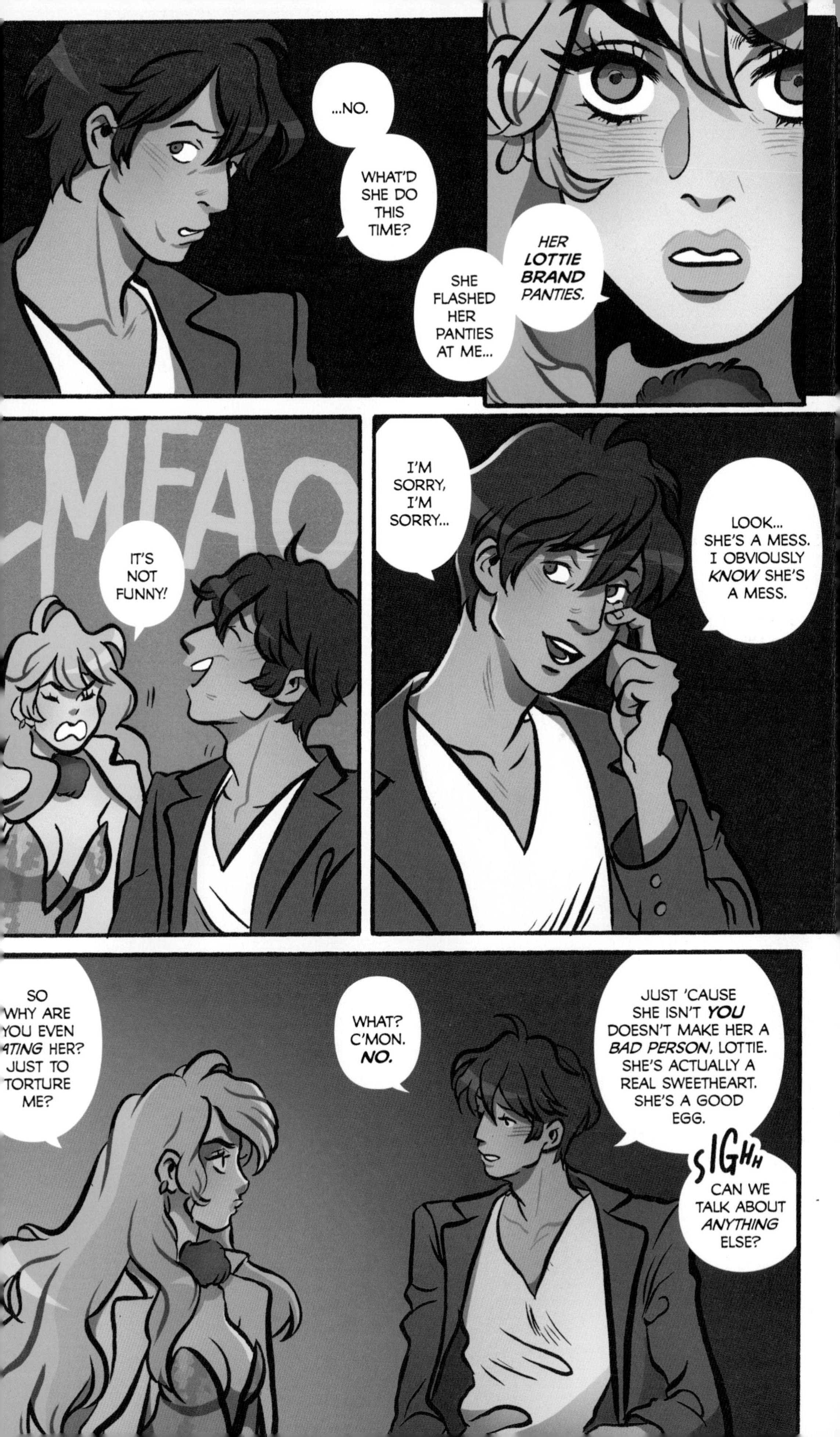

...NO.
WHAT'D SHE DO THIS TIME?
SHE FLASHED HER PANTIES AT ME...
HER LOTTIE BRAND PANTIES.
MFAO
IT'S NOT FUNNY!
I'M SORRY, I'M SORRY...
LOOK... SHE'S A MESS. I OBVIOUSLY KNOW SHE'S A MESS.
SO WHY ARE YOU EVEN ATING HER? JUST TO TORTURE ME?
WHAT? C'MON. NO.
JUST 'CAUSE SHE ISN'T YOU DOESN'T MAKE HER A BAD PERSON, LOTTIE. SHE'S ACTUALLY A REAL SWEETHEART. SHE'S A GOOD EGG.
SIGHH
CAN WE TALK ABOUT ANYTHING ELSE?

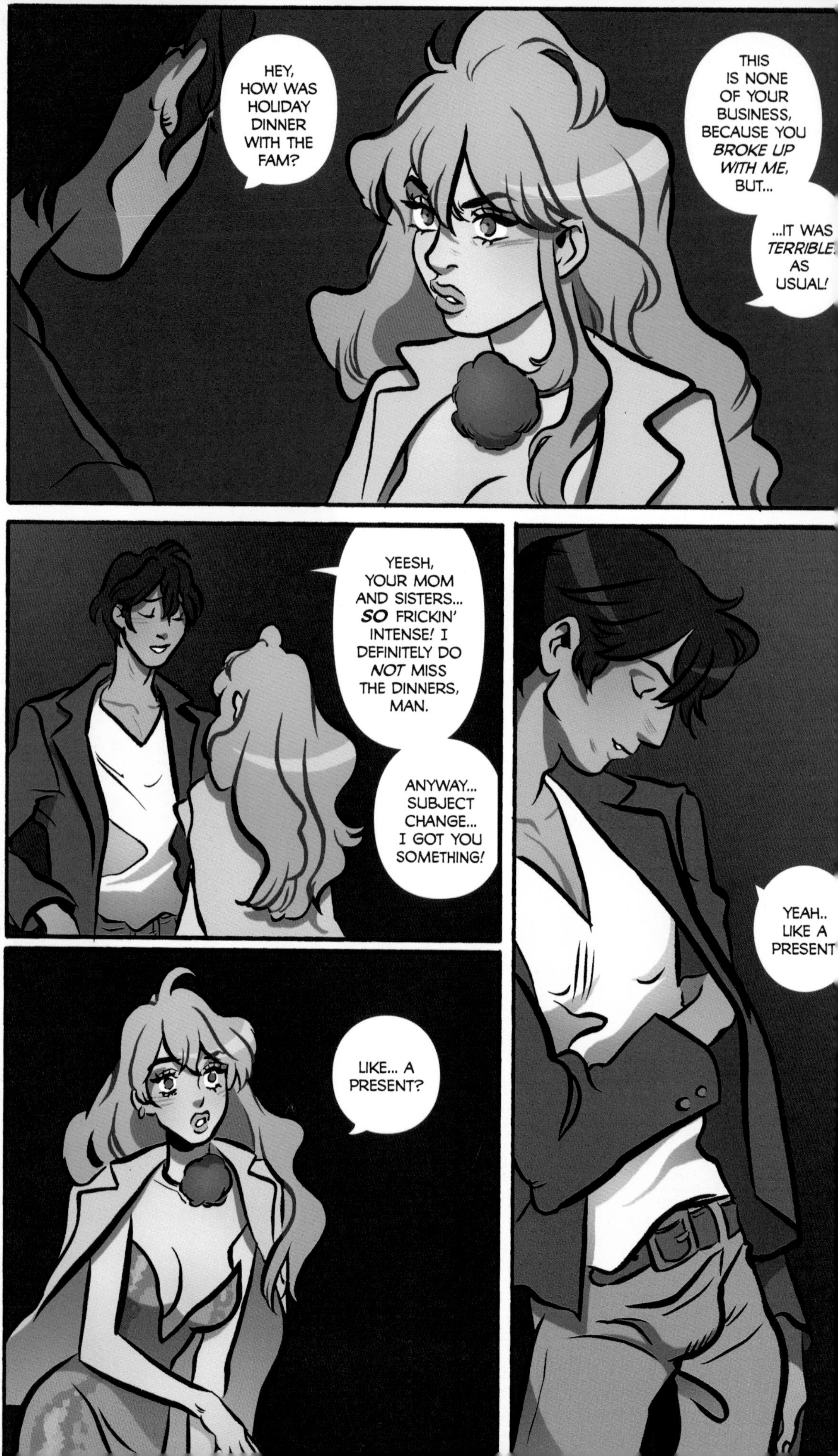
HEY, HOW WAS HOLIDAY DINNER WITH THE FAM?
THIS IS NONE OF YOUR BUSINESS, BECAUSE YOU *BROKE UP WITH ME,* BUT...
...IT WAS *TERRIBLE!* AS USUAL!
YEESH, YOUR MOM AND SISTERS... ***SO*** FRICKIN' INTENSE! I DEFINITELY DO *NOT* MISS THE DINNERS, MAN.
ANYWAY... SUBJECT CHANGE... I GOT YOU SOMETHING!
LIKE... A PRESENT?
YEAH.. LIKE A PRESENT

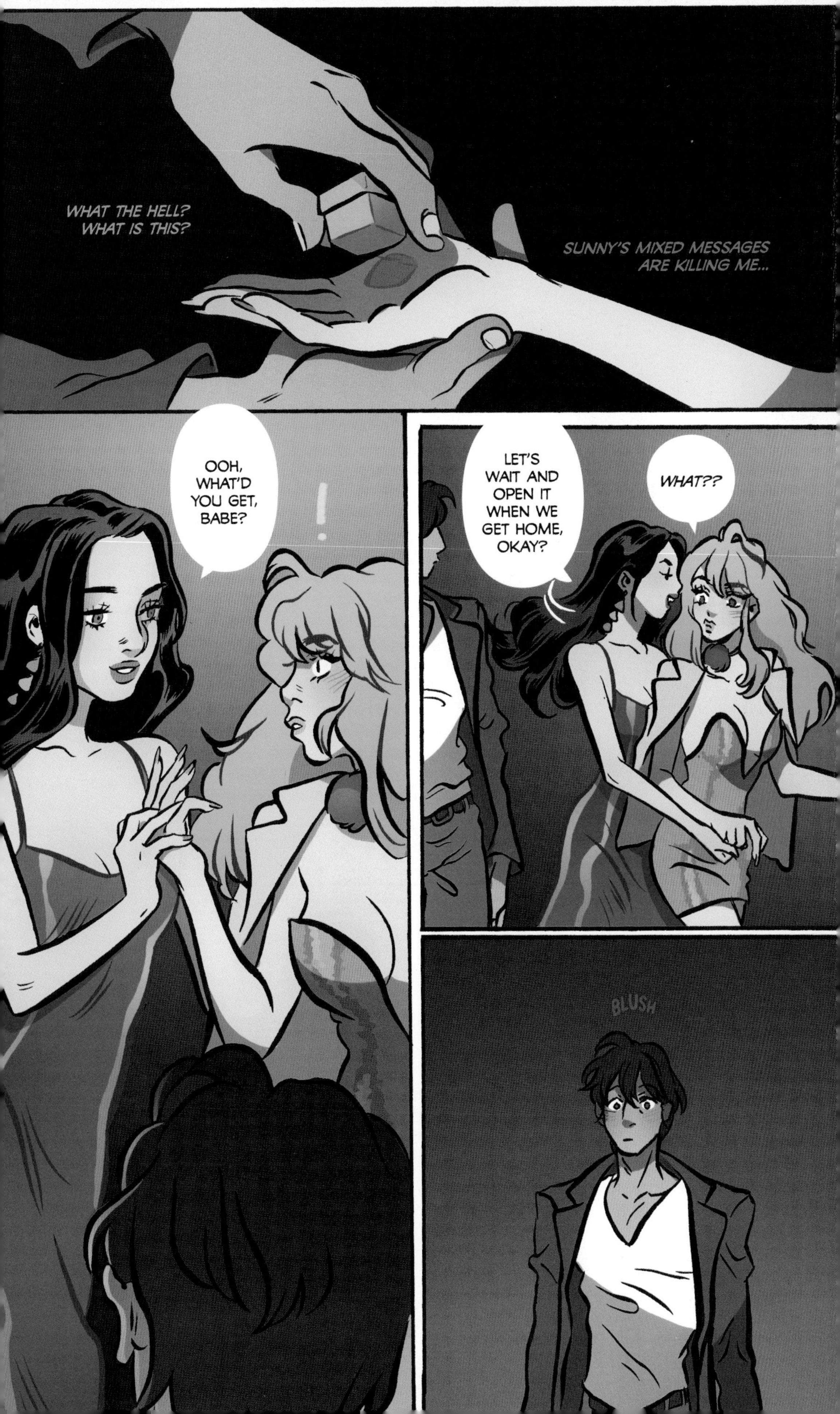
WHAT THE HELL? WHAT IS THIS?
SUNNY'S MIXED MESSAGES ARE KILLING ME...
OOH, WHAT'D YOU GET, BABE?
!
LET'S WAIT AND OPEN IT WHEN WE GET HOME, OKAY?
WHAT??
BLUSH

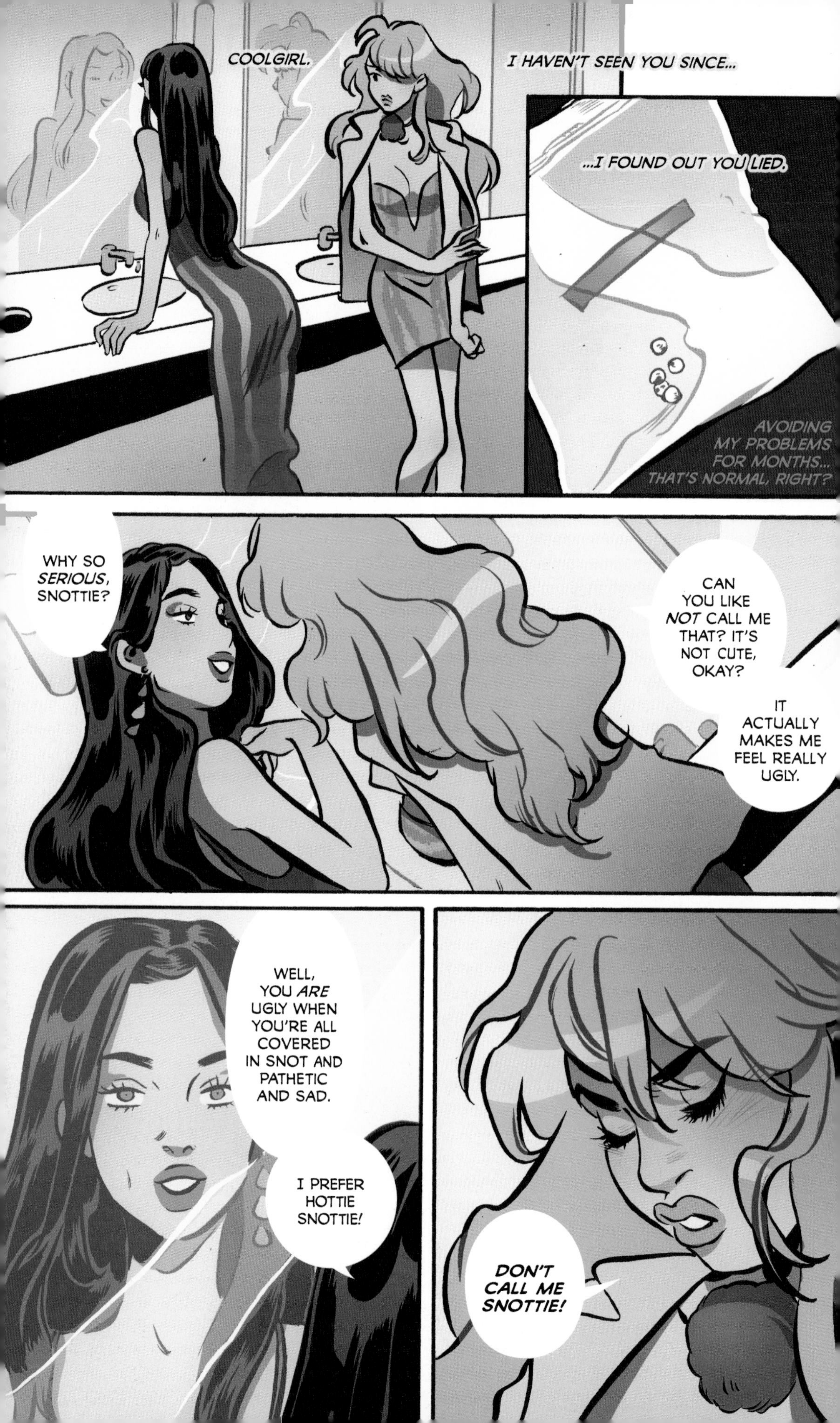

COOLGIRL.
I HAVEN'T SEEN YOU SINCE...
...I FOUND OUT YOU LIED.
AVOIDING MY PROBLEMS FOR MONTHS... THAT'S NORMAL, RIGHT?
WHY SO *SERIOUS*, SNOTTIE?
CAN YOU LIKE *NOT* CALL ME THAT? IT'S NOT CUTE, OKAY?
IT ACTUALLY MAKES ME FEEL REALLY UGLY.
WELL, YOU *ARE* UGLY WHEN YOU'RE ALL COVERED IN SNOT AND PATHETIC AND SAD.
I PREFER HOTTIE SNOTTIE!
DON'T CALL ME SNOTTIE!

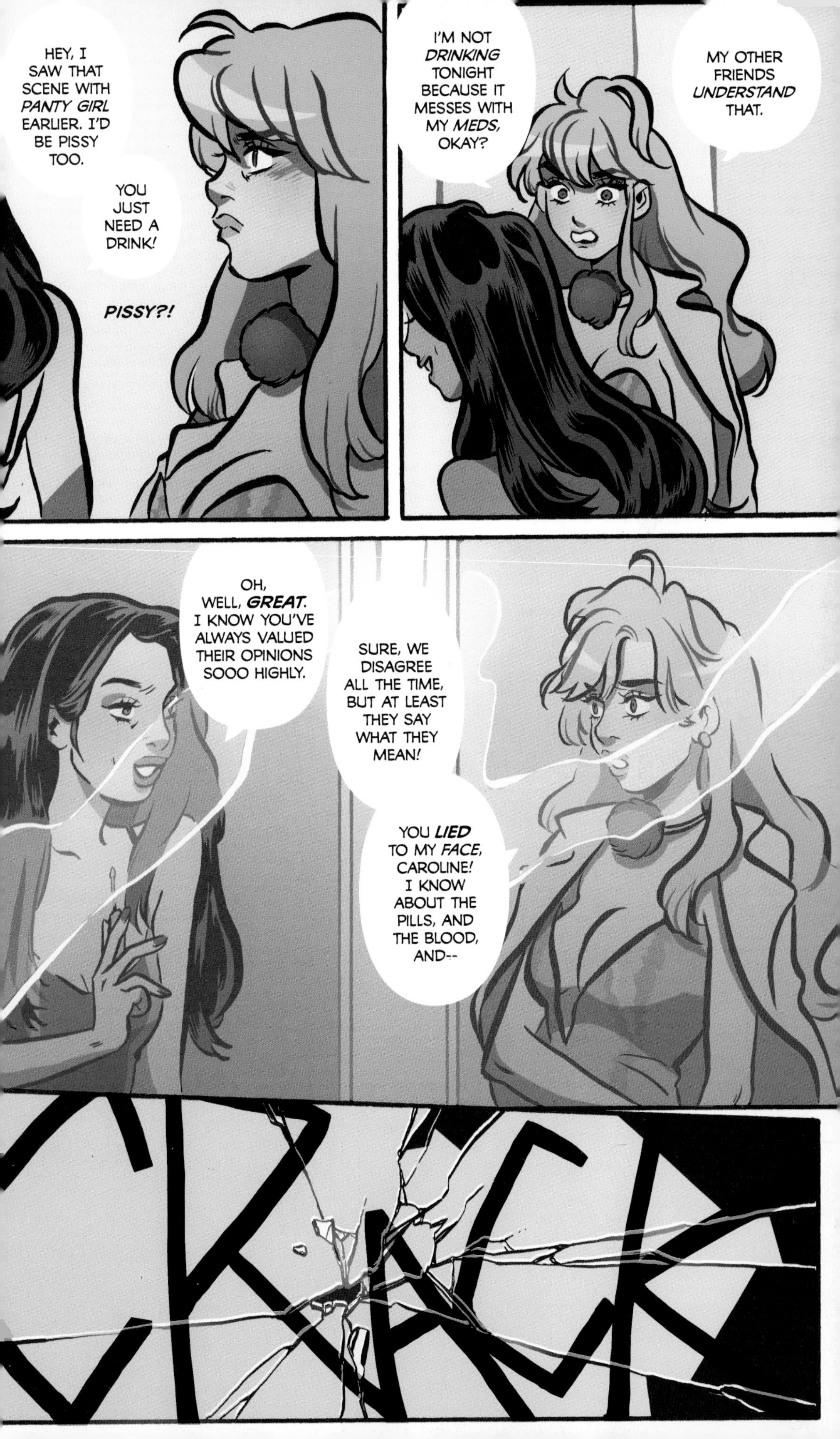

HEY, I SAW THAT SCENE WITH *PANTY GIRL* EARLIER. I'D BE PISSY TOO.
YOU JUST NEED A DRINK!
PISSY?!
I'M NOT *DRINKING* TONIGHT BECAUSE IT MESSES WITH MY *MEDS*, OKAY?
MY OTHER FRIENDS *UNDERSTAND* THAT.
OH, WELL, ***GREAT***. I KNOW YOU'VE ALWAYS VALUED THEIR OPINIONS SOOO HIGHLY.
SURE, WE DISAGREE ALL THE TIME, BUT AT LEAST THEY SAY WHAT THEY MEAN!
YOU ***LIED*** TO MY *FACE*, CAROLINE! I KNOW ABOUT THE PILLS, AND THE BLOOD, AND--
CRACK

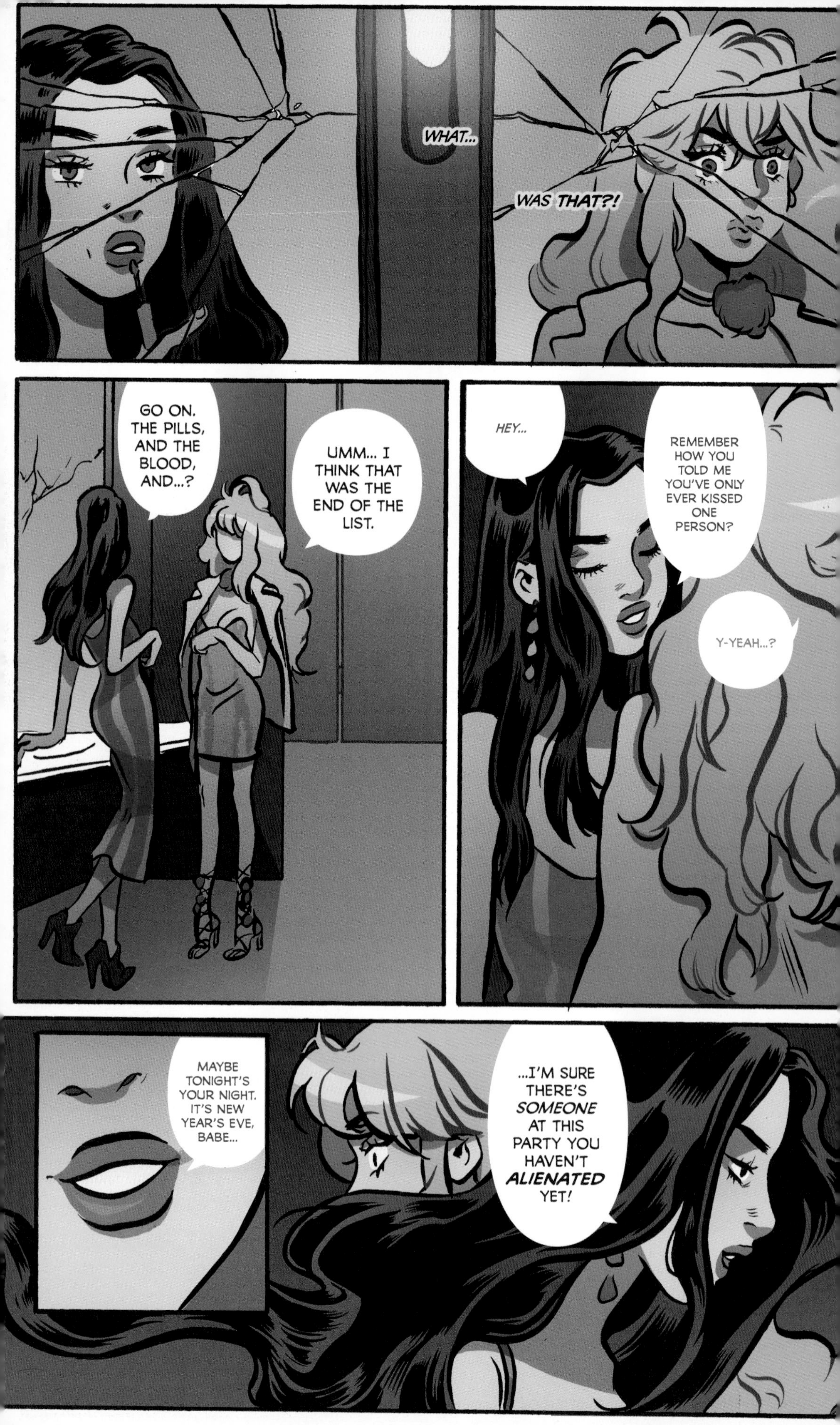
WHAT...
WAS THAT?!
GO ON. THE PILLS, AND THE BLOOD, AND...?
UMM... I THINK THAT WAS THE END OF THE LIST.
HEY...
REMEMBER HOW YOU TOLD ME YOU'VE ONLY EVER KISSED ONE PERSON?
Y-YEAH...?
MAYBE TONIGHT'S YOUR NIGHT. IT'S NEW YEAR'S EVE, BABE...
...I'M SURE THERE'S *SOMEONE* AT THIS PARTY YOU HAVEN'T ***ALIENATED*** YET!

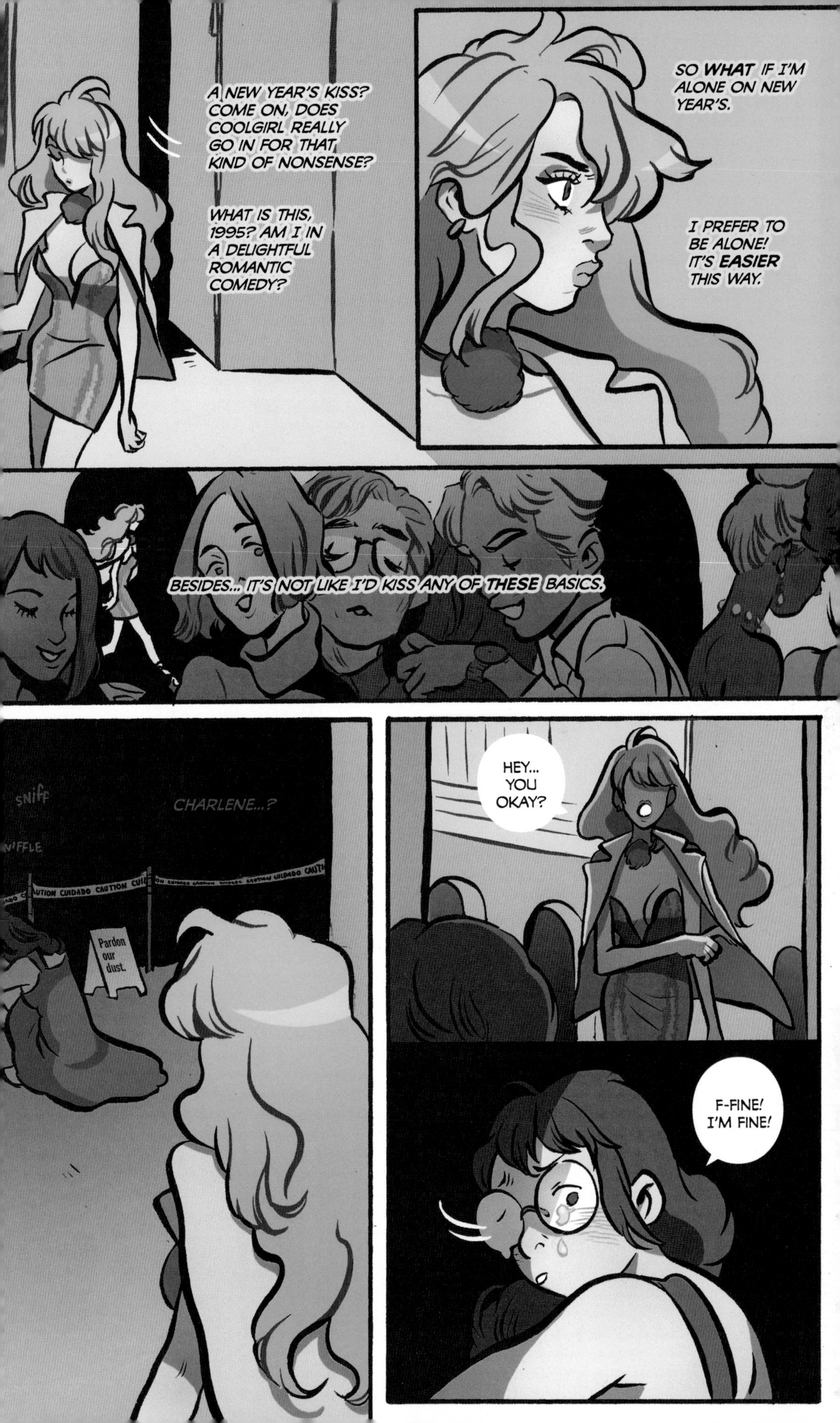
A NEW YEAR'S KISS? COME ON, DOES COOLGIRL REALLY GO IN FOR THAT KIND OF NONSENSE?
WHAT IS THIS, 1995? AM I IN A DELIGHTFUL ROMANTIC COMEDY?
SO WHAT IF I'M ALONE ON NEW YEAR'S.
I PREFER TO BE ALONE! IT'S EASIER THIS WAY.
BESIDES... IT'S NOT LIKE I'D KISS ANY OF THESE BASICS.
SNIFF
SNIFFLE
CHARLENE...?
CAUTION CUIDADO CAUTION CUIDADO
Pardon our dust.
HEY... YOU OKAY?
F-FINE! I'M FINE!

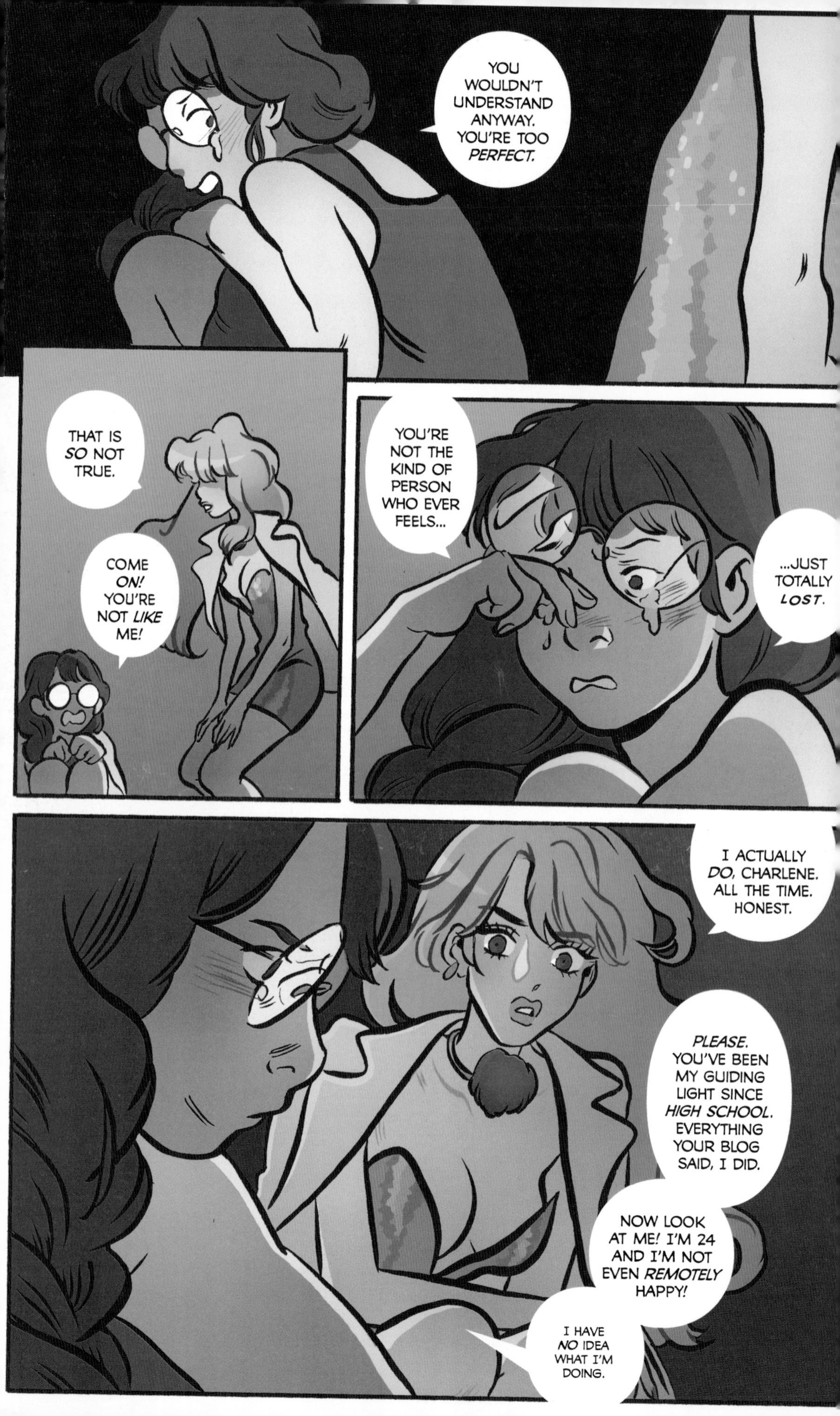
YOU WOULDN'T UNDERSTAND ANYWAY. YOU'RE TOO *PERFECT.*
THAT IS *SO* NOT TRUE.
COME *ON!* YOU'RE NOT *LIKE* ME!
YOU'RE NOT THE KIND OF PERSON WHO EVER FEELS...
...JUST TOTALLY *LOST*.
I ACTUALLY *DO*, CHARLENE. ALL THE TIME. HONEST.
PLEASE. YOU'VE BEEN MY GUIDING LIGHT SINCE *HIGH SCHOOL*. EVERYTHING YOUR BLOG SAID, I DID.
NOW LOOK AT ME! I'M 24 AND I'M NOT EVEN *REMOTELY* HAPPY!
I HAVE *NO* IDEA WHAT I'M DOING.

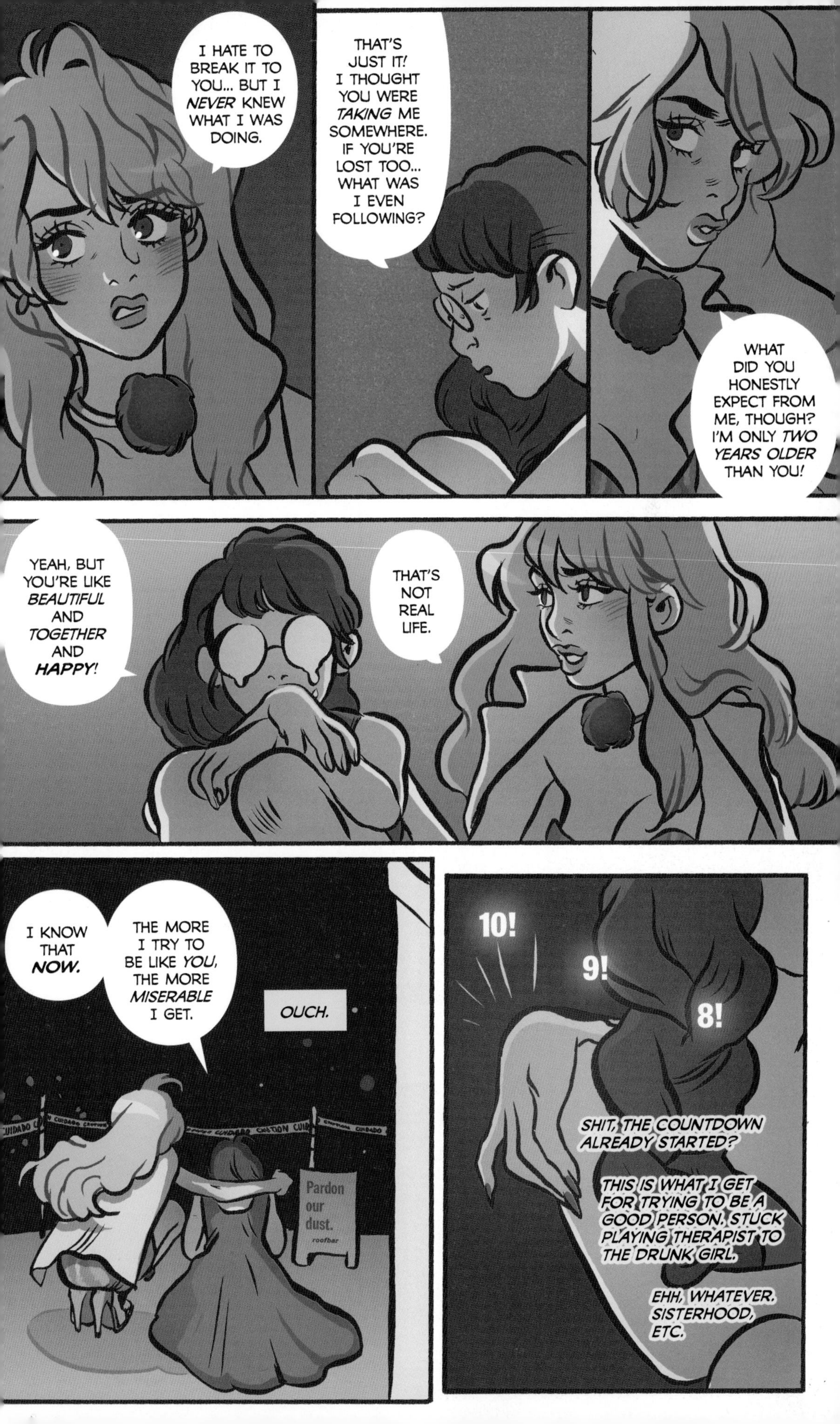
I HATE TO BREAK IT TO YOU... BUT I *NEVER* KNEW WHAT I WAS DOING.
THAT'S JUST IT! I THOUGHT YOU WERE *TAKING* ME SOMEWHERE. IF YOU'RE LOST TOO... WHAT WAS I EVEN FOLLOWING?
WHAT DID YOU HONESTLY EXPECT FROM ME, THOUGH? I'M ONLY *TWO YEARS OLDER* THAN YOU!
YEAH, BUT YOU'RE LIKE *BEAUTIFUL* AND *TOGETHER* AND ***HAPPY***!
THAT'S NOT REAL LIFE.
I KNOW THAT ***NOW.***
THE MORE I TRY TO BE LIKE *YOU*, THE MORE *MISERABLE* I GET.
OUCH.
Pardon our dust.
roofbar
10!
9!
8!
SHIT, THE COUNTDOWN ALREADY STARTED?
THIS IS WHAT I GET FOR TRYING TO BE A GOOD PERSON. STUCK PLAYING THERAPIST TO THE DRUNK GIRL.
EHH, WHATEVER. SISTERHOOD, ETC.

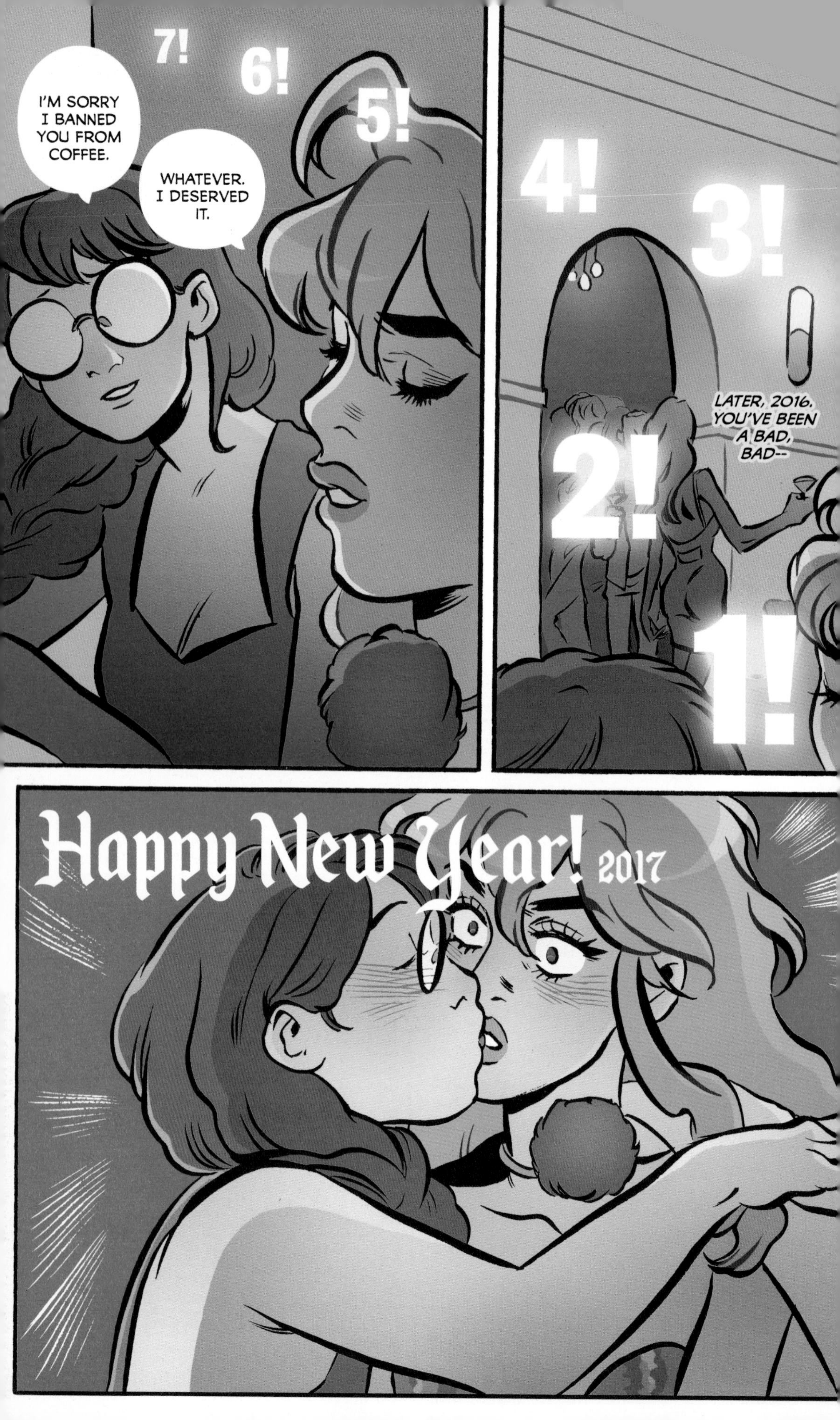
7!
6!
5!
I'M SORRY I BANNED YOU FROM COFFEE.
WHATEVER. I DESERVED IT.
4!
3!
LATER, 2016. YOU'VE BEEN A BAD, BAD--
2!
1!
Happy New Year! 2017

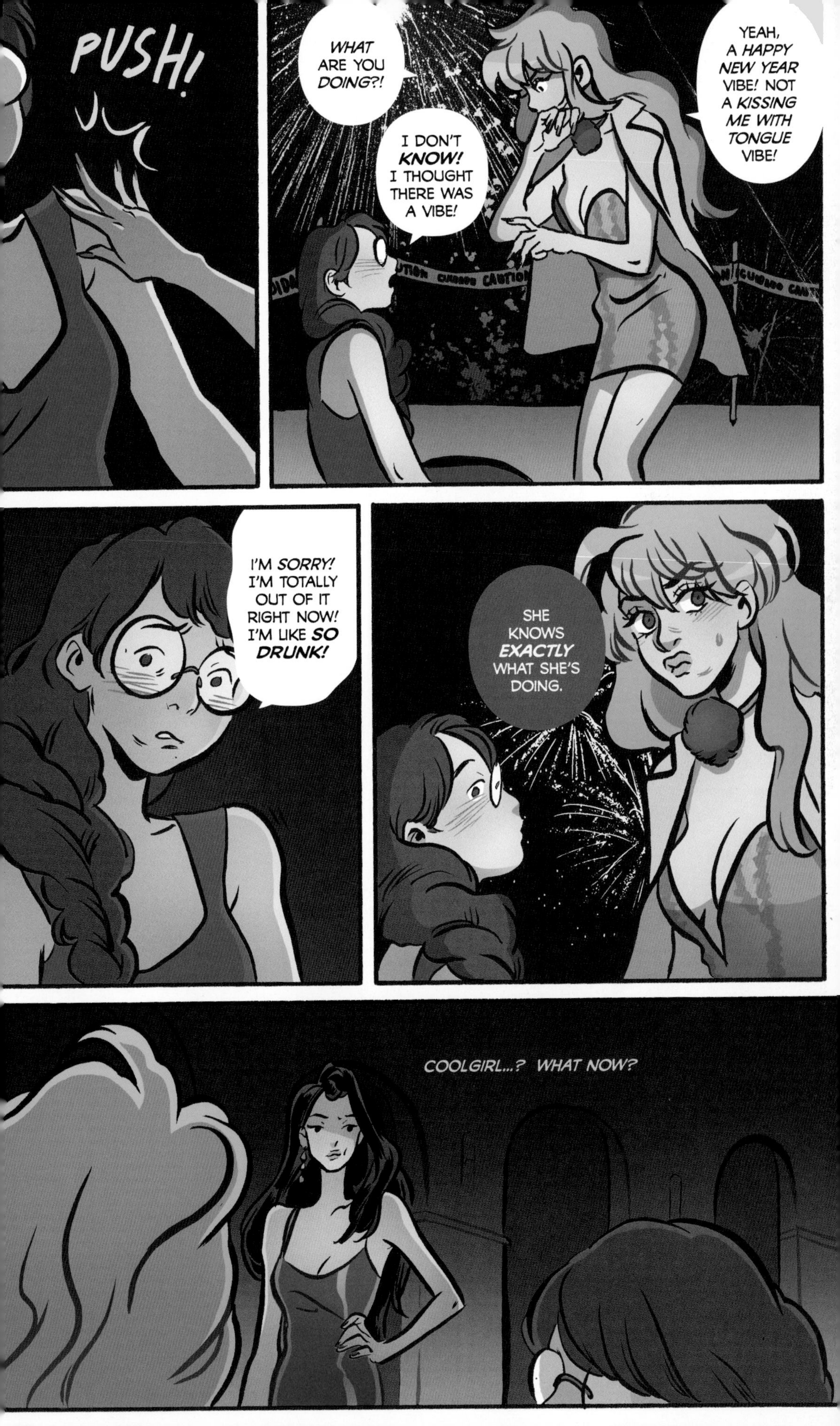
PUSH!
WHAT ARE YOU DOING?!
I DON'T KNOW! I THOUGHT THERE WAS A VIBE!
YEAH, A HAPPY NEW YEAR VIBE! NOT A KISSING ME WITH TONGUE VIBE!
CAUTION
I'M SORRY! I'M TOTALLY OUT OF IT RIGHT NOW! I'M LIKE SO DRUNK!
SHE KNOWS EXACTLY WHAT SHE'S DOING.
COOLGIRL...? WHAT NOW?

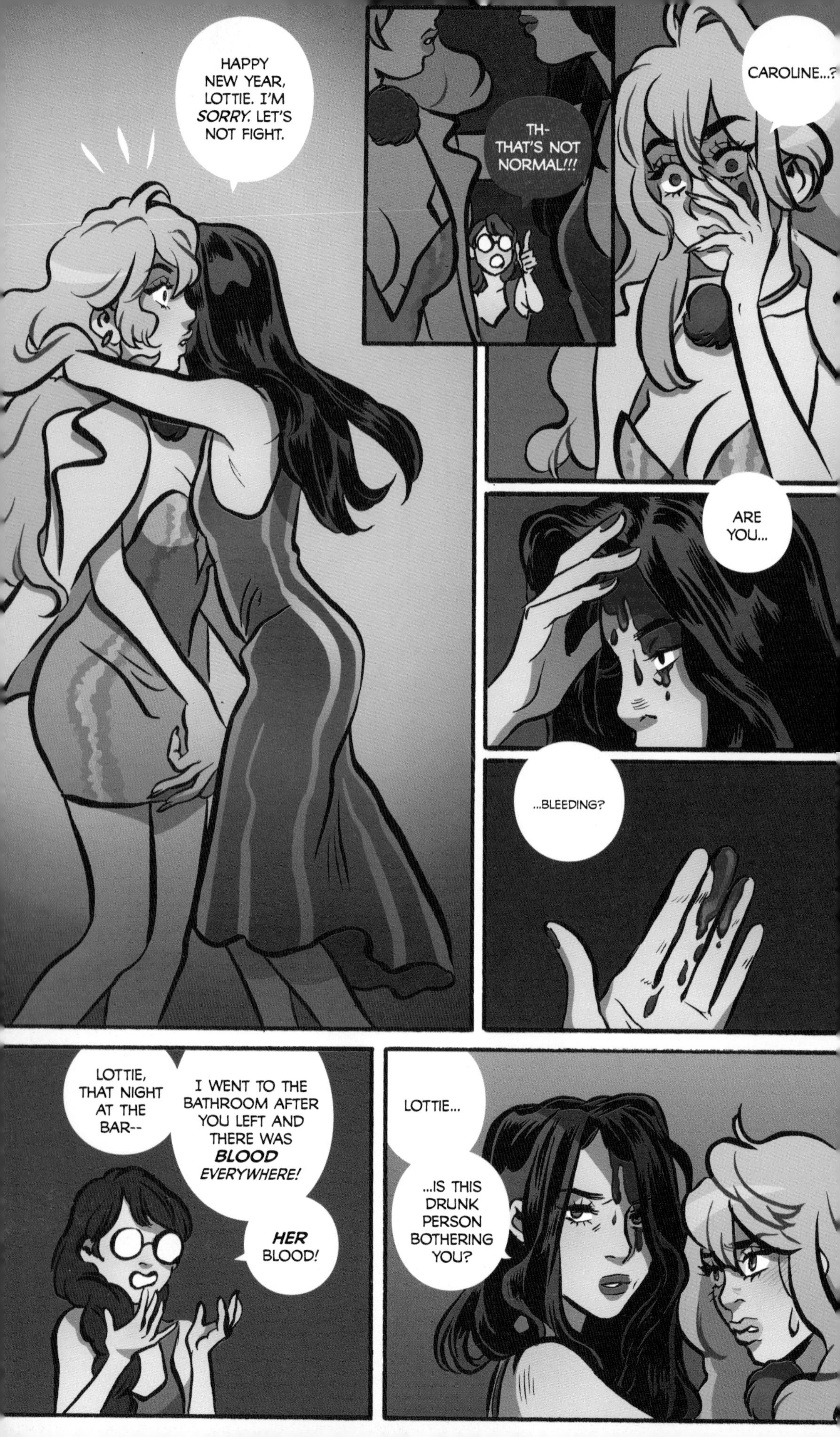

HAPPY NEW YEAR, LOTTIE. I'M *SORRY.* LET'S NOT FIGHT.
TH- THAT'S NOT NORMAL!!!
CAROLINE...?
ARE YOU...
...BLEEDING?
LOTTIE, THAT NIGHT AT THE BAR--
I WENT TO THE BATHROOM AFTER YOU LEFT AND THERE WAS ***BLOOD*** *EVERYWHERE!*
HER BLOOD!
LOTTIE...
...IS THIS DRUNK PERSON BOTHERING YOU?

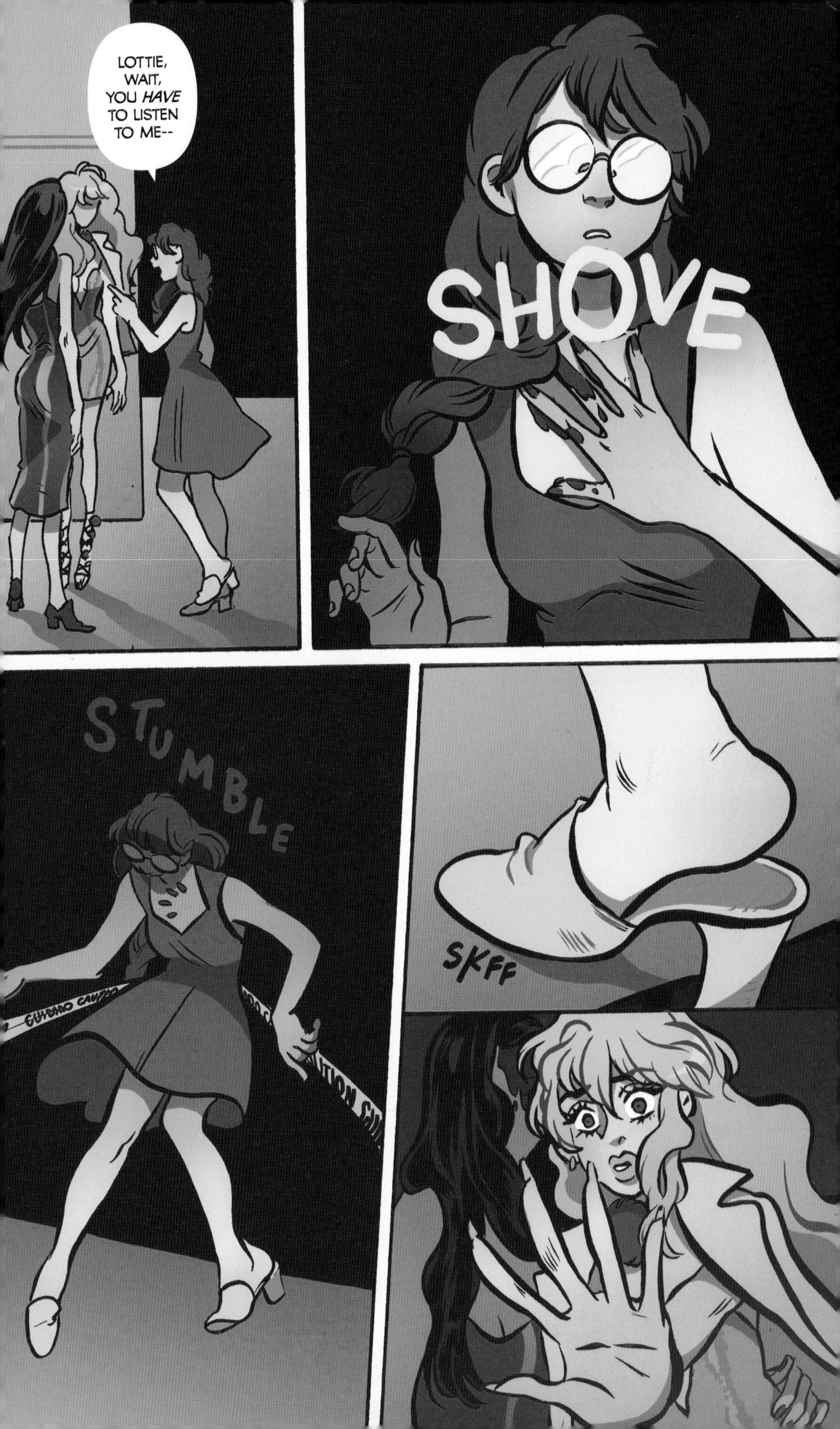
LOTTIE, WAIT, YOU *HAVE* TO LISTEN TO ME--
SHOVE
STUMBLE
SKFF

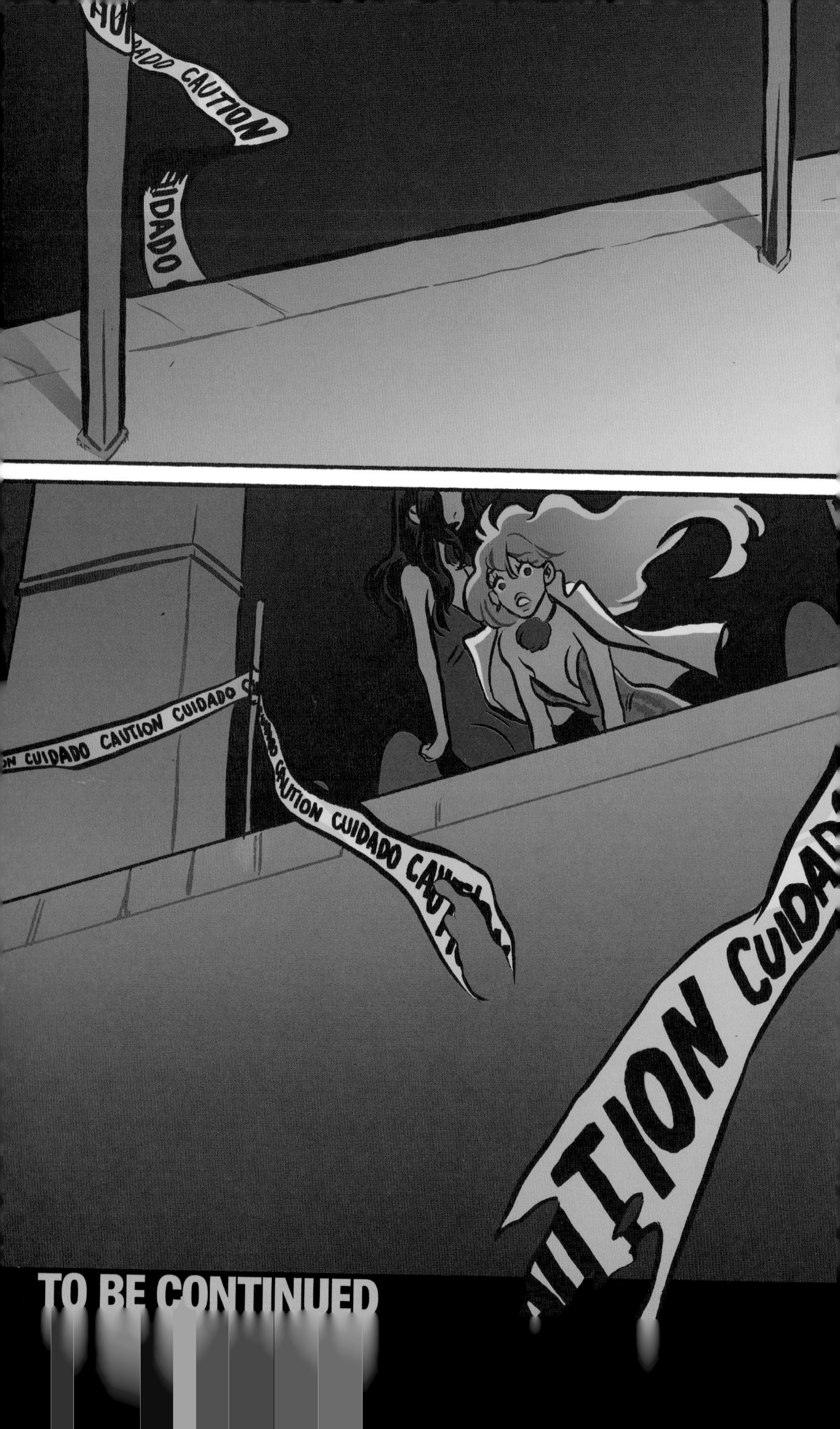
CAUTION
CUIDADO CAUTION CUIDADO
CAUTION CUIDADO
TION CUIDA

TO BE CONTINUED

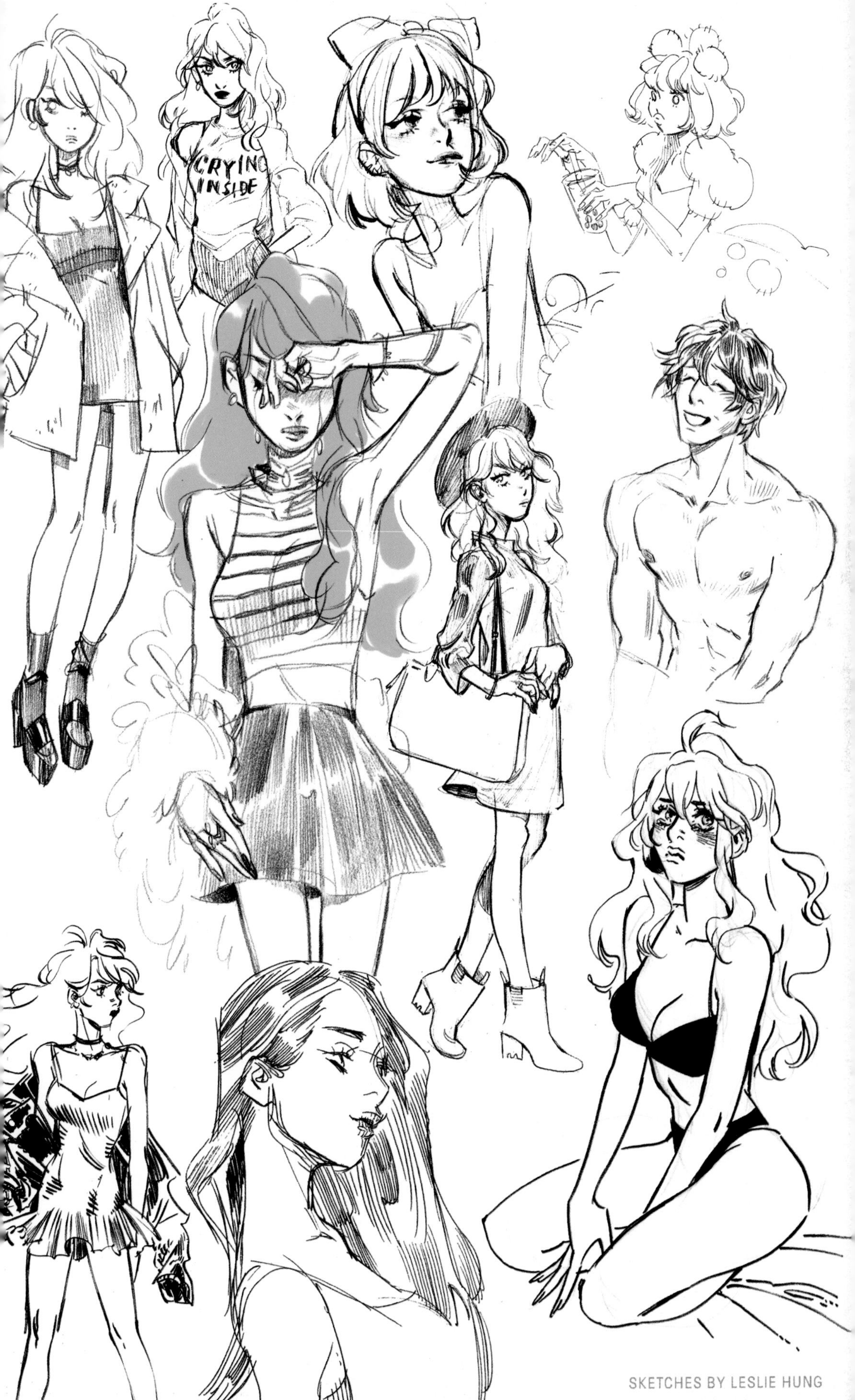
CRYING
INSIDE

SKETCHES BY LESLIE HUNG

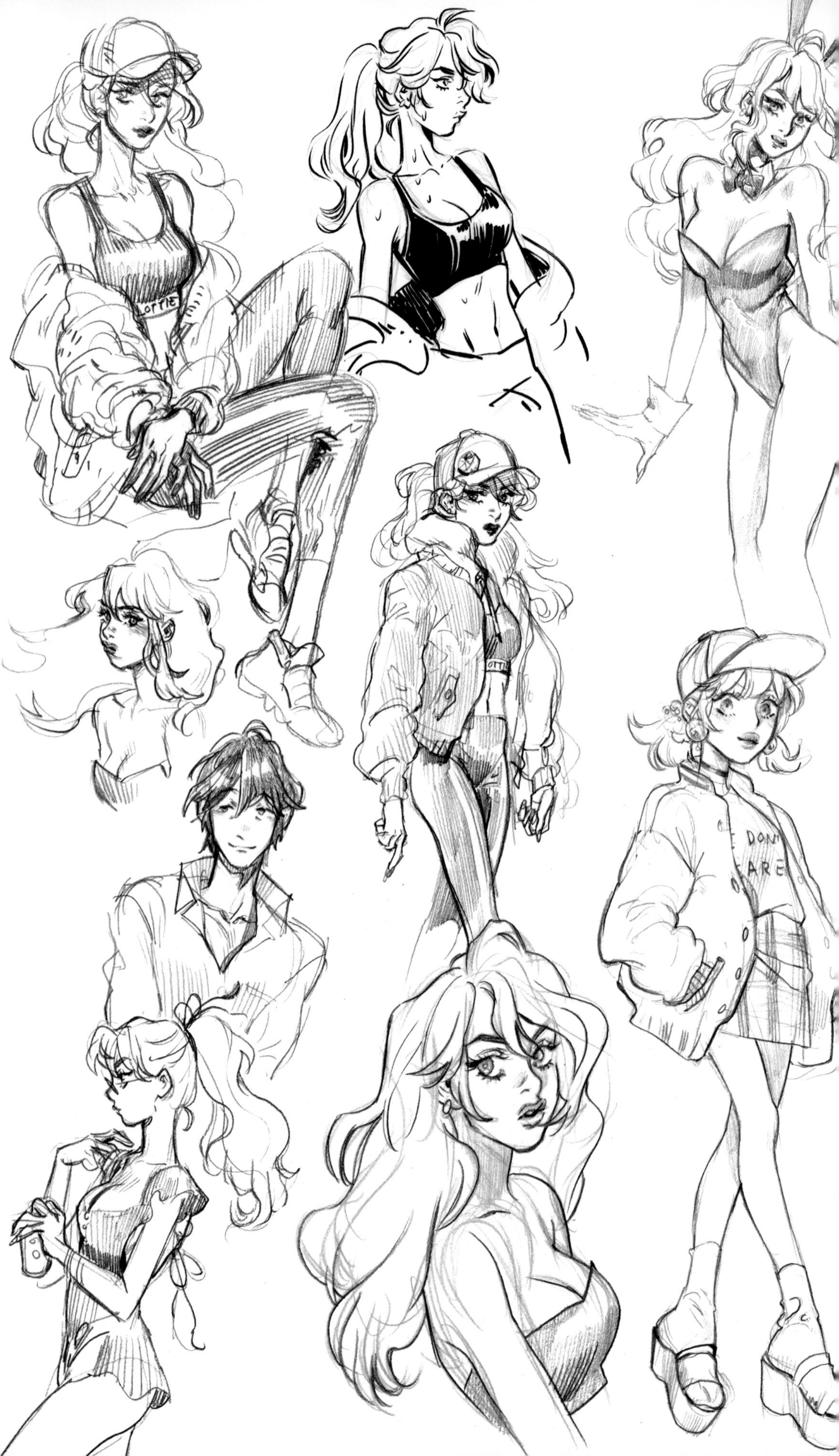
LOTTIE

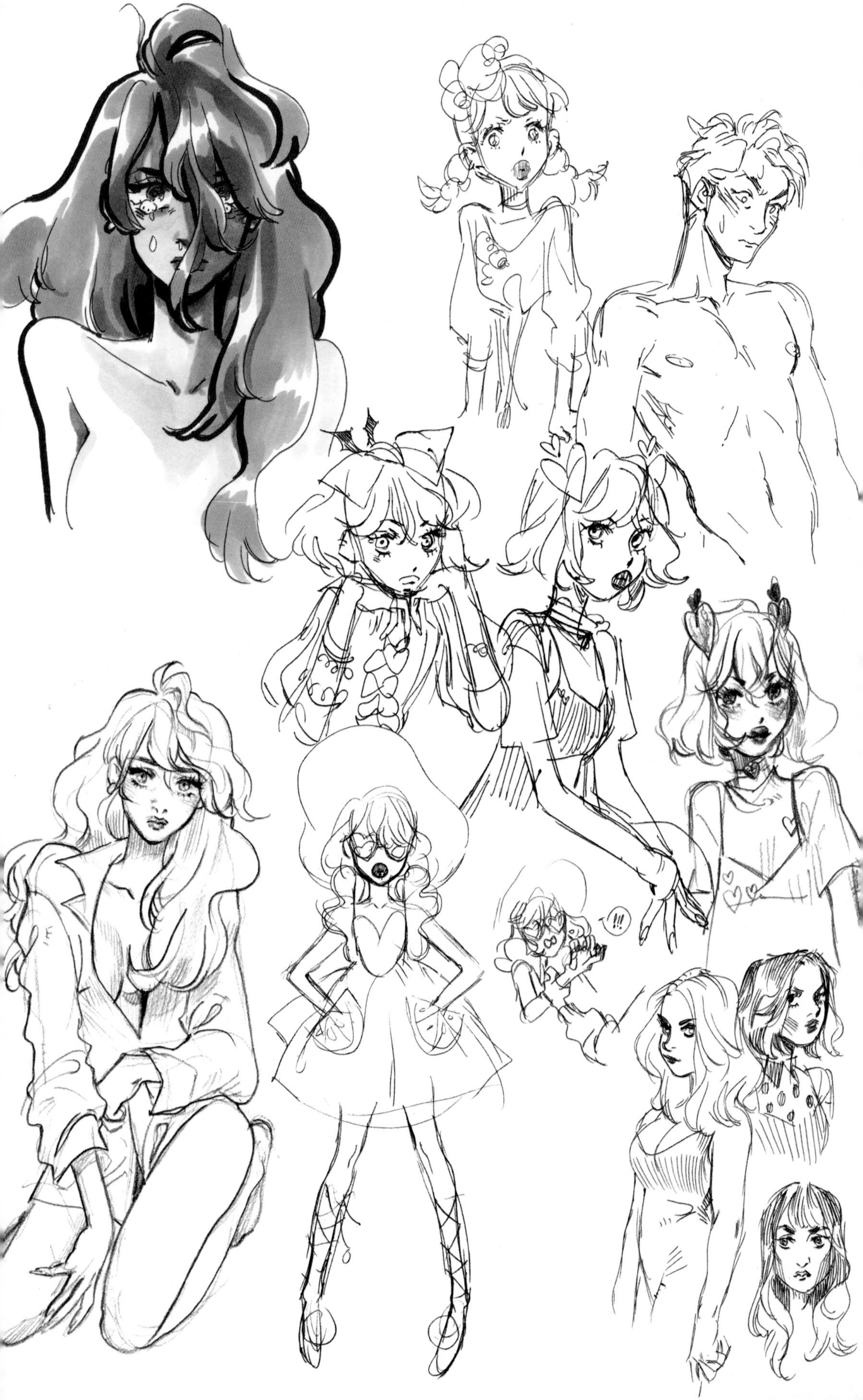
!!!

COVER GALLERY
ISSUE 1
LESLIE HUNG

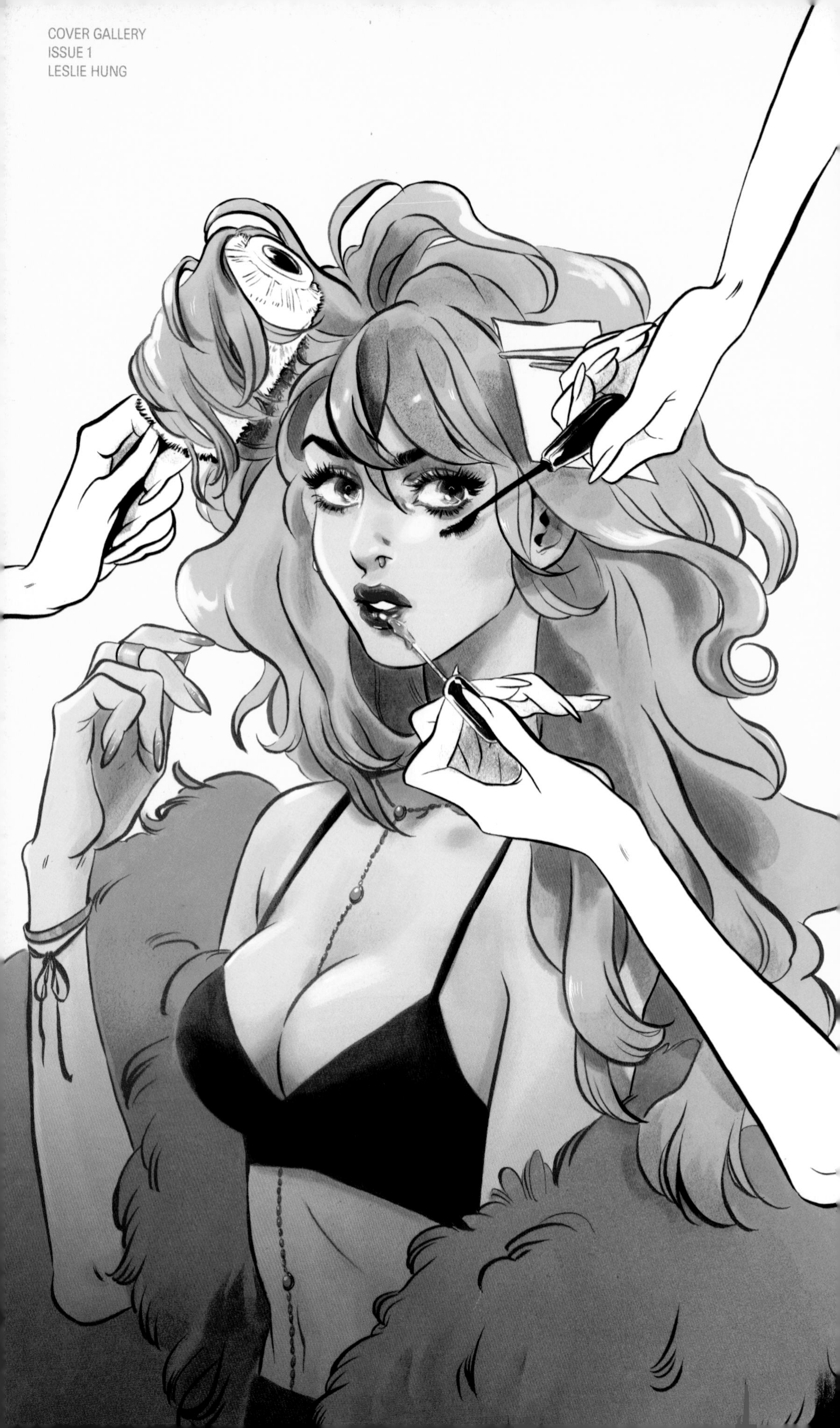

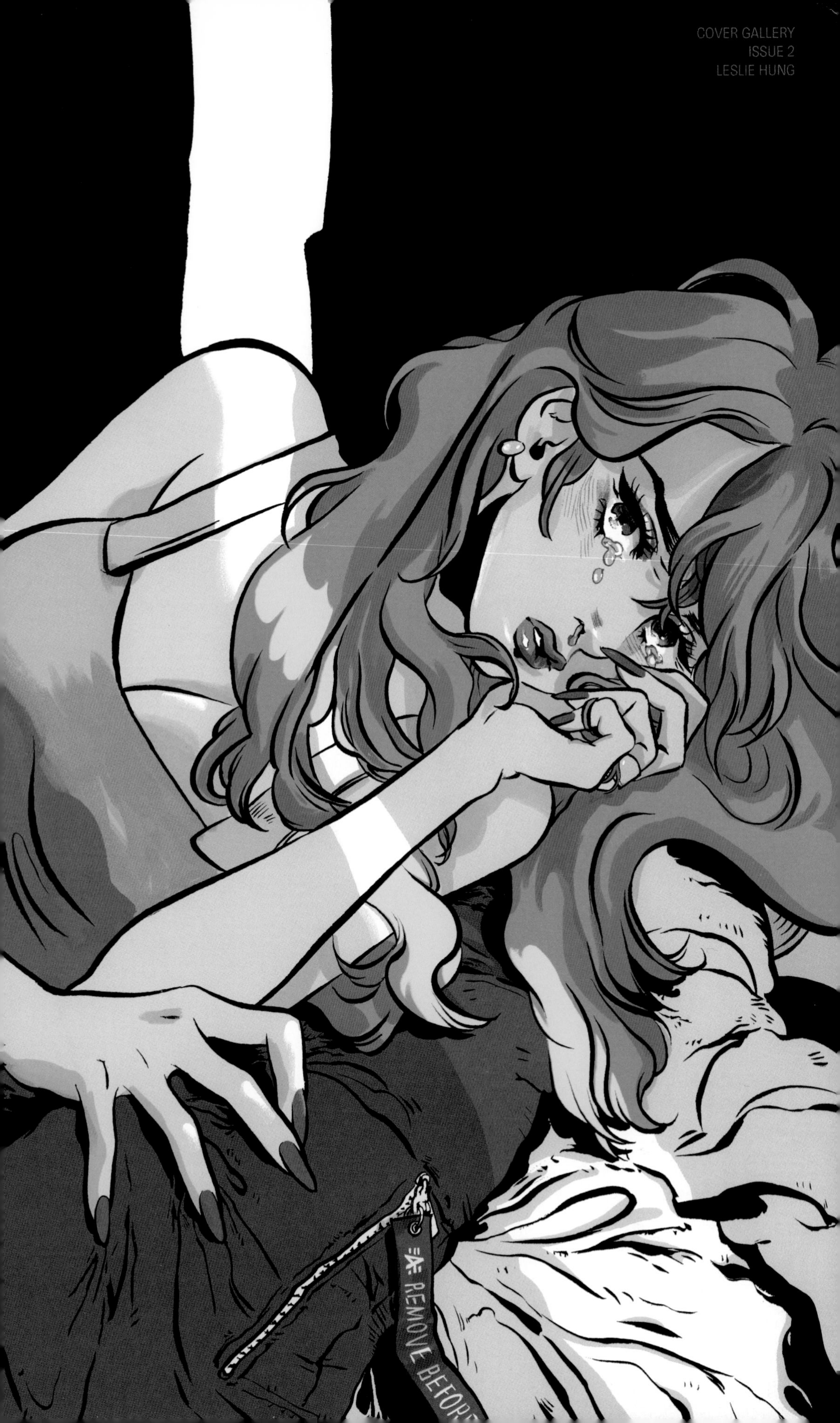
REMOVE BEFOR

COVER GALLERY
ISSUE 2
LESLIE HUNG

COVER GALLERY
ISSUE 3
LESLIE HUNG

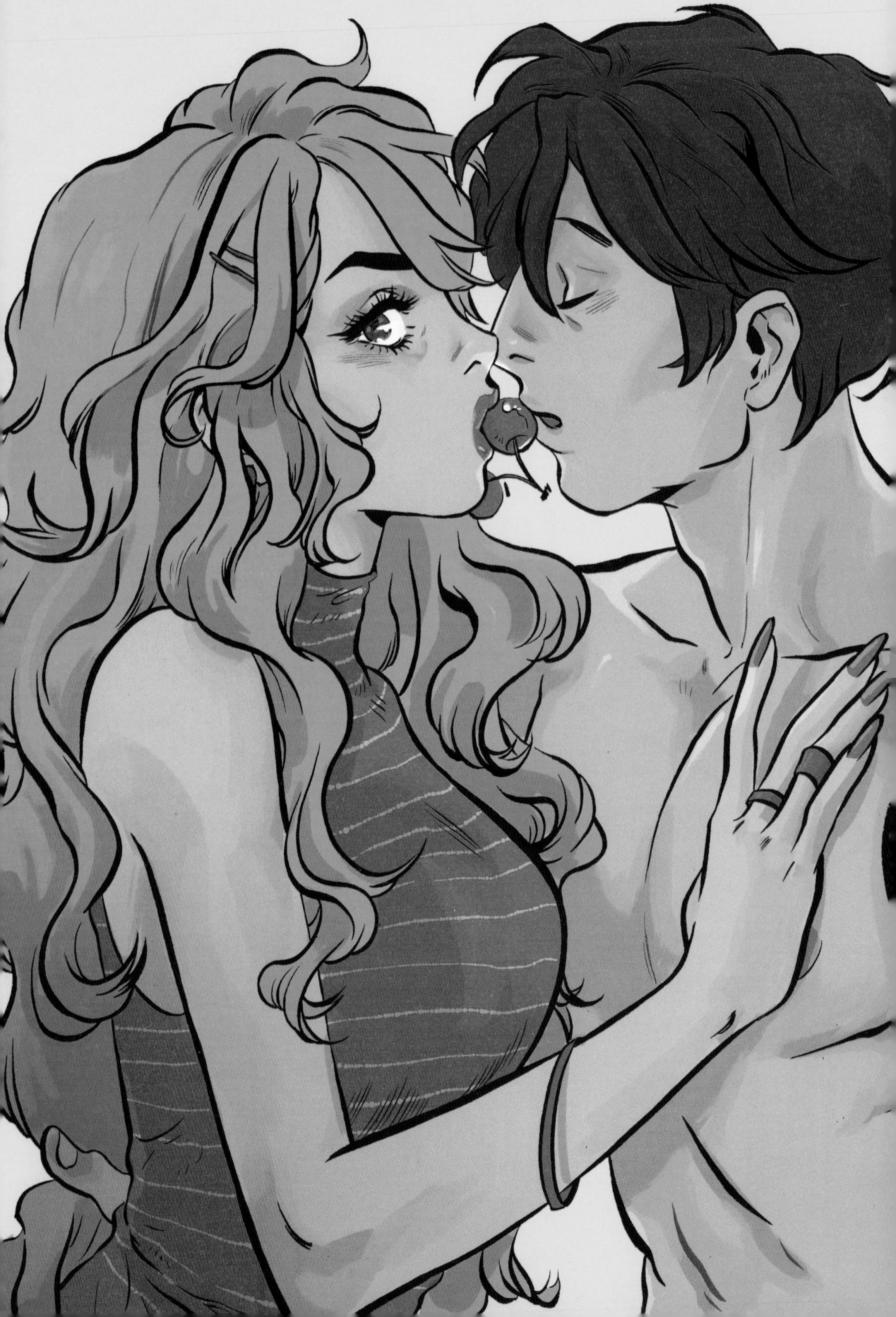

COVER GALLERY
ISSUE 4
LESLIE HUNG

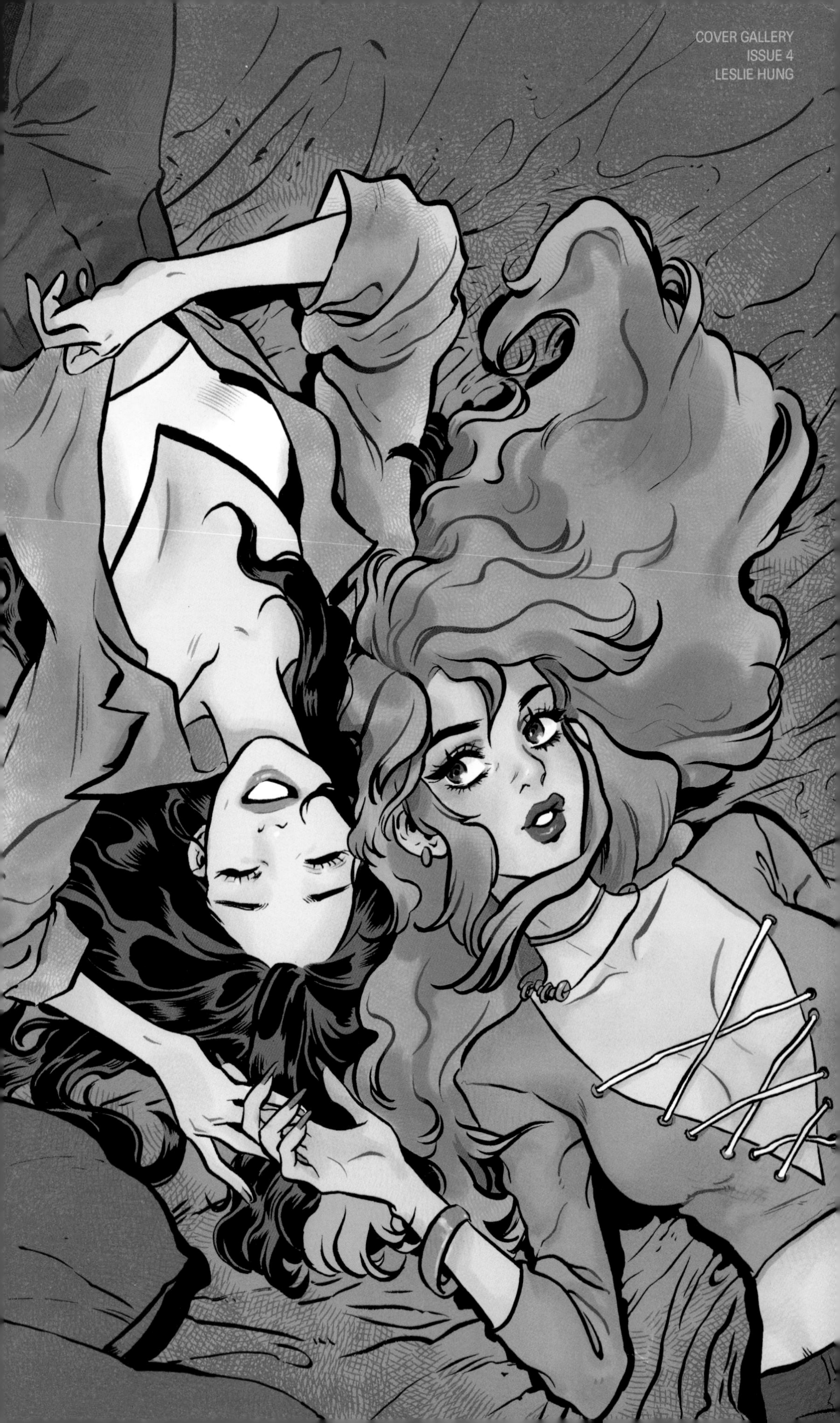

COVER GALLERY
ISSUE 5
LESLIE HUNG

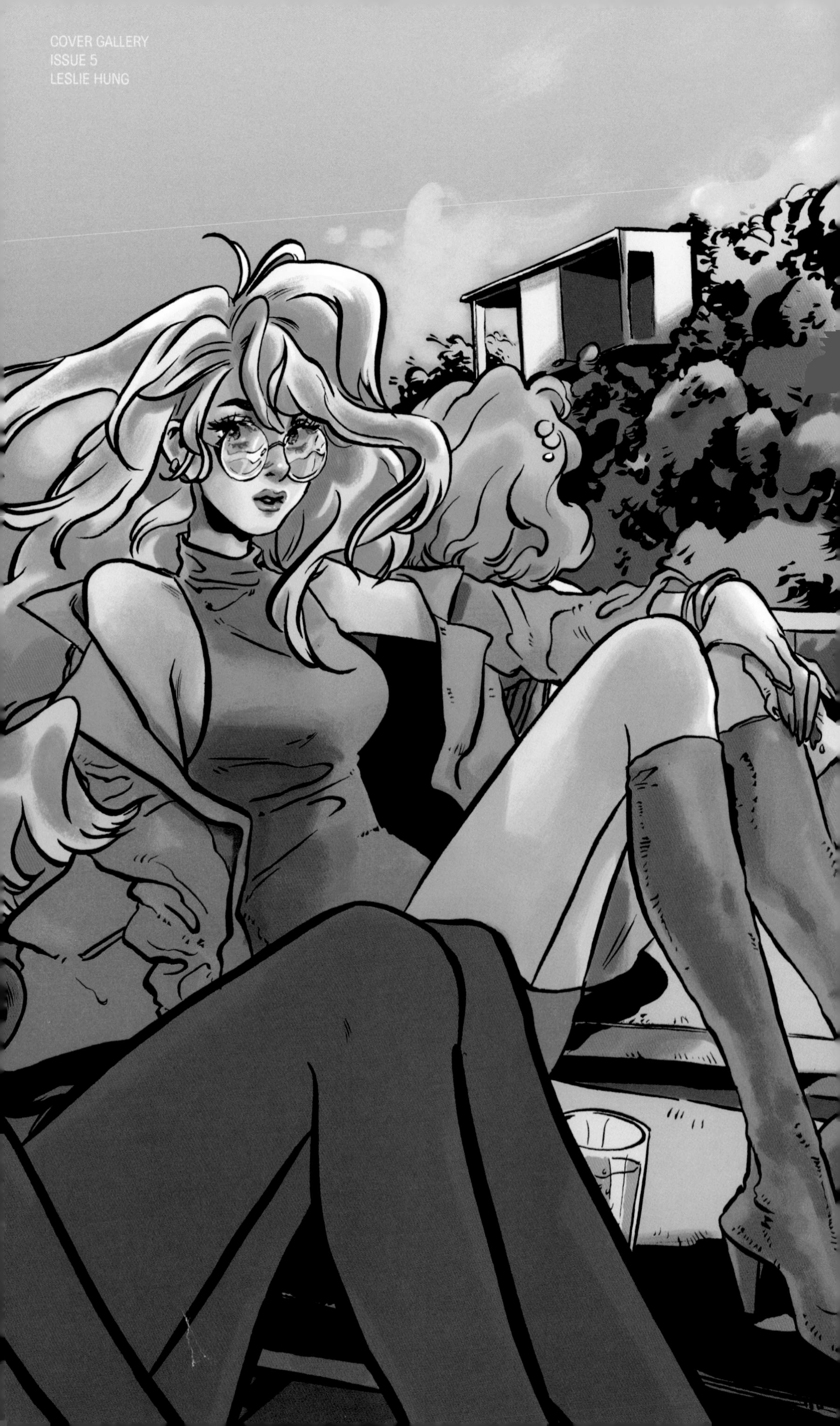

VARIANT COVER GALLERY
ISSUE 1
BRYAN LEE O'MALLEY & NATHAN FAIRBAIRN

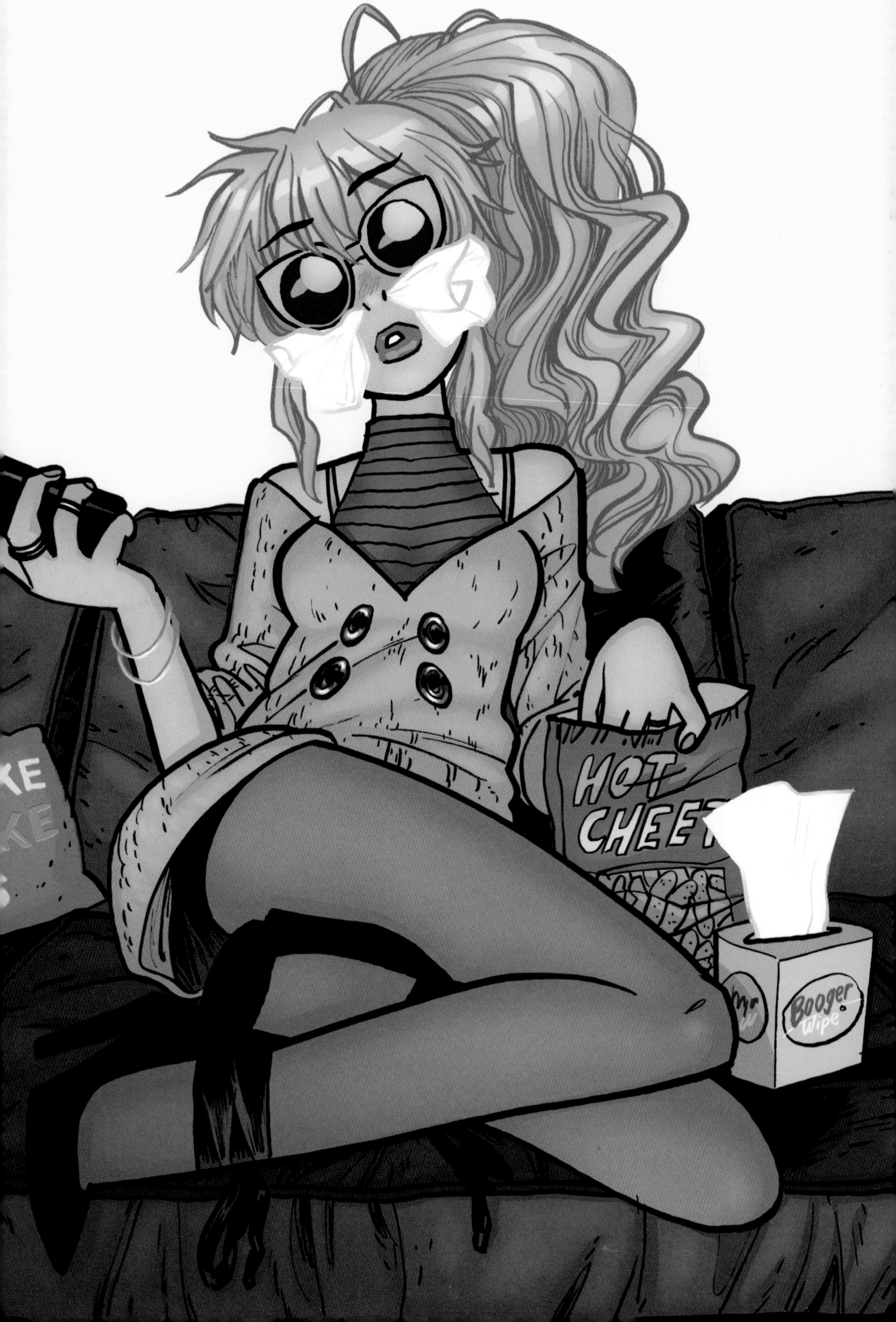
HOT
CHEET
Booger
Wipe

VARIANT COVER GALLERY
ISSUE 2
BRYAN LEE O'MALLEY & JASON FISCHER

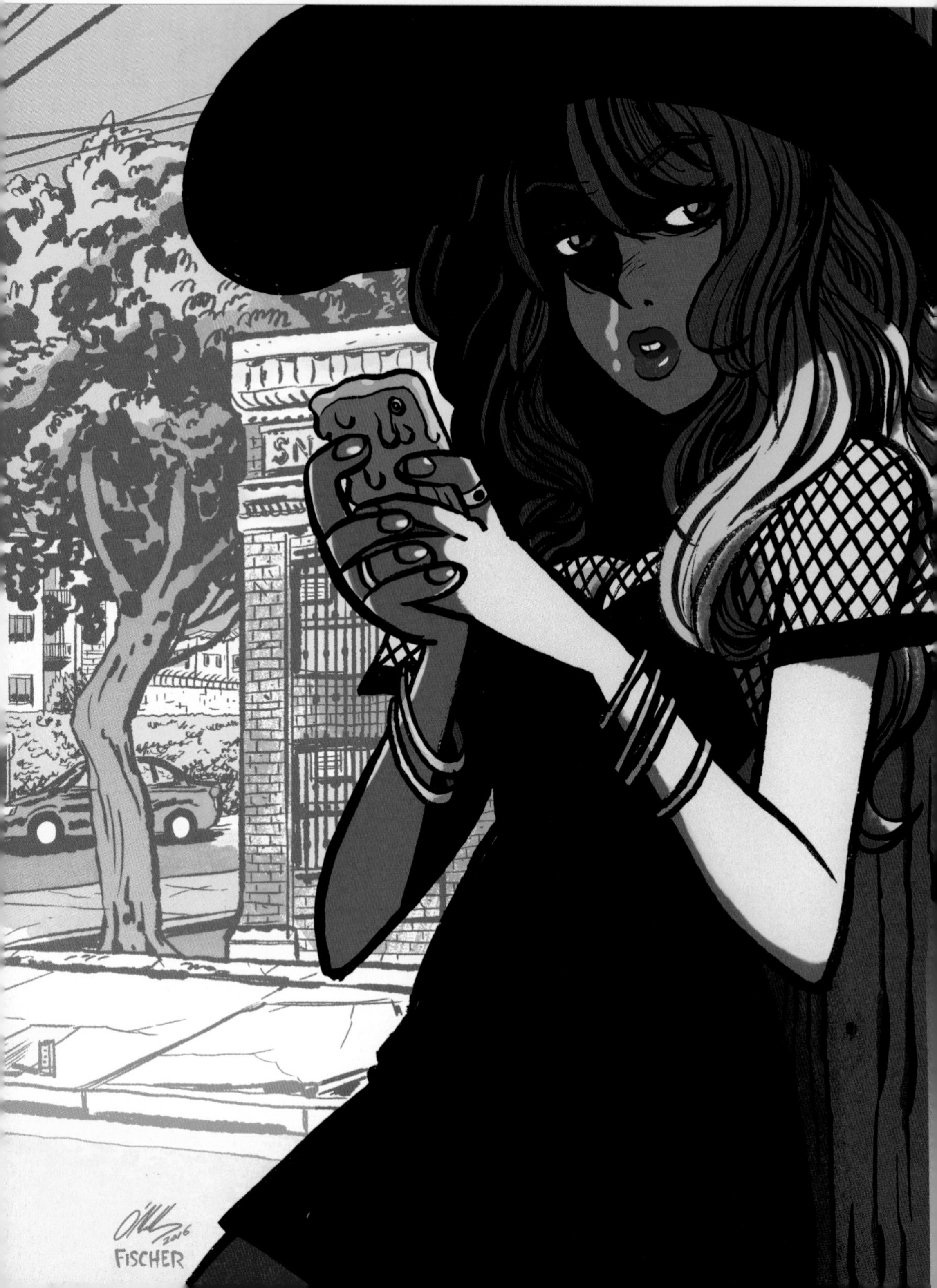
2016
FISCHER

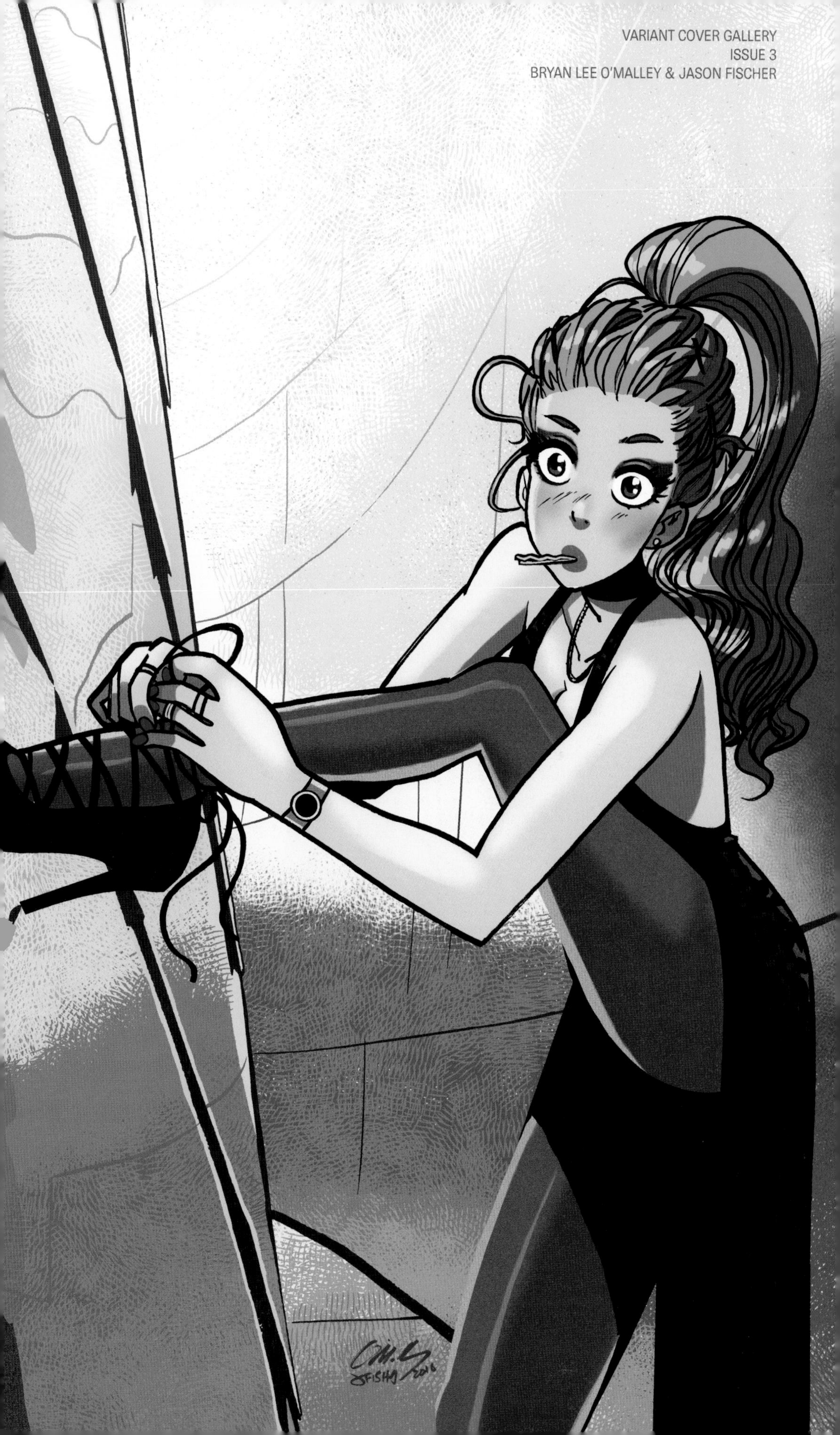

VARIANT COVER GALLERY
ISSUE 3
BRYAN LEE O'MALLEY & JASON FISCHER

VARIANT COVER GALLERY
ISSUE 4
BRYAN LEE O'MALLEY & JASON FISCHER

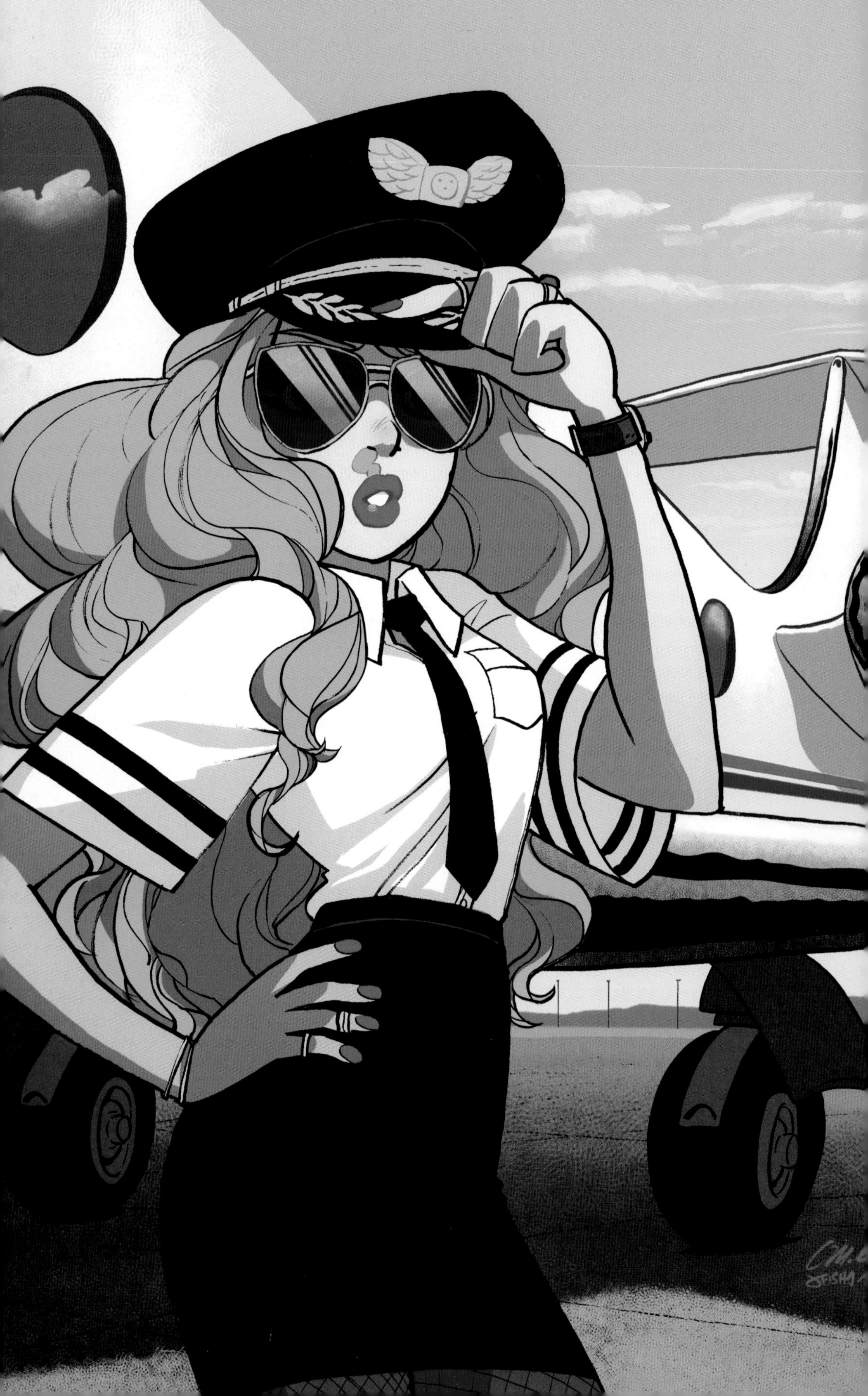

VARIANT COVER GALLERY
ISSUE 5
BRYAN LEE O'MALLEY & JASON FISCHER

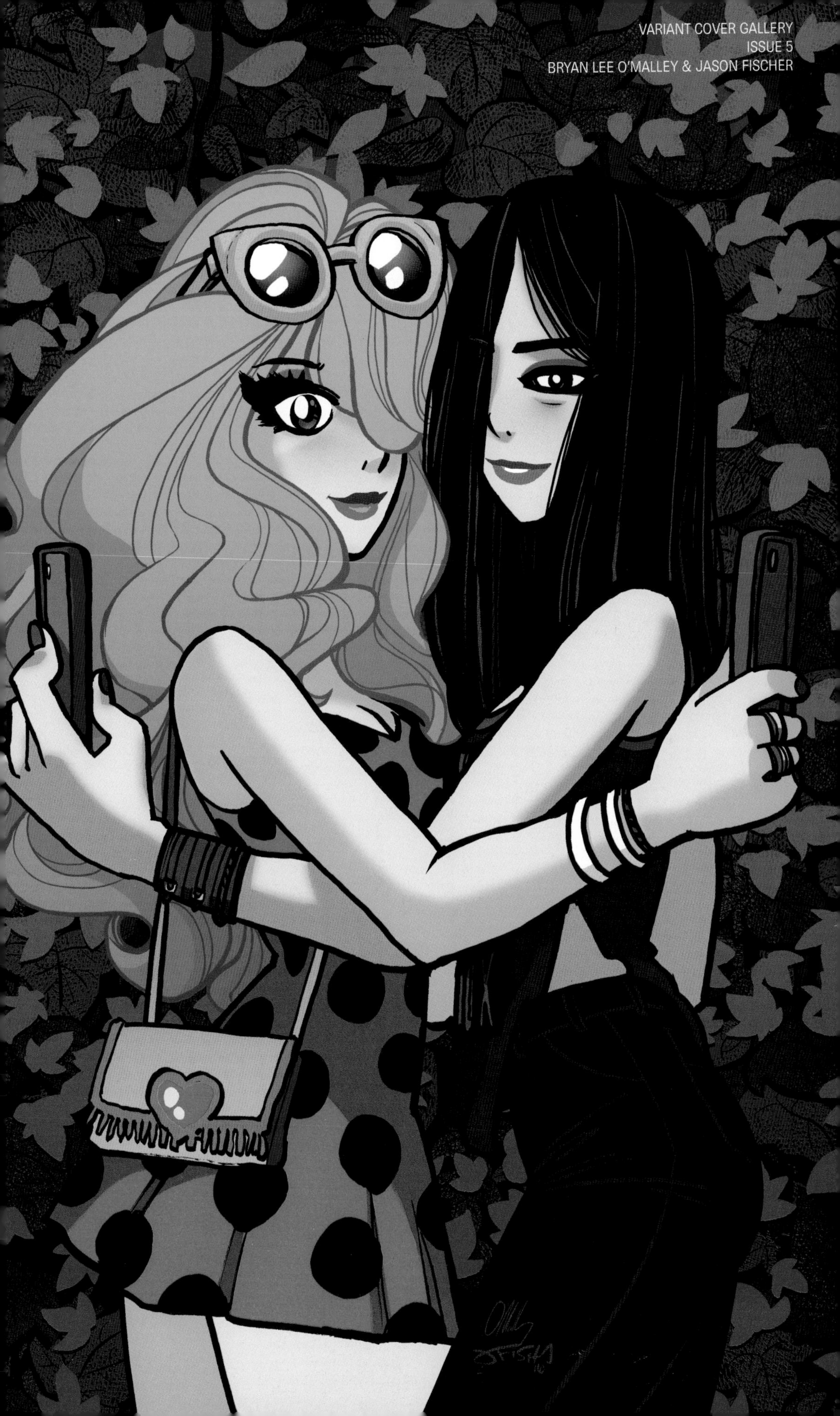

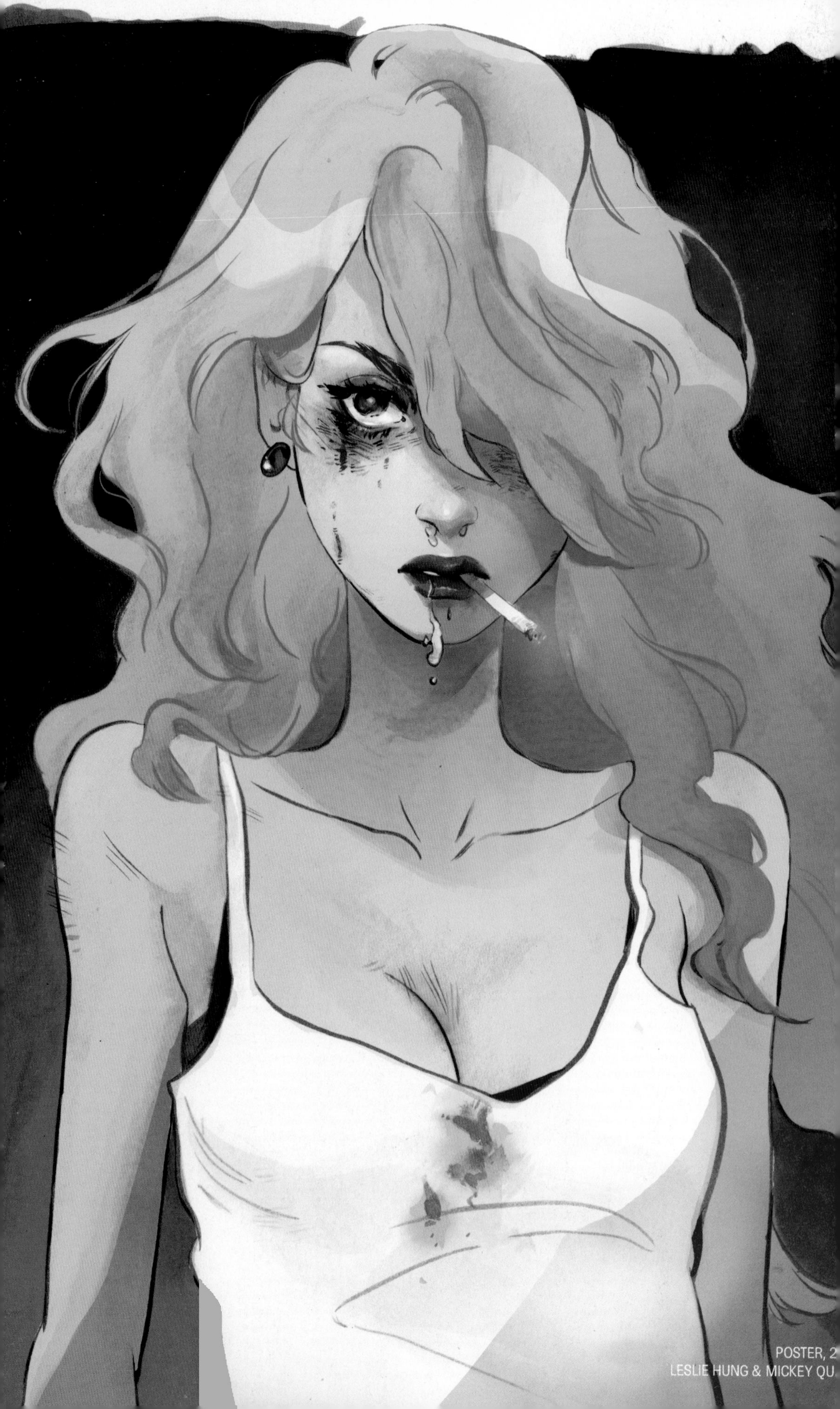

POSTER, 2
LESLIE HUNG & MICKEY QU